Blood Rites

By: Quinn Loftis

ISBN-13: 978-1475233636

ISBN-10: 1475233639

Dedication

Always for Bo and Travis. Without you both none of this would mean anything.

Acknowledgements

First I want to thank God for blessing me with a creative spirit. He has blessed me beyond measure. I also want to thank my husband for all his support, for the teasing that he gives me for writing teen paranormal romance. I like to remind him that at least he's never bored being married to me. I also want to thank a friend who has been a blessing to me, Melinda Senter, for her help in the creative editing. Her wicked sense of humor and eye for details has truly been a help. I also want to thank her for the beautiful cover art she has created for me. I want to thank Rachel Carr for being a fantabulous editor. I have been so blessed to get to know Rachel and her help has been invaluable. Thank you also to Jennifer Nunez for also editing and encouraging me to keep writing. Thank you Tilisa Meredith for being an awesome creative editor and letting me bounce ideas off of you and for catching the changes I should not make. Thank you to all my beta readers and reviewers. I cannot express my thanks for all your feedback and help. Finally, most important in many ways, thank you to everyone who has taken a chance on an unknown, self published author and purchased my book. Thank you for the reviews good and bad. Thank you for taking your valuable time and spending it with my characters and their story.

Chapter 1

"You know I will look ridiculous in that, right?" Jacque asked Sally while staring at the red dress her two best friends had hanging on the back of her bedroom door. "I mean, why don't you just sew a hood on it, put a basket of cookies in my hand and send me off to see grandma?" Jacque asked sarcastically, if not somewhat dramatically. She didn't understand why Sally and Jen insisted that she wear a dress for the bonding ceremony. She had repeatedly reminded them, and would again, that it wasn't a wedding. Since the challenge everything had been moving so quickly that she didn't really have a chance to veto their decision and nobody else seemed eager to jump to her defense. So, alas, she stood in her room with her two best friends wreaking havoc on her life, trying to tell her she was going to put on this ridiculous red dress.

"So how did things with Fane go last night?" Jen asked, pulling Jacque out of her thoughts.

That simple question reminded Jacque that the challenge had only happened yesterday. It felt like it had been days ago, but it had merely been hours. Last night after the challenge, Fane had come to her to plead forgiveness for making her believe he had died during the challenge. He'd really thought that she would not understand why he made that decision. Jacque was not going to deny the fact that it hurt, but she understood the reasoning behind it, and if it kept Fane alive that was all that mattered.

"It's all good," Jacque said nonchalantly.

The two girls stopped simultaneously and stared at Jacque in disbelief.

"I chewed Fane up like a chew toy and spit him out. Sally about smacked him into next week. And that's all you have to say to us? Hate to break it to ya, wolf princess, but that ain't going to cut it." Jen folded her arms across her chest and began tapping her foot. It was very obvious that Jacque would not be leaving this room until she gave up the goods. She figured they did deserve it after all they had done for her. Go on, Jacque, throw them a bone she told herself.

"Fane came to my room and sat on the side of my bed while I was still sort of asleep. I woke up to him kissing my cheeks, my nose, my chin, and then my lips. I was sure I was dreaming, but it seemed way too real. Then I freaked out. I decided I must have jumped off the deep end after the week from 'folk lore stories come to life' hell. I was seeing my dead mate sitting on my bed."

Before Jacque could go on Jen interrupted. "Ok, that's all fine and dandy, but I want the main course, not the before-dinner rolls. Main course, Jacque, get to it."

Jacque rolled her eyes. "I have to build up to the main course or else it's not really the main course. However, for the sake of your sanity I will speed it up. After I realized he was indeed real, he hugged me and I accidentally groaned in pain."

"Oh, hell. He went into possessive, jealous, I-no-longer-have-a-brain mode, didn't he?" Sally asked sarcastically.

"Point to you. He saw the bruise on my stomach and nearly went all werewolf kung-fu on his pack. I can't believe ya'll didn't hear him yell. But I got him to pipe down when I pulled out the 'I'm bruised because you played dead' card. Works every time." Jacque winked.

"Nice," Jen and Sally said, bumping fists.

"Then we kissed. A lot. Yep, there was a lot of kissing. Oh, and there was purring. But all clothes stayed on, Jen, sorry to spoil your fantasy."

"You are so not sorry to spoil anything. At least tell me if he's a good kisser," Jen whined.

Jacque looked at her, emerald eyes narrowed with a wicked gleam. "My sweet, sweet Jen, he's a good everything."

"Ok ladies, both of you back into your corners. Jacque's getting hitched today so there has to be a cease fire." Sally indicated the corners she wanted Jacque and Jen to stand in.

"I am not getting hitched, there is no ring involved."

"Says the wolf princess who's never been bonded to a werewolf before," Jen pointed out.

"Details, details," Jacque quipped.

She suddenly felt claustrophobic, like the room was beginning to get smaller. It reminded her of Alice in Wonderland when she eats the cake and begins to grow until the room is so small she is squished into it. She needed air. Jacque walked over to her window and jerked it open. She felt the summer heat hit her face, and even though it was blazing hot, it was refreshing and helped clear her brain from all the worries that were slowly stacking up on shelves in her mind. Each deep breath she took felt like it was slowly pushing each stack of worry into a trash bag. Breathe-she pushed worry about leaving Coldspring into the bag, breathe- next was worry for her mom, will she come to Romania or stay here, breathe- worry for her friends, breathe- worry about the bonding ceremony, breathe- worry about the blood rites, breathe. Finally the shelves were clean, and there in her mind amongst the empty shelves was Fane.

"Hello meu inimă, doing some spring cleaning?" Fane asked her, using their bond.

Jacque couldn't suppress the smile that followed; she should have known he would be listening. Especially since she was more emotional than usual. Well, that was really not a fair statement because she had been emotional for the past 5 days. Meeting your werewolf mate tends to do that to a girl.

"Just needed to put things in their place, how are you?" Jacque felt the warmth he was pouring into her mind, the love he wanted her to feel and it only made her want to be in his arms more.

"Soon, love."

"You keep saying that wolf man, when does soon become now?" Jacque teased him. *"Now go away. Isn't it bad luck to see your mate before the bonding thingy?"*

She heard him chuckle.

"No meu inimă, you're thinking of it being bad luck for the groom to see his bride before the wedding. I can see you all I want. In fact I could come rescue you from those two if you want."

"That's okay, they mean well, they are just a little rough on the execution. What time is this shin-dig starting?" Jacque asked.

"It starts as 1:00 p.m. I'll see you there Little Red." Fane's voice faded out of her mind and she could feel his humor. Oh wasn't he just too cute, picking up on her two best friends' idea of a sick joke, to turn her into the little girl who almost wound up as the

wolf's dinner.

"My, what big eyes you have, wolf-man," Jacque said out loud, unable to stop her sarcasm from boiling up.

"The better to see you with my love," Jen chimed in.

"What big ears you have!" Sally continued their comic relief.

"The better to hear you with my love," Jen followed.

"What big teeth you have!" Sally mocked, her hands on either side of her face.

"The better to eat you with my love," Jen cackled, but she wasn't finished. True to Jen form she added her own twisted sense of humor. "My, what big -"

Sally slapped a hand over her mouth, quickly realizing where Jen was going with that statement. Jacque started laughing so hard she had tears running down her cheeks. As soon as Sally removed her hand Jen quickly added, "Thebettertoeatyouwith," before Sally could re-cover her mouth.

Jacque abruptly stopped laughing, "You already said that," she said, confused.

"So I did, my sweet, innocent flower," Jen started to explain but was once again thwarted by Sally.

"Jen, shut it. Jacque, just allow yourself to ponder on that statement at a later date in time," Sally told her, sounding everything but the part of June Cleaver.

"Ok, moving on from our weird impromptu skit. I get it, you want to dress me up all pretty for this ceremony and I can either play along or you two will make it hell for me. That's what the red dress is about, isn't it?"

"You're smarter than you look, Sherlock," Jen said as she stood up. "We will give you your real dress if you promise to play nice. Otherwise you're going to be Little Red washed out Riding Hood, cuz that red really does nothing for your skin."

"Gee, thanks for that keen observation, Watson. Fine, you win, bring out the big guns."

Jen stepped out of the room and was back before Jacque could ask her where she was going. She came back with a hanger with what she presumed to be her dress hanging on it, but she couldn't tell for sure because it was covered in one of those zipped clothing protectors. As Jen hung it on the back of Jacque's bedroom door, effectively covering the dress that would have made her the living version of a sick fairy tale, Sally began to unzip the bag while humming the bridal march song.

"Cute, Sally, that's just real cute," Jacque told her sarcastically.

"Watch it Red. I'd hate to have to incorporate more of the famous fairy tale into your ceremony, but I'll do it if you force my hand," Sally threatened as she pulled the dress out from the hanging bag.

Jacque's breath caught at the sight, so simple yet very elegant and eye catching. She had to admit she was impressed with her friends' taste. The dress was primarily white, with a double flare skirt that came just above the knees. The waist had a green sash sewn into the dress and the green flared out into the skirt with some floral accents. To finish it off, they had added a hunter green, puff short sleeve bolero jacket made of satin with ruffled edges running up the high-necked collar and down to the sleeves. It was simply perfect.

"Hey wolf-man, they even thought of you and provided cover for my markings." Jacque sent the thought to Fane.

"How very thoughtful of them, Luna, although you can't honestly think I would have allowed you to come in that dress without the jacket," Fane answered.

"You are so lucky that you aren't with in my reach right now because that little comment would have earned you some retaliation and it still might if I'm not feeling generous later," she scolded him.

His only response was a soft chuckle in her mind and she thought she might have felt his hand caress her face. Geez, Jacque thought, he is going to be the death of me.

"Could you please stop talking to your hunky wolf and tell us what you think of the dress?" Jen said, snapping Jacque out of her thoughts.

"How did you know I was talking to him?" Jacque asked.

"You always get an intense look on your face, so I figure you are either constipated or talking to Fane. If you aren't talking to Fane then you ought to see a doctor because you are constipated a lot," Jen explained. Sally was cracking up at Jen and Jacque was giving Jen an un-lady like hand gesture.

"I have to admit, you guys have outdone your selves," Jacque told them. "It truly is beautiful and tasteful and the jacket was the perfect touch. Thank you guys so much. Oh crap, I think I'm going to cry," Jacque said, much to her chagrin.

"Don't start the water works, there will be plenty of time for that later," Sally teased her.

"Ok ladies, I need something to eat before I slide into that, if I might add, much more appropriate dress so let's head downstairs so I can get my grub on," Jacque announced.

"Please tell me you don't say 'get my grub on' to Fane when you are talking about eating," Sally pleaded.

Jacque waved her hands in the air in a whatever gesture. "He can either take me as I am, grub and all, or not."

"Oh I'm pretty sure he wants to take you, and quite possibly as his grub," Jen snickered.

Sally gave Jen their usual fist bump, "What would I do without you and your sexual innuendos, my sweet, nympho friend?"

"You would be square," Jen told her, her fingers tracing the shape in the air.

"Huh, so I would," Sally agreed thoughtfully.

The girls headed downstairs and threw together some PB and J sandwiches. They were quiet as they ate. Jacque finished first and just as she was going to head upstairs to change, her mom came into the kitchen. "You ladies need to hurry up if we are going to make it on time," Lilly told them.

"I've just got to fix my hair and throw on my dress and then I'm game," Jacque answered.

"Correction, *I* need to fix your hair. There is no telling what kind of mess you would put together on your head," Sally added

"Did you decide to cooperate with your partners in crime so you wouldn't be the world's first living Little Red Riding Hood?" her mom asked her.

Jacque glared at Sally and Jen, giving them her best 'if I was a wolf I'd bite your ass' stare. "Yea, they won this round, but you know what they say about payback."

Jen just laughed as she and Sally trailed her up the stairs to help her get dressed.

"Sit down, kick back and chill-out so I can fix this unruly mess you call your hair."

"You have to do it up off her shoulders because of the chomp, chomp thing, if you know what I mean," Jen said, her teeth snapping together.

"Gee, Jen. Thanks so much for the reminder of the fact that I'm going to be a chew toy later on tonight. I'm not nervous enough as it is or anything," Jacque told her.

"I'm just saying," Jen said with a roll of her eyes and shoulder shrug, "If it was me who was going to get chomped on by a hot, drool worthy, Romanian fur ball, let's just say I wouldn't make him chase me too long."

"Yeah, well knowing you, Jen, the so called fur ball wouldn't be the only one doing the chomping," Sally teased her dryly.

"No doubt, my sweet wall flower. But more to the point, it wouldn't be just my neck he would be chomping on!" Jen apparently cracked herself up with that one because she nearly fell out of her chair laughing, although the shoe Jacque threw at her head didn't help matters.

"Jacque, quit throwing shoes at Jen's head. Jen, if at all possible quite being a pervert for like 5 minutes."

"Make it 2 1/2 minutes and we have a deal," Jen volleyed back.

"Shameless," muttered Jacque, "the nyphmo is utterly, undeniably shameless."

"We all gotta be something, Jac." Jen just had to have the last word, so Jacque and Sally finally relented.

Sally pushed Jacque down into the chair by her desk and began to gather the various hair items she would need to tame the wild curls. As Jacque sat there staring off at nothing in particular, her mind was drawn back to the events of the past week. It was hard for her to believe that she'd only met Fane a week ago. She felt like she had known him forever and already couldn't imagine life without him. In one week she'd learned she was half Canis Lupus, her father was full Canis Lupus, and also that she was the mate of the Prince of the Romanian Canis Lupus. She had been claimed by the lunatic Alpha of Coldspring and had to watch Fane fight him for bonding rights. She even thought she'd watched Fane die. If someone had told her last week that all this was going to happen she would have said something along the lines of, yeah, and George Strait is selling me his ocean front property in Arizona as well.

"OWWW!" Jacque hollered as Sally's hair ministrations pulled her from her thoughts.

"Well what do you expect with this flaming mess on your

head?" Sally asked her as she continued to pull and tug on her hair.

"Just make sure you leave me some hair up there, okay?" Jacque said, rolling her eyes.

Jen walked over to look at Sally's handy work. "That actually looks pretty great, Sal. I like the little glitter bobby-pins you put in, very fairy tale-ish."

"Okay, okay, let me look already," Jacque said as she stood up and went to the mirror on her dresser. "Wow, Sally, it looks awesome. You made me look so much prettier than I really am. Sweet! Thanks, chickadee."

Sally grabbed Jacque by the shoulders and turned her so they were face to face. "You are beautiful, big, wild hair and all. All I did was bring attention to that fact. The way Fane looks at you, you should never doubt your beauty on the inside or out," Sally told her.

"Man Sal, why don't I ever get pep talks like that?" Jen asked.

"If ever you are in need of a pep talk, Jen, I will gladly deliver. As it is, you are a walking ego, so most of the time you need to be brought down a notch, not up. I say that with all the love in my heart," Sally teased her.

"Yeah, you are totally blowing me away with all your quote, unquote love. How 'bout don't give me so much love next time, huh?"

Jacque grabbed her dress and the jacket and began walking to the bathroom. "Ok, while ya'll work out your love issues, I'm going to get dressed. I expect ya'll to have kissed and made up by the time I get back."

"Brush your teeth before you put that dress on," Sally told her.

"Yeah and don't put perfume on your neck, you know because of the chomp…" Jen started.

"Chomp, chomp. Yeah I got it, Jen," Jacque interrupted.

Jacque closed the door to the bathroom and leaned against it. She took a deep breath and closed her eyes. "I can do this," she said out loud. It wasn't that she was scared of bonding with Fane, she wanted to be with him more than anything. No, she was just a big chicken about pain and wasn't really looking forward to being bitten. Then she remembered what it felt like when she thought he had died. She realized that in comparison to that feeling, a bite would be a piece of cake. On that thought she was able to move forward feeling much lighter.

"Are you ok, love?" she heard Fane ask in her mind.

She smiled at the warmth she could feel coming through such a simple question.

"I am excellent, wolf-man. Although, I am missing you," Jacque told him.

"I will see you soon, micul incendiu (little fire)."

"Fane, stay with me," Jacque whispered in her thoughts.

"Always," was his simple reply.

True to his word, Jacque could feel him like a shadow in her mind and it calmed her nerves and made her feel cherished.

Jacque soon stepped out of the bathroom and her two best friends stopped and stared, open mouthed.

"Well, how do I look?" Jacque asked them, a little unsure.

"You look amazing! Fane won't be able to take his eyes off of you," Jen told her.

Sally nodded her agreement but didn't say anything. Jacque looked over to her bed and saw that Sally had retrieved her suitcase and begun putting clothes in it for her.

"Sally, you don't have to pack a whole bunch it's just one night and then I will be back here," Jacque said.

Sally's face fell a tiny bit. "You will be back, but only for a few days. Then you will be packing more than an overnight bag," she told her, sounding so lost.

"I really hope you guys are considering coming to Romania for our senior year. Alina looked into the foreign exchange program, and found that it would look really good on college applications, and she has offered to be ya'lls host family. Have either of you talked to your parents about it yet?" Jacque asked.

"I mentioned it to my parents and once I pointed out that it could give me a leg up in getting into the international business degree programs I just happen to all of a sudden be interested in, they were surprisingly okay with it," Jen explained. " I kind of think my mom wants a break from me. You both know that if my mom and I are in the same room for too long it's like two pissed off cats who have been tossed in cold water and are ready to rip someone's eyes out. So I was going to surprise you later but now's as good a time as any. Romania won't know what hit them when I get done,"

Jen teased, although the statement was more true than not.

Jacque squealed in child like delight and hugged Jen tight. "This is so great!"

"You do realize that squeal is totally not sexy and if we are in Romania together and you are with me while I'm trying to get my game on that you are not permitted to make such a noise, right?" Jen told her, sounding put out.

"Oh, shut up and let me be all sentimental for a sec." Jacque hugged her for a minute more and then backed up, holding her hands in a surrender gesture. "Okay, I'm good, it's all under control."

Jacque turned to Sally, who had been watching the exchange. "So what about you, Sally? Have you talked to your parents?"

"I did and I told them the same thing Jen told hers, considering we rehearsed it with each other complete with back up guilt trips if the whole college reference didn't work, and hell must have froze over, pigs must have sprouted wings, and you must be half werewolf…wait, that last part is true, the point is they said yes!"

This time Sally and Jacque squealed in unison. "Oh come on, surround sound squeals? REALLY?" Jen whined. "You two are not invited when I go hottie hunting," she growled at them.

Sally and Jacque relinquished their squeals to turn and look at Jen. "Did you just say hottie hunting?" Sally asked her incredulously

Jen turned her chin indignantly. "Spot on, Sherlock."

"Just checking. I want to be completely clear on what I should say to your new beau when you finally nab him," Sally teased. "Something along the lines of, 'Hey Don Juan, did Jen tell you about her hottie hunting days back in the day, as in a couple of days ago back in the day?'"

"My sweet Sally, the point is you just admitted that I will be successful in nabbing a new beau, hence the hottie hunting will undoubtedly work. Ding ding ding, I win," Jen chimed.

Jacque rolled her eyes at her two best friends. "I'm thinking your parents aren't considering it a hardship to have you two go to Romania. I don't know, just a hunch."

Sally glanced at her phone and saw that it was 12:15. "We've got to head if we want to make it on time."

Sally and Jen each grabbed a bag and headed for the stairs with Jacque following.

"Wolf-man, we are heading your way, hope you're ready for this," Jacque sent to Fane.

"I have been ready for you since I laid I eyes on you. Be safe, I will see you shortly." Fane sent the words with a caress that caused Jacque to shiver.

As they pulled out of the driveway, Jacque leaned her head back against the head rest, closed her eyes, and pictured Fane's face, her future.

Chapter 2

Across two state lines in Denver, Colorado, Dillon Jacobs paced the floor of his office. The Alpha of the Denver pack was flipping through photos that Logan, his Beta, had taken of the daughter he hadn't even known existed until recently. He was struck with the fact that life as he knew it was irrevocably changed. Word had traveled fast in the Canis Lupis world that Vasile, one of the strongest Alphas of the Grey Wolves was in the States, not only in the States, but specifically in Coldspring, Texas. Coldspring just happened to be the town where Lilly Pierce lived, the woman whom he would have married had he not been a wolf who could only have one mate, the one nature choose for him. Not that Dillon didn't love his mate beyond words, but Lilly had been his first love. The loss had faded over the years, but the memories were still there, packed away in the recesses of his mind gathering dust. Until now.

As soon as he had heard about the Alpha Vasile being there, he had sent Logan to find out what had caused him to travel so far from home. Dillon had been in shock when Logan called to tell him that Lilly had a daughter, and that she was seventeen years old. It had been seventeen years since Dillon had last laid eyes on Lilly Pierce. Seventeen years since he had found his mate and packed his bags only leaving Lilly a note to say goodbye. It was the coward's way out, but he hadn't known how he could face her knowing he was going to rip out both their hearts. He had told Lilly that the day might come when he would have no choice but to leave. That hadn't make it any easier. The irrevocable proof though, was in the pictures. Lilly's daughter was the spitting image of himself. Dillon was not a large man, standing at 5'11", 190lbs. He was broad across the shoulders, as most Canis Lupis are, which was only enhanced by his narrow waist and the snug fitting tee shirts he often favored.

With auburn hair that had subtle waves in it and the same piercing green eyes as the girl in the photos, he could no more deny her than he could deny his reflection in the mirror. His face was more angular than the girl's, who Logan had said was named Jacquelyn, whose face was softer and rounder. He did see traces of Lilly here and there. Jacque had her mother's mischievous smile, and though her eye color matched his, they held the humor in them he so often had seen in Lilly. Like her mother she was as striking as she was beautiful. He thought momentarily on the fact that Lilly had named their daughter after Dillon's grandmother. Though Lilly had never met his grandmother, he had talked of her often, sharing with Lilly what an impact she had in raising him. He couldn't take credit for his quick wit and often wicked tongue that was all Grandma Jacquelyn.

"Your daughter is to be bonded to Vasile's son," Logan told him, snapping him out of his brief jaunt down memory lane. The dry indifference in his Beta's voice did not reveal if he cared one way or the other. Dillon turned to look at him, wanting to confirm that his body language matched his words. Logan was as serious and severe looking as ever. At 6'1", 250lbs of muscle, Logan was an intimidating being. He too was broad across the chest, had a narrow waist, and it was apparent in his snug black fatigues he had muscular legs. His dark brown hair he wore longer than most of Dillon's wolves, nearly touching his shoulders, but much of the time he had it pulled back. He had high cheek bones, a slightly crooked nose from being broken many times in his long life, and Dillon had heard more than one woman say Logan's lips were made for sin, whatever that meant.

"She is still a minor, how could Vasile even consider allowing them to mate?" Dillon thought out loud.

"Fane, the Alpha's son, had to compete in a challenge against another Alpha who was trying to claim Jacque. Perhaps it is Vasile's way of keeping his son from having to fight others from claiming your daughter," Logan offered

Dillon thought about this. It would make sense, for if Fane was indeed Jacque's true mate then he would walk through hell itself to keep another from claiming her.

"I will admit it is impressive that Fane, being as young as he is, was able to defeat such a strong Alpha," Dillon acknowledged

"He did have the benefit of his Alpha's counsel, surely that had an impact on his victory," Logan responded in his usual indifferent tone.

Still the idea of his little girl mated at 17 rubbed his fur the wrong way. Although he didn't really have a right to say what she could or could not do, she didn't even know who he was. Maybe, he decided, the best thing to do for now is to watch from a distance.

"Logan, I want you to go back to Coldspring and keep an eye on my daughter. Don't let yourself be known, just observe from a distance and report back to me. I will let you know if and when I will be coming myself. For now I will wait," Dillon told his Beta

"It will be done as you have said, Alpha," Logan responded in the formal address

Dillon excused Logan to depart, leaving him alone in his study with his thoughts. He had been keeping these thoughts blocked from his mate. He didn't know how she would respond to the news that he had a daughter with another female. No, for now he would keep this secret just a little longer.

Logan was sitting outside of Lilly Pierce's house when she pulled out of the driveway. He had barely made it back into town to see them off to Jacque's bonding ceremony. Luckily, he had put his plan in motion before he had reported back to his Alpha. It had been so easy to get information out of the Coldspring pack, considering there were none more dominant then him. Then he just did a little eavesdropping outside Jacque's window to get all the information he needed on her schedule and timeline for the bonding ceremony. He hated to be insubordinate, he usually prided himself on his faithful obedience to his Alpha, but in this situation he didn't think his Alpha was taking the appropriate action to protect his pup. Logan had decided it was his duty to step in since he wasn't emotionally vested in Jacque. He felt he was able to look at the situation more objectively. That was what he kept telling himself, anyway. The truth was Jacque Pierce was unique. She was special, and too new to this world to decide that the first wolf she met was her mate. It was his job as her dad's Beta to protect her and to show her that there was more than one wolf in the den. Again, that was what he kept telling himself. Shaking off those thoughts, he pulled out into the street to follow Lilly's vehicle. He knew the direction she would be heading because he had insured her route. All it took was a little money and he had been able to convince one of her employees to help implement his plan. Humans were so easy to sway without any sense of loyalty, they had no problem betraying those who had been kind to them. But that wasn't his problem, and it had worked to his advantage. Just as Lilly was turning on the street that would take her to her book store he turned off and drove to the spot that he knew they would have to pass once they continued on to Vasile's home.

His plan was simple, the best laid ones always were. All he needed to do to insure that Dillon would intervene was show that Fane could not protect his mate. There was nothing more disgraceful than a wolf who could not protect his own. Insuring that Lilly's tire would not only blow, but also cause a minor accident hadn't been all that difficult. He had placed a military device on the inside of the tire that simultaneously punctured it and wrapped a cable around the axel, pulling it once the tire blew, causing the axel to become unstable and theoretically cause her to lose control of the vehicle. It wouldn't be a devastating wreck, but it would be enough. The kink in the plan was the bonding ceremony. Logan had to make sure his plan happened before Jacque and Fane were able to complete the bonding and blood rites. Once the blood rite was completed all bets were off. The idea of Fane performing Blood Rites with Jacque made his skin crawl. Fane was just a pup, there was no way he could adequately provide and protect a mate. If Logan had any say, Fane would be leaving Coldspring, Texas empty handed.

Chapter 3

Fane had spent the morning doing absolutely nothing other than conversing periodically with Jacquelyn. Verbally sparring with her was one of his favorite things to do. No one would let him help prepare for the ceremony, his father saying that Fane needed to take this time to prepare himself for his Luna, for tonight. In all honesty, Fane was trying to avoid thinking about it, or at least about one part of it: the blood rites. He knew that Jacquelyn was nervous about it and he was as well. He had asked his father what he needed to do and all he had said was that instinct would take over and the magic of the mate bond would help. As nervous as he was about performing the blood rites, his wolf growled low at the thought of their mark on Jacquelyn's neck for all Canis Lupus to see. He realized his wolf was restless, eager to finish the bond. Fane decided he needed to let the wolf out for a little while, let him run off some of his energy.

He went out the back door and stood on the porch of the guest house on the property his parents were renting. The whole estate was 85 acres of woods, no prying eyes around. Fane stripped out of his clothes and felt the change pour over his skin, reshaping him inside and out, and within moments where a man had stood was now a large black wolf. Although he was a Grey wolf, his grey undercoat was tipped with black, the effect making him look nearly solid black unless his fur was rubbed the wrong way. The wolf shook his whole body as if he were wet and trying to expel the water from his coat. He put his nose in the air and, breathing deep, filled his lungs with wild flowers in bloom, fresh cut grass, and damp earth from a recent rain and finally let out a long howl. Fane heard a twig snap to his left and his howl cut off as he snapped his head in the direction of the noise. He saw a rabbit take off and just like that the chase was on. He took off like a bullet, eyes glued to the bouncing prey that wove in and out of bushes, around trees, and over fallen logs. Fane stretched his legs and lengthened his stride, the wolf reveling in the hunt, the air flowing through his fur rippling every strand. As Fane chased after his quarry, he realized that this hunt felt different than others. He felt whole, the emptiness that was every unmated male's constant companion was being filled. Because of that the wolf was able to focus more thoroughly on the hunt, his thoughts no longer divided between man and wolf. If he felt this good just from finding his mate, how good would he feel once the bond was complete, once their mating was consummated?

Fane lunged one final time, pushing his long body to its limit with his hind legs and landed jaws first on top of his prey, breaking its back instantly. The wolf enjoyed the spoils of the hunt and once he had his fill he found a sunny spot, the grass warm from the rays and laid down, rolling to his side. Feeling the warm air ruffle his fur, Fane's mind reached out for Jacquelyn's without intending to. It was like his soul needed to feel its other half and if he went too long without that contact, he became bereft and restless. He didn't say anything to her; he just sort of slipped into her thoughts, enjoying being with her even if he couldn't physically touch her. Once his wolf was content that their mate was safe he got up, shook off the grass and dirt, and began the run back to the guest house. He would need a shower after his run and he still had his vows to write. He was really struggling with what to say to Jacquelyn, he knew what he felt, but he just couldn't find adequate words to tell her.

After a shower and sitting and staring at a blank piece of paper, trying in vain to put his emotions into words, Fane decided to take a break. As he was lying on the bed all he could think about was a certain fiery red head and that tonight she would be all his. He had really been hoping that Jacque would be willing to incorporate the human wedding vows into the bonding ceremony, but she wasn't ready for that. He had explained that their bonding was permanent, unlike a human marriage, but the idea of being married at 17 seemed to make her nervous, so he would wait. Fane was quickly learning that waiting really sucked.

"Wolf-man, we are heading your way, hope you're ready for this." Fane heard Jacque's voice in his mind. He grinned at her playfulness, which was one of the things his wolf really liked about her: she played, something that even wolves in the wild did as a part of the mating dance.

"I have been ready for you since I laid I eyes on you. Be safe,

I will see you shortly," he told her as he imagined himself caressing her soft face. He sent her that feeling as well and felt her shiver in response. That made him smile even bigger.

Looking at the time on his phone, 12:15, Fane got up, deciding it was time to get dressed just as he heard a knock at the front door.

"It's open," he said loudly.

Fane's mother Alina came through the doorway. "I brought you the vows you are to say during the ceremony, and I was wanting to ask you if you had gotten Jacque an offering yet."

"I actually got her two things. The first is an autographed book she told me she loved as a child but no longer owned a copy of. I hope that it shows her that I listen when she speaks and the things that she feels are important to her are important to me as well. The second I think I should show you." Fane walked out of the living room and went back to the bedroom, returning with a small black box.

"Fane, is that what I think it is?" Alina asked.

"I know that she isn't ready to go through the human ritual of marriage. I have tried to explain to her that bonding is more permanent than marriage, but still she wants to wait. Through the bonding ceremony she will have my mark, my scent, and that will tell all *Canis Lupus* that she is mated, but human males will not recognize this. They will, however, recognize an engagement ring," Fane explained.

Alina was shaking her head when she said, "Barbarians, all of you. Possessive, bossy, over-reacting wolves." Fane knew she was teasing because she was beaming from ear to ear. "Well, let me look at it."

Fane opened the black box to show his mother the ring he had chosen to put on the finger of the one woman who would complete his soul. The ring was a wide platinum band and engraved all the way around the band in Romanian were the words 'finalizarea, absolut, chiar, intreg' (complete, absolute, unmovable, whole), and in the center was a very rare red diamond in a marquee cut.

"Fane, it's beautiful. I recognize the band as the one that I gave you to hold onto until you met your mate, but where did you get the stone?" his mother asked him.

"The day I spoke with Da and he told me Sorin was coming, I

called Sorin and asked him to look in the vaults in the pack mansion for a red stone for the band. I figured with the vast size of the vault and the centuries of things accumulated he could surely find one. I knew the bonding ceremony would be taking place sooner than we originally planned and I wanted the ring to be ready. The day that Sorin took Lilly to her book store he made a stop at a jeweler while Lilly was working and had the stone set. I wanted red for two reasons. One, she is my *micul incendiu (*little fire), with so much personality packed into such a small package, and two, it will be a reminder of this day when we both shed blood to bind our souls to each other."

Fane suddenly fell onto the couch, face held in his hands. "Mama, how is it possible to love someone so intensely, so much that at times it feels like it's going to make your heart explode because you just can't contain it?" Fane looked up at his mother, his eyes drawn together, mouth tight.

Alina sat down next to him on the couch, handing back the black box, taking his free hand in hers. "I don't know if there is any way to explain or truly understand the bond between mates. It's not human; it's beyond the realm of reason and that makes it hard to believe it is even possible. I know you haven't known her long, I know you are both young, but you will grow close faster than you can imagine. She will become your best friend and you will become hers. Even now I know you feel it, that no one in this world will ever love you as she will. You were born to love each other and that love will grow stronger as time goes on." Alina wiped a tear from her cheek as she looked upon the face that she had watched grow from an infant to a strong Alpha male.

"What if I don't make her happy?" Fane's voice was so soft, laced with fear and worry.

"Oh, Fane." Alina began wrapping her arms around her only son, pulling him close. "You will make her happy. You will also make her mad, sad, and annoyed, probably a little claustrophobic at times, but you will make her happy. Your wolf will step in when your human side steps out of line. The wolf only sees black and white, all he understands is that she is your mate, that you must love her, protect her, provide for her, play with her, and make her content. Your human side will fill in the gap of emotions the wolf does not understand. She will make you a better Alpha, a better man. You will give her what no other man ever could: the other half of her soul."

Alina stood up to go, but first handed him a piece of paper. "These are your vows, you can add to them but the first part must be said, for it solidifies the bond." Then she turned to go.

Fane stood up, and before his mother could make it out the door he said, "Mother, my Alpha, thank you." And he turned his head, baring his neck.

Alina looked Fane in the eye and held his stare as she told him, "Te iubesc fiul" (I love you son), and she turned and walked out the door, closing it behind her.

Fane unfolded the piece of paper and with hands shaking read:

On this day I kneel before you, my mate, to ask if you will make me whole. Will you give yourself to me, finally calming the beast inside, bringing order to chaos, shining light where there has been only darkness? Will you bind your life to mine, your fate to mine, and your soul to mine and in doing so complete the mate bond?

After Fane read that it would be Jacquelyn's turn to respond with her answer and her vows. Once they read the formal vows, if they so chose they could recite their own vows. Up until a few moments earlier, Fane hadn't been sure what to say, but his mother had remedied that. Everything his mother had said was what he was feeling. Fane grabbed a pen, sat down, and quickly wrote out the words he would pour from his heart to his mate.

Checking his phone for the time, he saw that he only had fifteen minutes until he was to be in the garden where the ceremony would take place. He grabbed the suit hanging on his bedroom door, stripped faster than he thought possible, and was slipping into his jacket when he suddenly heard a scream in his mind. He fell to the floor from the force of the emotions coming with that scream. He felt confusion, pain, and most of all fear, all-consuming fear.

"JACQUELYN!" Fane sent the thought through their bond. *"Where are you? What's happened?"* Fane waited for her response but no words came through, only fear and pain. She was scared and she was hurt. Fane took off at a dead run through the house and out the front door and nearly collided with his father.

"Something is wrong, I can feel it in in the pack bonds. What is going on?" Vasile asked.

"I heard Jacquelyn scream and felt her fear and pain and now I can't get her to answer me," Fane answered.

"When was the last time you spoke with her?"

"She told me around 12:15 that they were headed our direction. She sounded fine, in no distress," Fane answered. He couldn't keep from looking at his surroundings, expecting at any moment to be ambushed, but by what, he didn't have a clue.

Vasile was halfway back to the main house before Fane even realized he had walked away. Running to catch up, he heard his father on the phone with Decebel.

"Get the vehicles started and the pack loaded. Skender and Boian together, Sorin and you together, I will have Alina and Fane. I want each vehicle to take a different route going towards Lilly's house. Keep your phones on, be prepared for anything. We don't know if they were just in an accident or if this is the act of an enemy." Vasile didn't wait for a response before he hung up. Just as they reached the door to the house Fane's mother stepped out dressed in black cargos, a fitted black t-shirt, and combat boots, her fighting gear. She threw Fane a gun and then turned to her mate.

"We ready?" she asked him.

"Yes, let's go. You drive, Mina, just in case we have to engage anyone. Fane, you keep trying to get in touch with your mate. Do you have her cell phone number?"

"No, I never asked for it because we've always just spoken through our thoughts," Fane said in frustration, shoving the gun in the waist of the back of his pants. "Wait, I can call the Henrys and see if they know anything."

Brian picked up on the second ring. "Hello?"

"Brian, it's Fane. Did you see Lilly and the girls leave today?" Fane spoke in clipped tones, holding it together by a thread.

"No Fane, I didn't see them leave. Is something wrong?"

"I don't know, but I think something may have happened to them. If you hear from them please call me right away." Fane hung up before Brian could respond. His hands shook as he set the phone down on the seat next to him. He closed his eyes and concentrated as hard as he could on Jacquelyn, on her face, the sound of her voice, the color of her hair, every detail he could think of and he reached out with a push of his power. *"Jacquelyn, tell me where you are."*

Nothing. *"Luna, please answer me, if you can't with words give me something, a feeling, a picture in your mind, something to tell me you are still with me."* Fane was getting more and more desperate the longer he went without hearing a response from her.

He laid his head on the head rest, frustration threatening to pour out in the form of a huge black wolf. Fane just wanted something even if it was just a memory of the last thing she saw. As they got closer to town, Fane called on the wolf to use his superior hearing and heard the faint sound of sirens.

"Da, do you hear that?"

"Yes, it sounds like it's coming from downtown," Vasile answered

"Lilly's book store is downtown," Fane told his mother.

"Were they planning to go there on their way to our home?" his mother asked.

"Not that I know of, but I still haven't been able to communicate with her. When she let me know they were on their way she did not mention stopping by the book store," Fane told his parents.

Vasile's face looked somber when he said, "If you are unable to communicate with her it more than likely means she is not conscious."

At the thought of his mate so helpless Fane struggled to hold onto his wolf, and his father, realizing that he was about to lose it, turned to him and placed his hand on his shoulder and let out a low growl. Fane's wolf submitted reluctantly, but only just, by the presence of his Alpha. Finally they turned the corner and were on the street of Lilly's book store. As they drove in front of it they didn't see any sign of Lilly's vehicle but could hear sirens up ahead. The further on they drove they began to see smoke and then bright orange flames surrounding an SUV that lay upside down in the ditch. As soon as Fane saw the fire, and before his mother could stop the car, he was out the door running at wolf's speed, not caring if it drew attention, not caring if people realized that there was no way a human could run that fast. As he got closer to the vehicle he saw four figures across the ditch close to the road, as far from the burning wreck as they could get without being in the road. Four figures, two sitting up, two lying down, neither of the latter moving. Fane's wolf pushed forward, his eyes going wolf blue, his teeth getting longer as he struggled to hold his form, running to his unconscious mate.

Chapter 4

Lilly's phone rang as they turned off their street onto the service road, headed towards the estate Fane's parents were renting. Shc answered it without looking to see who it was.

"This is Lilly."

"Lilly, it's Jeff from the store," she heard her employee say and she noticed that he sounded nervous.

"Jeff, is everything okay? You sound a little tense," Lilly told him.

"Well, there is a little problem. We have an irate customer demanding to see you, saying something about being ripped off. He won't go into details, but he is really angry and I didn't know if I should call the police or what so I called you."

"If he hasn't hurt anyone don't call the police, we don't need to bother them with this if I can solve it by me coming up there and talking to the man. Give me five minutes and I will be there," Lilly told Jeff.

Lilly hung up the phone and took the first turn that would lead to her bookstore.

"Mom, what's up? Is everything okay at the store?"

"I'm not real sure. That was Jeff, he is one of my assistant managers, and he says there is an irate customer demanding to see me. Jeff seemed pretty apprehensive about it so I think I need to stop by, but I will make it quick."

"It's no big thing, wolf-man can wait a few moments. I'm not going to tell him we are making a detour, let's make him sweat a little when I don't show up exactly at 1:00," Jacque said with a mischievous smile.

"I don't think you and Jen should be allowed to hang out any more, Jacque, she's beginning to rub off on you and I can't handle more than one evil witch at a time," Sally said sarcastically.

Jen rolled her eyes. "There's nothing wrong with making the man sweat a little. I mean, come on, he did fake his death and nearly drive our sweet little Jacque out of her mind. All's fair in love and war, baby."

"Well, there is that," Sally conceded.

They pulled up to the curb in front of the book store and all four of them piled out of the car. It was way too hot to sit in the car even with the air on and besides that Jacque didn't want her mom facing some lunatic by herself. Once they were in the store, Lilly started looking around, expecting to see or at least hear this so-called irate customer, but there was nothing. Everyone in the store was quiet, perusing through the store, some talking softly to one another. She walked up to one of the employees and asked where Jeff was.

"He said he had to leave, something about an emergency," the employee named Lisa answered.

That's weird, Lilly thought. "Well what happened to the customer who was so upset?" Lilly asked.

"What customer? There haven't been any upset customers this morning."

Although Jacque had noticed that she hadn't been picking up emotions lately, she could feel something wasn't right. "Mom, I'm not really liking the sense of this whole situation. Let's go, okay?" Jacque told her mother.

"Yea, I'm with ya, Jac. I'm getting a bad vibe," Jen added

Lilly felt the same way; something was wrong. They needed to leave but she didn't feel comfortable leaving the store open. She turned back to Lisa and told her to politely tell the customers there had been an emergency and that the store needed to close, and then asked her to lock up.

As they all got back into the car, Jacque couldn't stop the chill that ran through her body. She was blocking her thoughts from Fane and even trying to block her emotions because she knew if he thought she was even in the tiniest danger, or that there was even a potential for danger, he would come flying to the rescue and she didn't feel like the situation was that dire.

As Lilly began to pull away from the curb, Jacque asked, "So mom, what do you think that was about?"

"I'm not really sure. Jeff has always seemed honest. I don't understand why he would lie about an irate customer," Lilly answered.

"Maybe he's one of those disgruntled employees who's

gotten his panties all in a twist because he didn't get that raise he wanted. Or maybe he's got one of those problems where you hallucinate and see things that aren't there. Or maybe he's on crack so he's hallucinating and seeing things that aren't there, or hmphmm -" Before Jen could continue, Sally slapped a hand over Jen's mouth.

"We really need to work on that whole brain, mouth filter, Jen," Sally said morosely.

"Hmm hmm hmming" Jen grunted around Sally's hand.

"Yes, yes, we know you're just saying," Jacque translated for her.

"Well, whatever his panties are in a twist about, as Jen so eloquently put it, they just became the least of his problems considering he lied to me and then left in the middle of his shift." Lilly pinched her forefinger and thumb on the bridge of her nose. It was times like these that owning her own business seemed like the least brilliant of all her bright ideas.

Jacque was looking at her mom, seeing the tiredness seeping into her like water searching for cracks in a foundation when she heard Jen whistle.

"Check out that tall drink of somin, somin."

All of a sudden Jacque heard a huge bang. Lilly began to swerve. She jerked the steering wheel to the right to compensate but it was too hard. The SUV began to spin and as they hit the ditch on the side of the road, the car began to roll. Over and over it rolled like a barrel down a hill until it finally came to an abrupt stop, landing upside down with its wheels in the air. Jacque was screaming, hell, they were all screaming. She could feel the passenger side door crush into her side, the side of the front dash slammed into her leg and she felt a bone shattering crunch shoot up her leg and the seat belt was like a noose across her neck. She was so confused she didn't understand what had happened. Finally the rolling stopped and as the car came to a jarring halt Jacque felt her head hit the side glass window and then it was quiet.

For a few moments it was eerily quiet except for the rapidly growing fire crackling in the air, smoke rising like a beacon declaring their crash site to all around. Finally Sally groaned and began to try to move. She shifted her legs, experimenting to make sure she was still intact.

"Everyone okay?" It was she who spoke first.

"If by okay you mean are my ears ringing out of my head, is my leg all scrapped to hell, did my seat belt cut a gash in my neck, and did our stinking car just do the tango down the side of a ditch, then yes Sally, we are okay," Jen answered.

When Jen didn't hear Jacque respond with a snarky come back she knew something was seriously wrong.

"Jacque, are you with us?" Jen asked. There was still no answer.

Then Sally spoke up. "Ms. Pierce, are you okay?"

"I hit my head pretty hard but otherwise I'm good," Lilly answered. She looked over at Jacque in the passenger seat and saw that she was unconscious, very pale and had blood trickling down her face. Lilly sucked in a deep breath and let it out slow as she reached over, hand shaking, to check for a pulse and although she could feel one she didn't think it was as strong as it should be.

Just then they all jumped as a loud popping sound erupted, drawing their attention to the front of the car. The engine was on fire and the flames seemed to be growing hotter and getting taller.

"Ok, so I'm thinking that's not a good thing," Jen said, her voice quivering despite her resolve to hold it together.

"Jen, I must say your powers of observation astound me," Sally said dryly.

"Dammit girls, neither of you are helping with the smart ass remarks," Lilly growled, which was completely out of character for her. "I'm sorry, that was uncalled for," she told them.

"It's okay Ms. P. Not many of us handle being burned alive very well, it's a little traumatic," Jen said, trying to lighten the mood, "Okay, here is what we are going to do." Jen started taking charge, realizing that Lilly was going into shock and Sally was, well, being Sally. "Ms. P, I need you to get your seat belt off and crawl to the back seat to climb out because the fire is going to keep you from climbing out the front. Sally, you need to get your seat belt off as well and crawl out your window. I'm going to crawl to the front next to Jacque and help get her turned so we can slide her out of her window. Sally I need you to go around and pull her from the outside."

"But what about the fire? We will get burned. How will we slide her? What if her neck is broken? You aren't supposed to move someone who might have a spinal injury. What, OWWW HOLY

CRAP! What was that for, you psycho cow?" Sally screamed as she placed a hand across the cheek Jen had just slapped.

"GET A HOLD OF YOURSELF, MAN! Do what I tell you. We can't worry about her spine because it won't matter if she burns to death, dammit!" Jen yelled, snapping Sally out of her spaz attack.

"Okay, okay. I'm good. I just needed a minute to lose it but I'm good now," Sally said as she began to climb out the passenger side window. Lilly was also making her way to the back seat to climb out the window. She didn't say anything, she was moving on auto pilot, numb from shock. Once Sally and Lilly had made it out and Sally was going around the back of the SUV, Jen began to climb to the front of the vehicle.

"Jacque babe, you with me?" Jen asked gently, pushing Jacque's fallen hair from her face. Jacque didn't respond. "Okay, chickadee, here is what's going to happen." Jen was talking to Jacque as if she were conscious because it was the only way she could keep from falling apart. She couldn't believe this was happening, couldn't believe that her spunky friend was lying limp, all spark gone out of her. "I'm going to grab you under your arms and turn you so your legs are facing the passenger window, then Sally is going to grab your legs and help me drag your ass out of this royally screwed SUV. Do you hear me, Jacque? You have to be okay, you have to be because someone has to argue with me, and tell me when I'm being a pervert. Jacque, Fane will go crazy without you and we both know how much damage a crazy ass werewolf can do." Jen continued to talk out loud to Jacque as she began to reach around her, sliding her right hand behind her back and underneath her right armpit. She then slid her left arm under Jacque's left armpit, and bracing her back against the side of the driver's seat to gain leverage, she lifted and began to turn Jacque's body. "Holy crap, your little frame is deceiving, hoss. Did you hear that, Jacque? I basically just called you a fat ass, so wake up and chew me out already!" There was nothing but silence to answer Jen's monologue. Sally was trying to get close enough to grab Jacque's legs but the flames from the engine kept jumping out. Sally almost felt like they were alive and determined to keep her friends trapped in the burning tomb.

"Jen, what do I do? The flames are going to burn all of us if we pull her out," Sally yelled over the roaring fire.

Jen was wracking her brain for ideas, knowing time was running short. “Hey Sally, is there water anywhere in that ditch?” Jen asked, remembering that it had recently rained. She watched as Sally took off at a run. As Sally ran, Jen temporarily let go of her burden and stripped off her shirt. Good thing she had decided to go with a sports bra today. Then as gently as she could, which wasn’t very, but crap the car was on fire, she pulled Jacque’s jacket off.

Sally was back, winded. “Yes, there’s water.” She was bent over, hands on her knees, gasping with all the smoke swirling around.

Jen threw her shirt and Jacque’s jacket at Sally. “Take off your shirt and take these and get them wet, then put your shirt back on and then throw me these two back. We will cover Jacque’s body in them to protect as much of her as possible as we pull her out.”

“What about you?” Sally worried

“DAMMIT SALLY JUST GO!” Jen hated yelling at her but she had to keep her focused, she was also beginning to realize that she cursed a whole lot more when she was under pressure. Oh well, could be worse, Jen thought.

Sally was back, dripping wet in her shirt. She threw the jacket and shirt to Jen and did her best to cover Jacque. She figured her face and stomach, where there were vital organs, would be the most important which left Jacques arms partially bear and her legs completely uncovered, but it couldn’t be helped. Jen once again got her arms underneath Jacque’s armpits and lifted. Sally grabbed Jacque's legs and on Jen’s count of three Sally pulled and Jen pushed. With strength that neither could have ever dreamed they got Jacque’s limp form moving forward out of the window. Jen saw the flames leap forward and scorch Jacque’s legs. She figured this would wake her friend up but Jacque never stirred. Finally, Jacque's upper body was making it through the window which put Jen directly in the line of fire, literally. Jen felt the flames on her bare skin and couldn’t help the scream that forced itself from her lungs. The flames hitting her skin acted like a whip slashing her forward into motion. She heaved with all her might, lunging forward, but just before she could get her and Jacque far enough from the flaming SUV, there was a huge boom, a flash of light, searing pain, and then Jen saw no more.

Sally screamed as the engine exploded; the smell of gasoline permeated the air. She suddenly felt part of Jacques body go slack and she realized the explosion had pushed Jen forward and onto her stomach. Both of her friends were unconscious and laying on the ground next to a burning vehicle.

"MS. PIERCE!" Sally yelled. When she didn't get a response she turned, looking for Jacque's mom. Finally she saw her through the haze of smoke billowing from the burning vehicle, sitting and staring into the flames, her face as blank as a freshly painted white wall. "LILLY! GET UP AND GET YOUR BUTT OVER HERE AND HELP ME!" The urgency and desperation in Sally's voice snapped Lilly out of her shock and she ran over, realizing what was happening.

"Grab Jen's arms, flip her on her back, and start pulling as fast as you can. Don't worry about her skin, it will heal. We have to get them as far away from that vehicle in case it blows again." Lilly jumped into action, finally realizing that the stuff had hit the fan and she had to pull it together.

"Okay, okay, let's do this," Sally said as she grabbed Jen and flipped her on her back and began to pull and walk backwards as fast as she could.

Lilly grabbed Jacque by the arms and began to drag her back away from the flames as well. When they had finally gotten a good distance away, they fell down next to the two unconscious forms. Sally immediately checked to see if Jen was breathing. She was, but it sounded labored. Both girls were severely burned, but they were alive, and at that moment that was all that mattered. Sally could hear sirens blaring and figured somebody who had seen the smoke must have called 911. The sirens seemed really close but that wasn't what she saw first. Suddenly through the smoke Sally saw a form racing towards them, moving faster than she thought possible. Fane came to an abrupt stop in front of Jacque's prone, still form. He knelt down next to her and, taking a deep breath, he let out a mournful howl of sadness and fury.

Chapter 5

Fane was sitting quietly next to Jacquelyn as the ambulance, fire trucks, and police came blaring onto the scene. He didn't dare touch her for all her burned skin. The ache in his chest felt as if a sharp wire had been wrapped around his heart and was being pulled tighter and tighter. He hadn't even heard his father walk up, nor did he realize when the rest of the pack had arrived. Not until he heard Decebel's deep growl did he finally snap out of his grief. Fane's eyes jerked up as he saw the huge wolf kneel down next to Jen's unconscious body. She was only in a sports bra and every inch of her exposed skin was burned, red, angry, and blistering. Fane didn't know what to make of Decebel's behavior but that could be dealt with later, after Jacquelyn and Jen were taken care of.

Fane walked beside the gurney the EMTs had loaded Jacquelyn's damaged body on. He wasn't letting her out of his sight. He didn't care that he wasn't a family member as the EMTs kept telling him, he was riding with her, and once he let them see the wolf in his eyes they quit arguing with him. Fane heard his father tell Decebel to ride with Jen. Fane could only assume that he had picked up on Decebel's earlier show of emotion and decided to use it to his advantage for now. After all, a good Alpha always utilized his wolves to the best of their ability. Fane could only hope that his Alpha was utilizing the other wolves to figure out exactly what had happened. Sally and Lilly were being taken in another ambulance and Fane saw his mother climbing in to ride with them.

Fane's father walked up to him just before they closed the ambulance doors. "I will follow you to the hospital. Sorin, Skender and Boian are going to stay here and see if they can get some idea of what happened and if it was truly an accident or not." Fane simply nodded. His wolf was on the surface and Fane did not trust himself to speak for fear that he might let lose the barely contained rage that boiled close to the surface. In truth, at this moment anyone near him was in potential danger. That's what you get when an Alpha's mate is injured. The EMTs shut the ambulance door and a few moments later Fane felt the vehicle begin to move.

The ride to the hospital was tense, the air thick with Fane's fear and anger. Being in the small enclosed area without much room to move if he needed to defend his mate was making the wolf restless. The EMT who was riding in the back with Jacquelyn and Fane kept shooting Fane nervous glances. Humans often knew they were in the presence of predators when around werewolves, even though they didn't know werewolves existed. When they finally arrived at the hospital, Fane was more than ready to get his mate out of the enclosed box and into a more defendable place.

The EMTs lowered the gurney to the ground and began rolling Jacquelyn quickly into the ER. They had a mask over her face, providing her life-giving oxygen to her deprived lungs. Her face, despite the burns on the side that had been closest to the flames, was ashen. Her arms hung limp at her sides and were covered in blisters from the flames that had raked over them. Fane felt a growl rising in his throat again and only kept it in check when he felt a hand come down on his shoulder and his Alpha's power roll over him. His wolf submitted immediately. Fane continued to follow the gurney that carried its precious cargo and even continued on when they rolled her into the operating room. Just as he stepped into the room a hand came up on his chest, pushing him back. His response was swift. He snarled at the one who would dare come between him and his mate. Fane's father was there in an instant. "I apologize for my son's behavior. That is his fiancé' and he is really worried," Vasile told the doctor who was still brave, or stupid enough to have his hand on Fane's chest.

"I understand he is worried but he cannot be in here, it's a sterile environment. As soon as we have information you will be the first to know."

"Thank you," Vasile told him as he grabbed Fane by the arm, pulling him out of the operating room. Vasile let out a low growl, pushing his power into Fane to force his obedience. Fane reluctantly backed out of the room, never taking his eyes off Jacquelyn's still form until the doors closed and he could see her no more. Just then they heard a loud crash and a ferocious growl down the hall. Vasile backed Fane against the wall and glared at him, using his Alpha power he told him, "Stay." Fane's wolf met Vasile eyes for three counts before they finally dropped in submission. With that, Vasile turned and took off, moving towards the vicious snarls. He came around the corner into another operating room to find Decebel crouched in front of Jen's body which lay still on the gurney. "What the hell?" Vasile growled. Decebel was snarling uncontrollably, his eyes glowing gold. Several humans in blue scrubs stood in front of him in defensive postures trying to explain to him that they were trying to help her and had to touch her in order to do that. Decebel wouldn't budge. His wolf was in control. Vasile stepped forward, gently pushing one of the blue dressed humans out of his way. He growled at Decebel and just as with Fane pushed his Alpha power forward. "Stand down Decebel, they have to help Jen." Decebel didn't move, he turned his head slightly giving a small view of his neck but it wasn't total submission. "DECEBEL, MOVE. NOW!" Vasile snarled, throwing power at his Beta. Finally, with the Alpha order given, Decebel had no choice but to move out of the way. It was almost as if an invisible force was pushing him aside to allow the medical staff access to Jen. As soon as he was out of the way the humans moved into action quickly and efficiently, like a well oiled machine. Decebel watched, shaking with suppressed rage as they stuck Jennifer with needles and put a mask over her face that he assumed would give her oxygen. As soon as they started cutting off her clothing he snarled and turned, pushing Vasile out of the room, pulling the doors closed behind him.

"Decebel, what was that about?" Vasile calmly asked his Beta.

Decebel averted his eyes in submission as he answered his Alpha. "I was just watching out for her. You were with Fane, Alina was with Sally and Lilly. There was no one but myself to make sure the humans didn't harm her." Decebels words sounded true to Vasile, but he picked up an underlying emotion that he didn't think Decebel was even aware of.

"Her family will be here soon, Alina has called them. When they get here you can let them take over her care. Until then I would ask that you stand outside this door and if the doctor comes out before her parents are here, get any information he has so you can pass it along. Are we clear?"

"I will deal with her family when they get here. We are clear," Decebel responded, his voice emotionless, his expression hard.

"One more thing, Beta. Keep your wolf under control," Vasile warned.

"Yes, Alpha," Decebel answered as he backed up against the wall, folding his arms across his chest. He stood as a sentinel to the operating room where Jen was being cared for.

Vasile turned to walk away. Decebel watch him go, seeing him shake his head in confusion. Decebel was confused as well but he wasn't in any shape to look too closely at why. Just leave it alone Dec, he told himself.

"What was that all about?" Fane asked his father as Vasile walked up to him. Fane was still standing exactly where Vasile had left him, in front of the operating room where Jacquelyn was being treated.

"Decebel was protecting Jen. He felt responsible for her since all the rest of us were elsewhere." Vasile noticed his own voice didn't sound like he believed what he was saying.

"Really? That's what he said?" Fane asked skeptically

"I don't know what to make of it either, but when I came around that corner into the room Decebel was guarding her, not letting any of the staff near her. When they began undressing her he shoved me out of the room," Vasile explained, his brow furrowed, his voice heavy with disbelief even though he had seen it all with his own eyes. Fane didn't know how to respond to that, but he knew he couldn't worry about it right now because all he could think about was his mate. He just kept seeing her limp form, the only sign of life her breathing and pulse. No spunky attitude, no gentle touch. He closed his eyes, shutting off his emotions so he could keep his wolf in check.

"Fane, Vasile, where is Jacque and Jen?" Fane heard Lilly ask as she was walking towards them.

"Jacque is in this operating room and Jen is just down the hall. Decebel is guarding her door," Fane told her. Lilly's shoulders slumped and her head fell forward as silent tears fell to the floor. Fane walked up to the woman who had brought his precious mate into the world and folded her into his embrace. She squeezed him tight as if her life depended on it. Fane couldn't help but think it should have been Jacquelyn's father standing here consoling Lilly, but what had happened wasn't his fault. He and Lilly had made the choice to stay together knowing that he would probably one day have to walk away. It still sucked.

Finally Lilly pulled back, she looked up into Fane's face and patted his cheek, "Thank you Fane, thank you," her voice hoarse with emotion.

Lilly backed up against the wall across from the operating room and slid down to the floor, prepared to stay there until the doctor came out with news of her daughter. Vasile walked over and knelt down in front of her. "Lilly, can you tell me what happened? What do you remember?" he asked her.

Lilly tilted her head back against the wall, looking up at the ceiling, then squeezing her eyes shut. She tried to picture herself driving away from her book store, then she began to talk. "I had gotten a call from one of my employees." She told him all about Jeff and the supposed irate customer that didn't exist and how Jeff was gone when she arrived at the store. Then just before she started to tell him about the loud noise and losing control of the car she remembered the man that Jen had pointed out on the side of the road.

"Wait, did anyone see a tall man on the side of the road standing next to a blue car?"

Vasile shook his head. "There were no other cars Lilly, just yours. Did you see a man?" he asked her.

"Just before the loud noise and then me losing control, Jen pointed out this good looking guy on the side of the road. It looked like he might have had a flat tire or something. He couldn't have been far from where the wreck was, he had to have seen it." Lilly was beginning to sound frantic.

Alina and Sally had just arrived, hearing the end of Lilly's comments. Alina knelt down on the opposite side her husband and took Lilly's hand. "We will figure it out Lilly, it's going to be okay," Alina told her gently

Sally spoke up then. "She's right, there was a man on the side of the road. He was tall, and big. I didn't get a good look but according to Jen he was what she classified as a tall glass of somin somin," Sally explained

Vasile looked up at Fane, who had been quietly listening to the girls describe what had happened. "Did you see anyone driving away as you approached to the girls? You were the first one there."

"No, there was no one, only the girls," Fane told him, bringing the image of Jacquelyn's damaged form to the forefront of his mind. He closed his eyes and willed the image away.

"Sally, Lilly, you both are okay?" Fane asked them, trying to get his mind off the images of the accident.

"Just a few cuts, minor burns other than that we are both fine," Sally answered. "I'm sure Lilly asked, but how are Jen and Jacque?" she asked

Vasile spoke before Fane could. "Jen is down the hall in the other operating room and they are treating her. Decebel is standing guard outside the door. Jacquelyn is in this one here. The doctors have said they will let us know something as soon as they can."

"If you all have it in control down here I think I will go keep Decebel company while we wait for news on both of them," Sally told them.

"I think that would be a very good idea," Vasile agreed. Sally found this comment odd but didn't respond, she simply turned and walked down the hall to find Decebel.

Everyone was quiet, none daring to break the silence as if the breach would somehow cause harm to Jen or Jacque. So they waited, like silent sentries waiting for news on their fallen comrades.

Once again the thought crossed Fane's mind that waiting didn't just suck, it was a complete and total bitch.

Chapter 6

Sally stood across the hall from Decebel. She knew he was a big guy but in this hall, with his stone like features revealing nothing of his thoughts or emotions, he seemed positively huge. His only acknowledgment of her when she walked up was a slight nod of the head. Sally couldn't help but think that at any moment he was going to bust out with "me Decebel, you Sally" type language. That thought brought a slight smile to her face. She knew it was a comment that Jen would have appreciated. Since she could tell he wasn't going to suddenly become the conversationalist of the century, she could at least try to get a little out of him. "How are you doing, Decebel?" Okay, Sally would admit that under the circumstances maybe that was a 'did you really just ask that' question, but hey, it was all she could come up with.

Decebel raised a single eye brow at the brown headed human in front of him and considered the question. How was he? Did he even know how he was? The answer to that was simple, there was a whole lot of 'I'm hanging on by a thread' raging inside him. So naturally, he lied. "I'm doing fine. How are you?" See, Decebel thought to himself, I can be approachable when I put my mind to it.

"Huh," Sally acknowledged. "Are you always this reticent?"

Reticent? And here Decebel thought he was being so not reticent. Go figure.

"I am guarding this door, I am not being reticent. I am being sensitive to my surroundings which can make me seem aloof."

"Well I'll be, that's the most I have ever heard you say," Sally said in honest astonishment. "Wow, you were like, explaining yourself to me and stuff. Jen would be so proud of you." Decebel visibly tensed at the mention of Jen. "You know, I think she thinks you're like the chocolate bunnies they sell at Easter, you know all yummy on the outside but hollow on the inside." Now Sally was pulling a Jen, her brain, mouth valve just would not seem to close.

"She compares me to a bunny?" Decebel asked

incredulously.

"Not in so many words. You have to understand, Jen likes guys. Well, she likes hot guys." Sally noticed there was that slight tensing in his features again, but this time it was the mention of Jen and guys that seemed to bring it on. I'm going to have to do some sleuthing, she told herself. "But she doesn't date much because, despite her rough edges, she's really smart and she gets bored easy. So if the outside package is interesting but the inside is crap, she's just content to ogle the package from a distance."

Before Decebel could consider her words or respond, the operating door swung open. Decebel turned abruptly, standing directly in front of a balding, middle aged man with beady eyes and a severe chin. His eyes suddenly widened when he looked up at Decebel, who realized his wolf must be looking out through his eyes because the doctor's jaw dropped open. Sally stepped up in front of Decebel and put on her sweetest smile. She looked at the doctor's name badge before speaking. "Doctor Thomas, how is Jen doing?" Sally couldn't help the slight waver in her voice. Fear of the unknown was sometimes worse than reality.

Dr. Thomas looked at Decebel and then back at Sally. He seemed to be trying to make a decision. "Does Jen have any family here? Parents, aunts, uncles?"

"I'm her betrothed," Decebel spoke up.

Sally nearly broke her neck when she whipped around to look at him, her jaw nearly hitting the floor. Decebel glared at her, daring her to contradict him. She didn't. Sally simply turned back around to the physician, skepticism written across his face.

"Decebel is from Romania. They do things differently there and their marriage has been planned for a long time, if you get my drift." Sally was scrambling for some sort of reason that would justify this 20 something looking mountain being engaged to a 17 year old. Honestly, what the hell was he thinking?

"An arranged marriage?" Dr. Thomas still didn't sound convinced.

"Yes well, things are different in other countries. But you see, Jen will be turning 18 in just a few weeks and that is why Decebel is here now, because…"

Before Sally could continue to dig her deep, dark grave Decebel stepped in. "You will tell me how she is." Sally glared at him and he reluctantly added, "Please."

Sally decided Dr. Thomas just wanted to be done with them because he finally relinquished. "Your friend is not conscious yet and I have no way of knowing when she will become so. It is actually a blessing for her to not be awake to experience the healing process of burns. She has suffered burns over 70% of her body." Sally couldn't help the squeak that emitted from her throat, she felt her knees go weak and might have hit the floor had Decebel's hand not steadied her. "Most of the burns are on her left side and her back. There was quite a bit of glass and small bits of metal imbedded in her back and arms that we had to remove one at a time, that is what took the longest. She will need to be transferred to our burn unit where she will have daily debridement. I'm not going to sugarcoat it, she is in for a long, painful road to recovery."

"What about scarring?" Decebel asked. Sally realized she should have been the one asking the questions since Jen was like a sister to her, but she couldn't seem to get her mouth to work.

"It will be extensive. What? Will she no longer meet your desire for a mail order bride?" Dr. Thomas said in obvious disdain for the idea of Decebel and Jen's impending marriage, which was fake of course.

Sally felt like cold water had been splashed on her face at the doctor's comment. She felt anger like waves rolling off of Decebel. Damn temperamental werewolves. She reached up and placed a hand on his arm, a gesture she hoped would convey her desire for him to bring it down a notch.

"Ok, well, thank you Dr. Thomas. Can we follow them as they transport Jen to the burn unit?" Sally asked, her arm still on Decebel in silent warning.

"That will be fine. The nurses will notify me as soon as her parents arrive and I will be going over her treatment with them." Dr. Thomas gave Decebel one last sharp look, for good measure Sally assumed, but when Decebel narrowed those yellow eyes on the doctor he abruptly turned around and, with hurried steps, walked away.

They brought Jen out on a gurney shortly after the doctor's nervous departure. After the little display Decebel had put on, Sally was surprised when he gave her only a passing glance. Decebel looked away quickly and turned to look Sally in the eye. "I am going to go let Vasile know what is going on with Jen. You will go with her, I will send Alina to come up with you."

"Ok, can we pause this little sitcom for just a second because just a moment ago you were all, this is my betrothed, blah blah blah, and now you are just leaving her in my care? I don't get it," Sally told him.

"You don't have to get it," Decebel almost growled at her.

"Just one, all I want is one blasted wolf who isn't a bossy, grumpy hair ass butt head," Sally muttered to the ceiling as she turned to follow the gurney. "Is that too freaking much to ask."

She wasn't positive but she thought she heard a muttered yes from Decebel.

Fane saw Decebel coming down the hall towards them. He assumed this meant they had given him news on Jen. Why was it taking so long with Jacquelyn? Just as he was going to ask Decebel what he knew, the door to the room Jacquelyn was in opened and a short woman who looked to be in her mid to late thirties emerged. She wore her hair short in a practical manner, and her eyes spoke of someone who had seen too much grief in her life. None of that held Fane's attention as soon as he caught the woman's scent. His head spun around to his father. He saw that Vasile's stare was intent and he too was assessing the air. At his father's barely apparent nod Fane confirmed what he had initially thought, this woman was a *Canis Lupis*.

"Who is the guardian of Jacquelyn Pierce?" the woman asked, scanning the group that had gathered around her. As her eyes fell on Vasile, Fane thought he saw a slight recognition in them.

Lilly stepped forward, her steps heavy with worry and fear."I am her mother Lilly Pierce," she answered.

"I'm Dr. Cynthia Steele." Lilly's quick intake of breath did not go unnoticed at the sound of that name. After all, it had only been 24 hours since Fane had killed Lucas Steele. "I need to discuss your daughter's condition with you. Would you like to go somewhere private?"

Fane let out a low growl that had Dr. Steele's head jerking around to look at him.

"We don't have to go anywhere," Lilly explained, "everyone here is family to Jacque."

Before the doctor could continue Vasile stepped forward. "Dr. Steele, we need you to be clear with us about everything you know about her condition. Do you understand what I am saying?"

"You don't have to pull that Alpha crap with me, Vasile Lupei, I know who you are and I know who your pup is, considering he killed my brother only a day ago," she snapped at him. Fane and Decebel tensed at the tone of voice the woman was brave enough to use on their Alpha. Vasile just took it in stride.

"You are correct," Vasile confirmed, "my -"

Fane interrupted him. "Yes, I killed your brother and I am sorry for your loss, but I am not sorry for protecting my mate from someone who tried to take her from me."

"Protecting your mate? If she is so protected Fane Lupei, then why is she laid up, burnt to a crisp in my hospital?" Dr. Steele's voice was like a slap in the face.

Fane's eyes were glowing as power lashed around him, causing Dr. Steele to lower her head although it was not in true submission.

"Could we please get back to my daughter? We can deal with the werewolf crap in a minute," Lilly said as stress laced her voice.

"My apologies," Dr. Steele told her. "Jacque has suffered burns over 65% of her body, most of which are third degree, but some are second degree burns. Her right leg is broken in two places below her knee, her hip dislocated, and fragments of glass had to be pulled out of her arms. She is stable at this time, but she has not woken up from the anesthesia we gave her for surgery. I don't know that she will wake up anytime soon." She paused for a moment and when nobody said anything she continued. "I haven't done anything to her leg, I wanted to wait to see what her body's healing process is. Since she is half wolf she is going to heal faster than a human. Her skin should heal completely with no scars, her leg I'm not sure, but I was worried that if I put pins in it that it would heal too rapidly and those pins would be a hindrance not a help. There is one problem that I'm not sure what the outcome of will be."

"What problem?" Lilly whispered

"Jacque was given a human blood transfusion before I was able to get here. I don't know how her blood will interact with it, or if it will hinder the healing process. It's not something I've ever encountered."

By the time the doctor was through talking, Alina was holding a weeping Lilly in her arms. Fane had reached out to the wall for support as he felt the air sucked out of him. “I need to see her. Now.” Fane's eyes were glowing and his hands shaking at the amount of effort he was having to exert to keep his wolf under control.

“That isn’t going to be possible until she is transferred to the burn unit,” Dr. Steele told him.

“I don’t think you heard me right. I need to see my mate now.” Fane’s eyes continued to glow and his skin tingled with the need to change.

Dr. Steele’s jaw tensed briefly but she quickly composed her face. “Mate? Don't you think you both are a little young to be deciding something permanent?"

“I cannot, nor do I want, to change what fate has chosen for me. She is mine and you will either take me to her or I will tear this hospital apart to find her.”

She stood still, defiant, before she finally said, “Fine, follow me." Fane grabbed Lilly’s hand as he went to follow the doctor, giving her a small smile of reassurance.

They entered the operating room and then walked past the table that he had seen Jacquelyn on when they had forced him out of the room. Dr. Steele then pushed open another set of double doors bringing them into an area where there were multiple rooms encased in glass so that those who occupied them were clearly visible. There was a large round desk in the middle of the room that seemed to serve as what Fane would consider the command center. Fane took in a deep breath and although there were tons of smells of sickness, cleaner, worry, he could still pick out the cotton candy fragrance of his mate. He pulled Lilly along as he followed the path of her scent, no longer worrying about following the doctor's lead. He passed three glass rooms before he finally was standing in front of hers. He slid the door open to her little room and let Lilly step in before him. She rushed to Jacquelyn’s bedside and immediately started talking to her, holding her hand, brushing the hair from her face. Fane stood back and watched silently, giving Lilly time with her daughter. His wolf was so restless, anxious to be close to their mate, to touch her and feel the life flowing in her. He nearly growled at the idea of waiting even a minute more. At last Lilly turned to Fane. “Do you want me to step out?” Fane hated to ask that of her, but he needed a few minutes alone with his Luna.

"Yes, please." His voice was strained as he held himself back. Lilly nodded, gave Jacquelyn a quick kiss to her bandaged hand and then stepped out of the room, sliding the door shut behind her. At last it was just him and Jacquelyn. He walked slowly to her bedside, afraid that the moment was just a mirage and would evaporate before his eyes if he so much as breathed too deeply. But when he got to her side she was still there, not a figment of his imagination, but real flesh and blood. Fane leaned forward and gently brushed some hair from her bandage wrapped face. He placed his nose as close to her neck as possible without touching her and breathed her scent in deep. Her scent was like a soothing balm, it caressed his wolf, calming him and helping him to clear his mind of the dread that had been his constant companion since he had felt Jacquelyn's pain and fear through their bond. Then he kissed her lips so lightly that he barely felt their heat and whispered her name. "Jacquelyn." First out loud and then through their bond. *"Jacquelyn. Please hear me, my love, wake up for me."* Fane didn't know if it would help but he had to try. After waiting several minutes, Fane realized that she wasn't going to wake up, at least not right then. He heard the door behind him open and turned to see Dr. Steele and Lilly waiting patiently.

"We are going to transfer her to the burn unit, her friend is there as well. They will both have to undergo multiple debridements to remove the dead skin so that the new skin underneath can heal," Dr. Steele explained to them.

"Can I stay with her?" Fane asked, never taking his eyes off of Jacquelyn.

"You may visit, but you cannot stay in the same room with her. There is too great a risk for infection."

Fane didn't like that answer but he wanted what was best for his mate. Whatever it took for her broken body to heal was what he wanted for her.

"When do you think we will know if the human blood is going to affect her, or how it will affect her?" Fane asked the doctor.

"There is no way to know, Fane. I know that is not what you want to hear. Over the next few days as her body begins to heal, her wolf blood should increase the speed of that process. If it doesn't then we will know that quite possibly the human blood is hindering it."

Chapter 7

Jacquelyn's wounds showed much improvement over the next week, but Fane still continued to pace the waiting room area as he had since the day of the accident. He was beginning to feel like a caged lion ready to pounce on easy prey. He could tell that everyone was picking up on his edginess because they all seemed to be avoiding him like the plague. He couldn't help it, it had been a week since the accident and still neither Jen nor Jacquelyn had woken. They were both going through daily debridement's and although it did appear that Jacquelyn's body was healing a little more quickly than that of a human's, it wasn't quick enough for Fane. He felt helpless. His wolf was restless and desired to be near their mate. He hated not being able to be by her, protecting her while she was in such a vulnerable state, but there was nothing to be done about it. He continually tried to reach out to her through their bond, but all he got was darkness and silence.

***

Dark silence occupied the space his Luna's voice once filled, but he spent the second week attempting to pull her from the enigmatic place she resided. His concentration was broken when Decebel said, "I wish there was something I could kill," as they sat in the family waiting area on the burn unit floor, the same chairs they both had taken up residence in for the past two weeks.

"I could go for a kill right about now," Fane agreed.

Fane was pleasantly surprised to discover that he and Decebel, despite a huge age difference of 107 years, got along quite well. Up until now Decebel had always just been his father's Beta to him, a powerful wolf, and when he was younger actually quite scary. But as they had spent the past two agonizing weeks waiting in the hospital, they had at times been each other's only company and so had begun to get to know one another. Fane was glad for Decebel's company, otherwise he might have already torn down the door to where Jacquelyn lay too still for his own liking. Fane wasn't sure how much more waiting he could take before he demanded to be allowed to be with Jacquelyn all the time. It was getting harder and harder to convince his wolf to be patient.

***

Two more weeks passed and Fane marked the four week anniversary of the accident on the calendar he placed at Jacquelyn's bedside, praying the strength of tonight's full moon would return his Luna to her rightful place at his side. He gratefully stood next to Jacquelyn's bed during one of the limited visits allowed and couldn't tear his eyes from her. It was amazing how much she had healed in the past month. Her skin was raw and pink where the burns had been but you could see the new skin was knitting together rapidly. Dr. Steele had told him that her leg was completely healed. She had gone back through Jacquelyn's medical records to alter some of the past findings because there was no way she could justify a person's broken leg healing completely in four weeks. She had also told him that they still weren't out of the woods regarding the human blood she had received. Jacquelyn had been running a fever constantly for the past 3 weeks and Dr. Steele also said that her white blood cell count was elevated, which meant her body was fighting an infection. Whether that infection was from the burns, or had something to do with the blood, she didn't know. So he continued to wait, and wait some more.

Before he left, he leaned down and kissed her forehead, and as he did everyday he whispered her name through their bond. "*Jacquelyn, come back to me.*" He longed to see her emerald eyes staring into his.

And finally someone heard his pleas. *"Fane?"*

Fane leaned closer, as if proximity would help with their mental bond. *"I am here, Luna. Can you open your eyes for me?"* he asked her, desperate to bring her back to this world.

She didn't answer him, and he thought maybe she had slipped away again, but then suddenly he was looking into a sea of green. His breath left his lungs as he saw the light in them slowly return. Fane didn't realize he had shed any tears until she whispered in a dry, hoarse voice, "Don't cry wolf man, you didn't think you could get rid of me that easy, did you?"

He could barely contain the relief he felt at hearing her speak, seeing her awake. "I want to hold you, Luna, but I don't know where to touch you without causing you pain," he confessed, it was his deepest desire that moment.

"I'm so doped up I can't feel jack right now, so lay it on me," she told him with a weak grin.

Fane leaned forward as gently as he could and placed one arm around her waist. He laid his head on her shoulder, effectively placing his lips right against the bend in her neck to her shoulders. He kissed her as gently as he could and felt his wolf rumble in contentment.

"I missed you," Jacquelyn told him in a strained voice.

"I messed up, Jacquelyn. I left you unprotected, I could have lost you. It is inexcusable. How can you even want me near you?"

"Fane, this is not your fault. Don't go all Alpha on me right now. I need you more than ever," she told him without shame at her own dependence on him.

"I'm here, and I'm not going anywhere."

The door to the room slid open and, true to his wolf nature, Fane took up a defensive posture in front of his mate. Okay, so maybe he was going to overreact for a while, but everyone would just have to deal with it. Lilly walked in with Dr. Steele at her side.

Lilly let out a shuddered breath and tears tumbled down her cheeks as she looked at her daughter. She walked forward as Fane stepped aside to allow her access to Jacque.

"So nice of you to return to the living," Lilly teased, even though her voice quivered.

"Yeah, well, you would be lost without me so I had to come back." Jacque leaned into her mom as Lilly kissed her gently on the forehead.

"I love you, Jacque."

"I know you do, mom," Jacque responded with her usual remark to her mother's words; it was an inside joke between them. Lilly always said that Jacque was too big for her britches and Jacque continued to prove her right. At the sound of Dr. Steele's voice, Lilly turned away from Jacque to look at the doctor.

"Good, she's awake," Dr. Steele acknowledged. "Jennifer has woken as well, about an hour ago."

"How long have we been out?" Jacque asked apprehensively. Somehow she knew it hadn't been only a few hours.

"A month, Luna," Fane told her gently as he brushed some hair from her forehead.

"A month?" Jacque's eyebrows rose with question in her voice.

"I have had it arranged that she will share a room with her friend, Jen. Lilly has consented to that. Jacque, is that okay with you?" Dr. Steele asked her.

"Nothing would make me happier," she told the doctor, a weak smile joining her words.

Fane and Lilly stepped out of the room when transport arrived to move Jacque to the room she would share with Jen. As she wheeled past, she gave Fane a quick wink and challenged, "Race you to the room."

Chapter 8

Dillon was joined by his Beta, Logan in his office to go over the weekly update on how Jacque was healing. It had been four weeks since the accident and finally Logan had some good news to pass on.

"Jacque has awoken from her coma," Logan informed him.

"Do you know anything else about her well-being or just that she is awake?" Dillon's voice was gruff with emotion despite the wreck having been a month ago.

"From what I can gather she is healing rapidly, nearly as well as a full blooded wolf."

Dillon couldn't help thinking for the thousandth time how Fane could have left her, or any of them for that matter, completely vulnerable especially after the challenge he had taken part in. Then a thought that he kept coming back to occurred to him again. He spun around, glaring at Logan. "You were there, why didn't you help her?"

"I was going to, Alpha, but Fane got there so quickly and he would have known what I was had I revealed myself. I realize now Jacque's safety should have been my first priority, not my cover," Logan told him, eyes down, neck exposed in submission

Dillon appreciated the gesture as he was hanging on to his wolf by a thread and any defiance on Logan's part would surely forfeit his life.

"I was going to stay out of this. I was going to trust Lilly to know what was best for our daughter, but these past weeks the more I go over it in my head, I just can't, not now. Jacque could have been killed and all because her supposed mate, who is little more than a kid, didn't protect her as is his responsibility." Dillon knew in the rational part of his brain that maybe he was being too hard on Fane, but he couldn't help it, that was his daughter, and had she died he would never have had the opportunity to know her. That was unacceptable in his book. Jacque was still a minor, he could invoke his rights as her Alpha, that he take her under his care until she was an adult. Lilly would probably hate him for it but she would eventually see that it was better for Jacque this way. She was too young to mate, and worse, Fane was too young to be her mate. He didn't understand what it meant to be a mate, the responsibility that came with it.

Dillon turned to look at Logan. "You said there were four wolves besides Vasile and his son?"

"Yes, Alpha."

"Get the pack's first four, with you and myself that will make six. We will be walking in with an even number of wolves so as not to appear like I am challenging Vasile, but enough to show that I have support. Also have Colin charter a private plane, I want to get there as soon as possible."

Colin was Dillon's assistant, for lack of a better word, and took care of any pack business and acted as a liaison to other packs. Because of his Omega status, he wasn't considered a threat or a challenge to other packs, nor was he a submissive which would allow other packs to walk on him.

Logan nodded at his Alpha's request and turned to go.

"We leave in an hour," Dillon told his retreating back.

His plan could not be working out any better, Logan thought to himself. Although he hadn't wanted Jacque to get hurt, how was he supposed to know that a simple blown tire would cause the car to roll, and then catch fire? Logan's heart had been in his throat when he had watched Jacque's still form being pulled from the burning SUV. He had nearly rushed forward to help but he had picked up the sound of the other wolves' vehicles and had gotten in his car and driven across the median to the opposite highway. He had been driving the opposite direction as Fane and his family. They'd never even looked his direction, their eyes only on the wreckage. Logan had thought that over the past few weeks Dillon's anger would abate, but much to his dislike it had only increased.

Dillon walked into the pack defense room where he knew the 4 top members of the pack would be this time of day. Each was in various states of cleaning their assigned weapons and monitoring the parameter of the mansion on the various TV screens that were wired to the cameras all around the grounds. It seemed like an archaic thing to do as they had not had another pack attempt to challenge them on their territory in over a century. Old habits die hard, and as Dillon told them you can never be too prepared.

"Lee, Phillip, Dalton and Aidan, I need you with me. Assemble your weapons. At this point you will not carry them on your person, but I want them available in case they are needed. Go pack enough clothes for three days' time and then meet me and the Alpha in the main garage. I will explain what is going on while we are en route to our destination. Move out." Without a word the 4 wolves assembled their weapons and then left the room to comply with their Beta's instructions. Logan always felt a sense of pride when the pack obeyed without question, it was a sign of trust, trust that he was going to have to betray. Better not to think of that now, he told himself, just do what needs to be done, ask for forgiveness later.

Dillon stood in the main garage, waiting on his pack to join him. He was trying to be calm knowing that the pack would feel what he felt, he didn't want them to have to shoulder his burdens. It was his job as Alpha to protect them from unnecessary stress, but this was a situation that he had never dealt with before, and for the first time he didn't really know how to handle it. He called on his wolf, knowing that he would be less emotional and more practical; he would do what needed to be done. Dillon could worry about the emotions when the situation was under control. Logan had just shown up and right behind him were his top four pack members, all dressed in black fatigues.

"Have you briefed them on the situation yet?" Dillon asked Logan.

"No, Alpha. I figured I could do that en route."

Dillon nodded his head in agreement. "Alright, let's load up into the Hummer. Phillip, you drive."

Once on the road, Logan began to fill the wolves in on the situation in Coldspring.

"It is imperative at this point that this information stay within this group. Dillon will be the one to decide when the rest of the pack will know," Logan told them.

Dillon spoke up then. "It may make you all uncomfortable since she is your Alpha as well, but I have chosen at this time not to disclose this to my mate. Speaking of, excuse me from the conversation for one moment, I need to inform her that I will be gone for a few days." He said no more on the topic.

Logan heard Dillon tell Tanya that he was taking a business trip to discuss pack relations and ways to improve pack communications and that he would be meeting with some of the Texas packs. She didn't question him and once again Logan noted the simple trust, trust that was being broken even as the Alpha spoke to his mate. It was for the best, Logan decided, and just like he needed to take matters into his hands regarding Jacque, Dillon had to make the difficult decision of dealing with this situation without the added stress of his mate's emotions. Once the situation was contained, then Dillon could sit down with Tanya and explain things. Logan would be sure to be busy when that conversation took place. Tanya was hot-headed, and more often than not spoke before she thought. It was going to be a volatile mess when it came time to explain things to her. Yea, good luck with that, Alpha, he thought to himself.

"So the plan at this point," Dillon began after he had disconnected with his mate, "is once we arrive in Coldspring I will contact Vasile first per pack law and let him know we are there. I am sure he will tell Lilly, who will in turn tell Fane who you now know has declared himself Jacque's mate. You will not engage Vasile's wolves unless I command it. Is there any confusion about this?"

Each of the wolves shook their heads and bared their necks in submission.

"After Lilly is notified I will set up a time to meet with her to discuss my meeting Jacque. At this point I am not going to say anything about the fact that I am there to invoke my rights as her Alpha. I will do that after I have met her. I will also only do that in front of Vasile, his pup and his Beta. During that time only Logan will be permitted to be with me," Dillon explained.

By the time he was done telling his pack what would take place, they had arrived at the airport and were boarding the charter plane that Colin had secured for them.

As the plane took off, Dillon sat back in his chair and closed his eyes. He tried to envision what Jacque would say when he introduced himself to her. Would she be angry that he had not been a part of her life? Would she be happy to finally meet him? He was usually so confident in himself but at this moment he couldn't remember ever being so unsure of himself.

Logan was trying to work out in his mind at what point would be the best time to take Jacque from the hospital. He decided he was going to suggest to Dillon that after he invoked his Alpha rights to have Vasile pull his wolves from guard duty and instill his own. Since he was the head of the pack enforcers he would set the guard rotation for the night, which would be the most vulnerable time, when the staff was minimal, and the cover of darkness would aid him in his task. He was so close to his goal, so close to having the first thing he had truly wanted in a long time, and he would have her. No matter what it took, Jacque Pierce would be his.

Chapter 9

Once the plane had landed at a small private air strip Colin had found, they had a rental car waiting. Dillon found himself wondering, not for the first time, what he would do without Colin, he seemed to think of everything.

Logan knew the location of the hospital so he drove while Dillon found Vasile's number in the directory of Alphas. Yes, they had a book with all the Alpha's numbers in it. Dillon couldn't help but think that somebody else had a Colin as well who had come up with the idea. Dillon dialed the number and as he listened to it ring all he could think was how this was going to be interesting. Vasile answered on the fourth ring.

"Vasile," he answered with his name instead of a hello.

"Vasile this is Dillon Jacobs, Alpha of the Denver Pack. I wanted to inform you that I am in Coldspring. Is there another Alpha I need to call?"

Vasile was silent for several beats before he responded, "No, the pack here in Coldspring is not official yet. I will notify the Alpha that you are here." Dillon heard Vasile take and audible breath and then let it out slow.

"Do I want to know why you are here, Jacobs?" Vasile asked, using his surname.

"I have a feeling you know. I want to speak with Lilly and I want to meet my daughter. It is my understanding that she has been in an accident." There was a slight growl in Dillon's voice as he answered Vasile.

"How, may I ask, did you learn about Jacquelyn, or the accident for that matter?" Vasile asked, his voice laced with skepticism.

Dillon decided to let Vasile draw his own conclusion by giving half truths to his questions.

"Pack members talk, Vasile. You know how it is. A group of wolves together is worse than a beauty shop when it comes to gossip. So naturally, when I heard that there had been a challenge given to the strongest Alpha's pup, and it was in Lilly's home town, I checked into things."

Dillon did not mention that he'd had Logan following Jacquelyn, or that he'd been at the scene of the accident. He didn't think Vasile needed those details.

"We are on our way to the hospital now. Would you please ask Lilly to meet me in the entrance? And I would ask, Vasile, that you not let Jacque know I am here yet."

"I will let Lilly know, however, I will not guarantee that she will see you." Dillon started to interrupt but Vasile cut him off. "Jacque has been unconscious for a month. Lilly has been through hell for that month, she is stressed out enough right now. Nevertheless, I will let her know. If you get here and she isn't waiting in the lobby, then call me tomorrow, we will go from there. However, I must know, how is your mate going to feel when Lilly sends you home in a pine box, because you have to know this isn't going to go well," the Alpha told him.

"I will deal with Lilly. I have five of my wolves with me, my Beta and my first four. We are not here as a challenge in any way to you or yours. I simply want to meet my daughter," Dillon told him, his voice never betraying the subtle lie. He didn't just want to meet her, he planned to take her home with him.

"Understood," Vasile answered. "I would ask that you and your wolves lay low, and treat this as if it were my permanent territory. In other words, don't give me a reason to regret having let you remain here. My Beta, Decebel, will be waiting with her as he is the most neutral party when it comes to Jacque and I think you will need some neutrality while you are, as you said, *dealing* with Lilly. You will have to let me know how that goes," Vasile said in sarcastic amusement. "What is your ETA?"

"My Beta says we will arrive in ten minutes."

"Ten minutes, how courteous of you to give ample notice of your arrival." Vasile had hung up before Dillon could respond to the jab.

"Did that go as you expected?" Logan asked him.

"Pretty much, although Vasile seems very calm for such a dominant Alpha. Those are often the most deadly ones. They never betray their emotions, so one never knows what their next move is."

"Sounds like he would be a good poker player," Logan said

dryly.

Dillon didn't acknowledge his Beta's words, instead he thought about the best way to keep Lilly calm enough to let him see Jacque before he dropped the whole 'I'm here to take my daughter away' bit. Unfortunately there were no bright ideas that fell from the sky, nor had he come across a book called *how to appease the lover you scorned for dummies*.

They pulled into the hospital parking lot. It was packed, so Logan had to park the rental a good ways away from the front entrance.

"I'm going to go in and talk with Lilly. I want all of you to stay here. She is already upset about Jacque being unconscious for so long and having me here is adding insult to injury, so I don't want to freak her out more by having a pack of unknown wolves descend on her." Dillon knew that talking with Lilly would probably be harder than talking to Jacque. He had history with Lilly. The kind of history that leaves a wound on your heart that will never heal. It scabs over, often repeatedly, but when the scab comes off it is just as raw and painful as the day the wound was inflicted. Dillon was lucky, he had his mate, whose presence often held the scab in place. Who did Lilly have, he wondered.

Dillon was brought out of his thoughts at the sound of Logan's voice. "At what point to you plan to claim the rights of an Alpha regarding a minor?"

"I will decide that after I meet with Lilly," he told him.

Without another word Dillon opened his door and stepped into the warm Texas heat, and though it was hot, that was not what had him sweating. He shut the car door and turned to walk to the entrance of the hospital. At that moment he truly couldn't say what would be worse, facing a lover that you had hurt, or chewing on a mouthful of thumb tacks. When Dillon reached the entrance and opened the door the first thing he saw was Lilly's beautiful face. He knew then that he would much rather chew thumb tacks any day over facing the betrayal in her eyes.

Chapter 10

Sally was waiting in the hospital room as her two best friends were brought in. She stood anxiously, twisting her fingers together. The worry she had been feeling for the past month was etched on her tight lips and raised eyebrows which put wrinkles in her forehead.

"Oh, come on Sal. If you keep looking at me like I'm a sick puppy you found in a ditch I'm going to smother you with a pillow in your sleep." Jacque winked at her friend despite her tough words.

"Bloody hell, here I thought I was the reigning female dog in this posse." Jen grinned at Sally.

"Bloody hell? Female dog?" Jacque raised her eyebrows at her usually snarky friend.

"I'm trying to clean up my potty mouth, you know how near death experiences change how you live and what not." Jen shrugged.

"Jen, bloody hell is profanity. You know this, right?"

Jen looked at Sally and rolled her eyes. "Only to the English so it doesn't count."

"I don't even know how to respond to that," Jacque said dryly.

"I thought you two would never wake up. Jen still looks like a mummy all wrapped up and you look like a freshly cooked lobster," Sally told them as she pulled up a chair in between their beds.

"I was just getting my beauty sleep." Jacque looked over at Jen and grinned wickedly. "So what took *you* so long?" Her implication was clear.

"Oh, Jacque, your innocent little mind wouldn't be able to handle what was going on in my head that kept me from returning to reality." Jen yawned and patted her mouth demurely.

"You don't know, maybe my subconscious is more adventurous than the conscious version."

"Well in that case, as a favor to Fane, we will be sure to knock your ass out the night of your bonding ceremony," Sally said dryly.

Jen laughed, but it came out more like a strangled cough. "Don't make me laugh, my lungs are char broiled. I feel like a Burger King hamburger, always cooked over an open flame."

"Your way, right away, baby," Jacque added.

"There are so many better ways to use that comment than on a stupid hamburger commercial," Jen said in chagrin.

"And she's back," Sally teased as she watched life slowly seep back Jen's eyes, body, and overall demeanor.

"I need to say thank you. You guys saved my life and I just want you to know I love you both and I will be forever grateful," Jacque told them as she wiped a tear from her cheek.

"You would have done the same for either of us, Jac," Sally told her.

"Well, now that you are forever in my debt I will have to think of ways to put your gratitude to good use," Jen teased dryly.

Sally and Jacque both laughed and rolled their eyes at their forever obstinate friend.

Jen looked around the room, noticing that it was just the three of them. "So where is the wolf entourage?" she asked Jacque.

"They all stepped into the hall just before they wheeled you two in. Vasile took a phone call and when he came back he beckoned for everyone, but told me to wait here for ya'll," Sally explained. "I figure it must be important if it got Fane away from his woman. He has refused to leave the hospital for even a minute since she was brought out of the operating room," she told Jen.

"For some reason I can't say I'm surprised her hottie Mcwolf man is glued to her side. She was nearly freaking killed," Jen exclaimed.

"You did not fare any better." A gruff voice had them all turning towards the door. Jacque saw Fane push around Decebel to come to her side. It was Decebel who had addressed Jen's words, and Decebel who stared at Jen like she had grown a extra appendage on her head.

Jen glanced at Jacque and then at Sally, looking for some sort of clue as to what to say, but neither could throw her any bones because they knew about as much as she did about Decebel, and it added up to zero, zilch, and nada.

"Ooookay, and you would be here why?" Jen asked him with obvious confusion

"I'm here to guard you. I mean guard all of you. Not just you, but each one of you at the same time, not alone," Decebel stumbled along.

"Yeah, I got it, no need to hurt yourself further," Jen told him sarcastically.

Decebel's head jerked up to look her in the eyes. Jen saw what she could only describe as hurt. Had her words hurt him? She swallowed and felt a knot forming in her throat at the cold look in his eyes. After several seconds he turned and looked at Fane. "I will be downstairs for a few minutes. The Alpha will be standing guard with Alina." Without another word or glance back, he strode out of the room.

Everyone in the room let out a deep breath none of them had realized they'd been holding.

"Would one of you yahoos like to explain to me what has his tail in a twist?" Jen asked, looking from person to person, waiting for some plausible explanation.

"Okay, one," Sally said holding a finger up, "we have no clue, he has just been like that since we got to the hospital. And two, did you just say his tail was in a twist?" Sally asked with repressed laughter at her friend.

"If I did it's only because half my body has been deep fried and I feel like someone beat me with a sledgehammer. So, that said, I am allowed some dumb ass remarks. Lay off, Polly Perfect, or I'll have M&M's personalized with your phone number on one side and *for a good time* on the other," Jen threatened irritably.

"And she's back again," Sally grinned.

Jen flipped her off.

Yep, Jacque thought, we're going to be okay. Jen's being a female dog, as she put it, Sally is egging her on, and I'm in the corner staying out of the line of fire laughing my butt off. Things will be back to normal in no time. Jacque looked up at Fane as he leaned down and kissed her on the forehead.

"What was that for?" she asked him.

"For every smile I see on your face I will kiss you," he told her lovingly.

"What do I get for a laugh?" she asked, her voice thick with suggestion.

Fane grinned at her, flashing those amazing dimples. "I don't think now is the appropriate time to demonstrate that love."

Jacque thrust out her bottom lip, attempting to pout, which only made Fane grin bigger.

"So what was so interesting in the hall?"

Fane hesitated just long enough for Jacque to wonder if he was being totally honest. He had his thoughts closed off, which also made her wonder what was up.

"It's nothing big. My father got a call from a pack that is driving through the area, and he likes to make us aware when another pack is about."

Something in Fane's nonchalant tone told Jacque that Fane was hiding something. It didn't make her mad because at this point she knew he was going to try to protect her, even if it was just from a fly wielding a toothpick as a sword. Fane would not leave her unprotected ever again. She had a feeling the number of fights they were going to have in their long lives had just increased exponentially.

"So Jen, how'd it go with your parents once you woke up?" Sally asked. "They were here constantly while you were checked out."

"Oh, it went fine, but I can't handle my mom being all emotional and hovering. You both know I don't do hovering." Jen rolled her eyes.

"Ah, yes, the hovering. Your mom does tend to hover when she is upset," Jacque agreed.

"I wouldn't call it hovering, actually," Sally said thoughtfully. "It's more like full blown nose diving. You almost have to duck for cover when Jen's mom comes at you and she's worried."

"Hence why she is no longer here," Jen acknowledged."It took some convincing, but with a little help from Alina we got her and my dad to think it would be better for them to let me get some rest and unless something is wrong they will come up tomorrow night."

Jen looked at Fane thoughtfully before asking, "Does your mom have some sort of ability to make people do what she wants?"

Fane chuckled but shook his head no. "Not unless she hasn't told me. My mother has always been able to get people to see things from her point of view. My father says it's an art the way she can work people around her. I don't know, you will just have to ask her."

Fane squeezed her hand. *"How are you, Luna?"*

"Considering I've been burnt to a crisp, my leg crushed like it was run through a blender and glass sprinkled in my skin like I was

a cupcake, I'm pretty stinking good," she told him with her lips turned up in a smile that nearly melted his heart.

"I love you," he whispered.

"What's not to love?" she teased.

"Indeed," Fane muttered under his breath.

Decebel stepped back into the room and without looking at anyone he walked across the room to Jen's bed. "Are you alright?" The words revealed some sort of emotion but his tone of voice was just as gruff as ever.

Jen was beginning to get frustrated with his odd aloofness towards her. What the hell, she thought, if he doesn't care why even freaking bother to ask. Just like earlier she decided to handle his coldness with what she did best, flirting.

"I could be better," she told him with a slight pout. Out of the corner of her eye she winked at Sally, who was giving her a questioning look.

"What does that mean?" he asked even more gruffly if that was even stinking possible.

"It just means that my circumstances could be improved, which in turn would make me feel better," she told him innocently.

Jacque was in her bed with her hand over her mouth trying to muffle her laughter as she watched her friend work her magic. The funny part was that Decebel had obviously never met anyone like Jen. He didn't look like he knew what to do. Jacque had a feeling that uncertainty was not an emotion that Decebel often felt.

When he didn't respond to her, Jen crooked her finger at him, indicating that she wanted him to move closer. When he acquiesced and leaned down, Jen grabbed the front of his shirt and pulled him until he had to support himself on the bed with his hands and his ear was next to her mouth. Sally and Jacque watched her whisper to him and suddenly Decebel's body tensed, his muscles rigid with statuesque grace. After a moment he stood up, took one last look at Jen, and without a word turned and walked out of the room.

Jen busted out laughing as soon as the door clicked. "Man, that was rich," she said, still giggling.

"Would you like to share, my wicked little friend, what you did to poor Decebel?" Sally asked her with one eyebrow raised.

"A lady never kisses and tells." Jen grinned and winked at Sally.

"There are two very obvious problems with that statement," Jacque started.

"Yah, yah. I'm not a lady, and I didn't kiss him, blah blah. Details, details my dear Watson," Jen said sarcastically.

Jen grinned to herself. She couldn't believe the boldness in the words she had whispered to Decebel, but it served him right for being such a butt head to her. She was just messing with him after all, it didn't mean anything so what was the harm. She ignored the nagging little voice that was trying to contradict her thoughts.

Chapter 11

After Fane had gone back into the room with the girls, Lilly had her mini panic attack and was able to calm down when Alina told her she would slap her if she didn't. "So he's on his way here, as in now?" Lilly asked Vasile.

"Yes, as in now. He will be here in about 10 minutes," he told her.

"Did he say what he wanted?" This time her voice was stronger, more determined.

"All he said was that he wanted to talk with you and that he wanted to meet Jacque."

"Yes, but we both know there is more to it than that, Vasile. He has to have an ulterior motive to travel all this way. I'm sure he wants to meet Jacque, but that's not the only reason he has come," Lilly told him.

"Decebel is going to go down with you. Even though I don't think he would hurt you or allow harm to come to you I want Decebel to get a feel for things. I have called Sorin, Skender and Boian to see if they could scout around the hospital parking lot and get a look at Dillon's men," Vasile explained.

"I'm ready when you are, Lilly," she heard Decebel say, which was really weird because she couldn't recall a time when Decebel had ever spoken *to* her. There was a first time for everything.

"Ok, let's do this," Lilly said, rolling her shoulders as if she were getting ready to fight.

"She has worn off on you, too," Decebel said to her as they got into the elevator to go to the lobby.

"Who has worn off on me?" Lilly asked him.

"Jen. She always says these weird comments that make no sense to the situation, and I notice you do it too. She's like a virus that just keeps spreading." The last part was said more to himself than Lilly.

"If she is a virus than she is the only one of her kind in existence, and she's a virus I would catch any day," Lilly told him, looking at him out of the corner of her eye.

Decebel growled something imperceptible but said nothing else. As the elevator doors opened, Decebel put a hand in front of Lilly so that she would not exit before him. He stepped out and looked around and then motioned to her to emerge, evidently deciding it was safe.

"What happen to ladies first?" Lilly teased, just trying to expel her nervous energy. She knew what the answer was but she just needed something to keep her busy for a few minutes before she saw the man she had once loved with every fiber of her being.

"I don't know what idiot thought it was smarter to let a woman enter a room before him. How does he know if it is safe for her to enter if he does not check it out himself? It's actually a much more caring act to go before her, therefore ensuring that nothing will harm her," Decebel explained, his tone of voice at first sounded with disgust and then it was almost tender when he finished speaking. He might just make a fine catch one day, minus the grumpiness and bossiness that seemed to plague all things furry, Lilly thought.

They hadn't been standing in the lobby long when the front door opened and Dillon Jacobs stepped through. Decebel started to move in front of Lilly, one of those 'I must protect hear me roar' moments, but Lilly pushed him aside, never taking her eyes off Dillon. She couldn't help the hurt tinged with betrayal that bled into her eyes. It was 17 year old hurt, but hurt nonetheless.

Lilly straightened her spine and strode forward, trying to cloak herself in confidence that she didn't feel. Decebel trailed just behind her, a silent reminder to Dillon that she was protected.

Dillon spoke first. "Lilly, it's good to see you," he said with sincerity dripping from his voice. That only made his presence worse, to know that he really meant what he said, but regardless of any words he could give her, the fact was he belonged to another woman. Sometimes Lilly just wanted to give life the finger.

"It's good to see you as well, Dillon," Lilly managed to force that out, fake smile and all without vomiting all over his shoes. "I don't want to do small talk ,Dillon. We both know you aren't here to catch up, or to reminisce about old times, so just get to why you are here," Lilly told him, realizing that she didn't have the patience for bush beating today.

"I know about our daughter. I sort of know why you didn't tell me about her, but I want to meet her, I think I deserve that much." Dillon's voice held honest hurt.

"I was going to tell you *that* night." She didn't have to specify what night it was. "But I came home and telling a note you are pregnant isn't quite the same as telling the father." Lilly knew she shouldn't be a butt head, she had made the choice to stay with Dillon after she knew that he would one day have no choice but to leave her.

Dillon tilted his head to the ceiling, closing his eyes. He inhaled a deep breath and let it out slowly. When he looked at Lilly again she could tell that he was struggling to keep his emotions in check.

"I didn't want to leave. You know that I didn't have a choice. Lilly, I would have stayed, I would have married you, been the father Jacque deserved. I would have."

Lilly cut him off. "I know that, ok, but that is not what this is about. You want to meet Jacque, well, that will be up to her. I will tell her you are here, and if and only if she wants to, you can meet her. But you're going to have to give her some time to process this, Dillon."

"I know it's a lot, but I want to see her today. I need to speak with her about some important things she needs to know about being a wolf."

"She has people to tell her about being a wolf," Lilly snapped at him, letting her frustration at the situation get the best of her.

"Right, the pup who allowed her to be harmed." Dillon's voice held obvious contempt for Fane.

Decebel growled low and stepped forward, pushing past Lilly's arm. "You will not disrespect the prince, he has done nothing wrong."

Dillon seemed to gather himself and back track. "I was wrong to assume it was his fault, Beta. I meant no disrespect, but you have to understand that as her father it was difficult to learn that your daughter was injured while in the care of another wolf."

"You may be her father, but only in blood," Decebel shot back at him, then turned to Lilly and took her arm. "We will go back and discuss this with Jacque and let you know something in the next hour." Decebel didn't give Lilly a chance to say anything more, he simply took her by the arm and started dragging her to the elevator.

"Bossy much?" Lilly glared at him as the elevator doors closed with a ding. "Why did you tell him we would contact him in an hour, Decebel? That isn't going to give Jacque much time to think about whether or not she even wants to consider meeting her father."

"The longer it takes for her to decide, then the longer he is here, and he has plans. He wasn't being completely honest about why he is here," Decebel explained.

The elevator gave a slight lurch as it made it to the floor where Jacque and Jen's room was. The doors slid open and once again Decebel exited first and then motioned for Lilly to follow.

"What do you mean he has plans?" Lilly ground out.

Decebel continued to walk towards the girls' room without answering her question. As they approached the door, Vasile and Alina stood from the chairs they had been sitting in front of the room where Jacque and Jen were recovering.

"What did you learn?" Vasile directed the question to Decebel.

"He wasn't telling the whole truth. He does want to meet her, his emotions are sincere, but he is definitely hiding something," Decebel explained.

"I don't understand how you could tell all that," Lilly spoke up

"When a person is dishonest their body gives off cues. Human senses cannot pick up on them, but wolf senses can, and are highly attuned to them," Decibel explained. "When you lie, generally your heart rate is quicker, your body gives off a slight odor from perspiration that you might not even know is on your skin, but it's there, your pupils dilate slightly, and your nostrils flare out. Dillon being a wolf can hide some of that, but I think seeing you threw him off and he wasn't protecting his emotions as well as he normally could, especially for an Alpha."

"So the million dollar question is, what does he want with Jacque?" Alina asked.

Just then the door to the room they had been guarding opened with a slight, but noticeable creak. "What does who want with Jacque?" Jen asked as she stepped out of the room into the hallway.

Chapter 12

Jen walked slowly, it was awkward because of all the bandages and the I.V. pole she had to drag around with her.

"Why exactly are you out of bed?" The question came from Decebel.

"I tried to tell her to stay put, but she's about as cooperative as a wet cat," Sally told them as she too came out of the room.

Jen hobbled over to where Decebel stood and stopped right in front of him. "I'm out of bed because there is nothing fun going on in bed," she teased. After her earlier encounter with him she couldn't help but feel brave and she could tell it made him uncomfortable for her to flirt with him, which only made her want to flirt more.

Decebel glared at her and took a step back. "You should be resting, not traipsing around in a hospital gown with an I.V. pole," he told her, sounding completely indifferent, just as if he were talking to a total stranger. Jen turned away and looked at Sally to hide the hurt in her eyes, which she didn't even know why she was feeling but there it was.

"What did I tell you, Sal, there is something going on and we are always being left out. So Ms. P, who wants to see our little wolf princess?" Jen asked, keeping her back to Decebel but not moving away either.

It was Vasile who answered. "Dillon Jacobs is here to see Jacque."

Both girls stared at Vasile blankly, "Right, right, and Dillon Jacobs would beeee?" Jen prompted.

"Jacque's father," Lilly spit out.

"Oh, snap," "Shit fire and hold the matches," Sally and Jen said at the same time. Vasile and Decebel coughed, both trying to cover up chuckles at Jen's vocabulary. Jen had the good grace to look slightly abashed at her outlandish statement, but only just.

"That doesn't even begin to cover it." Lilly's voice was distraught and frustration was written across her brow.

"So when were ya'll planning on dropping this nuclear bomb on Jacque's lap, because I think I am going to be needed elsewhere in the hospital at that exact moment," Jen told them. Sally stood next to her, nodding her head in agreement.

"We are going to tell her now," Decebel answered, giving Jen the perfect excuse to turn and ogle him without being obvious that she was indeed ogling.

Or so she thought until she heard Sally whisper in her ear, "So, Decebel is looking drool worthy I see."

Jen whipped her head around so fast that she knocked foreheads with Sally. "Freaking A, Jen, your head is even harder than I originally thought," Sally whined.

"Yea, well, Sherlock yours ain't so soft either," Jen snapped. Sally gave her a knowing look, reminding her that she had caught her checking out Decebel. She shouldn't be bothered that Sally had called her out on it, she checked out guys all the time. This was different though, this was a freaking hot as sin werewolf. Yeah, okay, maybe the burns were going to her head. That must be why she would suddenly be fixated on the unattainable. Although, she thought, werewolves can have flings can't they? She looked at Decebel again, who was studying the floor like it had the answers to life written on it in Aramaic. A fling with him, hmmm, could be interesting. She didn't realize she had spoken that last part out loud.

"What kind of fling would be interesting?" Sally asked.

"What? I didn't say fling, I said sling. A sling for my arm, because of the burns and what not." Jen stumbled over her words.

"Uh huh, right, a sling. We'll have the nurse get right on that, Jen." Sally's look of 'you're full of b.s.' matched her tone of voice.

Jen turned to Lilly then, for once not wanting the attention directed at her. "Okay, well I say we get this over with Ms. P, just rip it off like a band aid, nice and fast." As she was talking she was hobbling back to the room with her I.V. pole in tow. Before anyone knew what she had planned, Jen swung the door open, saying, "Jacque, dear old dad has come to pay his respects to the nearly departed."

Jacque's head snapped up. "What?"

"Crap, why did nobody tell me someone with a freaking I.V. pole could move that fast?" Sally blurted out.

Lilly came into the room, followed by Vasile, Alina and at last

Decebel, who was just as broody as ever. Jen crawled back into bed with Sally's assistance and turned to look at Jacque, who at the moment looked at a loss for words. That's a new one, Jen thought.

"Mom, tell me that Jen inhaled one too many smoke fumes, or that she is high on morphine, or even that she is just saying that to be a butt head."

Lilly shook her head. "How I wish I could give you any one of those excuses, but she was being just as brutally honest as she always is. You father is here and he wants to meet you."

Fane let out a low growl and Jacque laid her hand on his to help calm him. He looked at her and used their bond to talk to her. *"You don't have to meet him, you know that right?"*

"Yes, I know. But Fane, it's my father and he's here to see me. I can't tell you how many times I have dreamed that I would get to meet him one day," Jacque told him, and then she thought of what she had asked him earlier when she felt like he wasn't being totally honest.

"Wait, did you know about this? Is this what you weren't telling me?" Jacque glared at Fane skeptically.

Fane kneeled down so that he was face to face with her. *"I'm sorry, love. I just didn't want to upset you and I didn't know what he wanted. I wanted to wait to tell you when we had more information."* Fane's eyes were pleading with her to understand.

"Never keep things from me, Fane. It will never end well for you, we clear?"

"Crystal, Luna. Please forgive my thoughtlessness." Fane bared his neck to her out of respect for his mate.

"Man, that is so freaking yummy," Jen said, watching the exchange between Fane and Jacque along with everyone in the room. "I want one Sally, go find me one."

"One hot, loving, passionate, furry werewolf coming up," Sally said sarcastically. "Would you like fries or tots with that?"

"I prefer whipped cream actually," Jen said wistfully.

Decebel coughed and sounded like he was choking, while Jacque and Fane stared at the two girls in perplexity.

"I swear my two best friends have no shame. Absolutely, utterly, completely and wholly without indignity," Jacque's voice was full of mystification.

"Jacque," Lilly's voice brought Jacque back to the reality of the situation.

"Oh, right, so my father is in town…not sure what to feel about that to be honest."

Fane wished he could hide the worry that something wasn't quite right but she picked up on the thought before he could block it.

"What do you mean you don't think something is right?" she asked him out loud.

Fane turned and looked at Decebel. "Did you confirm it?"

"Yes, my prince, he is hiding something," Decebel answered.

Fane looked back at Jacque and he gently held her bandaged hand. "Love, he is here to meet you, but he is hiding another motive and we don't know what it is. It's making us very leery of him. I can't say that I like the idea of him near you."

"You will be with me, right?" she asked.

"Of course." He nodded.

"Then I won't be in any danger." Jacque said it with complete confidence in him.

He leaned down and kissed her gently. *"Thank you, Luna. I will always keep you safe."*

"I know wolf-man, I'm counting on it," Jacque smiled at him and gently ran her fingers down the side of his face.

Jen cleared her throat. "I don't mean to bust up an obviously promising interlude, but we kind of need to figure out what you want to do, Jac."

"I'm going to meet him," Jacque said bluntly.

Lilly looked at her daughter and gave one nod of her head that she understood. Vasile stepped up to Jacque's bed and placed a hand on Fane's shoulder, "Why don't you get some rest, Jacque. Sleep tonight and then your father can come meet you tomorrow."

Fane nodded his head in agreement with his Alpha, "I think that is a good idea, Jacquelyn. You've been through a lot today, you need to rest."

"I know I have, but I feel amazingly better. Aside from the fever I can't seem to kick," she told him in astonishment.

"That's your wolf genes coming out, we heal really fast. You are obviously going to heal much faster than a human but not quite as fast as a werewolf."

"Jen, how you be over there?" Jacque asked, using the slang that was nearly second nature with her best friends.

"Wait for it," Jen said as she began the process of unwrapping her legs and arms. Sally had started humming the song from the game show Jeopardy.

"Sally, wow, it's you! I've always wanted to meet you."

"It's me what?" Sally asked Jen, curiosity thick in her voice.

"The mayor of Smartassville of course. You should carry a sign that says welcome to Smartassville, population: 1."

Everyone in the room was trying to cover their laughs with coughs when Lilly finally gave it up and laughed out loud. "I'm sorry, Sally, but you have to admit that was pretty funny."

"I guess, for someone whose brain cells have been cooked recently, it'll do."

Jen finally had her legs and arms unwrapped and there was a collective gasp in the room.

"I must not have been burned as bad as you because I don't even have blisters on my legs anymore, the skin is just raw and really red. The ones on my chest are almost completely healed as well. Somebody will have to look at my back and shoulders to see if they have healed as well," Jen said, sounding dumbfounded.

"What?" Vasile, Alina and Decebel all spoke at the same time.

Jen looked around the room at each of them, unsure. "I said, I don't even have blisters on my legs or chest anymore." She nearly squeaked when Decebel was at her bedside in a flash. For someone so big he was surprisingly gentle as he examined her skin.

"You will tell me if I hurt you." Decebel held her blue eyes with his golden wolf eyes.

Jen couldn't say anything, she just nodded. All she could focus on were his hands touching her leg and she didn't even try to hide the soft sigh that came out as he ran his finger across her skin. He went to pull the front of her shirt down just enough to see her collar bone but Jen slapped his hand away. "You didn't buy tickets. You don't get a free show, fine, drool worthy werewolf or not."

"Alpha, it is true, her skin is healing rapidly. Too rapidly," Decebel said, looking at Jen.

"Why are you looking at me like I've grown a second head again?" Jen asked him, confusion marked her face.

Decebel just stared before finally turning and walking away. As he walked past Vasile he said, "I will take first watch tonight at the door." And then he was gone.

Jen was confused and frustrated at the little scene that took place but she couldn't worry about that right now, she had bigger fish to fry. If there was anything bigger than Decebel that is.

"Why would I be healing so fast?" she asked Vasile.

"I don't know. We will just have to continue to monitor you. Maybe have Dr. Steele run some blood tests on you," Vasile told her.

"Okay, well, I guess I will call Dillon and let him know that he can come tomorrow if you're sure, Jacque," Lilly told her.

"I am sure. Avoiding him won't do me any good. I think I need some sort of closure or whatever else it is that psychologists call it." Jacque's voice betrayed the fact that she really was tired even though she was feeling better.

The rest of the afternoon consisted of Jen and Jacque taking naps and when they were awake they continually bantered with one another with Sally as the mediator. There was never a moment when Jacque wasn't touching Fane or vice versa, both of them constantly seeking comfort from the other.

Finally, when it was time to call it a night Sally secured some sheets and a blanket from a nurse and slept on the couch by the window. Fane pulled up two chairs and sat in one while propping his feet in the other.

"You are not going to sleep like that," Jacque told him skeptically.

"You are right my love, I am not going to sleep at all," Fane told her. "Don't try to convince me otherwise, we have a group of strange wolves in your town, one of which is the father you have never met. There is no way I will sleep under those circumstances."

"Well, tell us how you really feel there, white fang," Jen said sarcastically, laying down and pulling the covers up. She felt really cold for some reason and was beginning to shiver.

"Are you okay, Jen?" Sally asked, noticing that her friend was acting like she was cold when it was not cold in the room.

"I'm just cold all of a sudden. Could you get me another blanket, Sal?" Jen asked, her teeth chattering together.

Sally walked over and opened the hospital room door and stuck her head out. Decebel was standing just to the right of the door.

"Hey Dec, could you get Jen another blanket please?" Sally asked him. She could have done it herself but she was experimenting. What could she say? She was an opportunist.

Decebel stood up straight and turned to face Sally directly. Trying to look past her into the room he asked, "Why, is she okay? Is something wrong?" Sally raised a single eyebrow at him. "I mean if something is wrong we might need to get Dr. Steele or something, that's why I'm asking," he said, trying to look nonchalant.

"Uh huh, right. Well, I think maybe she just has a little fever. That usually makes me shiver. So if you would be so kind," Sally prompted.

"I will bring them in to you," Decebel said as he turned away to search for her request.

A moment later the door opened to the room, letting a stream of light in that shone across the white floor, making the room seem harsh and uninviting.

Decebel walked over to Jen's bed instead of handing the blanket to Sally. He spread the blanket out over Jen while she simply watched him in silence. Once the blanket was in place he turned and walked out, closing the door quietly behind him.

"Is he bipolar, schizophrenic, or is there some weird werewolf gene that makes you a jack ass one moment and then somewhat nice the next only to then throw you back into jack ass mode within a single breath?" Jen asked, turning to direct her question at Fane.

"I don't know what is going on with him, Jen. I apologize if he is causing you distress. I can talk with him if you'd like."

"Na, it's all good. If he keeps it up I will gladly tell him to get the proverbial stick out of his fine, furry butt." With Jen's final statement the room fell quiet and Fane began to hear one by one the even breathing of each girl that indicated they had fallen asleep.

Chapter 13

Standing in front of the window in the hotel suite that Colin had reserved for them, Dillon ended the call he had just received from Lilly and turned to his wolves. "I'm going to meet Jacque tomorrow morning at 10:00 a.m. All of you will accompany me to the hospital but only Logan and I will go up to the floor she is on, and only I will go into her room. Right now they are insisting that Fane stay with her while I speak to her, which I guess I understand. She doesn't know me, I would be leery as well."

"It will all work out, Alpha," Logan told him in an unusual display of emotion.

Dillon nodded his head once in acknowledgment of his Beta's words. There was a small part of him that felt that something was off with Logan but he just shook it off. Logan was his most faithful wolf and he'd never given Dillon a reason to doubt his trust.

"I'm calling it a night. We need to leave here at 9:15 in the morning so make sure everyone is ready," Dillon instructed Logan.

"As you say, Alpha," Logan responded. He watched his Alpha walk towards the room he was staying in until the door closed behind him. Logan told the other wolves that he was going to go get something to drink, they didn't question him. Why would they, he was second to the Alpha. In reality he needed to finalize his plan. He was going to have to make sure that Jacque wasn't conscious when he took her because she would be able to alert the pup who was trying to claim her. Much to his surprise, when he had contacted the Coldspring pack and sniffed around to find out which members were still loyal to their dead Alpha, he had discovered that the doctor treating Jacque was Lucas Steele's sister. And wouldn't you know it the dear old doc was very forthcoming about her anger towards Vasile and his pup, so upset in fact, she offered her assistance. Things could not be going better. Doctor Cynthia Steele was going to come in and check on Jacque during his guard shift and give her and Jen extra doses of morphine. He also assumed that the third girl,

Sally, he thought he remembered them calling her, would be in the room. The only way to keep her knocked out without chemical use would be to use a pressure point in the neck to keep her unconscious. She would wake with a horrendous headache but it was better than having to harm her to keep her subdued.

Next, he had to procure transportation and a place to take her. That was what he was going to do tonight. Once again the Coldspring pack was willing to accommodate this for him as well, and thanks to a few disgruntled wolves who were angry at the death of their Alpha, they had offered up their assistance. One of the wolves, he didn't know his name, he didn't want to know names, was giving him a car and once again Dr. Steele stepped up and loaned him the use of her ski lodge in Colorado. He thought that would work out well because he figured once they knew what had happened they would never think he would take her back to his home state. The tricky part was going to be keeping Jacque from knowing where they were so she couldn't send Fane any clues. Until he had bonded with her and done the blood rites she would have that mental connection with Fane.

The wolf loaning him the car was going to meet him at the back of the hotel to give him the keys. He had parked the car in the hospital parking lot closest to the ER. The plan to get Jacque out was simple. Dr. Steele would transport her on a stretcher to a side door that physicians used right next to the ER. Since there was always commotion late at night in the Emergency Room, no one would notice a doctor wheeling a gurney out the side. Logan would pull the car right up and slip her inside. If things continued as they were he would be on his way to Colorado with his mate in tow in no time. He smiled to himself, quite impressed with his ability to plan all of this on his own.

He walked out the back exit to the hotel and, true to his word, the wolf waited with the keys.

"It's a tan Ford Escape, so it won't stand out. I parked right where you told me to," he told Logan.

"Thank you, I appreciate all of your help." Logan's voice was full of truth, he really was appreciative. Without the Coldspring pack's help this endeavor would have been much more difficult.

"We are just glad that the Romanian mongrel isn't going to get to keep our Alpha's chosen mate. We want him to suffer for taking our Alpha from us." The wolf's voice was dripping with malice.

Logan didn't want to linger here so he thanked the wolf again and then headed back to his room. As he entered the suite, he saw that the others had turned in already. He decided to take a quick shower since he didn't figure he would get another one for a couple of days.

As he laid down in his bed, the crisp hotel sheets itchy against his skin, he couldn't get comfortable. He had a feeling it had nothing to do with the itchy sheets and more to do with his conscience. He shut the door tight in his mind, not daring to examine the black spot that this choice was placing on his soul. His wolf approved of what the man was doing and that was enough. They both knew that Jacque would be better off with a mate who could protect her, one with experience. Logan closed his eyes, trying once more to fall asleep, but it eluded him for many hours into the night.

Dillon woke to the sound of his phone alarm going off. He reached over to the bedside table and picked it up to cancel the alarm. He took a deep breath, sat up, and rubbed his hand across his face, trying to dislodge the sleep from his brain. Standing up, he stretched and grinned. Today he would meet his daughter for the first time. He was scared out of his mind, but he was happy as well. He took a quick shower, shaved and dressed quickly in plain Levi's, a black t-shirt, and black boots. When he emerged from his room he saw that all of his pack were up and dressed and ready to go.

He looked at his watch and saw it was 9:15 on the dot. "Let's head out," he told them and headed for the door. Logan and the other wolves fell in line and followed Dillon out.

Once in the car and on their way to the hospital, Dillon turned to Logan. "I made a decision while I was getting ready this morning."

Logan nodded his head in encouragement for Dillon to continue.

"I've decided that after I've introduced myself and spent a little bit of time with Jacque, I will announce my Alpha rights and let Lilly know my intentions to take Lilly to her true pack. The shit is going to hit the fan, so be ready. Dr. Steele is going to make sure security is ready if need be."

"We will be ready," Logan assured his Alpha.

Chapter 14

Fane watched as Jacquelyn sat fidgeting in her hospital bed. Her skin was healing so fast and it was itching like crazy. So on top of bcing nervous about meeting her father in just a matter of minutes she was also itching like she had a bad case of fleas.

"Are you okay, Jacquelyn?" Fane asked her.

Jacquelyn looked at him sheepishly. "Just nervous and itching. My skin is healing so fast and the scabs are driving me crazy."

"Do you want me to see if they can give you something for the itching?" he asked her.

"No wolf-man, anything they give me will probably make me sleepy. I will just havc to deal."

Fane and Jacque turned their heads at the sound of a growl from a human throat. The sound was coming from Jen. She was rubbing her back vigorously against the wall. She actually looked like a horse scratching itself against a tree. Jacque thought about pointing this out, but held her tongue when Jen started spewing expletives.

"I feel like my skin is crawling with little ants it itches soooooo bad!" Jen ground out as she continued to attempt to assuage the itching by rubbing her back against the wall. Sally opened her mouth to say something but promptly shut it when Jen's head whipped around. "One word, one word Sally Michelle and so help me you will have to sleep with one eye open for the rest of your life for fear that I will steal all your dolls and make them do unholy things, take pictures, and then put them on your Facebook page with the caption 'I still play with dolls'." Jen was breathing hard after her rant.

"Jacque, I think we should tie her up when she spends the night with us, just to be on the safe side," Sally told Jacque dryly.

"Word," Jacque answered, using the slang she and her two best friends were so fond of.

"I think I would have to agree with your sentiment, Sally," Fane added.

"Watch it, Cujo. Just because you're hot doesn't mean I won't retaliate," Jen growled, still trying to allay the itching of her healing skin.

"Wolf," Fane muttered, as Jacque patted his hand, "I'm a bloody wolf."

The door to the room swung open and Decebel walked in and froze. He stopped cold at the sight of Jen growling and rubbing against the wall. She looked at him and nearly snarled. "Do you not know how to knock? And what the hell are you staring at? Haven't you ever seen a girl being groped by a wall before?"

"Not one who was so obviously enjoying it," Decebel answered without inflection.

Sally looked at Decebel, shaking her head from side to side. "The safest road at this point is to maintain neutral, in a non-threatening stance, and for the love of all humanity do not engage the beast. Just keep your mouth closed."

"Right, well I just came to get you and Jen and take you to another room so that Jacque can visit with her father," he told Sally.

"He's here?" Jacque squeaked.

Decebel looked at her and nodded. "He is on his way up now." He turned back to Jen and Sally and simply said, "Come."

Sally began to follow. Jen, of course, could not be that cooperative. "Oh, I'm sorry, did I miss something? Am I wearing a dog tag that indicates I should be walking on all fours and responding when a big grumpy ass werewolf tells me to come?"

Decebel turned and growled, "One of these days your mouth is going to write a check that your cute little ass can't cash." Decebel thought this would render her speechless but he should have known better.

"Oh, don't worry fur ball, I plan to be writing that check out in your name." With that she winked at him and hobbled past a dumbfounded Decebel, IV pole and all.

Sally turned and patted Decebel on the arm. "Good try, chief, but you are sparring with a master in her craft, and didn't we just discuss not provoking the beast? Geeze, try to save someone's life and they just throw it out the window," Sally continued to mutter as she walked past Decebel, her hands in the air as if to show her surrender to another's stupidity. "I'm done, finished, and if you hairy, testosterone filled, egotistical, snarling, drooling, flea infested werewolves want Jen to neuter you in your sleep than far be it from me to stand in your way."

Decebel turned and looked at Jacque. "Your friends have issues. Serious issues."

"You have no idea," Jacque said, shaking her head as Decebel turned to follow her two best friends out. "Good luck with that," she hollered before the door closed.

"Well, that was interesting," Jacque told Fane.

"Interesting definitely, but something is up with Decebel and he isn't exactly the most forthcoming wolf. Figuring it out is going to be like trying to figure out who shot Kennedy."

Jacque looked at Fane and grinned, "You know about Kennedy?"

He laughed, "Why wouldn't I?"

"You're from Romania," Jacque said with a 'duh' look.

"Like I told you, I studied American history. My parents wanted me to know more than just Romanian history."

"I guess that once we are in Romania and start school, I will learn all about Romanian history?" Jacque asked him.

"You will learn a lot about Romanian history as it pertains to the pack. It is a lot of information, but important since you will one day be the Alpha female."

"Ugh, don't remind me, it really freaks me out," she whined.

"My silly Luna, you are going to make an amazing Alpha. Don't doubt that." Fane leaned down and kissed her gently on the lips.

"Mmm, there is not enough of that going on lately," she teased him.

"Yes, well, I didn't think you wanted to give Jen free entertainment."

"How right you are wolf-man," Jacque joked.

There was a knock at the door causing Jacque to sit up straighter. Fane stood up and walked to the door to open it. Before he did he turned and looked at Jacquelyn. *"You ready, love?"*

"You are with me, so yeah, I'm ready."

"Always, meu inimă (my heart)."

"Oh, and Fane?" Jacque started.

"Yes?"

"Try not to kill my father, okay?"

Fane's eyes glowed blue and he growled low.

"Stop it, wolf-man, answer the door." She laughed at him,

thankful for the brief distraction.

Fane opened the door and a man stepped in. He wasn't nearly as tall as Fane, but he had broad shoulders, red, wavy hair the same color as Jacque's, and he had the same piercing green eyes. Fane felt like he was looking at the male version of his mate, he had to admit it was a little creepy.

The man held out a hand to Fane politely. "You must be Fane Lupei. I'm Dillon Jacobs, Jacque's father."

Fane took Dillon's hand and shook it. "I am Fane, Jacquelyn's mate," Fane told him without looking away from the Alpha wolf's eyes.

Jacque realized that neither of them was going to relinquish before the other, she had to step in before one of them did something stupid. So she cleared her throat. Okay, it wasn't much but she figured telling the two Alphas to get their heads out of their butts wouldn't go over real well.

"It's probably best that you did not say that, you are right, my love," Fane told her, obviously listening to her inner dialogue. He had told her once that her thoughts fascinated him. Her response had been that she was glad she could entertain him.

Dillon turned his head in response to Jacque. "You must be Jacque."

"In the flesh. Well, at least what's left of it," she answered.

Dillon let out a soft growl but caught himself quickly. "Yes, we will get to that shortly. First I just want you to know that had I known about you, I would not have stayed away. You don't have to believe me, but I at least want you to know that I would have been here and a part of your life."

"I believe you," Jacque told him, tears gathering in her eyes, and before she could stop them they were pouring down her cheeks.

"Oh, little one, I'm sorry." Dillon walked quickly to her side, he felt awkward for a moment until Jacque made the first move, she reached out to him and just like that Dillon was holding the little girl he'd always wanted. He pulled her close and she cried harder. He rocked her and whispered over and over, "I'm so sorry little one, so, so sorry."

Jacque couldn't believe she was blubbering like a baby, but crap, he was here. The one man she had always wondered about, where he was, what was he doing. If he had been around would he have taught her to climb trees, or change a tire? Would he have taken her to the movies the way Jen's dad did with her or taken her fishing? It just all sort of hit at one time and she couldn't hold it back any longer. It was pure instinct that had her reaching for a complete stranger, a stranger, but still her dad.

Fane stood back, his wolf pacing as he watched a stranger hold his mate, his mate who was hurting. He hated that she was hurting and that he couldn't be the one to comfort her. Call him selfish, so be it, but she was his, his alone.

"I'm sorry, wolf-man. Please don't take it personally," Jacquelyn told him

"I know, love, don't worry about me. Spend time with Dillon. I will be fine." He sent the thought to her as well has a picture in his mind of brushing his finger tips across her neck where his mark should be by now. That just made him growl again.

Jacque finally composed herself and pulled back from Dillon. He gently brushed her hair out of her face.

"I know I wasn't there for a long time, but I'm here now. I want to be a part of your life if you are okay with that."

"I would like that," Jacque said honestly.

"Why don't you tell me about yourself: favorites, dislikes, and all the stuff a father should know." Dillon smiled reassuringly.

"Well, where to begin?" From there for the next few hours Jacque and Dillon talked about anything and everything. Fane could tell that they had very similar personalities. Their likes and dislikes, even their sense of humor was alike. He was happy for her, he really was, but his wolf still did not trust Dillon Jacobs.

Finally, Dillon stood up. He looked at his watch, realizing that they had been talking for four and a half hours. Lunch had come and gone and the entire time Fane had stood against the wall opposite Jacque's bed, never moving, just standing and watching her. Jacque looked up at him and smiled, that smile was worth every minute he had stood there keeping her safe.

"I'm all yours as soon as he leaves," she told him through their bond.

"I'm going to hold you to that, Luna." He winked at her and saw her cheeks turn pink. He loved it when she blushed, loved that he was the cause of that blush.

"I'm going to let you get some rest. I will be back later, though, if that's ok?" Dillon asked her.

"Yea, I'm good with that," Jacque answered.

"Okay, great." He turned to Fane and once again held out his hand, "Fane, thank you for your patience and letting me spend some time with Jacque."

"If it makes her happy and she is safe, I will always be okay with you spending time with her," Fane told him, letting his wolf show through his eyes just a little.

Dillon took a step back before he could catch himself. Interesting, Fane's wolf thought, Alpha, but not over him. Good to know.

Fane was on his way over to Jacque before the door clicked closed. He sat down on the edge of the bed next to her. "How are you, really?" she asked him.

Fane leaned forward and placed his lips on her neck and breathed her scent in deep. His wolf growled in contentment. "I'm better now," he admitted.

Jacque laughed and brought his lips to hers and kissed him gently. Fane deepened the kiss enjoying the way she tasted, reminding him that she was safe, and she was his. Jacque moaned as he pulled back. "Will it ever be enough?" she asked him with a grin.

"I hope not. I hope you always want more of me. I must prepare you now, I will never get enough of you," Fane told her without shame at his need of her.

"Duly noted, wolf-man," she teased him.

Chapter 15

Dillon stepped out into the hall after having spent the morning and part of the afternoon with Jacque. He could tell that Fane really did care for her and he was beginning to rethink invoking his Alpha rights. If he didn't he would lose her, she would bond with Fane and then go off to Romania, just when he had found her. Maybe it was selfish but he didn't want to let her go. Not yet.

He hadn't taken but a few steps when Lilly, Vasile, his mate, his Beta, and Logan were walking towards him. This was not going to be pretty.

"How did it go?" Lilly asked him.

"Really well, she told me all about herself. She's not shy at all." They all chuckled at that remark, obviously in complete agreement.

"So what now?" It was Lilly who asked again.

"I think we need to talk." Dillon looked her in the eyes. "All of us." He addressed everyone standing in front of him.

Vasile lead the way to a private family area. Nobody sat, not wanting to put themselves in a vulnerable or submissive position.

"Speak," Vasile ordered. This was the Alpha talking, not Fane's father.

"I'm invoking Alpha rights in regards to my daughter, who is a minor," Dillon announced with complete confidence.

Vasile growled, causing Dillon's confidence to waver momentarily, but then he remembered that he had every right to step forward, it was pack law.

"You know I have every right, Vasile. She is still a minor, she is my daughter, and it has been made apparent that Fane is not ready to protect her the way a mate should." At that last part Decebel lunged forward. Vasile caught him before Logan could intercept him.

"How dare you speak about our prince with such disrespect again," Decebel growled.

"Decebel, stand down." Vasile spoke calmly, but there was a pulse of power in his words that poured over the room, pushing everyone to their knees, including Dillon.

Dillon fought the command and managed to get to his feet.

"I will ignore the disrespect you have just shown my family, Jacobs, and only address the pack law that you have brought to our attention," Vasile told him.

"What is he talking about, Alina?" Lilly whispered.

"Just listen Lilly, and whatever you do, stay calm," Alina told her firmly.

"Calm, okay, got it," Lilly responded.

"You are correct it is pack law that you have the right to invoke Alpha rights, but you need to be sure that this is really what you want to do. You do realize that having a pissed off teenage daughter will make your life difficult, to say the least?" Dillon didn't respond.

"Have you thought about what she wants, that she wants to be with Fane?" Alina asked him gently.

"I have, but then kids do not always know what is best for them. If she comes with me I will get to spend time with her. She can use the time away from Fane to figure out if he really is the best thing for her."

"Go with you? What the hell are you talking about, Dillon?" Lilly's jaw was clenched in anger.

"Calm, remember," Alina told Lilly.

"He just said he wants to take my daughter."

"OUR daughter." Dillon interrupted.

"No, that is not how it works, Dillon. You don't get to come and say you're her parent and that she should come with you when she doesn't even freaking know you!"

"Lilly, she is half wolf. You can't possibly know everything that is best for her," Dillon tried to reason.

"Everyone out." Lilly's voice was like a whip. "Out! Everyone!"

Vasile nodded to Decebel and his Mate.

"Logan, go," Dillon told his Beta.

Once the door closed and Dillon and Lilly were the only two in the room Lilly straightened her spine and looked Dillon dead in the face.

"I don't know who you think you are, Alpha or not. If you try to take her she will hate you. She loves Fane, they are mates, and you of all people know what that means. If you try to keep them apart you will rip their souls in two."

Dillon took a deep breath. "I'm not taking her from him indefinitely. She's only 17, Lilly, she isn't even an adult."

"She will be eighteen in two months, Dillon, which you might know had you been around when she was born."

"Fine then, I will have her for two months, because once he bonds with her she will be gone, Lilly, and I just found her." Dillon's voice was soft and Lilly could hear the pain in it.

"Why do you even want her so bad? Surely you have full-blooded werewolf children with your mate, which I do not begrudge you by the way."

Dillon looked at the ground when he spoke. "We were never able to conceive."

The words hit Lilly like a punch to the gut, pushing all the breath out of her.

"Jacque is your only child?" she asked him.

"Yes."

Neither of them spoke for several minutes. It was Dillon who broke the silence.

"Lilly, I'm not trying to be the bad guy. I could have lost her in that wreck. She should have been protected, and I'm not blaming you. Fane is responsible for her, he just isn't ready, they need time to mature. If all I can get is two months with her, then so be it, but maybe if they step back for a little bit they will see that it would be good to wait to bond."

"You're trying to intervene what fate has ordained. It's going to back fire on you, Dillon. If Jacque doesn't want to go with you, I swear to you I will do everything in my power to keep it from happening. God help you when Fane finds out." Lilly turned abruptly and fled the room, slamming the door behind her.

Logan walked in just after Lilly's departure.

"That went well," Dillon said sarcastically.

"Vasile wants to speak with you," Logan told him.

Dillon nodded his okay for Logan to let Vasile in.

Vasile came into the room and his power followed him. Dillon could feel it and it grated on his wolf as if being petted against the grain of his fur.

"What are you going to do?" Vasile asked.

"Just what I said, Jacque is coming home with me at least until she turns 18. If she wants to be with Fane after that, then I can't stop her. So from now until she leaves my wolves will guard her. You will pull your wolves back, and Fane can be here during the day but I don't want him sleeping up here."

"So be it. You had better keep her safe, Dillon. If anything happens to my son's mate while in your care I will take it out of your flesh." Vasile's voice was that same deadly calm, but Dillon's wolf had no choice but to submit.

Vasile turned to Logan. "You need to come introduce yourself to Jacque. While you are doing that I will get Fane." Vasile turned and looked back at Dillon. "Hold your wolves back until I get Fane away from the hospital. You have no idea what you have provoked. You will be lucky if my wolf can make him submit."

"Logan, go with Vasile and meet Jacque, I will call the rest of the pack and tell them to wait until I say to come in," Dillon ordered his Beta.

Vasile left the room with Logan behind him. Dillon took a deep breath, wondering for the hundredth time if he was doing the right thing.

Chapter 16

Vasile opened the door to Jen and Jacque's room and walked in without knocking. At this point politeness was not at the top of his agenda. Decebel was standing against the wall, his look cold and promising death. Jen and Sally were sitting on one bed looking very confused, and Fane and Jacque were on her bed. Fane stood up abruptly when he saw the other wolf enter the room with his father.

"Alpha, who is this?" Fane asked him.

"This is Logan, Dillon's Beta. He has come to introduce himself to Jacque because he will be helping with guard duty," Vasile explained.

Jacque smiled and said hello but could tell something was wrong. She looked at Fane, who was still staring daggers at his father.

"Fane, I need to speak with you in the hall while Logan introduces himself."

Fane growled.

"Stop!" Vasile ordered. "Decebel will stay here, she will be fine."

Fane turned to Jacque and leaned down to kiss her. *"I will find out what is going on, love. Will you be okay?"*

"I'm fine, Fane. Go, do what you need to but then come back to me." She kissed him gently and smiled into his blue eyes. Fane gave her hand one last gentle squeeze and then turned to follow Vasile out of the room.

Logan stepped up to Jacque's bed and held out his hand. "Jacque, I am Logan, it's so nice to meet you."

Jacque smiled politely but her words were tense. "It's nice to meet you as well." Jacque had barely gotten the words out when they heard a loud growl and things being slammed about outside of the hospital room door. Jacque started to get up. "What the hell is that."

Decebel got to her before Logan could touch her. "Jacque, stay here please. Logan and I will be right outside to see what is going on."

"Okay, please make sure Fane is okay. He is blocking his thoughts," Jacque told him.

Decebel nodded and then turned back to Jen and Sally. "You two stay put."

"Once again I am reminded that I should be wearing a collar that says 'if found please call the bossy werewolf who thinks he is my owner at 1-800-butt-head'," Jen said sarcastically.

All three girls heard Decebel mutter under his breath, "Little, mouthy smart ass." As he followed Logan out of the room and into the hall, it was a complete wreck. Chairs had been thrown, glass in the family area broken, Fane had gone crazy. Decebel turned to Logan. "If anything happens to any of those girls, you will die by my hand after I have declawed and neutered you."

"I will protect them," was Logan's only response.

"HE CAN'T HAVE HER!" Fane yelled. His voice had gone guttural, his wolf pushing to take over. His claws had pushed through his fingers and his eyes were glowing wolf blue. His canines had begun to elongate.

"Fane, STOP!" Vasile growled at him.

Vasile had taken him down to the Emergency Room and was using one of the family holding areas to talk to his son. Alina and Lilly had gone with them.

"Ea apartine cu mine, cu ranita noastra (She belongs with me, with our pack.)," Fane pleaded with his Alpha.

"It's pack law, Fane. I cannot stop him."

"ARRGGGHHH!" Fane slammed his fist into the wall, punching a huge whole. "Nu ma intereseaza despre ranita legea, ce ti-ai legii. Ea este colega mea, sufletul meu si ma intrebi pe mine sa mearga intr-o parte din ei (I don't care about pack law, about your law. She is my mate, my soul and you ask me to walk away from her)." Fane grabbed a chair and threw it across the room, shattering the glass windows. He didn't even pause before a ripped the television out of the wall and threw it out the window, following the chair to its fate.

"Fane este de ajuns (Fane that is enough)." Vasile's power flowed over the room, driving Fane to his knees. Fane's shoulders slumped in defeat, his head hung. His hands were balled into fists, the claws that had begun to shift digging into his hands, cutting deep.

"What would you do if it was mama?" Fane's voice was so low that Vasile only heard it because of his wolf hearing.

"I would kill anything and anyone who kept her from me," Vasile admitted. "But Jacque is not in any danger, and it's not for forever, it's just two months and then you can complete the bond and blood rites." Vasile knew he was asking the impossible, he wouldn't want to be separated from his mate for even two days let alone two months, but Fane and Jacque were both still minors and not bonded. By pack law, Jacque's father had every right to do what he was asking. What could Vasile do?

"You can be with her during the day, but he asks that you don't spend the night with her," Vasile told him, trying to speak as calm as possible, knowing he was prodding an already angry beast.

"El solicită? Vrei să spui că ţi-a spus, Alpha la cel mai mare pachet de lupi gri din lume, el vi sa poruncit, că nu am putut sta cu partenerul meu pe timp de noapte? (He asks? Do you mean he told you, Alpha to the largest pack of Grey wolves in the world, he commanded you, that I could not stay with MY mate at night?)" Fane growled.

"Înţeleg că sunteţi supăraţi, am înţeles sunteţi doare, dar eu sunt încă în stadiul alpha-ul tău, vă va prezenta la mine, Fane. (I understand you are angry, I understand you are hurting, but I am still your Alpha, you will submit to me, Fane). You know I will not let anything happen to Jacque, trust me. If not as your Alpha, then as your father."

After a few moments of silence Fane finally stood up and looked at his father. "I don't know if I can do that. You ask too much, Dillon Jacobs asks too much. I may not be the Pack Alpha of the Romanian Greys, but I'm more dominant than Jacobs.He will not take what is mine. I'm sorry, Alpha, but in this I cannot obey." Fane didn't wait for his father to respond as he turned and left the waiting area, headed back to Jacquelyn's room.

Jen and Sally came over and climbed onto Jacque's bed. "You got anything coming in on your reception, Jac?" Jen asked her.

"If you mean is Fane talking to me, then no, he's blocking his thoughts. I am getting intense anger, though. Whatever it is, Fane is royally pissed off," she answered.

"No pun intended, but" Jen laughed, "get it? Royally pissed, cuz he's a prince…anyone, no… no takers? Okay then."

Sally patted her on the leg. "Any other time, I would have totally given you props, but a werewolf just nearly tore the hospital apart, so right now props are all on hold."

"Noted." Jen clicked her tongue and winked in acknowledgment to Sally's statement.

Jacque was beginning to get a little panicked over the fact that Fane would not respond to her through their bond. What could be making him so mad?

"This is ridiculous," Jen grumbled as she began to rise off the bed and trudged slowly toward the room door, her IV pole in tow. She pulled it open and stuck out her head. Decebel was standing to the left of the door in his usual pose, arms across his chest, looking for all the world like he would be happy to rip someone's arms off given the chance. Be that as it may, Jen had to take two seconds, okay, maybe three to acknowledge that the man had a nice chest. Not an option, she told herself and decided that would have to be her mantra when she was around Decebel.

"Is there something wrong, Jen?" he asked her in an annoyingly calm voice.

"We just heard what sounded like a tornado ripping through this hall and you really want to ask me if something is wrong? Really? That's all ya got? Are you seriously going to stand there and act like everything is peachy keen jelly bean?"

Decebel raised a single eyebrow at her. "Which question would you like me to answer first?"

Jen growled at him. "Oh forget it," she said as she grabbed her IV pole and began to walk past him. "I'll find out what the hell happened without the help of Mr. 'I'm a big bad werewolf, I will eat you'." Her voice got deeper with each word.

As she passed him, in a voice so low she nearly missed it, she heard him mutter, "You might like it."

Jen whipped her head around, nearly losing her balance and knocking her IV pole over.

"Did you just make a joke? Because if you did then we need to get on the phone with air traffic control to tell them to be on the lookout fat little pigs with wings, and maybe even channel hell to see if the lakes of fire have frozen over."

"I don't know what you're talking about," he told her, his face dead pan as he gently took her arm and led her back to the room. He gently pushed her inside and pulled the door shut behind her.

Jen stood there completely dumbfounded.

"Did you find anything out?" Sally asked. Both her and Jacque were looking at their friend in expectation.

"I..." Jen couldn't get her mouth to spit out what her brain was trying to piece together, so she just stood there looking thoroughly confused.

Sally got up and walked over to Jen and began to help her back to the bed. "Is it just me, Jac, or does it look like little miss thang has been rendered speechless?"

"Never thought I'd see the day," Jacque agreed. "But for clarification purposes, Jen, snap out of it and tell me if you found out anything."

Sally snapped her fingers in front of Jen's face. This finally brought her brain back online. "Okay you," Jen pointed a finger at Jacque, who in turn pointed to herself and mouthed "me" to Sally. Sally just shrugged her shoulders. "I have no information to give you other than the hall is a mess, that is all I know." Jen then turned and looked at Sally. "I did however find out Decebel has a sense of humor…I think, maybe, sort of, crap I don't know."

Before Sally and Jacque could ask Jen to clarify, the door to their room opened and Lilly walked in, looking very tired.

"Mom, what's going on?" Jacque asked her mother.

"We need to talk."

"That's never a good sign," Jen said.

"Sally, Jen, you both need to stay and listen, this will affect you both."

"No Jen, *that* is never a good sign. The last time she asked you guys to stay I found out I was half werewolf," Jacque said, her voice wavering.

Before Lilly could get started there was a light knock on the door.

"Come in," all three girls yelled.

Alina walked in apprehensively. "Lilly I thought maybe I could help explain things if there were any questions."

"That would be great, Alina, thank you," Lilly told her.

"Ok," Lilly said, pulling up a chair to sit down. She placed her elbows on her knees and leaned her head down, running her hands through her hair. "let me get this out before Fane gets here because once he gets here no one will be getting near you, Jacque."

"Mom, you're making me nervous, what's wrong?"

"Dillon is invoking Alpha rights as your father because you are a minor," Lilly told her, frustration from her earlier encounter with Dillon leaking into her voice.

Jacque stared at her mother blankly, knowing she should be outraged she just wasn't sure about what exactly. "Alina, translation please," Jacque asked, turning to look at Fane's mother.

"First, I want you all to promise not to say anything until I have explained completely," she told them. "Do I have your word?"

"Word," all three said dryly.

"Dillon does not think you and Fane are old enough to mate."

Jacque started to interrupt, her face full of obvious outrage, but the look in Alina's eyes was pure Alpha and Jacque's mouth snapped closed. Alina nodded her head in approval and continued. "Since he is your father, it also helps that he is the Alpha of his pack, and you are under the age of 18, he can invoke what is called Alpha rights. Basically, he is saying he can keep you and Fane from becoming bonded until you are 18. He wants you to go back to Colorado with him and his pack for the next two months until you turn 18. He thinks that you and Fane need to mature some, that Fane is not ready to be a mate and protect you as you ought to be protected." After Alina finished talking, she waited for the inevitable but it didn't come. Instead, Jacque sat still as stone, her breathing even, her lips drawn tight in a straight line.

"Fane, I know you can hear me. I need you." Jacque sent the thought to Fane, allowing him to feel her anger, her fear and worry.

"I am on my way. You need to know, Jacquelyn, I will kill anyone who tries to take you from me. Anyone." Fane's voice was like death itself, cold, dark and unrelenting.

Jacque shivered at the sound of it in her mind. *"Just hurry, please,"* was her only response to his edict.

"Well, if Jacque is not going to share with the room the fury which she is undoubtedly feeling, by all means allow me," Jen announced. "Dillon Jacobs and what furry army is going to try, and let me just reiterate that, as in will, endeavor, strive, aim, seek, and albeit unsuccessfully attempt to take Jacque away from us?"

Sally looked at Jen and couldn't help the grin that spread across her face. "Your vocabulary never ceases to amaze. Just when I think all you know is profanity and perversion you come out with a speech worthy of Braveheart. Well done."

Jacque would have acknowledged her friends efforts to defend her had the door not flew open and a raging, pissed off werewolf prince walked in. His power swirled around them so strong that Alina let out a whine, sounding alarmingly like a wolf in pain. Even Jacque felt the dormant wolf gene in her wanting to submit to the power of the Alpha wolf in Fane. It was getting hard to breathe the air was so thick with his anger. He walked over to Jacque, whose head was bowed and turned so that her neck was bared. It was like she knew instinctively to submit so as to not provoke the dominant wolf and hopefully she would subdue him in her surrender. Fane's wolf must have been the one in control of the wheel because he leaned down over Jacque and growled low. He placed his face against her neck, breathing deep, and his voice was guttural when he spoke. "Mine."

Jacque turned her head slightly and did what no other would ever be able to do when this Alpha was at this point, she looked him in the eyes. "Yes, I am yours." As soon as the words were out of her mouth, Fane pulled his power in and all of a sudden it was like a weight had been lifted and they could breathe again.

"Note to self," Sally coughed to clear her throat, still trying to drag air in, "never anger an Alpha."

"Good call, Sherlock," Jen said sarcastically as she fell back on the bed, taking in deep breaths. She threw her arm across her face and tried to calm her racing heart.

Jacque looked around. "Everyone okay?" When everyone nodded in agreement she turned and looked at her mate.

"Sit," she told him firmly.

Fane's eyes continued to glow and Jacque noticed his human hands had claws. His wolf was still here to play. Good to know, she thought.

Fane growled, or rather his wolf growled. Jacque blew her breath out in exasperation. "Mate, you have made your point, we all submit and yadda yadda, now will you please sit down next to me?" When Fane didn't acquiesce, Jacque turned and looked at Alina as if to say 'fix it'.

Alina walked over to where Fane stood and he turned and growled at her. Alina bared her throat, careful to keep her head lower than his and to not make eye contact. "The wolf is in control right now, Jacque, so until Fane can pull him back some he is going to respond just like an Alpha wolf in the wild."

"What do we do then?" Sally asked.

"Everyone just stay calm," Alina told them. "Nobody but Jacque can look at Fane in the eyes right now, and keep your head lower than his," Alina explained.

"Well that's not hard to do, he's a mountain with legs, albeit a hairy mountain," Jen muttered to no one in particular.

Jacque turned her notice back to Fane. She took his hand, drawing his attention from his mother. He looked down at her and she could see his eyes soften. She stood up slowly, gingerly, because despite her rapid healing she was still in pain, especially when she moved.

"You sit," his mate told him.

"No, I stand."

"Me Tarzan, you Jane," Sally mumbled.

"Snap, you beat me to it. Nice going, Thelma." Jen grinned at Sally.

"I learned from the best, Louise."

"Damn straight." Jen and Sally bumped fists and turned to look at Jacque who had cleared her throat louder than necessary.

"What?" they both said in unison, shrugging their shoulders.

"I swear I have my own tweedle dee, and tweedle dumb." Jacque rolled her eyes and turned once again to her mate. *"What can I do to help you?"* Jacque spoke through their bond, hoping to soothe the wolf, who was still the one manning the boat.

"Touch," was the wolf's response.

Jacque nodded her head in acknowledgment to his response. She took his hands and placed them around her waist, she wrapped hers around his waist and then put her hands up under his shirt so that her skin was touching his, then she lay her head on his chest and listened to the beat of his heart. She felt him lay his cheek against her hair, and could hear him breathe in. Jacque knew he was taking in her scent, which for some reason comforted him. She ran her hands up and down his back enjoying how smooth his skin was, how strong he felt.

"I love you," Jacque whispered into his mind, pouring every ounce of emotion into those three words. She felt his deep rumble in his chest and knew that this was what he needed, just as wolves sought comfort through touching each other, Fane's wolf needed to feel her, a physical reminder that she was his, she was safe.

"Mulţumesc, Luna, doar poţi să-l calm (Thank you, Luna, only you can calm him)." Jacque exhaled a deep breath at the sound of Fane's voice in her mind.

She pulled back just enough to be able to look at his face. "Welcome back," she whispered to him. Fane turned her so that his body was shielding her from view and he placed his hands on either side of her face and just looked at her, like he was trying to memorize her every detail.

"Dragostea mea, Aş dori să vă sărut acum (My love, I would kiss you now)." Fane spoke so softly that Jacque nearly missed it.

"What did you just say?" She asked, cocking her head to the side quizzically.

"I said I wanted to kiss you now."

"Then why are we still talking?" She asked with a wicked look in her eyes.

Everyone in the room ceased to exist at that point, the only thing Fane could see was Jacquelyn's waiting lips. He leaned down at the same time that she stretched up on her toes to meet his eager lips. Usually when he kissed her it started gently, but not this time. Fane let go of her face and wrapped his arms firmly around her, pulling her close to his body. Jacque ignored the stinging pain that having him so tight around her caused because for this she would burn all over again. She wrapped her arms around his neck and stretched even higher on her tiptoes trying to get closer, if it was even possible. She felt his tongue slide against her lips and a moan escaped her lungs. She heard Fane's low growl in response. Jacque pulled back, and breathing hard she looked around Fane's shoulder, remembering they had an audience.

"They're gone," he whispered, his breathing just as labored as hers.

"No wonder you were getting hot and heavy." She grinned.

"The key words there Luna are 'were getting,'" he told her as he gently led her to the bed where she had spent the last month while her body desperately tried to heal. Healing was not the thing her body needed right now.

"I'm sorry if I hurt you when I held you."

"Wolf-man, if you are gonna hurt me like that, by all means hurt me." She laughed when he fake growled at her and bared his teeth.

She sat down on the bed and leaned back against the pillows at Fane's prodding. He leaned across her, propped up on one arm, careful to not put any weight on her legs. With his free hand he reached up and pushed her hair away from her neck, he ran his fingers down her collar bone and back up to her neck. Jacque shivered at the sensation of this hand on her skin. He continued to trace this same pattern from one collar bone to the next and back up to her neck.

"I love touching you." She heard his deep voice in her mind.

She smiled at him and ran her fingers through his hair, pulling a groan from him.*"I love hearing you make those kinds of noises, and I love even more that I'm the one who causes them."* Jacque couldn't believe how candid she was being with him, and how unembarrassed she was. But she wasn't, not anymore, this was Fane, her mate, her best friend, her love, and the last person in the world she would ever need to feel embarrassed in front of.

"I'm glad you're finally catching on," he said in response to her thoughts.

Jacque tugged at his hair in retaliation to his eavesdropping.

He laughed. "It's not eavesdropping, love. I've told you it's being attentive."

"So do I have your attention?" she whispered as she traced his lips with her fingers.

"Undivided," he said, lips barely moving. He was mesmerized by his mate, her touch, the only thing that could bring his wolf to heel.

"Good, cause you might want to pay extra close attention to what I'm thinking right," she paused as she pictured in her mind what she wanted, needed from Fane, "now," she finished.

"I think I can handle most of that," he said as he kissed her fingers.

Jacque's brow furrowed. *"Not all?"*

"You're a wicked, wicked woman. You know that, right?" Fane teased her as he leaned forward and kissed her neck, nipping gently where his mark would soon be.

"There we go with the whole 'soon' thing."

"Hush, my love. No more words," Fane said in between kisses on her neck, collar bone, and lips.

And there were no more for a long while.

Chapter 17

"I understand what you need me to do, Logan. I don't need you to explain it twelve different ways." Dr. Cynthia Steele's frustration at the wolf showed clearly on her face.

"If something changes in the plan, if for some reason Fane is able to stay with her tonight, we have to have a plan B," he told her.

"Plan B is I come tell them that the blood tests I took from Jen are abnormal and that I want to take Jacque to the lab and draw more blood so I can compare the two. They will be focused on the fact that I've said Jen's blood is abnormal," she explained.

"And is it abnormal?" Logan asked her.

"That's patient confidentiality, Logan, you know I can't tell you that."

"You are helping me abduct a future Alpha's mate and you are worried about patient confidentiality?" he asked her disbelievingly.

"I don't have anything against Jen, therefore yes, I'm worried about her privacy. You only need to worry about Jacque."

"Fine," Logan growled. "Just make sure that one way or another we get Jacque away from those mongrels and that she is sedated for our departure."

Dr. Cynthia Steele watched the wolf leave her office. She wondered, not for the first time, if she was doing the right thing. Then she would see her brother's face in her mind. He had been so unhappy the last few years. She had known that his wolf was growing uneasy at being unmated for so long, especially an Alpha who could be more than dangerous. His death was a perfect testament to what could happen when a wolf went after a female that wasn't his true mate. So why was she helping Logan? It was obvious that Fane was indeed Jacque's mate. The truth was she was angry and hurt and Fane was the cause of that anger and hurt. She couldn't challenge Fane for killing her Alpha, but she could hurt him just the same. That's all there was to it. Fane had taken what was hers and now she would take what was his. The papers she held in her hand drew her from her thoughts as she once again went over the lab results that belonged to Jennifer Adams. Although Jennifer looked ordinary enough, but there was nothing normal about her blood, and she knew if Logan knew, Jacque wouldn't be the only female he would be trying to take to his pack.

"Dillon, just let him stay the night with her," Lilly was saying, "I don't see what the big deal is."

"The big deal, Lilly, is that she is only 17 and you're saying its okay for her to have a guy spend the night with her. What else are you okay with our daughter doing?" Dillon's nostrils were flaring as his frustration at the situation rose.

Jen, Sally, Vasile, Alina, and Decebel all sat in the family waiting area that had become the undeclared meeting spot. They all looked on as Lilly and Dillon squared off.

"Does he realize what a major no-no he just made?" Sally whispered to the group.

"Ahh, you are right Sally. He criticized her parenting. That was probably the dumbest thing he could do," Vasile agreed.

Alina patted her mate's leg. "I knew you were smart when I met you."

"Come now, Mina. Don't be too shy to admit that you were so taken with my good looks that you could not focus on anything else."

"He's remembering it backwards," she whispered conspiratorially to Jen and Sally. "The first time we met the only words he could say were Luna and mina, and even then he didn't say them in the correct order." The girls laughed with Alina.

"Ahh, my love, now you are just being mean," Vasile whined, and to hear an Alpha whine only made them laugh harder. Jen caught Decebel watching her but he quickly looked away when she caught his eye.

A loud slap brought their laughing to a halt as they all turned to see a shocked Dillon Jacobs standing with a red hand print across his face.

"You can go to hell, Dillon Jacobs, and take all your damn smelly, flea infested wolves with you." Lilly turned on her heel, slamming through the waiting room door. They all jumped when it slammed closed.

"Do all of you think we have fleas?" Decebel asked as he looked at Jen and Sally.

"I think we just make an assumption because of the hair and what not, that you, ya know, might have a problem with the little buggers when you are in your wolf form." Decebel's face got more dubious with every word Jen spoke.

"Well, crap! Everything else with fur has fleas what did you expect us to think?" she snapped at him.

Decebel's only response was a slight lifting of his lips that might have even passed for a smile…maybe.

Sally looked at Decebel with an obvious question written across her face. When Jen was no longer looking, Decebel winked at Sally, a silent acknowledgement that she knew something was up, and he wasn't sharing.

Vasile walked over to Dillon and took a deep breath. He placed his hands on his hips and looked at the ground for a long moment.

"Are you sure this is still what you want to try and do?" he asked Jacobs.

"I don't know any more," Dillon admitted. "Lilly's angry with me, Jacque probably hates me, and your son would just as soon kill me as look at me. But Vasile, she's my daughter, she's so young."

"She is young, and so is Fane, but that does not change the fact that they are true mates. His marks are on her skin."

"What?" this remark had Dillon's head snapping up.

"You didn't know?" Vasile asked him.

"No," Dillon said, shaking his head in disbelief.

"If you try to separate them Fane will just come after her, and he will kill every wolf that gets in his way. He may be young, Dillon, but he is more dominant than any wolf I know, myself included," Vasile admitted.

Dillon clenched his jaw and ran his hand through his hair, he felt like he had aged twenty years overnight. He still hadn't told his mate what he was really up to. That conversation was going to add another twenty years to his shortening lifespan. He took a deep breath, let it out, then looked at Vasile. "Let me think about it tonight. I'm tired, everyone's tired. Fane can stay with her tonight. Your wolves can guard her if that's what you want. I will talk to all of you about it in the morning." Dillon paused as he was opening the door to leave. "Tell Jacque goodnight for me, I have a feeling it wouldn't be the best idea to go see her right now."

"Considering she's probably thoroughly lip locked with white fang, then, no it would definitely *not* be a good idea to go see her. Oww, WTH Jen?" Sally rubbed her arm where Jen had smacked it.

As Dillon stood very still in the open door, Jen glared at Sally. "Did you have to point out to him that his daughter was making out with a boy, alone, in a bed, alone?" she muttered.

"Jen," Decebel grumbled.

Jen continued as if she hadn't heard. "I mean, geeze, Sally, why not suggest he go give them a condom just to, ya know, be on the safe side and while he was at it he could take a banana and demonstrate how to put it on, and-"

"JENNIFER!" Decebel finally snarled.

Sally and Jen both jumped and turned to look at him and they heard the guest room door clang shut. "What?" Jen growled right back.

"I think he was just trying to say that we all got the point, Jen," Alina said gently.

"Oh," Jen said taken aback. "Well, why didn't you just say so? You didn't have to snarl at me," she huffed.

"I didn't snarl at you." Decebel's voice was low and tight.

"Yes. You. Did," Jen argued.

"I have to agree Dec, there was definite snarlige going on," Sally said, nodding her head.

"Okay," Decebel said calmly. "I'm sorry I snarled at you," he told her.

"My name."

Decebel cocked his head and looked at her quizzically. "What?"

"My name," she told him. "If you are going to apologize to *me*, than you need to say my name." The look on Jen's face was completely wicked.

Decebel clenched his jaw. His eyes were beginning to glow gold, but he managed to say politely, "I'm sorry, *Jennifer*, for snarling at you."

Jen grinned and held up the phone she had been holding. "That's going to be my new ring tone, the big bad wolf apologizing to widdle ole' me." She batted her eyes innocently.

Sally was coughing back a laugh, at the same time hoping that Jen had not just prodded a sleeping lion.

Decebel didn't say anything as he rose. He walked towards Jen who had the good sense not to run from a predator, although her eyes did get a little wider. He stopped just beside her and leaned down so that his mouth was next to her ear. "A banana, Jen, really?" He whispered and then was walking away.

The door was nearly closed by the time her brain started functioning again. "Oh, Come On! It was all I had!" She yelled, knowing his wolf hearing would pick it up.

Alina and Vasile had sat quietly through the exchange. "Have I ever told you how glad I am that we don't have a daughter?" Vasile asked her under his breath.

Aline slapped his leg. "Hush, did you just see what I saw?"

"Yes," Vasile answered sounding very tired. "I saw it. I haven't decided what to do about it."

Alina looked at him dubiously. "Do about it? Alpha, you're going to leave it be and let fate take its course."

"Mina," Vasile started to argue, but Alina was already turning her attention back to Jen and Sally. Obstinate woman, he thought to himself.

"I will be home in a few days, Tanya," Dillon was telling his mate over the phone. She had called his cell phone several times and sent him text messages as well, all of which he had not responded to. To say the least she was ticked off.

"Why can't you tell me what you are doing? And don't tell me its pack crap, you always tell me what's going on between the packs." He could almost see her snarling at him as she spoke.

"It's not something to discuss over the phone, you are just going to have to trust me." Dillon was losing his patience.

"Dillon, just tell me."

"Enough!" Dillon growled.

Silence came across the phone, all he could hear was her breathing. "Tanya, I'm sorry love, I didn't mean to yell at you. I'm just a little stressed at the moment, will you please trust me? It wasn't right of me to leave without talking to you first, but what's done is done."

She didn't respond right away and Dillon was beginning to think she just might have hung up on him.

"I trust you, but you won't do this to me again, Mate. I am your Luna and deserve more than that." Her voice was calm and unwavering; she once again showed why she was his Alpha female. She was deceivingly small and quiet, but when Tanya needed to be Alpha she had no problem delivering.

"You are right, Luna. I won't let it happen again. I love you," Dillon told her just before he hung up.

He stood in his hotel room, nursing the scotch he had poured himself. He had called Logan and told him to pull the wolves back for now, that they would regroup in the morning. Logan insisted on staying at the hospital just to keep an eye on the Romanian pack. Dillon told him to make sure he stayed out of sight and didn't cause any problems. Dillon had underestimated Fane's reaction to his announcement that he would be taking Jacque home with him. He had no doubt what Vasile said was true, Fane would kill anyone or anything that kept him from his mate. Which is the way it should be, right? He would move heaven and earth for Tanya, the only reason he hadn't told her about Jacque was because he knew it was going to be one more reminder that she was not able to conceive. He didn't want his mate to hurt, to feel inadequate that she had not been able to bare him any pups. Dillon didn't care, he was perfectly happy with their life, or was, until he found out about Jacquelyn.

In truth he was once again being a coward, just like when he walked out on Lilly without a word. And now he had left without a word to his mate about a child he didn't know he'd had because he was afraid she wouldn't want him to have a relationship with Jacque. He had a lot of groveling to do when he got back. First he had to set things straight with Jacque and Fane. He didn't want to lose her, but forcing her to come with him wasn't going to make her stay, he realized now, it would only drive her further away. He would tell her tomorrow that he had been wrong, and weren't those the hardest words for any Alpha to choke up. It seemed like those were the only words Dillon needed to say to the women he cared about.

Logan stood in the parking lot of the hospital. He had been watching and listening to any information he could get about what Vasile or Fane's plans were regarding Jacque. They didn't suspect anything of Dillon or his pack, even after Sorin, Fane's apparent childhood bodyguard, had found the mechanism he had placed on Lilly's vehicle. Vasile had decided it must have been the Coldspring pack retaliating, and sent two of his other wolves out to meet with their new Alpha. Of course, the new Alpha had no clue of the mutiny taking place in his own pack, so Logan was safe on that end. His next move was going to be to call Dr. Steele as plan B was going to have to be executed. Fane would not be leaving Jacque tonight, so they would just have to get Jacque to leave Fane. He pulled out his phone and mashed the number two where he had put the doctor on speed dial.

"Dr. Steele," she answered.

"You're going to have to get Jacque by telling them about her friend's blood. Fane is staying," Logan told her.

"Ok," she paused. "It's 5:30 p.m. now, so, give me a couple of hours. I will have to wait until one of the labs is clear. Once I have her in the lab and under sedation you can come help me put her on the gurney to wheel her out. I will have to get you some hospital scrubs to put on so you don't look suspicious pushing what appears to be a dead body through the hospital."

"I will wait for your call." Logan didn't wait for her response, he simply hung up.

Taking a deep breath, he turned his face up towards the setting sun, feeling the heat even this late in the day. He hated the heat, it depressed him, even his wolf. He would be glad to get back to his mountains in Denver. An iniquitous smile stretched across his face, his wolf eyes glowing. He wouldn't be returning to his mountains alone. That thought perked him and his wolf right up.

Chapter 18

After Decebel had left the waiting area, Jen and Sally had decided to find a deck of cards and chillax, as Jen liked to say.

"So, do you think Fane and Jacque have…" Sally let the word draw out in a question.

"Have what?" Jen asked as she looked at her cards. "Do you have a two of hearts?"

"Go fish," Sally said absently. "Have, ya know, done it." Sally whispered, leaning across the table.

Jen was looking at her cards with such concentration it was almost as if she were willing the one she needed to appear in her hand. "Done it? What, you mean has he bitten her? Three of spades?" she added.

"Go fish. No, Jen, that is not the 'it' people refer to when they are talking about 'it'." Sally was making quotations signs with her fingers as she spoke, which effectively gave Jen a look at her cards.

"Six of clubs, excellent. Give it up, I saw it," Jen told her, holding her hand out, making a 'give me; gesture.

"It's not even your turn, you cheat. Now listen to me," Sally tried again

"Sally, good grief. How you and Jacque have stayed so pure with me as your best friend I'll never know. Sex, say it with me. S-e-x," Jen said, sounding it out letter by letter.

"Shhh! Don't say it so loud." Sally looked around to see if anybody had heard.

"Why? It's not like people don't know what it is, or don't know that everyone is doing it. Now give me your six of clubs, hussy."

"Fine, here," Sally growled, slamming the card on the table.

"Touchy, touchy," Jen muttered as she placed her own six of clubs on top of the one Sally had laid down.

"The answer's no," Jen said absently.

"No what?" Sally asked and then added, "Jack of diamonds."

"Damn," Jen mumbled and handed Sally the card she had

requested.

"No, I don't think they have done the deed."

"Why not?" Sally asked, surprised.

"One," Jen said, leaning back in her chair, tilting her head to the side as she looked at Sally. "Jacque won't until she's married."

"Yeah, but it's Fane. I mean look at him. You're telling me if you got that alone you wouldn't throw those ideas out the window?" Sally interrupted.

"Do you really want to talk about what I would do if I got that," Jen nodded her head toward the direction of the hospital room where they knew Fane and Jacque were, "alone?"

Sally shook her head and waved her hands. "Point taken. Okay, move along, what was number two?"

"Two, Fane is too chivalrous with all that, 'I respect your choice to wait' crap. He could seduce her if he wanted. Jacque would fold like a bad hand of Texas hold 'em. And three, we'd know if they had." Jen began to look at her cards again as if she had just cleared up the mysteries of the world.

"What do you mean we would know?" Sally asked her, laying her cards down. Jen lifted her eyes to Sally and slowly reached across the table and picked up her cards. She picked out the ones that matched hers then laid them back down."I don't have anything you need, so go fish."

"Jen, I'm serious. How would we know? I don't think Jacque would tell us, she's too embarrassed about that kind of stuff. She never told us about what she and Trent did."

"Trent was not Fane," Jen began. "We would know because it would be written all over her. She would have the morning after glow, the little grin on her face of knowing that her innocence is gone and she lost it to a freaking Greek god."

"Huh," Sally said thoughtfully. "I've never seen that look on you before." She looked at Jen questionably.

"Of course you haven't, I'm a virgin. That and no Greek gods have offered themselves to me lately, but I haven't lost faith." Jen threw that out there like it was no big surprise.

Sally's jaw dropped. "You're a WHAT?" Sally's words came out just as Decebel walked up.

"Yes, Jen, you're a what, exactly?" He asked her, voice serious as ever, eyebrow raised.

Jen glared at Sally. "One word, Sally,"

Sally held her hands up in surrender. "Oh, believe me, I have not forgotten what you will do if I say a word when I'm not supposed to. I knew I should have gotten rid of those damn dolls," she grumbled.

"Hi Decebel," Jen said, grinning innocently and acting as if she had just noticed his appearance.

Decebel narrowed his eyes at her, then his face wiped clean like a cloth running across a dry erase board. "Vasile and Alina wanted me to invite you both to come eat with everyone in the hospital cafeteria."

Jen tossed down her cards. "I could eat. What about you, Sally?"

Sally was still staring at Jen with shock-filled eyes. "You, you, Yoooouuu," Sally kept saying to Jen, with different inflections in her voice.

"Sally, let's move past this and get on to more important things, okay?" Jen took her IV pole in one hand and Sally by the other hand and began pulling a reluctant Sally away with Decebel to follow.

"What could be more important than the fact that you're a mmrrm." Jen had slapped her hand across Sally's mouth. She was trying to keep from losing her balance and knocking her IV over and she looked back at Decebel, who was watching in curiosity.

"You will have to excuse us for a sec, Dec, she swallowed her tongue. I'm just going to help her cough it up. We can meet you down there," Jen said sweetly while she continued to keep Sally's mouth covered.

"Okay then." Decebel sounded unsure as he walked past the two girls. He looked back at them one more time before turning and walking away muttering in Romanian.

"What is wrong with you?" Sally sputtered when Jen finally uncovered her mouth.

"I have a reputation to maintain. You can't just go flapping at the lips that I'm as pure as you and Jacque," Jen said, hands on her hips, lips set in a tight line.

"Oh, believe me, Jen, no one would ever confuse you with being pure, virginity be damned," Sally shot back at her sarcastically. "Out of curiosity, does Jacque know?"

"No and she doesn't need to know. What's the big freaking deal, Sally? So I'm not as experienced as I let on. What does it even matter?" Jen was getting irritated at her friend's curiosity in her sex life, or lack thereof.

"It's not really that it's a big deal as much as it's just, kind of disappointing," Sally said, sounding deflated.

Jen looked at her through half-hooded eyes. "Okay, so what I'm hearing you say," Jen started then paused, shaking her head in disbelief."You're disappointed that I'm a virgin? Did I misunderstand you? Is my hearing going bad or are you just a dumbass?"

"Okay, let me *esplain* it like this, Lucy."

"By all means, Ricky, *esplain* away," Jen responded dryly.

"So, you know how when you are a kid and you see Disney World on T.V.?" Jen nodded her understanding as Sally continued. "It's so amazing and bigger than life, they show you the fireworks above the big beautiful castle that every little girl dreams of living in, and you think 'wow, I want to go there'."

"Are you seriously comparing me to an amusement park?"

Sally shushed her. "Wait for it."

Jen motioned for Sally to get on with it.

"Finally your day comes and your parents take you to Disney World. You're going to see the beautiful castle you've seen so many times on T.V. Only when you get there and walk up to the big castle, you realize it's just a big castle-shaped building with a hole going through the middle where people are walking in and out." She blew out a deflating breath. "Even though it was still a pretty awesome place, it was a little disappointing that the castle wound up being a fake."

Jen just stood there staring at Sally. She didn't really know what to say, she was truly baffled by the fact that this news was having such a detrimental effect on her best friend. "Sally, you do realize that you just compared the news of my virginity to an amusement park castle right? Just want to be clear on that."

Sally nodded, biting on her bottom lip. "Yeah, now that you put it like that it's really kind of disturbing," she said, closing her eyes and shaking her head. "I guess I was just expecting you to be the one to tell me what it was like, ya know? Kind of like how you were the first one of us to shave your legs, and try tampons, and wax your bikini line," Sally said wistfully.

"Well, the night's still young my sweet, innocent flower. Who knows what could happen between now and tomorrow morning?"

Jen laughed at Sally's dubious look.

"Come on, Virginia, let's go get something to eat." Sally darted out of Jen's reach, knowing she was going to try and hit her at the sound of her new nickname.

"Sally," Jen growled out a warning, unable to move quickly due to the annoying IV.

"Did you say something. Virginia?" Sally continued to tease. darting here and there to stay out of Jen's slapping hands.

Fane and Jacque looked up from the table when they heard Sally's singing all through the cafeteria. She was belting out at the top of her lungs Train's "Meet Virginia". A very pissed off looking Jen was dragging her IV pole as quickly as she could without falling, trying to catch up to her quarry. By the time Sally had reached the table, she had tears streaming down her face from laughing so hard. She leaned over the table, panting, finishing her serenade. "Her confidence is tragic, but her intuition magic, and the shape of her body, unusual, meet Virginia!" Sally ended dramatically, arms in the air like Vanna White indicating where Jen now stood. Much to Jen's chagrin the entire cafeteria broke into applause.

Jen pasted on her most dazzling smile and waved at everyone adoringly, but to Sally she muttered under her breath, "This is war."

Sally bowed to her audience and then to the table where all friends sat clapping as well. Decebel stood up and walked over to Jen. It was obvious he was trying not to laugh, and Jen was disappointed because she really wanted to know what he looked like when he was cracking up, but it was at her expense so she could stand the disappointment.

"Why don't I help you to your seat?"

Jen grabbed Sally's hand. "That would be nice, thank you, Decebel." She drug Sally behind her as she followed Decebel to the seats he indicated. As he was pushing Jen's chair in behind her while she sat down, Decebel leaned forward and whispered in her ear. Jen's body went rigid. Sally looked at them curiously, then looked at Jacque to see if she was seeing this. Jacque shrugged her shoulders in an 'I have no clue what's up' manner. Sally watched as Jen tilted her head up to look at Decebel. She batted her eyes sweetly and smiled a very sensual smile. Sally noticed Decebel's eyes begin to glow. "Hey, Fane," Jen raised her voice about the noise in the room.

"Yes, Jen?"

"Didn't you say something about your kind healing fast?" She asked him, never taking her eyes off of Decebel. It was then that Sally noticef Jen had placed her hand around Decebel's wrist of the hand that he was propping himself up on the table with. It looked like a flirtatious gesture unless you were seeing it from Sally's view and could see that Jen's other hand was wrapped around the butter knife next to her plate.

Fane cleared his voice, unsure of where Jen was going with this. "Yes, that is correct, we do heal a lot faster than-" Before Fane could finish what he was saying, Jen interrupted.

"Okay thanks, that's all I needed."

Jen moved faster than Sally had ever seen her move, but it was like everything was happening in slow motion. Jen raised the knife as her grip around Decebel's hand tightened. At the same time, Sally and Jacque yelled, "Decebel, run!" Decebel realized what was happening and moved quicker than the eye could see grabbing Jen's wrist before the knife could make contact with his flesh.

To Decebel's credit, he didn't give any indication that a knife had just nearly been stabbed into his hand. His golden eyes were glowing and Sally thought she could see flames in them. "Jen, you might want to, um, go sit by Jacque, or ru-ru-run. I'm just saying," Sally stuttered.

Jen's gaze never wavered from Decebel's. The whole table sat frozen, waiting for his reaction. Decebel slowly pulled the knife from her hand, he smiled slowly, showing Jen that his canines had lengthened. "You're running out of checks, Jennifer."

"Depends on whose checkbook you're looking at, now doesn't it, Decebel?" Jen matched his cold sarcasm.

Before they could continue their sparring, Dr. Steele walked up to Vasile and asked to speak with him in private, so naturally the whole table got up and followed them.

They ended up back once again in the family waiting area. Jacque was beginning to think that no other families came to this floor because they were the only ones ever using this room.

"Vasile, when I said privately, I meant just you," Dr. Steele told him.

"I understand, Dr. Steele, but everyone in this room will know what you have told me in a matter of hours."

"More like minutes," Sally added.

"Good call," Jen said, going to bump fists with Sally. But she stopped just short, remembering that she was supposed to be mad at her. Sally just rolled her eyes.

"Fine," Dr. Steele said, giving up on trying to persuade him otherwise. "I got Jennifer's blood results back."

The whole room seemed to hold their breath. Jen stepped forward slowly, forgetting about the IV attached to her, and had Sally not caught it, would have fallen on Jen's head. Jen never even noticed.

"What were my results?" Jen asked apprehensively.

Sally and Jacque both stepped up on either side of Jen in a show of silent support.

"Jennifer, do you know anything about your genealogy?" Dr. Steele asked her.

Jen just looked at her blankly. Sally nudged her. "Jen, she wants to know if you know about your ancestors?" Still no answer.

This time Jacque tried. "Jen? Your lineage, descent, forebears, pedigree-"

"I got it, Jacque," Jen cut her off.

"If you mean, do I know of any non-human blood in my family, then the answer is no," she told Dr. Steele.

"I'm not sure if it is a were-gene or not. Since Jacque is not full blooded I need more of her blood to compare it to Jennifer's. I will come by her room later tonight to get her after the lab techs have gone home. I don't want anyone to ask questions."

Chapter 19

"Um, Sally?" Jacque said absently as they sat on the bed in the hospital room she had been sleeping in.

"Yep."

"While Jen is taking a shower, why don't you tell me exactly what happened between you two."

"What makes you think something happened?" Sally asked, sounding utterly guilty.

"Really Sally? You were singing at the top of your lungs 'Meet Virginia' with Jen chasing you, IV pole and all." Jacque lifted an eyebrow at her. "You still want to go with that answer?"

"Okay, fine, you win. She's mad at me because I was teasing her." Jacque waited for Sally to continue, she didn't.

"She's mad because you were teasing her, that's it, nothing else?" Sally shook her head and continued to look guilty. "So if I go in there and start singing 'Meet Virginia' she won't come out here and throttle you?" Jacque made as if to get up off the bed and go towards the bathroom.

"WAIT! Ok, you win, Jen is mad because I was teasing her because she'savirgin." Sally said the last part so fast that Jacque nearly missed it, nearly.

"Jen's a what?" Jacque asked in complete shock.

"Mother of pearl! Did you guys think I was a slut and just hanging out with you two wall flowers in my spare time, ya know, in between tricks and what not? Why is everyone so surprised I'M A FREAKING VIRGIN? If you are so interested let me just throw out my reason and you can swallow it or choke on it okay?" She continued before they could answer. "I actually think sex is supposed to be for that one special person, and not just 'hey I love you let's do it'. I mean the one you decide to take on for life." Jen stood in the open bathroom door, wrapped in a towel.

"Are you saying you're going to wait to have sex until you're married?" Sally asked in complete shock.

"Geeze, Sally, is it really that hard to fathom? I know I joke about it a lot. I like to joke about it to see the shock on people's faces. But personally, my forever man is the only one getting a piece of all this hotness."

Jacque had just developed a newfound respect for her perverted friend. "Okay, three things. First, I'm totally digging what you're saying. I get it and I think it's great. Second, don't change. Because out of us three only you could get away with the things you say and we desperately need the comic relief. And last, I'm dying to point this out technically, Jen. You couldn't be a freaking virgin, it's an oxymoron."

"Good one, Vern." Sally bumped Jacques fist.

"I know, right?" Jacque smiled. "We learned from the best, Sal."

"You two hussies better not forget it, either," Jen growled at them.

"Are you done being mad at me?" Sally asked.

Jen glared at her for a minute. "Yeah," she said, waving her off. "I was having a really hard time staying mad anyway. I have to give you serious props for the whole 'Meet Virginia' bit, that was pure genius."

"I know." Sally dusted off each shoulder. "I got mad skills, yo."

"Had I known you were singing that because you had just found out about our perverted little friend's deep, dark secret, I seriously would have peed on myself from laughing so hard."

"So, Jen. You going to fess up to what Decebel whispered in your ear that caused you to stab the poor wolf?" Jacque asked her petulant friend.

"Where's Fane?" Jen asked, ignoring Jacque's question.

"He's sitting on the other side of that door, growling at anything and anyone that comes within a few feet of it," Jacque said, nodding her head towards said door. "Now answer the question, Jen."

Jen didn't answer right away, she wasn't sure how to answer if she was being honest with herself which was a practice that she liked to avoid because it usually lead to being reasonable, and frankly, where was the fun in that? Sally and Jacque waited patiently, not wanting to provoke Jen's as-of-late testy temper.

"I don't really know what it means," Jen told them.

"Well, if you tell us we might be able to help you figure it out. You know we are good at figuring stuff out and what not."

"Oh, yes. How could I forget the mighty Sally and Jacque, super sleuthing divas," Jen said sarcastically.

"Hey, that has a ring to it," Jacque said thoughtfully.

"Jacque, focus." Sally elbowed her.

"He said," Jen began, and much to her amusement her two friends edged towards her, bodies leaning forward, hanging on her every word."You two are like two monkeys waiting for the tourist to throw you a banana peel."

"Jen, you do remember what monkeys like to throw back at those tourists, don't you? Spill it now," Sally growled.

"He dared me to give him a reason to kill someone if the time came that he called me Virginia and it no longer pertained to me." When Sally and Jacque didn't say anything, Jen looked up at them and saw that they were both wide eyed with their mouths hanging open. "Are you going to say something?"

Sally got up and began to pace the room, chewing on her bottom lip and muttering under her breath. Jacque continued to look dumbfounded.

"Hello? This is mission control calling out to all pushy, know it all friends who bullied me into telling them something I didn't understand myself and are now acting like the monkeys earlier referenced."

That effectively got Jacque to shut her mouth and finally acknowledge Jen.

"I'm sorry, I was sort of thrown off for a moment. I just can't believe he said that."

"What does it mean?" Jen asked, her voice uncharacteristically soft.

Sally looked at Jen and then at Jacque. "Does it mean what I think it means?"

"I don't know, Sal. I mean why else would he care what her virginity status was?" Jacque answered.

"Maybe it's a little sister thing, like he feels he needs to be her big brother," Sally said, nodding her head as if that would somehow make it true.

"I've seen him looking at her, and if he sees her as a little sister then Fane needs to beat the crap out of him cuz he looks like he's considering incest."

Jen watched the exchange between her two friends as they

communicated as if she wasn't sitting right in front of them.

"Hey, Ricky, Lucy, I'm sitting right here. Would you please stop talking like I'm not in the room."

"Right, sorry Jen." Sally kneeled down in front of Jen and placed her hands on her knees for balance. "Jacque and I think Decebel's being possessive towards you."

"That's your sleuthing in action? Really? Well bloody hell, why don't you guys go clear up the mystery behind Stonehenge seeing as how ya'll are so good at figuring things out and all."

"There's more to it than just possessiveness, Jen." Jacque stood up and started the pacing that Sally had abandoned. "He's treating you like…" Jacque was motioning her hands as if trying to encourage someone to spit out what she couldn't get her mouth to say.

"It's like he thinks, maybe…" Sally began but then aborted her thought.

"Just spit it out already. He thinks and is treating me like what already?"

"Mate," Jacque blurted out so fast it looked like someone had slapped her on the back to make the words come out. "He's treating you like a mate would."

Jen felt like she had been punched in the gut. She tried to take in air but her lungs wouldn't work. She thought she could hear voices but they sounded muffled, as if coming from the other side of a closed door. Her thoughts were jumping from one image to another like one of those flip picture books making the pictures look alive the faster you flipped them, only this wasn't a book, this was her life. She saw Decebel coming towards her bed when he asked her if she was alright, flip, he was kneeling next to her looking at the skin on her legs, flip, he was standing in the hall of the hospital all but growling at her, flip, he was laying a blanket over her as she lay in the hospital bed shivering. On and on the images came. There was one common denominator in each image: Decebel was nearly snarling at her in all of them. All of a sudden, she felt cold wetness on her face. She gasped, trying to get her bearings, filling her lungs with precious, life-giving oxygen.

"Crap, Sally," Jen sputtered. "There better be a stinking, world-changing reason that you threw water in my face."

"You weren't breathing and you wouldn't respond to us saying your name. I was going to slap you, but Jacque decided a hand mark marring your skin might not be the wisest thing right now," Sally explained nervously.

"I have found a flaw in your reasoning," Jen said, looking for all the world like they had better agree with her. As Jacque handed her a towel to dry her face, she explained her theory. "Any time Decebel is in the room with me he looks at me like he wants to throttle me. Not once has he ever appeared to be interested in me in *that* way."

"You of all people should know that a look of intense desire can be mistaken for the look of throttling," Jacque said, matter of fact like.

Jen cocked her head to the side, one eyebrow lifting. "Oh really, do tell, Jac. At what point in your long, full of incredible opportunities, mystifying life have you experienced a guy looking at you where you thought, is this desire for me, or for the throttling he just might be thinking about giving me? Really, please tell me so that I could possibly fan the tiny flame of hope that my common sense is desperately trying to douse with the cold reality that Decebel is NOT AND NEVER, IN MY 'I'M NOT A FREAKING WEREWOLF' LIFE, WILL BE AN OPTION!" Jen cursed the damning tears that revealed the depth of her emotions regarding the brooding wolf who was a constant shadow in her mind.

"Jen, I'm sorry," Jacque whispered as she sat down on the bed and wrapped an arm around her shoulders. "I didn't know you had feelings for him."

"Of course I have feelings towards him. I feel like he is a pompous, hairy, flea infested butt head." Jen thought if she said it out loud then maybe she could believe it. No such luck.

The room was quiet without Jen's loud voice to fill the empty spaces.

"So, how 'bout this weather we've been having?" Sally said, forever the one trying to smooth things out.

Suddenly Jacque stood up, causing Jen to nearly fall in the floor. "What the crap, Jacque?" Jen spat. Then she looked at Jacque's face and could see something was very wrong.

"I'm going to be sick." Jacque's voice was desperate and pained.

Jen put her hands on Jacque's shoulders and began guiding her towards the bathroom, all the while shouting orders at Sally. "Go get Fane, get some towels and cold washcloths, then get Dr. Steele."

Sally headed for the door but it flew open, thankfully before she was close enough to be hit with it. Fane came in a storm of power. He walked past Sally, following the painful sounds of the sickness coming from his mate. Decebel came in behind Fane and stopped beside Sally.

"What's going on?" he asked, his voice as authoritative as ever.

"We were just sitting, talking about," Sally paused, remembering what they had been talking about before Jacque had gotten sick. "Nothing important, and then Jacque stood up and said she was going to be sick. Jen took her into the bathroom and I was coming to get Fane but he was already coming into the room." Decebel just nodded in response. Sally realized then she was supposed to get towels and a wash cloth. She headed out the door of the room and then paused to look back at Decebel. "Can you get in touch with Dr. Steele somehow?"

"Yes."

"A 'man of few words' would be an understatement in describing that wolf," Sally muttered as she continued on her quest for towels.

"What happened?" Fane growled at Jen as he maneuvered himself into the spot she had just occupied. He took over holding Jacquelyn's hair as she retched up anything and everything from her body.

"I don't know what happened. We were just talking and everyone was fine and then bam, Jacque was getting sick." Jen slapped her hands together in emphasis.

"Luna, can you tell me what's wrong?" Fane asked her, his voice full of the anguish he was feeling at seeing her so sick.

"It feels like my insides are trying to crawl out of my mouth. How's that for descriptive?" Jacque sent her thoughts and moaned out loud at the same time as another spasm gripped her stomach, and she began to dry heave because there was nothing left inside her.

Fane placed his hand on her forehead as she began to shiver. *"You're burning up, Jacquelyn."* Fane didn't know anything about fever but he was sure that her temperature was beyond the point of being just a minor fever.

"Here, I have washcloths." Sally came into the bathroom and turned on the cold water, pushing the washcloths under the flow, then she squeezed out the excess and handed one to Fane.

"Put it on her neck," Jen instructed, then took a towel from Sally and folded it placing it on the floor and pushing it underneath Jacque so her knees wouldn't be on the hard, cold floor.

"Decebel got in touch with Dr. Steele, she is on her way here," Sally informed them.

Jacque finally slumped back against Fane, exhausted from being sick. Her face flushed from the fever, and her breathing was shallow. Fane picked her up and carried her to her bed. As he gently laid her down he spoke to Decebel. "Get my father."

"Done, my prince, I've already called him. He and your mother and Lilly were down in the cafeteria. They are on their way up now."

Fane nodded. "Thank you."

Without warning Jacque screamed out, "FANE!" Jen and Sally jumped. Decebel flinched because of his sensitive wolf ears.

Fane rubbed Jacquelyn's forehead."I'm here, love. What can I do?" Fane was gritting his teeth, frustration and fear coursing through his body.

"Make it stop," Jacquelyn whispered to him. "Please make it stop."

Chapter 20

Cynthia dialed Logan's number as she continued to examine the blood sample she had under the microscope. Her hands shook as she turned the dial to bring the slide into focus. She couldn't believe what she was seeing, but there it was in living color. Jennifer's blood matched Jacque's blood. The only difference being the amount of cells that carried the gene. Since Jacque was half wolf her blood was full of them. Jennifer, however, had just enough to be recognizable by a person who knew what to look for. Logan finally answered. "Tell me you have good news, Dr. Steele."

"Well, if you mean can I get Jacque by herself, then yes I have good news. I just received a call from Vasile's Beta. Jacque is sick. I'm going now to see her and will have her transferred to the ICU, where visitors of any kind are not allowed after 9:00 p.m. I have a pair of scrubs for you here in my office. I will leave it unlocked so you can get in. Wait in my office for my call." Cynthia was changing the slides in the microscope, putting Jennifer's up and sliding Jacque's sample under the scope. As she looked into the eyepiece she ceased hearing anything Logan said. She'd thought that this could happen, but thinking and reality are very different.

"Okay, Logan, I will call you when I'm ready. Bye." And without listening for his response she hung up. She continued to examine the blood as she watched the human cells attack the werewolf cells. Jacque had received a blood transfusion before she had been able to stop it. That was what she was watching on the slide in front of her. The human cells from the blood that did not belong to Jacque were attacking her cells. She had heard that this could happen when a wolf received human blood because human blood recognized the wolf cells as a virus and attacked accordingly. She knew of only one cure, one way to stop the human cells from killing the wolf cells and inevitably killing the werewolf.

As she stood up and put her lab coat on, she took one last look at the slide then turned to go to Jacque's room. She kept telling herself that it would be okay, that Logan would be able to heal her, that she wasn't putting Jacque in any real harm. Before her conscience could talk her out of it she was standing in front of Jacque's door. She'd been able to hear her cries from down the hall and she could only imagine how painful it was for your body to turn on itself. There, see? I will be helping her by giving her the morphine to keep her under, and then she won't feel the pain until Logan can heal her. Assuaging her guilt, she turned the doorknob and walked into a room full of worried people, an emotionally out of control Alpha, and the cries of a very sick girl. Thankfully, at the sight of a sick person the doctor in her kicked in and she focused on that role, on doing something to help.

By the time Dr. Steele walked into the room everyone was there, lining the wall of the room. Every face was draped in worry and fear for Jacquelyn. Fane heard the door open. He turned to see Dr. Steele walk into the room, and before anyone could ask her a question she held her hand up and headed for Jacquelyn's bed. The only sound was the whimpering and cries of his mate.

"Please do something for her." Fane found himself pleading with Dr. Steele desperate for something, anything to help Jacquelyn.

Dr. Steele listened to Jacquelyn's heart, and then she shined a light into each eye. She moved Jacquelyn's hands away from her stomach and began pushing on it in various locations, causing a cry to erupt. Fane growled but Dr. Steele was not intimidated. "Save it, wolf. I can't help her if you expect there to be no pain." She reached into her pocket and pulled out something Fane didn't recognize. He watched her run it across Jacquelyn's forehead and then look at a small screen on the side.

"It's a thermal scanner to take her temperature. She's at 105.2, which means if we don't get her temp down she will either have a seizure, go into a coma, or both." Dr. Steele looked over to Vasile. "I'm going to have to take her to the ICU. No one is allowed in there, the patients are all too sick to be exposed to the germs people would innocently bring in. You understand what this means?"

Vasile nodded. "I will take care of it."

They watched as she pushed a button that caused an alarm to sound, then they all heard footsteps moving fast towards the room. The next thing Fane knew he was being pushed out of the way.

Decebel and his father grabbed him before he could lunge at the hospital staff as they transferred Jacquelyn onto a gurney. He couldn't focus on what Dr. Steele was saying as he watched his mate being taken from him to where he could not go...again. Once Jacquelyn was out of sight he finally looked at the doctor.

"What is wrong with her?" he growled.

"I don't know yet, Fane. You will have to be patient and let me do my job. You growling and throwing massive Alpha fits will not help Jacque get better."

Fane was taken aback by the doctors' boldness, but found that he respected her for it.

"Just make her well again. Please."

Dr. Steele put her hand on Fane's shoulder. "She will be fine." She stepped back then so she could look at the whole group crowded into the little room. "I will let you know as soon as I know something." And then she turned and walked out.

The room was quiet, no one daring to break the silence, for then they would have to acknowledge the fear that was threatening to consume them one by one. The silence was broken by a cursing Jen. Everyone turned to look at her and watched as she wrestled with the tape that held her IV in place. She wasn't paying attention to the fact that everyone was focused on her. "Hey, moron nurse number one said, look at this IV I just put in this chick, do you think I used enough tape? Absolutely not, said moron nurse number two, you have to wrap an entire roll around her arm so that nothing short of a miracle will get it off." Jen muttered the dialogue under her breath as she finally got the tape off of the IV in her arm. "Finally!" she announced triumphantly as she pulled the IV from her arm, blood trickled down towards her hand. She looked up and noticed everyone watching her.

"What?" she asked. Her eyes got bigger as Decebel began to walk towards her. He got so close that she had to strain her neck back to look up at his face.

"Why did you take that out?" His face was hard, unreadable.

"Because if I'm going to have to have a pole attached to me I would prefer it be one that I could get some use out of. But as it was this particular pole as my constant companion, it just wasn't doing it for me." Jen batted her eyes at him. "Besides, what the hell does it matter? My best friend has just been rushed off to the ICU and you're worried about my stupid IV?"

"Put it back," His eyes glowing gold as he took hold of her arm.

"Oh, yeah, sure thing. I'll get right on that," she said sarcastically as she pried his hand from around her arm. Paying him little more attention than if he were a gnat, she stepped around him so she could see the others.

"So what's the plan, Vasile?" She heard material ripping and as she turned towards the noise she watched as Decebel tore a piece of the sheet from the bed off and brought it over to her. He took her arm, gently this time, and wrapped the material around the spot that was still bleeding from where she had ripped her IV out. Without a word, he went back to the spot he had previously been standing while Jen watched his retreating back.

Vasile answered as if the peculiar scene had not taken place. "For now you and Sally will stay here and I will put a guard on the door. Fane and Decebel will stay in the waiting area for the ICU. Fane," Vasile looked directly at his son, "you will not attempt to defy what Dr. Steele has said. Are we clear?"

"As you say, so shall it be," Fane gave the formal response, neck bared in submission.

"Good," he continued, "Alina and Lilly will go home and rest." Lilly started to interrupt but Alina stopped her with a hand on her arm and gave a sharp nod of her head. Lilly swallowed the words she was about to say.

"Lilly, I understand that you want to be here for your daughter, but you need to rest and you won't get it here. Trust me, okay?" Vasile waited for her response before continuing.

"Okay," she answered, her voice resolute.

Vasile looked at his watch, it read 9:30 p.m. "I think it's time to call it a night. As soon Dr. Steele has information she will contact me and you will all know within minutes." Vasile turned to leave and Alina followed him. Lilly came up to Jen and hugged her and then did the same with Sally.

"Don't worry Ms. P," Jen told her, "Jacque's the most stubborn person I know. She will be fine." Lilly nodded and with eyes full of unshed tears, she left as well.

Fane gave them each hugs as well and told them to call him if they needed anything, to which Jen threw out, "I think Jacque would kick my butt if I called you for what I need." Decebel growled, but at least it got a small smile from Fane. That was what Jen had been aiming for. Jen turned to Decebel and stuck her tongue out at him like a petulant child.

As he and Fane left, Decebel turned back one more time. "You two. Don't do anything that you consider brilliant. The rest of us will consider it stupid." He shut the door just as Jen threw the nearest thing she could get her hands on, which happened to be the box of tampons that Sally had absently set out, so naturally tampons went flying everywhere.

"Arrrrrgh, I'm so going to skin him the first time I see him as a wolf and make him a nice rug to lay on in front of the fire place," Jen growled.

"Um, Jen, you don't have a fire place," Sally pointed out.

"My hypothetical fire place, Sally. Come on, keep up will you?"

"Oh, my bad. I forgot that I'm supposed to be taking notes on your hypothetical life so that when you make references to it I will know exactly what the freaking A you are talking about."

"Well, at least you are able to admit when you are wrong. That's a step in the right direction." Jen patted her friend, then jumped back just before Sally's fist could connect with her shoulder. "Man, it's nice not to have that stupid pole stuck to me."

Sally sat down on the bed and looked at Jen, her face no longer playful. "What's the plan, Jen? I know you're cooking one up because that's what you do best, so what are we going to do?"

"Sneak into the ICU of course," Jen said, matter of fact like.

"Nice." Sally smiled conspiratorially and then listened intently as Jen laid out her plan.

Chapter 21

"Start her on IV Vancomycin and Fentanyl twenty five micrograms bolus, f/b continuous infusion of three micrograms per hour. Then cover her with cooling blankets. Let's try to get her temperature down. If she starts shivering, replace them with regular blankets." Dr. Steele was issuing orders as she continued to monitor Jacque's condition. She had no problem deciding to sedate her given the amount of pain she was in; the fact that it would make it easier to move her was just a plus.

While the nurses followed out her orders, she stepped into an empty room and called Logan. He picked up on the first ring.

"I had to bring her to the ICU. I need to get her stable and then I will get the nurses out of the way so you can come up and move her," Cynthia explained.

"What do you mean get her stable? What's wrong with her?" Logan's voice was low, and Cynthia couldn't tell if it was worry in his voice or something else.

"The human blood she was given through a transfusion is attacking her body."

"Can you fix her?"

"Yes, I will tell you how once you are on your way to Denver. I'll text message you when I'm ready."

Logan heard the line cut off as Dr. Steele hung up. He couldn't believe that something really was wrong with Jacque. Was it his fault? No, he told himself, you didn't make them give her the transfusion. That was just something that happened, one of those no fault situations. Besides, Dr. Steele said she could fix it, that's all that mattered. Jacque would be fine, and she would be his. He sat down in a chair as he waited in her office for the text that would bring him one step closer to his goal.

"Are you sure this is going to work?" Sally whispered to Jen as they walked down the hall. They'd had a lucky break when Skender, the wolf Vasile put on the door had stepped away to go to the bathroom.

"Of course it's going to work, it's my idea," Jen said confidently.

"Right, like that summer you decided it would be a good idea to sneak out and go camping?"

"Hey, everything turned out fine. It was just a little fire," Jen said carelessly.

"A little fire, Jen? Really? You burned three acres, the freaking fire department had to get one of those crop duster planes to pour water over it, and you say *that* turned out fine?" Sally's whisper was now more of a whispered shout.

"Okay, so it got a little out of control. This is nothing like that. It's a simple in and out op."

"Did you just say in and out op?" Sally asked sarcastically.

"Yeah, you know, op like operation. We get in and we get out undetected."

"Oh, well once you put it like that, I don't know why I was ever worried." Sally rolled her eyes, clearly not comforted in the least by Jen's words.

They continued to walk down hall after hall. All of them were beginning to look the same.

"Do you even know where the ICU is?" Sally finally asked.

"No, but I figured they would have signs with arrows that said 'you are here', and then pointed you the way you needed to go. You know, like in the mall."

"Says the genius who planned our in and out op." Sally took a deep breath and let it out slow.

As Jen rounded a corner, she saw a guy in scrubs coming towards them. Before Sally could be seen she pushed her back. "Go," she whispered.

"What?" Sally gasped.

"Go, there is a nurse or doctor coming this way. I will distract him. You go on like we planned." Sally hesitated. "Are you going to let Jacque down, Sally? Leave her all alone, scared in that unfamiliar room?" Jen knew the guilt trip would do the trick and sure enough...

"Sometimes I want to punch you in the face, Jennifer Adams," she ground out as she turned and walked the opposite direction.

"I love you too," Jen whispered, then quickly added, "Its 11:00 p.m. Now, meet back in the room in an hour and a half." Sally lifted her hand in acknowledgment but kept walking.

Sally walked as quickly as she could down the hall and, rounding the corner, nearly ran into two huge doors with the letters ICU labeling them. Well, ask and you shall receive, she thought as she gently pushed on the doors to see if they would open. They didn't. Wishful thinking never did anyone any good but it was worth a try. She looked along the walls on either side of the door because she had noticed that a lot of the hospital doors were automated with a button so that you didn't have to push them open. As she examined the wall to the right of the doors, the hairs on the back of Sally's neck began to rise. She felt like she was being watched. She began to turn but before she could she felt pressure on her neck, and then darkness and silence engulfed her.

Chapter 22

Skender was standing in front of the room that Jacque's friends were staying in when he heard the elevator ding to announce its arrival. He couldn't help his natural instinct to take up a defensive posture when he was protecting something. When no one immediately exited the elevator, his wolf perked up. He sniffed the air and sharpened his hearing. He could smell a human and hear breathing. There was someone on that elevator, someone not conscious by the sound of their slow breathing. He moved quickly before the doors could close and a steady stream of curses in his native tongue began to flow from his mouth at the sight of one of Jacques' friends in still form in the floor, the one called Sally. He quickly scooped her into his arms and hurried towards her room. He knocked before opening, hoping that he would hear the other one, the mouthy one they called Jen, answer. The response was louder than any words could have been. Skender had learned that sometimes silence was the worst kind of noise. He opened the door slowly, only to confirm his fears. The room was empty. He carried Sally in and laid her on one of the beds, checked her pulse and watched her for a few seconds to make sure her breathing was steady. Then, as quietly as he entered, he left. All the while, the silence that filled the room screamed at him. Once in the hall he debated over and over in his mind whether to go search for Jen or call Vasile or Decebel and let them know what was going on. He could only imagine the wrath that Decebel would reign down on him. His actions towards Jen may not be obvious to him, but everyone else saw it, and if he found out she was missing he would tear Skender apart. Maybe I can wait just awhile to see if she comes back, if not then I will panic. In the back of his mind he knew he should call his Alpha, but fear stayed his hand.

Jen turned toward the guy approaching her. As he got closer, she realized that he was pretty cute and not much older than herself. The mischief gods were smiling on her tonight.

"You do realize you aren't supposed to be going to the ICU this late, right?" he asked her, totally throwing her for a loop.

"The ICU?" Jen said stupidly.

"Yeah, that's the only thing in the direction your friend just went." When Jen didn't respond but stood there looking back and forth between the direction Sally had gone and back at the cute guy, he spoke again. "I better go get her to keep her from getting in trouble. You need to head on back to whereever it is you are supposed to be."

The part about him going and getting Sally was what finally brought her out of her trance. Jen touched his arm to get his full attention and when he looked at her, she smiled her most seductively adoring smile. "Okay," she paused to look at his name badge, "Matt. You caught me. I was out roaming the hospital because I'm bored out of my mind. I was in a car accident and have been stuck in bed and I'm finally allowed to be up and moving. So here I am little 'ole pathetic me looking for a good time," she paused and winked at him, bringing on a full blush, "in a hospital. You wouldn't happen to know where I could find a good time that maybe came with a few drinks?" Jen said in her most hopeful voice. The guy named Matt looked at Jen, then at the hallway behind her, clearly torn about doing the right thing and the fun thing. Lucky for Jen, she was very good at convincing guys to do the fun thing.

"Well, I was just going to end my shift," he began, but Jen interrupted with a squeal.

"Yay! See, this was fate. You were going to leave work and be bored, and I was going to have to sit in my bed all alone and be bored, but instead we met. Pretty awesome if you ask me." Jen grinned at him adoringly. She wrapped her arm in his as she said, "Lead the way, handsome."

Matt took her to a room marked 'Dietary' in bold letters. "We have beer that is kept on the floors for people who come in and are alcoholics."

"Shut up! Really?" Jen asked.

"Yep, the docs have to write a script for it, though. It's not the greatest but it'll get the job done in a pinch." He grinned at her and Jen saw that he had dimples. She groaned inwardly, if only she hadn't given her heart to another. Wait, WTH, she hadn't given her heart away, what was she thinking? Matt interrupted her inner dialogue when he took her by the hand, and after he had filled his backpack with beer he pulled her out of the room and continued down another hall. They came to a small waiting area tucked around a corner where it was virtually impossible to see. Matt set down his bag and pulled out two beers. He handed her one and kept the other for himself. Jen sat down on the love seat and stared at Matt over the rim of the beer can as she took a sip. "So Matt, what do you do exactly?"

Four hours, 12 beers, and two bags of Cheetos later…

Matt was sitting on the love seat next to Jen while she rambled on about werewolves and how bossy they were. He figured she must've been into reading those paranormal romance books that chicks are so into. When she finally paused, Matt took advantage of her silence by placing his fingers under her chin and turning her face to him. Jen's eyes widened as he began to lean towards her.

"Has anyone told you how pretty you are?" Matt asked her.

Jen giggled. "On occasion." Jen turned her head, slightly cocking it to the side and asked, "What are you doing?"

"I'm going to kiss you," he answered bluntly.

"Huh, well I guess that's ok. It is for Jacque, after all."

Matt looked confused by her statement, but she wasn't refusing so he took that as an all clear. He leaned in the rest of the way and pressed his lips firmly to hers. Jen leaned closer into him and allowed him to part her lips with his tongue. This kiss lasted several seconds but Jen abruptly pulled back when she felt Matt's hand slip under the hem of her shirt and graze her skin.

"Oh, I don't think I'm quite drunk enough for that, big boy," she teased.

"Can't blame a man for trying when there's a beautiful girl sitting next to him, can you?" Matt winked at her.

Jen stood up then and would have fallen down if Matt had not steadied her. "Whoa, the floor is dipping. That can't be safe. You should probably tell someone to have that looked into," she told him as she continued to try and stay upright.

"Uh huh. Jen, I think it's time I got you back to your room."

"Room, shroom, I'm having fun. Aren't you having fun, Matty?"

Amazingly, drunk Jen was still able to flirt.

"I'm definitely having fun, but I don't want someone to be worried about you if they come to your room and you are gone. Come on, you point me in the right direction and I will escort you safely, my lady."

"Ooo, you're my knight with the shiny armor." Jen giggled.

"That's right, beautiful." Matt smiled and wrapped his arm around her waist to help support her, and began to walk with her in the direction she pointed. She rambled the entire way there and when they finally got close, Matt froze at the sight of a big man standing in front of the door she indicated, arms folded across a wide chest. Matt swallowed hard as he continued forward.

"Hey!" Jen waved at the man and giggled when he lifted a lip at her and snarled.

Matt stopped moving forward, and when Jen realized he was nervous she stepped out of his hold and pointed, "Matty, don't be nervous, that's just Splender." She turned and blew the man a kiss. "He's just grumpy."

Jen continued forward and when she reached the guy, she grinned big and pulled him into a hug, which looked awkward because the man remained stiff as a board.

"Hey Splender, how ya been?" Jen said as she relinquished her hold on him.

"It's Skender," he growled, "and what are you doing with that?" Skender pointed to Matt with a growl worthy of Decebel.

"Oh, that's Matty. He's my new friend, right Matty?"

"Uh, well yeah. But just friends, man, and I just wanted to make sure she made it back okay, so I'll just be going then. Bye Jen," Matt spoke rapidly and began backing away. He gave her a final wave and turned to hurry on his way.

Skender turned his scowl on Jen. "You had better get back in there before Decebel finds out you were gone with a guy."

"Oh, Slender, quit being a worry worrier." Jen stumbled forward and Skender caught her. He reached back and turned the knob on the door to her room, gently pushing her in.

"Go to bed and stay out of trouble," he growled again.

"What is it with you wolves and your bossy beingness? It gets old, you know. Hey Spender, is the room spinning or are you spinning? If it's you, could you please stand still." Jen was wobbling on her feet.

Skender took her by the hand and led her to the nearest bed. "He is going to rip my throat out with his bare hands," he was mumbling under his breath as he eased her to the bed and stepped back.

"Naw, he won't rip your throat out." Jen's inebriation did not keep her from understanding he was talking about Decebel, although her words were very slurred. "He won't be that quick about it. Geeze, Snipper. Don't you know him better than that? When he's in grouchy bear mode he wants to inflict pain. I see it every time he looks in my inspection, wait, that's not right. When he looks to my…well whatever it is ends in 'tion'. The points is pain. 'K, now stop spinning."

Skender went to the door to leave, but turned back before he closed the door behind him. "You going to be okay?"

Jen gave him a thumbs up. "I am better than good, Spenster. I'm fantabulishisness." Skender shook his head as he closed the door.

Jen stood up and wobbled over to the stack of clothes lying on the other bed. For some reason a shower seemed like a splendid idea. As she reached for her clothes, she noticed a lump under the covers. She leaned forward and poked the lump, there was a grunt and then nothing else. Well, she thought, it's a lump and although she should probably investigate she figured the lump would still be there when she was done with her shower. Nodding her head in agreement with herself, she headed off to the shower…without the clothes she had picked up and set down while she poked the lump.

Chapter 23

Fane paced the waiting room of the ICU while Decebel and Vasile played cards. He looked in their direction and growled.

"Fane, it's not that we don't care, but this room would get rather small if all three of us were pacing, and the cards keep our minds busy. So keep your snarling to yourself," Vasile growled back.

"It's just driving me crazy," Fane admitted. "The constant waiting, the not knowing. I can't pick up any of her thoughts, it's making my wolf very restless."

"The doctor must have sedated her, which is a good thing since she was in so much pain. She will be fine, Fane. You know I will do anything in my power to keep her safe and get her well."

"I know, thank you," Fane told his father.

Logan's phone vibrated, indicating he had a text message. He picked it up and looked at the lit-up screen.

Cme to 4th flr. Use staff elevtr 2 avoid wt rm, I will buzz u n the doors.

Logan stood up and put his phone in the pocket of the lab coat Dr. Steele had left for him. He grabbed the keys to the car the Coldspring pack had loaned him and headed to the fourth floor. He couldn't help but be nervous with Vasile and his wolves still in the hospital. When the elevator doors dinged and opened, he stepped out and immediately froze. One of Jacque's friends was standing in front of the doors that had the words ICU on them, trying to figure out a way to open them. If she was trying to sneak she was very lousy at it. He crept up behind her, his wolf helping him be silent while he stalked his prey. Just as the girl was about to turn around, Logan placed his hands on the point between her neck and shoulder and squeezed. She crumpled like a house of cards. He caught her before she hit the floor and the only thing he could think to do was put her in the elevator and hit the button that would take her back to her floor and hope she would be okay. He placed her limp body on the floor of the elevator and pushed the button to her floor and watched as the doors closed. That was a development he had not been expecting but he couldn't worry about it now. He walked back to the ICU doors and heard a loud buzz and the doors opened. Directly in front of him was the nurses' station, a circular desk that gave them a clear view of every glass-encased room. Dr. Steele stood waiting in the doorway of a room directly to his right.

"She's heavily sedated. I have her hooked to an IV drip to keep her under. I also figured that since she would have to have the IV attached that if stopped, we would need to have a reason to be wheeling her out of the hospital, so I forged transfer papers to the burn unit at Children's Hospital in San Antonio. Not really plausible but it may buy us some time if caught."

Logan was impressed with the doctors' forethought. "Thank you."

"Let's just get this done," she growled. Logan wondered if the good doctor's conscience was nagging her. He thought about reminding her about what Fane had done to her brother, but decided it would be better to just keep his mouth shut, get Jacque, and go. Dr. Steele had wheeled a gurney into the small room, right up against the bed that Jacque was lying in. Logan thought she looked pale, even with her still-pink healing skin.

"I need you to grab that end of the sheet and on my count, pull. It will slide her smoothly across," Dr. Steele was telling him as he stared at the woman he had chosen as his mate.

Logan grabbed the end as instructed and pulled smoothly on the doctor's count of three. He covered her with a blanket up to her neck and Dr. Steele placed and oxygen mask over her face. She said it was just to help make it harder to identify Jacque. They began to wheel the gurney out and it struck Logan that there was no one else around.

"Where are the nurses?"

"There are only two ICU nurses at night and I sent one to get me some more antibiotics from the pharmacy, and the other to my office to get my phone."

"But you have your phone," Logan said before thinking.

"Yes, but she doesn't know that now does she? Now hurry before they get back," she told him as she pulled the door to the room Jacque had been in closed. They pushed the gurney through doors opposite the ones that Logan had come in. It brought them straight to an elevator that had the doors held open by a large steel trash can. Dr. Steele was ahead of the game, Logan liked that. As they rode down, the sound of elevator music filtered through the speakers and although the music was meant to be calming, it was grating on Logan's nerves, and he really just wanted to rip the speakers out. Calm down, he told himself, it's almost over.

The elevator doors opened and they pushed the gurney into a hall with harsh fluorescent lights that shined against white walls and white linoleum floors. Logan could hear sounds emanating from the right end of the hall. The emergency room, he thought. They turned left and quickly wheeled the gurney away from the noise. The hall seemed to go on forever, although Logan knew that it really wasn't that long. At that moment, pushing the gurney with Jacque on it even five feet would be too long. Just when he thought he might have to take off in a sprint, they were finally in front of the doors that would lead to the car he had waiting for them. Dr. Steele pushed a button on the wall and the doors opened automatically.

Logan had parked the SUV directly to the left of the doors, and as they wheeled Jacque over to the back passenger door Logan realized that with Jacque sick, things just got a whole lot more complicated, so he made a split second decision. When Dr. Steele walked to his end of the gurney so that she could get the IV bag to hang on the clothes hanger hook above the back seat window, Logan grabbed her by the neck. She froze as she felt Logan's claws pierce her skin, a warm trickle of blood slid down her throat.

She didn't know what the hell Logan was up to, but she did know that her role in this game had just changed, and not to her benefit.

"I cannot manage all these medicines for Jacque, so until you tell me what I need to do to make her better you are going with us," Logan growled low, his eyes beginning to glow.

Her wolf naturally wanted to submit but she just wanted to spit in his face. She looked down at Jacque. The girl really was sick and she held no ill will against her, she just happened to be caught in the crossfire. Once again to help justify her actions, and allay her guilty conscience, she would comply with Logan. "Okay, I will go with you. But as soon as I have shown you what you need to do to heal her I'm out, got it?"

Logan gave her neck one more squeeze for good measure. "We'll see, doc," he told her, his look promising retaliation if she did not keep her end of the deal.

They got Jacque loaded into the back seat. She hung the IV bag from the clothes hook above the window, then climbed into the passenger side taking a deep breath and letting it out slow. What have I gotten myself into, Cynthia thought to herself. She watched as Logan pushed the gurney back on the sidewalk, not bothering to take it back into thc hospital. He walked to the driver side door and climbed into the vehicle. Without a word he started the SUV, put it in drive, and slipped off into the night while Jacque's mate waited in vain to hear of news of her well being. Cynthia couldn't have stopped the tear that slipped down her cheek if she had wanted to.

Chapter 24

Sally woke up groggily. It took her a moment to get her bearings, but then she remembered she was in the hospital because Jen and Jacque were both healing from the wreck. She put her hands to her head and moaned, her head felt like it was splitting open. As she stood up slowly, she realized that there was singing coming from the bathroom. She looked around and noticed Jen was not in her bed, and then she remembered that Jacque was really sick and in the ICU. She looked at the clock on the wall and saw that it was 5:00a.m. Walking over to the bathroom door, she tried in vain to remember what had happened last night. She gave up and knocked on the door. When the singing continued and no one answered her, she turned the knob experimentally to see if it was locked. It was. She pressed her ear to the door and realized then that it was Jen singing. Pressing closer, she strained to hear her.

"You're so hypno-something, could you be the devil, could you be an angel, your touch is something good, feels like going floating, leave my body glowing."

"Katy Perry? She's singing Katy Perry in the hospital bathroom. Just when you think you've seen it all," Sally mumbled. She knocked on the door again. Still no answer, so she started banging. Then she was banging and hollering, "JEN! OPEN THE FREAKING DOOR!" Wouldn't you know, she just sang louder. Why am I not surprised, she thought.

"They said I'm afraid, you're not like the others, futuristic werewolves'
different DNA, they like to command you," Jen continued.

"Can't you at least get the words right if you're going to be so stinking loud!"

Just as Sally was going to resume her, so far fruitless, banging the hospital room door flew open. She turned to face the would-be intruder. "Why don't you freaking wolves ever knock? Has ever occurred to you that we might be naked up in here?"

Decebel at least had the good grace to look embarrassed. "I apologize. I heard banging and yelling. Is everything okay?" He asked, glancing around the room. Before Sally could answer he spoke again. "Where is Jen?"

Before Sally could answer they both heard Jen.

"Kiss me, k-k-kiss me, infect me with your love, and fill me with your poison,
take me, t-t-take me, wanna be your victim, ready for abduction boy, you're a werewolf, your touch is so furry, its supernatural, extra-werewolf-iestrial," Jen sung as loud as she could.

Sally was shaking her head in disbelief, "This is gonna be good. I mean, she might actually be embarrassed when she finds out you heard all that."

Decebel cocked his head as if listening for something, then he sniffed the air, taking in a deep breath. "I smell alcohol. Have you two been drinking?" Decebel asked in disbelief.

"Of course not!" Sally said with obvious offense.

Decebel didn't acknowledge her answer but continued to ask questions. "Why were you banging on the door?"

"It's locked and Jen won't answer me. It's like she can't hear me."

"So, she might be drunk and she's trying to take a shower?" Decebel asked skeptically.

"That. could be. a bad thing, right?" Sally pushed out the words.

Decebel was already in action, he was banging on the door so hard the hinges shook. Werewolf strength, must be nice.

"JENNIFER, OPEN THE DOOR!" he yelled.

There was a pause in the singing and all they heard was the water from the shower. Both of them held their breath waiting for her response. One beat, two beats. "Knock, knock?" they heard her ask.

"Jen, open the door. This isn't funny," Sally tried.

"Jen, open the door, this isn't funny who?" Jen repeated and snickered.

"Okay," Sally said to Decebel. "You're right, she's tore up from the floor up."

"Jennifer, I want you to back away from the door," Decebel told her.

"What are you going to do, Decebel?" Sally asked him apprehensively.

Decebel didn't answer her, instead he braced both hands on either side of the door, pulled his leg back and kicked hard. The door didn't resist at all, it splintered where his foot hit and then swung open. Steam came flowing out of the bathroom looking like a living being, slipping around Decebel, seeming to pull him in towards Jen. He started to enter but before he could put a foot over the door jamb, Sally grabbed his arm. "Hey buddy, she could be naked all up in here so wait. If I need you I will call."

"You are right, I will wait here. But hurry," Decebel relented.

Sally stepped into the steam. Jen was standing in the shower, dancing to music that Sally couldn't hear until Jen decided to share, that is.

"There is this decibel, on another level, boy, you're my lucky werewolf, I wanna walk on your wave length, and be there when you vibrate, for you I risk it all. But you're not an option, wanna be a victim, ready for objection, and I don't remember the words, something about poison. You're an alien, wait I mean a werewolf, let me see your furry paws, don't know what rhymes with paws." All of this was to the tune of Katy Perry's E.T. song. Man, she is going to be so freaking embarrassed when I tell her she sang about Decebel and his paws. Sally actually laughed out loud at the though., Jen turned at the sound of Sally's voice. Sally saw more of Jen than she needed to in an entire lifetime.

"SALLY!" which actually came out more like Swally. "Hey chica, how'd you like my singing, pretty good right? You be my backup, the Sonny to my chair, or like the, um," Jen screwed her face up, struggling to come up with an adequate combination, which she didn't. "Like the black eye to my peas." Jen laughed and nearly fell over.

Sally jumped forward to catch her friend and keep her from cracking her skull. "Crap! Jen, stand still."

"Is everything okay? Do I need to come in there?" Decebel's raised voice caught Jen's attention. Great, just what Sally need, a drunk, horny, naked chick chasing a werewolf.

"No!" "Oooh, did you bring a boy home, Sally?" Sally and Jen spoke at the same time.

Of course, *now* Jen was eager to get out of the shower, now that

Sally was thoroughly soaked. Jen untangled herself from Sally and headed straight for the smashed-in bathroom door…naked…as in no clothes. Sally was slipping, trying to catch her. She wasn't going to make it.

"DECEBEL. Incoming, drunk, naked, crazy chick!" Sally yelled as loud as she could.

A second later she heard Decebel say something that sounded curiously like Romanian cussing and Jen say, "Oooh, you're freakin hot, as in h-o-," Jen was attempting to spell out hot, it obviously wasn't going to happen.

Sally finally made it out of the bathroom, water dripping off her. She imagined she resembled a very pissed off wet cat. Decebel had wrapped a sheet from the bed around Jen, who was at the moment trying to grope him. "Have we met?" she asked, "Cuz if we haven't then we should, and by meet I mean hook up." Decebel was gallantly trying to keep Jen's hands in appropriate areas. Sally supposed she should help but this was just too good to pass up. She walked over to her backpack and pulled out her phone.

"What are you doing?" Decebel's voice was incredulous.

"I'm videoing this. This is too good to pass up. Jen is going to have a freaking heart attack when she sobers up and I'm going to have it all on video. It will be like a Christmas present that just keeps on giving. Every time I need a pick me up, I just turn on the video of Jen drunk off her rocker, groping a werewolf who has no clue how to handle a drunk, horny teenager! This is like the best gift ever, someone in the galaxy loves me." Sally was laughing by the time she was done talking. Decebel, however, was not.

Jen turned to look at Sally as if realizing for the first time she was in the room. "Sally! Look it," Jen tried to whisper like Decebel wouldn't be able to hear her, but it came out more as a hoarse shout. "What's his name? He is so yummy!"

"Jen, that's Decebel, remember? Fane's werewolf pack member?" Sally watched Jen for any recognition.

Jen was studying Decebel closely, as in had her hands on his face. Then she ran her fingers through his hair, close, all the while staring at his face. "Hmm, he kind of looks familiar now that you say that..." she continued to study him, turning her head from side to side.

Decebel looked at Sally as if looking for instruction.

Inspiration hit. "Say something bossy to her," Sally grinned at her ingenious.

Decebel growled at her, she shrugged her shoulders. "Fine, be the first werewolf raped by a drunken teenage girl. Whatever dude, it's your rep."

Decebel grabbed Jen's hands and looked her straight in the eyes. "Jennifer, go and get dressed. Now." His voice was as cold and firm as always.

Jen froze, then giggled as she said,"Decebel. Oh yeah, I know you. You're so hot when you're bossy." Great, Sally thought as she rolled her eyes, inebriated Jen thinks Decebel is sexy when he's bossy, nice.

To Sally and Decebel's surprise Jen finally relented. "Fine, I'll put on some clothes. But only because you asked so nicely." Jen began to un-wrap the sheet and she was nearly naked again when Decebel realized she meant to get dressed right there in front of him. He moved faster than he ever had before and made a bee line for the bathroom. "Tell me when she's dressed," he told Sally.

"Roger that, little buddy," Sally said sarcastically.

"Do you think he likes me? I think I like him, but I shouldn't," Jen's voice sounded like a wounded little girl. Oh no, Jen was going from silly drunk to sad drunk. Sad drunks were the worst kind.

"Jen, look at me," Sally said in the sternest voice she could muster. "Why do you think you like Decebel?"

Jen's face was blank, then she grinned. "Why would you think I liked Decebel, silly? He's bossy, cold, mean, grumpy, pushy, yummy, sexy, strong, tall."

"Um, Jen." She snapped her fingers in Jen's face, which had gone all spaced out as she continued her description of Decebel. This was bad, so very freaking bad. Jen had a crush on a werewolf who she could never have. Damn, Sally thought, why can't she be like other girls and like the captain of the football team, or even some grungy high school dropout? But no, she had to fall for a werewolf.

Jen's voice was soft. "It's no big thing, he's not an option." She swung back to the other end of the drunken spectrum and was spinning in circles with her arms out, singing, "He's not an option," over and over in the same tune she had been singing earlier. Sally grabbed Jen and helped her into her clothes and then hollered for Decebel to join them again. When he walked back into the room, Jen immediately walked over to him and leaned on him, looking up at him dreamily. He walked over to the bed as Jen continued to keep herself attached to him. When they were both seated he looked up at Sally, "So what exactly happened last night?"

Sally closed her eyes and rubbed her face roughly with her hands, trying in vain to remember what happened but there was just a black spot in her mind.

"I don't remember, Decebel," she answered honestly.

"Okay, what's the last thing you remember?"

"Jen and I had decided to sneak into the ICU to see Jacque. We wandered all over the hospital until we nearly got caught by some guy in scrubs. Jen made me go on without her and said she would stay and distract the guy."

Decebel growled. "What do you mean she was with a guy?" He looked down to ask Jen about it but she was sound asleep, her head leaned against his arm. Decebel gently laid her back and swung her legs up on the bed, then covered her with the blankets. He turned back to Sally and pinned her with his gaze. "What the hell were you two thinking? Did I not specifically say to not do anything stupid?"

It was clear to Sally that nothing she could say would calm the pissed off werewolf in front of her, so she didn't even try. "Look, Jacque is our best friend, she's all alone in a room with tubes and crap stuck to her, she's in pain, and she's scared. We were not just going to leave her like that all by herself."

"I understand that, but you could have asked for help instead of attempting it on your own," Decebel told her.

Sally's jaw dropped open, baffled by what she had just heard. "Are you saying you would have helped us?"

"I'm not going to say that I wouldn't have tried to talk you out of it, but knowing this one," he nodded his head in Jen's direction, "she wouldn't have relented. So yes, I would have helped you."

"Wow. Well, next time we want to break some rules we will definitely recruit your expertise."

"Good, now do you remember anything else? Did you make it into the ICU? Do you remember coming back to your room?" Decebel fired question after question at Sally.

"Hold up, Dec. Let me think," Sally told him, holding her hands up in an effort to get him to stop. "I remember standing in front of the ICU doors and I was trying to figure out how they opened and then..." Sally furrowed her brow, trying so hard to remember what had happened.

"Hold on, you guys got past Skender, right?"

Sally nodded her head yes and watched as Decebel got up and walked to the door. He stuck his head out and she heard him ask Skender to come in. Skender walked in, shoulders slumped forward, and Sally could tell he was getting ready for his butt to be chewed on by his pack Beta.

"Skender," Decebels' voice was low and demanded truth. "Could you please explain to me how two teenage girls were able to get past you?"

Skender looked at Sally and then at Decebel. "It must have been when I went to the bathroom. I wasn't gone that long, and the room was so quiet I figured they had gone to sleep." Skender stumbled over his words as fear rolled off him.

"Why didn't you call me and ask me to come and take over for you?"

"I don't know, Decebel. I just didn't think they would try anything."

Decebel snorted. "Have you not been around these girls for the past month? Surely you've noticed their pension for trouble."

"Hey now, there's no need to be hating on us," Sally frowned.

"Speaking the truth is not hating, as you call it, it's just stating a fact," Decebel informed her.

"Okay, so we know how they left, now we need to know how they got back." Decebel glared at Skender. "Did you happen to be at your post when the girls returned?"

"Yes, I was here both times," he answered, no less nervous than before.

"What do you mean both times?"

"I mean both times. They didn't arrive back together at the same time," Skender explained, "they arrived separately. Sally was the first one back."

"I don't remember coming back," Sally told him.

"Well, I wouldn't expect you to. I found you knocked out in the elevator."

Sally gasped and covered her mouth. Decebel didn't say anything, he just waited for the wolf to continue.

"The elevator doors opened and no one stepped out, so I ran

over before they could close to see if someone was in there, and there you were on the elevator floor. So I picked you up and put you back in the bed. That's when I realized that Jen was gone as well." Skender flinched at the low rumble coming from Decebel.

"Pray tell, why did you not call me at this point, Skender? Don't you think it was a pretty big deal that you found Sally unconscious in an elevator and Jennifer missing?" By the time Decebel was done talking, he was pacing the room, looking like he was on the verge of throttling the poor wolf.

"I should have called you right away, but I decided to wait and see if Jen made it back on her own. If she hadn't returned shortly I was going to call you then. I see now in hindsight that wasn't the best idea."

"You think?" Decebel asked. "When did Jennifer get back?" he growled.

"She came back about an hour ago in the company of a guy in scrubs, she said his name was Matty. She was pretty drunk when I inquired her about the guy. He got scared and hurried off. Then I helped Jen back into their room and I've been sitting out here ever since," Skender finished.

Sally was convinced if he had been in his wolf form he would be cowering with his tail between his legs. Then again, as she looked at Decebel and the obvious rage he was battling, Sally had to admit she felt like cowering as well.

Decebel finally looked at Skender. "You can go."

Skender let out a breath that Sally didn't think he even realized he had been holding. He turned to go but before he could make it out the door Decebel told him, "Skender, I will not forget this, and it will be dealt with once everything else has been worked out. Understood?"

"Yes, Beta." And then he hastily shut the door.

Sally could feel the anger coming off of Decebel, it was nearly tangible.

"Are you okay?" she asked him.

"I'm not really sure at the moment," he answered honestly.

"Well, maybe you should take a time out. Jen's not awake for you to growl at and there's no sense in growling at me now when you're just going to do it again when she wakes up."

"That's probably a very good idea. However, I will warn you

Sally, a time out will not cool my temper. If anything it may become worse as I have time to dwell on all the possibilities of Jennifer's little adventure."

"Okay, well, let's just not worry about that right now. I mean, she obviously showed up fully clothed. Skender didn't mention that it looked like she was disheveled or whatever, so you can assume that she didn't let this Matt character de-flower her."

"Sally, you're not helping." Decebel turned away from both girls, taking a deep breath and letting it out slowly. "Look, I'm going to check on Fane and see if they've heard anything since I left. Please do not leave this room until I come back. Do you think you can handle that?"

"Okay, Decebel, since you asked so nicely," Sally responded, her voice thick with sarcasm.

Chapter 25

Fane and Vasile were discussing the fact that since Jacquelyn had gotten sick the situation with Dillon had changed when Decebel walked into the waiting area.

"How are Sally and Jen?" Vasile asked his Beta.

Decebel sat down in one of the chairs across from them and ran his hands through his hair in frustration. "You're never going to believe what those two got themselves into last night."

"What have the two troublemakers done this time?" Vasile asked.

"They came up with the bright idea to sneak into the ICU to see Jacque, but their plan didn't quite hash out, if you can imagine. Sally ended up unconscious in the elevator with no memory of how it happened and Jennifer was drunk off her ass after having spent the night with some mongrel named Matty." Decebel's voice had gone deathly low at his mention of Jen.

Vasile let out a slow breath before responding, "Are they both in one piece?"

"Yes, Alpha. Jennifer is sleeping off her wild night as we speak and Sally is with her."

Fane looked at Decebel and then his father, his brow furrowed in thought. "Why would Sally be unconscious in the elevator?" Fane got an uneasy feeling and his wolf perked up, something was wrong but he didn't know what it was. Suddenly the urgency to have news on Jacquelyn's well-being overrode his sense of propriety.

Fane stood up and walked towards the ICU door. He began banging on it forcefully, not pretending at politeness. After a few moments the doors opened and a nurse stepped out. "Can I help you?"

"I want to see Jacquelyn Pierce." Fane's tone left no room for argument, but apparently the nurse hadn't got the memo.

"Sir, I know Dr. Steele told you that family and friends are not allowed in the ICU due to the seriousness of the illnesses. It further compromises their immune systems."

Fane noticed that the nurse's heart rate was quickening and she had sheen of perspiration across her brow. Fane looked past the nurse into the room behind her and saw that there seemed to be a sense of urgency from the other staff. Several other nurses were on the phones and there was a doctor pointing towards a room, his face displaying obvious frustration. Fane called on his wolf's hearing to catch what the doctor was saying. "How does a patient just up and disappear? Have you tried to get in touch with Dr. Steele?" That was all Fane needed to hear. He pushed pass the nurse and her weak attempts to stop him. Fane heard his father behind him, and Decebel was only a step behind Vasile.

Fane followed the direction the doctor had been pointing to and stepped into an empty room saturated in his mate's sent. He instinctively reached out to her through their bond, but there was only silence in response. He turned back to the doctor and knew his eyes were glowing based on his expression. Fane grabbed the doctor by the front of his shirt and lifted him effortlessly off the floor. "Where is Jacquelyn Pierce?" he snarled.

"Fane, put him down," he heard his Alpha issue the command but his wolf wasn't listening.

The doctor grabbed onto the wrist of the arm that held him in the air, his mind threatening to shut down from the fear pouring over him.

"I d-d-don't know," he stuttered. "I just got here to do my rounds and when I went to see Ms. Pierce her room was empty. I had the nurses check to see if she had anything scheduled for this morning, but they can't find anything. We can't get a hold of Dr. Steele either."

Fane could tell the doctor told the truth but was reluctant to set him down, not wanting to give up an object to direct his anger upon.

"Fane, set him down now," he heard his Alpha say again and this time he obeyed. He turned and dared to look Vasile in the eyes, earning a growl in warning.

"We need to call Dillon Jacobs," he told his Alpha before he finally relented and dropped his eyes. Turning away from the doctor, he stormed past Vasile and Decebel and back into the waiting area they had just occupied. He didn't look to see if they would follow, he knew they would. Fane watched as his father dialed Dillon Jacobs' number and waited for him to answer. He picked up on the third ring.

"Dillon," Vasiles' voice was low, "have you anything to do with Jacque's disappearance?"

Fane and Decebel had no trouble hearing Dillon's response as he yelled into the phone, "What the hell do you mean she's disappeared!"

Vasile voice never changed in volume nor did it lose the deathly edge. "I mean just what I said, she is not here. They are unable to locate Dr. Steele as well. Are all of your wolves accounted for?"

"All of my wolves are here at the hotel." Dillon paused. "Wait, not all. Logan stayed at the hospital so he could let me know of any changes."

"Then you know that Jacque was in the ICU?"

"No, I haven't heard from Logan. I assumed everything must have been alright. Is she okay?" Dillon's voice was beginning to sound frantic.

"Jacque got sick last night. Dr. Steele thinks that because she received a blood transfusion of human blood her body is attacking the human blood and in turn attacking her body. They took her to the ICU, which was the last time we saw her, and now this morning she is gone."

Fane was losing patience. He needed action, needed to be doing something to find his mate. As Decebel placed his hand on Fane's shoulder, he told his prince, "We will find her."

"There is no other option," Fane told him.

Fane and Decebel looked at Vasile as he ended his conversation with Dillon. "He is on his way here. He said he would try to get in touch with Logan."

"What do we do until then?" Fane growled in frustration.

"Have you tried to reach out to her?" Vasile asked, referring to the mate bond.

"Yes, she isn't answering. I can't even get a sense of her presence like when she is sleeping."

"She must be unconscious. Dr. Steele probably sedated her to give her some relief from the pain," Vasile said, voicing his thoughts out loud. Then he reached out to his mate through their bond. *"Mina, you and Lilly need to come to the hospital. Jacque is missing."*

"How is Fane?" Her voice in his mind conveyed all the worry that she was feeling for her son and his mate.

"He is coping for the moment, although I don't know how long that will last. Come to me, meet us in Jen and Jacque's room. I will explain everything once you are here."

"We are on our way, don't let him do anything he will regret," Alina pleaded with her mate.

"As you say, my Luna, so it shall be done," Vasile answered formally, a vow to his mate to care for their son.

"She's missing? Missing, as in gone?" Sally asked for the third time.

"Yes Sally," Vasile answered for the third time, just as patiently as the first time.

"Crap, crap, crap," Sally snapped as she walked over to where Jen lay. She shook her friend none too gently. "Jen, wake your drunk butt up." When Jen didn't stir Sally headed towards the bathroom. "Desperate measures," Sally mumbled.

"This is going to get ugly," Decebel said, looking at Vasile, not attempting to hide the smirk on his face.

Sally came back into the room carrying a cup of water. She stood over Jen and shook her one more time. "Last chance, Jen. Wake up!" Still she didn't stir. Sally tossed the water right on Jen's face. Jen came to, sputtering and wiping the water from her eyes, trying to figure out where she was. Her eyes landed on Sally and the cup she held in her hand. The feral look that came over Jen's face was all the encouragement Sally needed to jump back just as Jen lunged for her. Decebel moved in a blur of speed, wrapping an arm around Jen's waist to pull her back.

"I'm weighing the pros and cons of beating the crap out of your skinny ass," Jen told Sally, her face still dripping with the water from Sally's cup.

"I'm sorry, Jen but it's important. Jacque's gone," Sally told her, eyes pleading with her friend to hear her.

Jen pulled out of Decebel's arms as she asked, "What do you mean she's gone?" She looked around the room until she found Fane. She noticed his lips tightened and his eyes were glowing a deep blue, which, had he not looked like he wanted to rip someone's head off, would have been beautiful.

"She was not in the ICU this morning," Vasile explained. "I

have Sorin, Skender and Boian searching the hospital and questioning the staff. Dillon is on his way and is going to have his wolves help with the search."

"Wait a sec," Jen said, shaking her head. "So you don't think Dillon has anything to do with this?"

It was Vasile who answered. "I won't know for sure until I can ask him face to face, but when I spoke with him on the phone he sounded genuinely caught off guard."

Just as Vasile finished talking, the door to the room opened and Dillon walked in and just behind him were Lilly and Alina.

"What is with werewolves and their lack of ability to knock?" Jen asked. "I mean, seriously, does it have something to do with the energy it takes to lift your hand and bang it against the door? Or is there a general rule that all werewolves are exempt from the common courtesy?"

The whole room stopped and stared at Jen. She looked around and shrugged. "Well, I'm just saying."

Dillon ignored Jen's outburst and turned to Vasile. "I did not have anything to do with this. I am not so low as to take my daughter away from her mother under the cover of darkness like some thief."

Vasile didn't say anything right away, but seemed to be weighing the truth in his words. Finally he nodded. "I believe you." Then he turned to Lilly. "Lilly, how are you?"

"Well, if you want the truth, I'm straddling the fence. One side being-what the hell and the other side- are you freaking serious. I just don't understand why we can't keep her safe. What are we doing wrong?" Lilly asked, on the verge of tears.

Fane walked over to her and wrapped his arms around her. "Îmi pare aşa de rău (I'm so sorry)," he whispered. "I should have demanded to stay with her."

"Fane, it's not your fault. You may be a prince in your world but in mine you're just a teenage boy. Here they don't give special treatment to teenage boys no matter how good looking."

"Regardless, I could have forced Dr. Steele, but I was trying not to disrespect her in her territory. I won't make that mistake again," Fane promised.

Lilly looked at Vasile. "So what do we do now?"

"We need to narrow down the possibilities," Vasile told her. "First, Dillon, did you get a hold of your Beta?"

"No, I've left him several messages but he's not answering nor has he called me back."

"Has he been acting strange lately?" Decebel asked him.

"Not really. I mean, I kind of thought he seemed a little off but I just brushed it off. Logan is my most faithful wolf. I can't imagine him betraying me."

"We've been trying to get in touch with Dr. Steele but she isn't answering her phone either, and none of the doctors or nurses know where she is." Vasile's voice betrayed the frustration that he was trying desperately to keep in check.

"Okay, so what I hear you all saying is that we really don't know jack crap and have no place to start. Am I getting it right?" Jen asked.

"Jennifer." Decebel gave a warning growl.

"Do not growl at me, fur ball," she snarled at him. "I just want to make sure we are all on the same page." She turned and looked at Fane and asked, "Have you not been able to speak to her through your freaky mind voodoo?"

"No, my father and I think Dr. Steele sedated her because of the pain. If I could just get through to her..." Fane didn't finish as emotion washed over him. He closed his eyes, bowing his head and shut the world out as he pictured his mate's face in his mind. *"Jacquelyn, can you hear me my love?"* He waited, but still there was no response. For the second time since he met her she was beyond his reach, beyond his protection. The hole that was left in her place threatened to drag him into the darkness. He vowed then and there that whoever had taken her would die by his jaws.

Chapter 26

Logan rubbed his eyes as he tried to push away the sleep that threatened to take over. He looked at the clock and saw that they had been only been driving for 2 hours. His phone had started ringing about an hour after they left the hospital and continued to ring on and off for an hour. He knew who it was without checking the caller I.D. By now, Dillon and Vasile, along with the others, were probably trying to piece together the events of the night that lead to the disappearance of Fane's mate. They might be a little confused by Dr. Steele's absence and he wondered how long it would be before Vasile decided to question her pack.

"We need to stop soon so I can check Jacque's IV. she probably needs another dose of sedative," Cynthia told him.

Just then, Jacque began to stir, letting out a painful sounding moan. Logan pulled the SUV over immediately, he couldn't risk Jacque reaching out to Fane. He had heard from Dillon that she and Fane were able to share their thoughts and although that might have deterred another wolf, Logan knew if he completed the Blood Rites with Jacque that bond with Fane would be broken. Or at least that's what he believed.

He watched as Dr. Steele got out of the vehicle and opened the back door where Jacque lay. While she administered more of the sedative, Logan was weighing his options on whether they should continue traveling by car, or if he should charter a small plane once they got to Dallas. He had his pilot's license and as long as he could find a plane to rent he would be able to get them to Colorado much faster.

Cynthia checked Jacque's pulse and respirations, making sure everything was within normal limits. Once she was satisfied that Jacque was settled and the sedative was working, she shut the door and climbed back into the passenger seat.

"So, do you have a plan for between here and Denver?" she asked Logan.

"As a matter of fact I've just decided that it would be better for us to fly rather than drive all the way to Colorado."

"Fly?" Cynthia asked.

"Yeah, I have my pilot's license, so once we get to Dallas we are nearly there already, just another hour and a half. I'll just rent a plane and we will fly the rest of the way. Is there any open land where your cabin is where I could land a small plane?" he asked her.

"There actually is an open field near the cabin."

"Excellent." Logan once again felt like things were working in his favor. He couldn't help but think that maybe this was fate because of how well things were going for him.

Cynthia sat back in her seat and closed her eyes, not wanting to encourage Logan to engage her in conversation. She was here for Jacque and that was all. Once Jacque was well she was getting the heck out of dodge.

"Vasile I'm ready to get out of this joint," Jen told him as she sat on her bed. "I mean, seriously, my skin is just really pink, no more blisters. I've already called my parents and told them that they are releasing me and Jacque, so now I just need you to work your werewolf mojo and get me released."

Decebel coughed, attempting to cover a laugh. Jen glared at him. "What are you laughing at, exactly?"

"I just don't understand where you learned to talk like that," Decebel told her honestly.

"It's a gift. Now quit laughing at me."

"As you say, Jennifer, so shall it be," Decebel told her, his eyes never wavering from hers.

Jen's breath caught as she noticed his gold eyes begin to glow. She turned away abruptly, needing to put distance between her and the wolf who was constantly ruffling her feathers.

"I will see what I can do about getting you released, Jen, if you think you are ready," Vasile told her.

"I'm sure. We've got plans to make. We can't be just sitting up here twiddling our-"

"JEN!" Sally abruptly cut her off.

"What? Twiddling our thumbs. Thumbs, Sally. Where is your mind?"Jen asked her with a wicked twinkle in her eyes. Much to

Jen's delight, Sally's face turned bright red.

"You might not want to mess with me, Jen. I've got the goods on you. So go on and rub me the wrong way, I dare you, and we all get to be serenaded by a highly inebriated Jennifer Adams," Sally threatened.

"What are you talking about, Sally?" Jen asked and there was actually worry etched across her face.

"Sally, maybe this isn't the best time," Decebel started but was quickly cut off by Jen.

"This doesn't concern you, Cujo," she snapped.

Decebel growled.

"Actually, it kind of does concern him since he was the object of your affection during your little performance."

Jen's face was beginning to turn a shade of red that Sally swore she'd never seen on her best friend, ever. She decided maybe Decebel was right and that she needed to save this ammunition for another time. "Jen, let's just call a truce, okay?"

"Fine, I'll let it go. For now," Jen relented.

Sally let out a deep breath, thankful to dodge that bullet.

Several hours later, they were all walking into Lilly Pierce's house, each looking thoroughly defeated.

"I can't believe how long it takes to get discharged from the hospital. I was beginning to think that at any moment they were going to tell each of you that you had to cough up a kidney before they would let me leave. I mean, seriously," Jen complained.

Everyone automatically made their way to the living room, all taking seats wherever they landed. Lilly looked at Vasile. "What now? I just feel like we should be *doing* something."

Vasile acknowledged Lilly's comment with a nod and then turned to the Denver pack Alpha. "Dillon, at this point is it safe to say that there is a possibility that your Beta is involved?"

"As much as I don't want that to be the case, the fact that he disappeared at the same time as Jacque and won't answer my calls is not boding well for his innocence," Dillon admitted.

"What about Dr. Steele?" Fane's voice was no longer his own as his wolf pushed for dominance.

"I think it's time to pay the Coldspring pack a visit and see if they know anything." Vasile looked at Fane, understanding filled his eyes. "Dillon, Decebel, and Fane will go with me to meet with them. I'll call the Alpha and arrange it. Skender, Boian and Sorin, you will stay here."

Fane watched his father step out of the room to make the call to the Coldspring Alpha. For what felt like the thousandth time he reached out to Jacquelyn and still there was nothing. He felt like his skin was too tight, and that at any moment his wolf was going to take over. He knew he could keep his wolf under control if he could just do something, take some sort of action to find their mate. This sitting and waiting the wolf didn't understand. He wanted to hunt the one who would dare to take what belonged to them. Vasile came back into the room, bringing Fane back to the present.

"We will meet them in twenty minutes at their pack head quarters," Vasile announced.

Alina met Vasile at the door as the wolves began to file out. "Please be careful."

"I will, Mina. I will also do whatever I need to get any information that will help us find Jacque."

"I would expect nothing less, Alpha." She leaned into his embrace and found comfort in his strength.

Jen and Sally stood at the door, watching as the men piled into Vasile's SUV. Jen was startled when Decebel appeared at her side, she didn't realize he hadn't left the house yet. As he passed her he paused briefly and leaned close to her ear, "We have much to discuss about your little escapade, Jennifer."

Jen's jaw dropped open but she quickly caught herself and shouted after him, "A lady never kisses and tells, Decebel."

That earned her a glare from him and a high five from Sally. "Nice one, Jen."

"I know, right?" Jen winked at Decebel as he continued to glare at her while getting into the vehicle.

"Sally, please tell me I didn't say the things I'm beginning to remember saying to him when I was tipsy."

"Okay, you didn't say those things," Sally obliged.

"I said them *and* I walked out of the bathroom naked in front of him, didn't I?" Jen's face was full of the mortification that she knew would be even worse when she had to face Decebel again.

"Butt freaking naked," Sally confirmed.

"Shit."

"I would say you're in deep," Sally agreed.

As Vasile pulled out of the driveway, Jen and Sally turned, closing the door behind them and Jen pointed a finger at Sorin. "Sorin! Where have you been, my man?"

"I've been around. You might say I've been working behind the scenes."

"Oooh, covert ops, sweet." Sally rolled her eyes at her best friend. Jen never could stay down for long.

Vasile pulled into the driveway of the Coldspring pack's head quarters. He had explained on the way that he would be the one to ask the questions and he wanted everyone else to remain silent. Well, his exact words were 'keep your damn muzzles shut', but who's being technical. They all exited the SUV and followed Vasile to the door. It opened before they could knock and Vasile recognized the wolf as the new Alpha he had appointed after Fane had won the challenge between him and their former Alpha.

"Vasile, I invite you and yours to come in. Be welcome." The Coldspring Alpha's words were a formal greeting that promised Vasile's pack's safety while in their territory.

"Jeff Stone, Alpha of the Coldspring pack, we accept your invitation and acknowledge your promise of peace, matching it with our own," Vasile responded just as formally.

Jeff stepped aside to allow the wolves to enter, then shut the door behind them. Vasile noted the sparseness of decoration and the lack of warmth that he had grown accustomed to in his own pack headquarters. They followed as Jeff led them down a hall. No pictures adorned the walls, which where a pale gray in color. He opened a door and ushered them into a room that appeared to be a meeting place. There were two couches arranged across from one another and several wing back chairs set on either side of the couches, forming a circle.

"Please be seated." Jeff took a seat first, willing to submit to Vasile's dominance over him. All the other wolves took various seats and Vasile was last to finally relinquish.

"We come to you with grave news regarding my son's mate,"

Vasile announced to the Alpha. "I need to know if you or any members of your pack are involved."

Jeff moved forward in his seat, straightening his back, indicating to Vasile he had his full attention.

Vasile continued, "Jacque was taken from the hospital last night where she had been recovering from a car accident. It appears that one of Dillon's wolves, he is Jacque's father and Alpha of the Denver pack, is involved."

"I'm sorry to hear this, but why would you think my pack would be involved?" Jeff asked.

"Dr. Steele was the physician treating Jacque."

Jeff's eyes widened at the news and it was apparent to Vasile that he had not been aware of this information.

"Cynthia has not been around the pack since Lucas fell. Do you think she is involved in Jacque's disappearance?"

"I think there are members of your pack who harbor anger towards Fane for taking their Alpha and I can only imagine the hurt that Dr. Steele must be enduring at the loss of her brother. It would make sense for Logan, Dillon's wolf, to seek out help from wolves that would do anything to take from Fane what their Alpha had failed to do."

Jeff didn't respond for several minutes, the lack of focus in his eyes making it evident he was lost in thought. Finally he spoke, but not to Vasile. His eyes settled on Fane. "I know of four wolves that are loyal to Lucas even now. I have had to force their obedience on more than one occasion."

Fane didn't hesitate. "Call them now. I will not wait any longer to get the information I need to find my mate."

"Give me five minutes."

Fane nodded, acknowledging the Alpha's request. The fact that Jeff would even seek Fane's approval revealed who the dominant wolf was between the two.

True to his word, Jeff returned five minutes later. "They are on their way. I told them it was a pack meeting. They do not know of your presence."

"That was wise," Vasile agreed.

Twenty minutes later the four wolves Jeff had called sat before Vasile, unable to move before the Alpha's power. Fane's growl as he stood beside his father had the wolves baring their necks in submission, although it was evident they did not want to.

"You will answer Vasile's questions honestly, be advised he will know if you lie." Jeff growled low at the four seated before him.

"Are any of you acquainted with a wolf named Logan?" Vasile asked.

At first the wolves did not answer but as Vasile's power began to squeeze their throats, cutting off their air, finally one relented.

"No, we don't know a wolf by that name."

"Truth," Vasile acknowledged.

"It would make sense, Alpha, for Logan not to reveal himself to them." Decebel spoke low, not affected by his Alpha's power flowing through the room.

"Did any of you aide a wolf in the abduction of Fane's mate?"

Again, the wolves did not answer right away. Vasile growled a warning promising discipline at their lack of obedience.

"We don't know what you are talking about." This time a different wolf spoke up.

Fane lunged forward, grabbing the wolf by the throat. "You lie," he growled, allowing his wolf to show. His eyes glowed a deadly blue, his canines lengthened, and his claws dug into the wolf's neck. For the first time, Vasile did not try to stop Fane.

"It is obvious that none of you learned your lesson about harming an Alpha's mate when Fane killed Lucas." Vasile's voice was sharp as a knife. "You will answer with truth or I will allow Fane to glean the information from you however he deems necessary."

The four wolves looked to their Alpha, pleading with their eyes for him to intervene. His response showed the ultimate disrespect as he turned his back, essentially saying he was turning a blind eye to the Romanian Alpha's actions.

Finally the wolf sitting farthest from Fane broke. "We gave him a car. He said he needed transportation that could not be linked to him in order to take Fane's mate." The wolf dared to snarl at Fane when he told him, "It's no less than what you deserve for taking one of ours."

Fane dropped the wolf he had been holding and to his father's surprise he stepped back. His gaze swept over each of them, and a power Vasile knew matched his own caused the wolves to fall to their knees in submission.

"Where did he take her?" he asked, his voice had gone low, the calm before the storm.

"That we don't know. He didn't say and we didn't ask."

"Truth." Vasile nodded.

"You will hear my Alpha's judgment for your actions and you will thank whatever god you serve that it is not me dealing out your fate." Fane once again pushed his power out and the four wolves grabbed their throats, trying in vain to breathe. Finally, after they began to turn blue Fane relented.

Vasile turned to Jeff. "Alpha of the Coldspring pack, this is my decision for these four wolves who are under your rule. I expect you to make sure it is carried out. If you do not you will share in their fate."

"So as you say, it shall be done," Jeff told Vasile as he bared his throat in submission.

Turning back to the condemned wolves, he told them, "You will be forced into your wolf forms by your Alpha. While in this state you will be declawed and your fangs pulled from your mouths. Your pelts will be shaved from your bodies." The wolves whined in fear and anger but Vasile was not done. "Once back in your human forms, the markings on your backs shall be distorted to show you have been stripped of your place in the pack. You will then be turned out to be lone wolves in your vulnerable states, without a pack to protect you. Do you understand that this is the price you will pay for your treachery and crime against Fane, the prince of the Romanian Canis Lupis?"

The four wolves had no option but to bow in submission and bare their throats. Vasile turned back to Jeff. "I thank you for your cooperation and if you find anything else out I would ask that you contact me immediately. Do you still have my card I gave you after the challenge?

"Yes, I will help in any way I can." Turning to Fane, Jeff averted his eyes to Fane's shoulder, not wanting to challenge him by looking in his eyes. "I'm sorry for the pain my pack has caused you again. I know that does not help, but I want you to know nonetheless."

Fane gave a single nod at the Alpha to show that he heard his words, but said nothing in return. He turned to follow the way they had entered, needing to think and process the information Jeff's wolves had said. He didn't know if it was enough to help them but it was something, and right now something was better than nothing.

Chapter 27

Cynthia held on to the handle on the roof of the small plane that Logan had procured once they had arrived in Dallas. She had never flown in one so small and had already decided after thirty minutes of the it rattling all over the place that she never would again.

"How long did you say this flight would take?" she asked Logan.

"We have about an hour and fifteen minutes left."

"Great," she muttered under her breath.

It hadn't been as difficult as she had thought to get Jacque loaded up into the plane. She did have to give her another dose of the sedative as Jacque had started to moan again. Cynthia was hoping that once they arrived at her cabin she could allow the sedative to wear off so that Jacque could tell her how she was feeling. There was no way for her to gauge the progression of her condition without Jacque's input.

Logan looked over at Dr. Steele and decided it was time for her to explain what exactly would need to be done to fix Jacque. He didn't want to have to wait to bond with her, he knew that even now Fane would be doing everything he could to locate her.

"Tell me again what is wrong with her," Logan said, more of a command than a question.

Cynthia took a deep breath and let it out slow, knowing it was inevitable that this conversation would take place.

"She received a transfusion of human blood. To put it simply, because she is half wolf that part of her blood does not recognize it. Therefore, it is attacking the cells. Cells that have already begun to flow through her heart, her liver, her kidneys, all her muscles. Blood is the nourishment of the body, taking nutrients and oxygen to the organs. Her body is trying to prevent that from happening because it thinks the blood she received is a virus."

Logan's face was somber when he asked what needed to be

done.

"She needs werewolf blood to replace the human cells that her body is attacking," She explained.

"That will be easily remedied."

"I don't know if it's that easy, Logan. I don't know if she has to receive it by biting and taking the blood through her fangs, I don't even know if she has fangs, or if a transfusion would work," she admitted.

"Still easily remedied, we will do it both ways," Logan said, complete confidence in his voice.

The rest of the ride was spent in silence. Cynthia worried about Jacque and how Logan had practically salivated at the idea of Jacque taking his blood. Cynthia wasn't paying attention to the fact that she wasn't seeing any of the mountain ranges that outline the Colorado skyline.

She was brought out of her stupor when she heard Logan on his phone.

"Is it ready?" she heard him ask. "Good, we should be there in a few minutes."

Realizing something wasn't right, Cynthia looked out her window and could tell by the landscape that they were not in Colorado.

"What's going on, Logan?" she asked, her voice wavering, betraying how nervous she was.

"Change of plans," was all she heard before everything went black.

Logan looked over at Cynthia's slumped form, feeling a small pang of regret at having to cause her pain, but it was necessary. After he had decided to take her with him he realized that she could tell Jacque where they were and then Jacque could tell Fane. He wasn't about to let her ruin all his hard work if she suddenly decided to have a conscience. So he had called one of his wolves, Sam, because he knew was loyal to him and wouldn't contact Dillon, and asked him to rent a cabin in the Ozark Mountains in southern Missouri and send him the coordinates as well as find a place to land. His pack mate had done better than that. He had found a cabin with an empty field right next to it. Again, Logan felt like fate was intervening. He told Sam to get on a plane and fly to the airport nearest to his location, then to rent a car and, after getting groceries. to meet him at the cabin.

As he closed in on the location of the field, he began his descent. He saw the cabin to the right of the field. As the wheels touched down to the earth, the plane bounced at the contact. Overall it wasn't too bad a landing, Logan thought.

Once the plane was fully stopped Logan jumped into action, not wanting Cynthia to wake up before he had her blindfolded and cuffed. He was still going to need her help with Jacque, so he figured he could allow her to be uncuffed under his supervision while she tended to her patient. He went around to the passenger side of the plane and opened the door. Cynthia's unconscious form tumbled out and he caught her just in time to keep her from hitting the hard ground. He grabbed a bag from the front floorboard and then headed in the direction he had seen the cabin.

When he got to the door he remembered Sam had told him that the place that rented the cabins would put a key under the mat. Gingerly leaning down to move the mat aside without dropping the doctor, he saw the silver key. To his eyes it was a small trophy proclaiming his victory at having finally arrived at his destination with his soon to be mate.

He stepped into the cabin, not bothering to look around, and hastily placed Cynthia on the first piece of furniture he saw. He reached into the bag he had brought in and grabbed a pair of handcuffs. He leaned her forward, pulling both arms behind her, and secured her wrists with the cuffs. Feeling like for now that would be enough, he headed back to the plane to get Jacque.

Logan grabbed the IV bag and laid it on Jacque's stomach for the transfer from the plane to the cabin. He lowered one end of the gurney onto the ground and then pulled it forward until the front wheels were at the edge of the doorway. Stepping into the plane, he grabbed the front of the gurney and lowered it to the ground as well. Logan grabbed the rest of the bags that Cynthia had brought with her and shut the plane door. He began to push the gurney forward as fast as he could without toppling Jacque from it.

Finally arriving at the front door of the cabin once more, Logan pushed the gurney into the cabin, and this time stopped abruptly, caught off guard by how open it was. The roof was pitched and rose at least thirty feet in the air. There was a loft across from the place where he stood that was open to look over into the main floor of the cabin. Below the loft there was long hall and he could see several doors that he assumed led to bedrooms. To his left along the back wall was the kitchen, the cabinets done in beautiful cedar. There was an old fashion Dutch oven in the wall to the right, and on the island that stood in the middle of the kitchen was a flat top stove. All of the appliances had matching cedar fronts that had to have been custom made. To his right he saw a huge rock fireplace and various chairs and a couch made out of cedar that appeared to have suede cushions, all forming a semicircle around the fireplace. There were blankets thrown across chairs and pillow stacked on the floor, making it obvious this was a place of comfort, to relax and push away the rest of the world. Logan's wolf rumbled in approval of the place he would call his den.

Needing to figure out the best place to put the women, he walked down the hallway towards the various doors. Two of them were just regular square bedrooms, each had a bed made of cedar and a bedside table. In between those two rooms was a small bathroom. The third door on the left was the master bedroom, it was larger than the first two and Logan could see double doors that opened into a spacious bathroom. Finally he walked into the door across from the master bedroom and stepped into an inviting space that appeared to be a library/study. There were shelves that lined the left side of the wall all the way across, filled with books of various sizes and colors. In the middle of the room was a fluffy rug that, at a second glance, he realized was a bear's pelt. Surrounding the rug were several cedar chairs with plump cushions and blankets thrown across their backs. On the furthest wall from the door was a beautiful cedar desk with a credenza with shelves that had lighting built into them. This was where he would put Jacque and Cynthia. They would be comfortable in here, and the best part was there were no windows in this room.

Logan went back into the living area and picked Cynthia back up. He carried her to the library and set her in one of the cedar chairs. Then he went and picked Jacque up off her gurney and placed her in one of the chairs that was more the size of a love seat. As he began to leave the room, he heard Cynthia moan and turned to see she was waking up. She moaned and tried to move her arms, her eyes snapped open as she realized they were stuck behind her. Looking around wildly, trying to get her bearings, her eyes landed on Logan.

"What have you done, Logan?"

"I couldn't have you telling Jacque where we were if you suddenly decided you couldn't go through with the choice you had made. So I decided it would be best not to go to your cabin. I regret having to cuff you, but until I can put a lock on the outside of this door you will have to say that way."

"You know, I could just shift and be out of these in a second," she challenged him, trying to hold his stare.

Logan growled and stepped towards her, his eyes glowing. Cynthia had to drop her gaze. Crap, he was more dominant than her. Of course he would be, he was a freaking Beta.

"You can try to change, but know this: there is only one reason I am not an Alpha of a pack. Can you guess what that is?"

Cynthia realized what he was telling her was that his power was strong enough to prevent her change. He would have to be Alpha material in order to do that. The only thing that would make him weaker than other Alphas of course, she thought, looking over at Jacque... "You don't have a mate," she answered.

"That will be remedied soon enough," Logan growled, his eyes still glowing.

Logan turned to leave the room, telling her not to move. Regardless of what he had said she tried to change, but Logan had been telling the truth. The power he had flowing through the house prevented her change.

Logan returned, carrying three more sets of handcuffs. He walked over to her and he grabbed one of her ankles and applied the cuff, then with the other end he cuffed the rail of the cedar chair. Cynthia glared at him as he watched him secure Jacque in the same fashion.

As Logan stepped away, he heard Jacque moan. He looked back at her and saw that her eyes were fluttering and she was trying to move. He stood frozen, waiting, but he didn't have to wait long as Jacque's eyes opened. She looked at him then tried to look around, her eyes finding Cynthia.

"Dr. Steele?" Her voice was hoarse and full of unasked questions. Jacque turned her head back to him. "Logan?" She groaned and tried to pull her legs up towards her chest but wasn't able since one was cuffed to the chair rail. When it seemed that the pain had passed she looked down at her foot, and then tried to pull her arms around, realizing she was handcuffed.

"Would someone like to explain to me why I'm handcuffed and not in the hospital?" Jacque asked, looking back and forth between Dr. Steele and Logan.

"You've been kidnapped, Jacque. Logan wants to make you his mate," Cynthia answered matter of fact like, and with much more truth that Jacque expected.

Once again, pain wracked Jacque's body and she closed her eyes, trying to shut it out. When she could breathe again she looked at Dr. Steele. "What's wrong with me?"

Cynthia explained to her the same thing she had to Logan in the plane, but stopped before she told her how she could be healed.

"Okay, doc. You can't possibly think that I don't know that you must know how to fix this. Why else would Logan bring you along?"

It was Logan who answered. "You need wolf blood. You will get it from me."

"Excellent," Jacque said sarcastically even as she reached for Fane with her mind.

"Fane!" She couldn't contain the fear that poured into the bond between them. She was in pain, she might die if she didn't get werewolf blood, and some crazy wolf had once again decided she should be his. Said wolf wanted her to take his blood and, yeah, scared was an understatement at this point.

Jacque felt arms wrap around her and a hand caress her face. "*Jacquelyn."* The desperate ache she heard in his voice was enough to bring tears to her eyes.

Chapter 28

Sally and Jen listened as Vasile told everyone what had happened with the Coldspring pack. When the wolves had returned from their meeting, eyes glowing and the power rolling off of each of them sucking the air from the room, it gave away that they had bad news.

"Now that we know who has her, how can we figure out where Logan took her?" Alina asked her mate.

"I've been thinking about that and the only thing I can think to do at this point would be to question Dillon's wolves." Vasile turned to look at the Alpha. "How do you feel about that?"

Dillon nodded his head in agreement. "I was thinking the same thing. I don't know if Logan would have confided in any of my pack, but the only way to know for sure is to question them." He turned to his wolves. "Lee, Phillip, Dalton, and Aidan, you will be first."

Vasile stood and turned to Lilly. "If you don't mind, I would prefer all of the women wait in the kitchen."

Before Lilly could object, Jen grabbed her hand. "Come on, Ms. P. Let the fur balls do their thing. I'm sure they will gladly fill us in once they have beaten the truth out of these four."

"Jennifer," Decebel growled.

"Save it, wolf," Jen growled back, holding her hand up in indication she didn't want to hear what he had to say, "you and I will dance later."

Lilly let Jen pull her into the kitchen while Sally and Alina followed. Sally went straight for the fridge and pulled out a Coke. Turning to Jen, who had hopped up on the counter, she tossed her one, knowing she would be expecting it. Then Sally grabbed her own and went and stood next to Jen, leaning back against the counter. Alina stood opposite the girls with Lilly next to her.

"Alina, why would Logan take Jacque?" Lilly asked the female Alpha.

Alina stared at the floor for a few moments before answering, "I can think of two reasons. One, he thinks he is helping Dillon by being the one to make the decision to take Jacque so that Dillon doesn't have to."

"If that's the reason he's dumber than he looked," Jen said in between drinks.

"The second would be the one I feel is probably the reason, he wants a mate. I'm not sure how old Logan is, but from the power I could sense on him he's old enough to be feeling the effects of not having a mate," Alina explained.

"What is with this mate business? Is it really so big of a deal that these werewolves are willing to gamble their lives?" Sally asked Alina.

"To a human it seems unrealistic," Alina answered. "The idea of a soul mate, what we call a true mate. There are so many facets to the magic behind our kind. I don't understand it all, I just know what I've seen to be true. There is a darkness in the soul of a male wolf. He is designed to be fierce, unrelenting, protective to an extreme, and unforgiving. If a male does not find his mate, this darkness begins to take over and gradually he begins to go mad, unable to control the darkness that was once something that kept his family, his pack safe. Often males will describe it as being at war with their wolf." All three women were listening so intently that they didn't notice the male wolves that had gathered in the background, listening.

"His mate is the light that keeps that darkness at bay. She fills the hole that has been growing ever larger in his soul. When the bond is completed between mates, their very souls merge, and the male will be able to leash the darker part of his nature and at last be at peace with his wolf."

There was a pause of silence before anyone spoke.

"What does the girl get out of it? I mean, that sounds great for him, but what about the hole in her soul?" Jen's question was nearly a whisper. Alina cocked her head to the side in a very wolf-like gesture, surprised that such a question had come from Jen.

Alina walked over to Jen and placed her hand under her chin and tilted her head so that she was looking right at Alina's face.

"She gets a man who will love her completely and faithfully. She gets a man who will not only save her life, but lay down his own to keep her safe. He will provide for her no matter the cost, he will shelter her against all the storms that come their way, he will be the one to bring a smile to her face when no one else can. She gets a friend, a lover, a mate, the only man in this world who can complete her and give her the other half of her soul."

Jen wiped the tears away that had begun to fall of their own accord, not understanding why Alina's words felt like they were etching themselves on heart. She smiled at Alina. "Is that all?" she half heartedly joked, trying to shake off the intense emotions Alina's words had stirred in her. Alina leaned forward and pressed a kiss to her forehead as she whispered, "In time, all will be revealed. Do not give up hope, for Jacque or for yourself."

When Alina had stepped back to her spot against the opposite counter, it was then that Jen realized the wolves had been listening to Alina's words. She felt like a hole was being burned into the back of her head and she knew who was watching her. She turned slowly and caught Decebel's eyes. They were glowing and never wavered from hers. After several moments she finally tore her gaze away, not able to think under his intense stare. As she turned around, she saw Fane and the look on his face threatened to rip her apart. She hadn't thought about how his mother's words would affect him when his mate, the other half of his soul, was in the hands of another wolf.

Vasile stepped forward and took Alina's hand as he addressed everyone. "The four wolves Dillon brought with him are innocent, they know nothing. So our next move is to go to Denver and speak with the rest of his pack." Vasile turned and looked at Lilly, his face softened as he stared into the face of a woman who was holding it together by a thread. "We are going to charter a jet. I'm not going to try to talk anyone out of going because it would just waste time."

"Finally a wolf who knows when he's been beat," Jen said, reverting back to her sarcastic self. Vasile shot her a look that dared her to say more. Jen wisely decided to be fascinated by the peeling nail polish on her fingers.

"The biggest hurdle will be Sally and Jen's parents. Lilly, you and Alina are going to have to go with the girls to let them know that we will be leaving immediately instead of in a couple of weeks. Tell them there has been a family emergency and we need to get back to Romania as quickly as possible." Lilly nodded, her face taking on a look of determination as she finally had a task, something to do instead of just waiting. She grabbed the car keys from the counter and motioned for the girls and Alina to follow her.

"How do you think your parents are going to take this, Jen?" Sally asked her voice low.

"Oh, probably about as good as that time we took tampons and hung them from the trees in front of Principal Stephens' house."

"That good?" Sally asked sarcastically.

"Remember, it's for Jacque. So do whatever it takes, Sally. I don't care if you have to pull out every guilt trip card in your arsenal, we will be getting on that plane to Denver. We clear?"

"I'm with you," Sally confirmed. For Jacque she would do whatever it took to make sure she was on that plane.

Fane walked up the stairs to Jacquelyn's bedroom and shut the door behind him. He took a deep breath, taking her scent in, letting it flow over him. He felt his wolf push, growling, looking for their mate in this place where they had whispered words of love, and shared their dreams for the future. Lying down on her bed, he buried his face in her pillow and it was there that he finally fell apart. Only with Jacquelyn could he ever let go. He remembered the night before the challenge when he had poured out his fears to her. He had laid his soul bare and she had welcomed him with open arms. His shoulders shook as the pain and emptiness threatened to break him. The past hours without being able to touch her mind, not knowing if she was okay had nearly brought him to his knees. He had listened to his mother speaking about the importance of a mate to the male Canis Lupis and now Fane felt like a knife was being thrust through his heart. The more she had talked the more it twisted, shredding muscle, arteries, veins that would send life-giving blood throughout his body. Jacquelyn was his heart and without her his soul would wither and decay, just like the muscles and organs without blood. Without Jacquelyn, the darkness he would unleash would be the likes of which has never been seen.

Fane took a deep breath, trying to bring his emotions under control. He needed to think clearly and not allow his actions to be dictated by anger or fear, which would not bring his mate home safe. He sat up and wiped the evidence of his pain from his face. He wouldn't show the depth of his emotions to anyone but his Luna. Only she had the right to his deepest hurts, desires, fears. Only his Jacquelyn. He stood and walked towards the door and as his hand grasped the door knob, he heard in his mind a voice he would have killed to hear again.

"Fane!" Jacquelyn's fear laced her words. Fane felt his heart in his throat as his soul reached for its other half. His wolf growled, snarling to be let loose.

"Jacquelyn." Though he tried, he couldn't keep the desperation at finally hearing her, at finally feeling their bond no longer empty.

"Are you okay? Are you hurt?" Fane had to know. Though he couldn't do anything about it at the moment, he had to know.

"I'm hurting, but not because anyone has hurt me. Logan has kidnapped me and Dr. Steele."

"Are you still sick?"

"Not as bad." Fane felt a pause before she continued. *"I'll be okay."*

"Can you describe your surroundings to me? Maybe it will give me some sort of clue as to where you are." Fane knew it was a long shot, but then again there might be something that Logan had missed that would be just enough to give himself away.

"The room we are in has no windows. It looks like a library or study."

Fane waited, feeling her intent to examine her surroundings.

"Okay, it looks like maybe it's a log cabin. The furniture is made out of some sort of wood and the walls are all wood like a cabin. I don't see anything else that would give any clue as to where we are." Jacquelyn's voice was beginning to sound panicky.

"Luna." Fane gentled his tone to a whisper in her mind as he pictured himself caressing her face, wrapping his arms around her and holding her close. *"I will find you. You are mine, I will always come for you."*

"Fane, hurry. Please."

The please is what got him. His Luna didn't say please even in the most dire of situations, his Luna commanded. There was something she wasn't telling him, but he wouldn't push her right now.

"Jacquelyn, I need to let my father know that you have contacted me. We are leaving shortly to go to Denver to question Dillon's pack.

We are hoping that he confided in one of the other wolves and maybe revealed where he was taking you," Fane explained, wanting her to understand if she didn't hear him it wasn't because he was gone.

"Okay. If I'm able to figure out anything that I think might help, I will let you know."

And because he could not tell her, he pushed the image of him kissing her to her mind as he whispered, *"I love you, my Luna."*

"Fane, stay with me."

"Always." His word was a solemn promise to her alone.

Fane threw open her door and rushed down the stairs. His father and the other wolves were all gathered in the living room. He didn't see any sign of the girls and assumed they had not made it back yet.

"Jacquelyn has contacted me through our bond," he announced, slightly breathless, not because of excursion but from the frantic beat of his heart, knowing she was alive and as of yet unharmed.

"Was she able to tell you anything? Give you any clues to where they might be?" Vasile asked his son.

"All she could tell me was that she thinks he has her in a log cabin. She said the room that she is in has no windows, but that the furniture is made from wood and the walls were wood like a log cabin."

"Did she mention Dr. Steele?"

"She said that Logan kidnapped them both. It sounded as if Dr. Steele was just as much a victim as Jacquelyn, but something about that doesn't sit well with me," Fane admitted.

Vasile nodded. "I agree with you. I don't see Dr. Steele as the victim type. She's an Alpha female, she makes her own choices." Vasile looked at each of his wolves. "If you are not packed then do so now, and be quick. Dillon, I will leave you to command your wolves. I will not step on your authority."

"I appreciate that, Vasile. I have already sent Dalton and Lee to get our things from the hotel, they should be back any moment."

"At this point the only thing left to do is wait for Lilly, Alina, and the girls to get back."

"Do you think Lilly can convince their parents to let them go with us?" Fane asked his father.

"If Lilly cannot, there are few who can resist your mother."

Vasile gave Fane a knowing smile, and for the moment because he could feel Jacquelyn's presence in the back of his mind, he was able to give a small smile back. It was true, after all. His mother always seemed to get her way. Somehow she was able to make people think that whatever it was she was wanting had been their idea in the first place. They went along with her with a smile on their face, completely oblivious. He had never seen her use it with ill intent, his mother was too kind-hearted for that. He nearly laughed at the thought of poor Sally and Jen's parents falling unknowingly under her spell.

Fane felt Jacquelyn stir in his mind. *"Share with me what is assuaging your anger, Fane."*

"My mother and your mother are at Sally and Jen's house trying to convince them to let Sally and Jen leave for Romania today. Obviously, that's not true but we have to tell them something so that Jen and Sally can come along, seeing as how they would hitchhike if we didn't bring them."

"I see you are learning," Jacquelyn teased.

"Funny, my love, but Jen said the same thing to my father." He could feel the humor she felt at this and he was glad he could give her some small amount of distraction.

"What I was thinking was how my mother seems to have the ability to get whatever she wants; people just go along with her. I almost feel bad for their parents, with my mom there, there is no way she won't get them to agree to let the girls come and on top of that, they will think it's the best idea of the century."

Jacquelyn was quiet for a moment. Fane couldn't pick up what she was thinking or feeling, her ability to block him was getting stronger.

"Luna, you would tell me if he has hurt you." Fane made it a command instead of a question.

"I see that distance doesn't affect your ability to be bossy."

It didn't go unnoticed by Fane that she had dodged his comment.

"Jacquelyn." He let her hear a growl in her mind.

"Under the circumstances I am as good as can be expected, wolf-man. Tell me when you are around Jen and Sally, I could use a dose of their kind of medicine."

"As you say, my love, so shall it be." Fane would give her the world if she asked it of him, and he would move mountains to make

it happen.

Jen and Sally sat in the backseat of Alina's SUV, both dumbfounded by what had taken place at their homes. One minute their parents were completely unsure about letting them leave and then the next Alina was hugging them and letting them know they were welcome to come to Romania any time. She even told them that Vasile and she would pay for it, and get this, their parents were eating out of Alina's hands like she was serving the best thing since sliced bread.

"Thelma, could you please tell me what happened back there?" Jen mumbled, her voice in a trance like state.

"I'm as lost as you, Louise," Sally said, looking just as confused as Jen.

Alina smiled at the girls in the rear view mirror. "It's all in the presentation, girls. If you can set a flawed diamond in front of someone, at first all they see is the flaws. But if you pick it up and turn it just right in the light, suddenly the flaws fall into the background, bringing forth the radiance that lies behind those flaws."

"Damn, she's good." Jen grinned.

Lilly looked back at Jen and Sally and allowed a small smile to cross her face though it didn't reach her eyes.

Alina suddenly got one of those far off looks that Jen and Sally recognized immediately.

"What's the boss man have to say?" Jen asked, not caring at this point if it was her business or not. If it pertained to Jacque, then as far as she was concerned it was most definitely her business.

"How did you know I was speaking with Vasile?" Alina asked, true surprise in her eyes.

"You got the same look that comes over Jacque when she and her fur ball are using their mind mojo. Although, I did ask her once if she was constipated because she just sort of got a constipated look on her face." Everyone's eyes were on Jen by the time she stopped talking.

"What?" she asked.

Lilly let out a small laugh. "Thank you, Jen. I needed that."

"That's what I'm here for, Ms. P. Your own personal comic relief." Jen looked back at Alina. "So seriously, what'd he say?"

Alina looked at Lilly, her face softened as she said, "Jacque contacted Fane through their bond."

Lilly took a deep breath and closed her eyes as she let it out. "Is she okay?"

"Vasile says that she told Fane that Logan had not hurt her but that she was still in pain from whatever it is that was wrong before."

"We never got a chance to talk to Dr. Steele about it," Lilly said to no one in particular.

"Did she say if Dr. Steele was with her?" Sally asked Alina.

"Jacque did say Dr. Steele was there and that they had both been kidnapped by Logan,"

Jen made a clucking noise with her tongue. "I don't know if I believe that. Dr. Steele had a back bone. I don't see her being bullied by any wolf."

"I'm with you, Vern," Sally agreed.

A few minutes later, they pulled into the driveway of Lilly's house. They all piled out of the SUV and headed for the front door, which opened before they even reached it. Decebel stood in the doorway, looking as ominous as ever, Jen thought.

"What, no kiss hello?" she goaded him, for some reason finding satisfaction when she could get a reaction out of him. Jen wasn't ready for the look he gave her in response to her remark. It actually looked as if he were considering kissing her. She scurried past him and heard him chuckle, which Jen decided not to acknowledge.

Once everyone was in the house, crowded once again into the living room, Vasile went over again what Jacque had told Fane. Finally, he told them the plan for once they arrived in Denver.

"Dillon and I decided it would be best if we did not stay at their pack headquarters, especially since we will be questioning his wolves and some might think they are being accused of something. So we will be staying in a hotel close by. We will be taking my SUV, which holds 9 and Dillon's SUV, which holds 6, to the airport. Boian, you will ride with Dillon and his wolves. It is 2:00 p.m. Now, so by the time we load the plane it will be around 3:00 p.m. The flight is a little over 2 1/2 hours, so we should arrive in Denver around 5:30 or 6:00 p.m. Any questions?" No one responded so Vasile turned to Dillon. "Do you have anything you need to say?"

"Not right now. I'm ready when you are." Vasile nodded his head and, without another word, headed towards Alina. Everyone took that as their cue to gather up their stuff and head out to their assigned vehicles.

Lilly was walking through the house, making sure all the lights were turned off when she felt a gentle hand on her arm. She turned to find Dillon looking at her with eyes that were as haunted as her own.

"I just want you to know I will do everything in my power to find her," Dillon told , and she could tell he meant every word.

"Thank you," was all she could say. She didn't know what else to say. Here the love of her life stood right before her, close enough to touch, and yet he was forever out of her reach. But it was enough, Lilly decided, that he loved their daughter. Even if he couldn't love her, he loved Jacque and that would be enough.

Once everyone was loaded into the vehicles, their bags all piled into the backs of each SUV, Sally took a minute to look at the seating arrangement. Vasile, Alina and Lilly were in the front, Sorin, Decebel, and Fane were in the back, and Sally and Jen were in the second seat with Skender sitting in between them. Sally looked around Skender to her wicked friend. "What are you up to, Lucy?" Sally whispered.

Jen had that look on her face that Sally was all too accustomed to. Sally thought of it as the face before the storm.

"Oh, Ethel, how could you possibly think I would be up to something?" Jen blinked innocently.

Sally shook her head and noticed again as she sat back that Decebel's location was directly behind Jen. Great, Jen was in one of her moods where she just had to poke the lion. She just couldn't leave well enough alone. Sally braced herself for what was sure to be an entertaining ride to the airport, no matter how brief.

Sure enough, not ten minutes in Jen let out a dramatic sigh. "Sally, I'm so freaking tired," she announced. She then tried to lean against the window, looking like she was trying to get comfortable. Once it was obvious that wasn't going to happen, she sat up and looked at Skender. She shrugged her shoulders in a very 'what the hell' sort of attitude and just before she laid her head on his shoulder,

Sally saw Jen wink at her.

Sally jumped when she heard the smack across the back of Skender's head, and turned to look at where the hit had originated. Decebel was glaring at the wolf, his eyes glowing dangerously. He only said one word, but it was enough to give Sally chill bumps.

"Move," Decebel told him. Skender was up so fast that he hit his head on the roof of the vehicle. He slipped around Sally and nudged her leg with his to indicate he wanted her to move over. Sally looked back at Decebel again to see that his glowing eyes were now locked onto the back of Jen's head.

"You are a very bad girl. I've told you that before, right?" Sally whispered in Jen's ear.

"Oh, chillax. I wouldn't mess with him if it wasn't so easy, but he just walks right into them, ya know? I mean, seriously, Sally. How can I pass that up."

"Well, you could do like the rest of us and grow up," Sally said in her motherly tone.

"Ahh, but Ethel, my dear, where would be the fun in that?"

"Where indeed," Sally muttered.

Chapter 29

Jacque reclined in the chair, slightly more comfortable than when she had first woken up now that Dr. Steele, or Cynthia as she insisted she call her, had given her some pain medication. She continued to reach out to Fane, although not always with words, mostly just to feel that he was still there, that the bond was still open between them. She had decided not to mention to Fane just yet what Logan had planned. She had been diligently trying to block part of her thoughts from him so he wouldn't know that Logan was going to try to get her to take his blood. Jacque was sure that if Fane had not killed anyone yet, that little bit of information would tilt the scale.

"Jacque, how are you feeling?" she heard Cynthia ask.

"The pain is tolerable right now," Jacque answered, turning to look at the doctor.

Jacque eased up into a sitting position in order to look directly at Cynthia without having to turn her head. Logan had taken the handcuffs off their hands when he told them that he had put a lock on the outside of the door. They each still had a foot cuffed to the chairs but at least they could move a little. After Logan had removed the handcuffs and left the room, Cynthia had told Jacque that she could hear another man in the cabin. At first Jacque was going to ask how she could possibly hear that, but then rolling her eyes, she remembered, oh yeah, werewolf.

"Who do you think it is?" Jacque asked.

"Maybe a member of his pack. There's no way Logan would leave us here by ourselves if he needed supplies. He has to have someone helping him and it's rare for a wolf to seek out a human's help."

Jacque thought about her words and realized that could be useful to Fane.

"Fane, there is another man here with Logan. We haven't seen him but Dr. Steele says she can hear him."

"Ask Dr. Steele to see if she can hear Logan use a name. Any

name Logan might say could be useful."

"Okay. Where are you?" Jacque asked.

"We are on the plane on our way to Denver. Sally wants me to tell you..." Jacque felt the reluctance in Fane tell her

"She wants you to tell me what?" Jacque prompted.

"This really should be a conversation that you have with your friends, but Sally won't let up, so, she wants me to tell you that Decebel saw Jen naked." Jacque could hear the embarrassment in his words and she could picture Jen threatening to throw Sally out of the plane.

"What!" Jacque actually spoke out loud as well as in her mind before she could stop herself. Cynthia gave a start at Jacque's sudden outburst. Jacque looked at her timidly. "I'm okay, just some technical difficulties."

"You're talking to Fane, aren't you?" Cynthia asked her.

Jacque nodded and then directed her thoughts back to Fane. *"I really want to know why Jen was naked in front of him, but I know what they are doing, they're trying to distract me."*

"Distraction is Jen's specialty, love."

"Keep me posted, wolf-man. I'm gonna try and see what Dr. Steele knows." Jacque tried to block out the pain that had begun to burn through her body, she swore it felt like someone was trying to cook her from the inside out.

"Jacquelyn, you're in pain, what's wrong?"

She heard the worry in his voice and felt him pouring love through their bond. She had to cut him off until she could get herself under control or she would drive him mad, knowing she was hurting and out of his reach.

"I'm fine, wolf-man, just some cramps. I'm gonna get some rest before Logan comes back. I love you."

"I'm with you, Luna."

"I know, wolf-man."

Cynthia watched as Jacque curled into a ball, her eyes squeezed closed as if trying to shut out the pain that was tearing through her. She didn't ask if there was anything she could do to help because she knew there wasn't. Until Jacque got wolf blood she would continue to hurt, and more than likely it would get worse. Finally Jacque's body relaxed, but the pain had left her breathless and she strained to drag air into her lungs.

"Be honest, doc," Jacque spoke, opening her eyes and fixing them on her, "how much worse is this going to get?"

She knew that she wouldn't want to be lied to, nor would she want the truth sugar coated, so she wouldn't do that to one of her patients either. "It's going to get a lot worse, Jacque. Your body is going to continue to attack itself and if you don't get the wolf blood your organs will begin to shut down. I know that's not what you want to hear, but I will always be honest with you."

Jacque nodded. "Do you know how long it could take? I mean, do you think I will be able to hold out until Fane gets here?"

"You sound so sure that he will find you." The look in Cynthia's eyes said she didn't think Fane had a hope in hell.

"He will find me, of that I have no doubt," Jacque said with confidence. "But the interim is what concerns me. You see, I'm not too keen on the idea of taking Logan's blood. So I'm just trying to prepare myself."

Jacque watched as Cynthia met her gaze and without ever blinking, told her, "Prepare for the worst."

Jacque didn't say anything more after that. She slept when the pain would abate but would come awake screaming when it returned. She was constantly trying to focus on keeping her shield up in her mind so Fane wouldn't know how bad she was hurting. Every now and then she would simply say his name through their bond just to hear his response. She remembered waking a couple of times to the sound of Cynthia telling her to eat, but food had no appeal because she knew she would just throw it up. Another time she was awake, Cynthia tried to get her to drink something but again Jacque refused. She didn't know how long she had been in this room with Cynthia, she didn't know if it had been hours or days. All she knew was the pain was getting worse and though she bit her lip fighting the need to scream, it didn't work.

"Ahhhhhhh!" Her scream died down into sobs that shook her body. The door to the room flew open and Logan came rushing in.

"Cynthia, what's wrong?" He looked over to see Jacque writhing in pain, her face so contorted it hurt to watch. "Fix her!" Logan yelled at the doctor who was sitting across from Jacque, syringe of pain medication already in hand.

"The pain medicine isn't lasting as long. Sedating her would be the only way to stop the pain," Cynthia snarled, her lips curling back to show her teeth.

"NO!" Jacque ground out. The thought of not being able to reach Fane was unbearable, she would rather endure her present torment. "No sedation, please, no."

Logan knelt down beside her and tried to take her hand is his, but Jacque jerked away. "Don't touch me!"

Logan growled, his eyes narrowed, and his lips drew into a thin line. He turned to Cynthia. "Tomorrow we will try giving her my blood."

"No, no blood," Jacque moaned as she continued to fight through the hurt.

"Jacque, the blood will make you better, you don't know what you saying," Logan tried to persuade her.

Jacque opened her eyes and looked directly at Logan. "Not *your* blood. Never your blood," she ground out through her teeth, but loud enough for him to hear.

Logan snarled at her as her rejection slapped him in the face. He felt a rage come over him and wanted to break something, anything. He grabbed Jacque's arm and jerked her forward so that her face was inches from his. The hold he had on her felt like at any moment her bones would snap in half.

"You will take my blood, you will be mine, and there's nothing that pup can do about it." His eyes were glowing dangerously as he snarled at her and although she knew she shouldn't provoke him more, all sense of survival went out the window.

"You may have taken me," her voice was barely a whisper, "but I will never be yours." As if to punctuate her words she snarled back and then spit in the wolf's face. Jacque watched as his canines lengthened, felt his nails turn to claws against her skin. Logan dropped her back to the chair and slapped her so hard she was sure some teeth came loose.

"LOGAN! What the hell is wrong with you?" Jacque heard Cynthia yell.

When Logan turned at the sound of her voice, Cynthia saw Logan's eyes looked wild, his breathing rapid and uncontrolled. Logan was being consumed by madness. She knew that males who lived too long without mates could go insane, but he seemed to be progressing at an incredible speed. In the four days she and Jacque had been with him she had noticed his hunched shoulders, the constant furrowed brow and narrowed eyes as his mood grew darker and darker. The only thing that Cynthia could figure was that maybe the idea of having Jacque wasn't truly doing anything to combat the madness because she wasn't his true mate. The woman he thinks is the one who will fill that dark abyss is rejecting him and the precarious dam that had been held in place by the promise of a mate had broken when Jacque had told him she would never be his. It was then that Cynthia realized that Logan would do whatever it took to have Jacque submit to him, even if it meant beating it into her. She lunged for him, trying to grab the hand that was rearing back to hit Jacque again.

Logan turned at the last minute and his fist connected with Cynthia's face. She felt her jaw break and then the lights went out.

Jacque saw Cynthia hit the floor from the force of Logan's fist. Before she could call out to the doctor, Logan had jerked her up by her hair. Jacque screamed at the sharp pain that burst through her scalp. She squeezed her eyes shut as she felt him lean into her neck, taking in a deep breath. She wanted to vomit at the idea of him taking in her scent, her skin crawled at the contact of his against hers.

Logan sat down on the chair and pulled Jacque onto his lap. He continued to grip her by her hair holding her in place. She watched in sick fascination as he brought the forearm of his free hand to his mouth and with the canines that had lengthened bit down. The bite was so deep that his blood ran freely from the wound. Logan turned and looked at her, the blood on his mouth dripped down his chin as he spoke. "You shouldn't have pushed me, Jacque. It could have been special, it could have been good, but you pushed, so now we do it the hard way." As soon as Jacque realized his intent, the pain was forgotten and her sole focus was on doing whatever it took to get out of Logan's grasp. She kicked, she clawed his arms and face, but he was too strong.

Jacque closed her eyes as she continued to struggle, she gagged as soon as the felt his arm against her mouth, the smell of iron hitting her nose just as she felt a warm, sticky substance touch her lips. She struggled harder, but Logan had moved the hand that had been holding her hair to her forehead to hold her head in place. He pushed his arm harder against her mouth and then she felt him clamp her nose shut. She tried so hard to hold her breath, determined to die from lack of oxygen before she would swallow his blood, but her body betrayed her. Almost as if against her will her mouth relaxed and she gasped for air. Logan took the opportunity to push his arm farther into her mouth. No matter how hard she struggled, she couldn't stop the blood she felt flowing from his arm down her throat.

Jacque's eyes jerked open when she felt the pressure from her mouth recede as Logan pulled his arm away. The look in his eyes was feral, dangerous. He continued to hold her head in place as he replaced his mouth where his arm had been. Jacque tried to squeeze her lips closed against the slot of his mouth and when that didn't work she bit him as hard as she could. Logan jerked back, but instead of the snarl she expected his lips were curled up into what was an unnatural smile. "If I had known all it would take to get you to bite me was a kiss, I could have saved myself a lot of trouble, Jacque."

His voice was deceptively calm, but Jacque could see the storm that lay just beneath the surface. He started to pull her up and she closed her eyes, thinking that maybe now he would leave. Her mind ached from fighting to keep Fane from hearing her, her body hurt from its own abuse as well as Logan's.

Logan must have sensed the small amount of relief that came over Jacque as he shifted her back to the chair because he leaned down next to her ear and whispered, "Your turn," as he ripped the neck of her shirt. Jacque instinctively turned away, attempting to hide herself, but realized her mistake too late when she heard Logan howl and his claws raked across her back, across her mate's markings. Jacque screamed as her flesh tore, she felt the warmth of her blood running across her skin. She felt Logan lean down over her and run his tongue across her. And as she felt his teeth pierce her skin, her lips screamed for the one who would save her, but couldn't.

"FANE!" She screamed as she clawed at the chair, trying to get out from underneath Logan, away from him, away from his mouth. "STOP! Please stop," she sobbed and in between her sobs she could hear him sucking greedily at her flesh and the sound made her so sick that she vomited all over the floor. The smell from her sickness must have pushed through the lust that had permeated Logan's mind as he finally pulled back. She felt his weight leave her body and heard the sound of his steps getting further away. She looked up at him as he opened the door to the room that had become her own personal hell. Through the tears in her eyes, she saw the blood smeared all over the front of his shirt, and on his lips, her blood. Logan looked back at her, "You may have his marks *on* you, but it's my blood that is *in* you." Jacque pressed her face into the cushion of the chair as she heard the door close, and as the lock clicked in place she felt something inside her break.

Her body shook uncontrollably as the tears poured from her eyes. She could feel Fane pushing in her mind, trying to get through, but she kept the walls in place. How could she face him when another's blood was in her, when another's teeth had pierced her skin? She could feel her stomach clenching, preparing to expel the poison Logan had made her swallow, but nothing would come up. No matter how hard she heaved, nothing would leave her body. She cried until she thought she couldn't possibly have any tears left. She was wrong.

"My love, I'm here."

The tears began anew at the sound of that voice in her mind, at the feel of the lips she felt press to her forehead through their bond. Shame washed over her as she thought about Logan's lips on hers and the retching began all over.

"I'm sorry, Fane. I'm so sorry."

Jacque pulled her knees as close to her chest as she could with her leg cuffed to the chair. She tucked her chin in to her chest as the blood dried on her back and the pain continued to pulse through her. She closed her eyes and shut the world out.

Chapter 30

Fane stood in the hotel room looking out over the city of Denver and off into the mountains. The soft murmur of Jen, Sally, and his mother was behind him. It had been two days since they arrived and still they knew nothing more than they had before. Fane's father had questioned over half of Dillon's pack and so far everyone had been truthful, no one knew anything about Logan's actions or whereabouts. To add to Fane's frustration, he was having trouble staying in contact with Jacquelyn. She kept blocking her thoughts from him and at first he figured it was to keep him from knowing how much pain she was in, but now he was beginning to worry that there was more to it than that. He closed his eyes against the thought of the other wolf putting his hands on Jacquelyn. He knew thinking like that wouldn't help him find her, it would only succeed in Fane wanting to kill something or someone. Fane reached out through their bond, and as he had been able to all the other times, he felt her but couldn't hear her thoughts. She was only letting him through enough to know she was alive, and okay…according to her. Fane didn't know he was growling until he felt Sally's hand come down on his shoulder.

"You okay?" she asked him.

Fane shook his head in frustration. "Something isn't right." Fane stepped away from her touch, not consciously realizing he couldn't stand the touch of another, not when it couldn't be his mate's hands. "I can feel her," he continued as he paced the expanse of the room, "but that's all. Every now and then she will give me a brief comment but then she shuts me out."

Sally could see the visible signs of Fane's frustration written across his brow. His eyes narrowed and he looked out the window as if he could see her if he searched hard enough. She turned to see Jen come stand beside her, arms folded across her chest in an identical pose to Sally's.

"What's up with lover wolf?" Jen asked Sally and, regardless of the words, her tone denoted how much she cared about Fane and Jacque.

"He says he thinks something is wrong with Jacque, but she won't tell him," Sally explained.

"Of course she isn't going to tell him. She knows he would go all claws and fangs up on someone if he thought she was being hurt. That's not to say I'm not royally ticked at her for keeping something from him, because that means she's keeping it from us as well."

Sally's reply was interrupted by a curt knock on the door, followed by an uninvited Decebel. Jen rolled her eyes and let out a huff of air. "You got the knocking part right, fluffy, but you forgot the part where you are asked to come in. You don't just knock and then walk in." Jen turned to Sally, shaking her head. "You would think they at least have some sort of puppy training class or something."

"If you aren't careful, he's going to be picking Jen-kibble out of his teeth after his next meal," Sally whispered under her breath as Decebel continued to stare Jen down.

Jen's gaze never wavered as she responded to Sally. "And what makes you think I object to being dinner?"

Sally choked, and Jen slapped her on the back as she winked at Decebel, finally breaking their standoff.

"Fane, Dillon has called and says he has two wolves who want to speak with you and your father," Decebel said as he turned his eyes from Jen.

Fane's head snapped around and met with his father's Beta. Decebel immediately dropped his eyes and stepped to the side to leave the doorway open. Fane began to say something as he passed Jen and Sally, but was cut off. "Don't even say it. We are going with you even if it means we have to hide in the car." To everyone's surprise it was Sally who made this announcement as she grabbed Jen's hand and tugged her along. Decebel looked to Fane who simply shook his head as if to say, just leave it.

Fifteen minutes later, Fane, Vasile, and Decebel got out of the rented vehicle to go into the Denver pack's headquarters. Fane looked back at the four remaining in the vehicle, Sally, Jen, Lilly and Alina. Worry was etched on each of their faces. "We will be back shortly," was all he said, then he was gone.

"Have I said yet how much this just sucks?" Jen muttered under her breath.

Lilly patted her hand. "We are going to find her."

"I'm the one who's supposed to be saying that to you, Ms. P."

"Vasile, these are the two wolves who wanted to talk with you." Dillon indicated the two wolves who sat across the table from them in the dining room.

"Michael, Sean, tell them what you told me, please."

Michael and Sean both looked slightly nervous, but only because they were sitting in front of one of the strongest Alphas in the world, not because they were guilty of anything.

"All we know is that Sam said he was getting a flight to Springfield Missouri a few days ago," Michael told Vasile.

"Why would you think that would be important information?" Vasile asked.

"Well, because Sam is Logan's best friend and we heard you were asking if anybody in the pack had helped Logan. If anybody did it would be Sam."

Fane growled low, showing that he was losing his patience. "What does Sam going to Springfield have anything to do with helping Logan?" he growled.

It was Sean who answered this time. "If Sam was going to Springfield then that probably means he is going to Ozark."

This time it was Decebel who growled. Vasile eyed both of his wolves and then turned back to Michael and Sean. "Please forgive their manners, they are a little stressed at the moment. Please explain the significance of Ozark."

"Oh, right. Sorry." Sean continued, "Sam owns a cabin in Ozark, Missouri and when he goes there he usually flies into Springfield."

Vasile grabbed Fane's arm before he could leave, cocking his head to the side, a very wolf-like gesture. "Excuse me for asking, but why would a wolf that lives in Colorado own a cabin in the Ozarks?"

Michael looked at Dillon for permission to answer. When Dillon nodded he turned back to Vasile. "Sam's father is the Alpha in Springfield, Missouri. When Sam goes to visit his family he usually stays at the cabin on the land that the Springfield pack hunts on."

"This just keeps getting better and better," Decebel grumbled.

Fane turned around slowly as Michael finished speaking. He looked at his father and then at Dillon. "So what he's saying is, my mate has been kidnapped and taken into the territory of an Alpha who doesn't know she is there and placed in the middle of his hunting ground?"

"Yes?" Michael's voice was nearly a squeak as he watched Fane's eye glow brighter and his canines lengthen.

"Dillon, do you know where this cabin is located?" Vasile asked, his eyes never leaving his son.

"No, but I will contact Sam's father. If I tell him what is going on maybe he will be willing to help."

"Or once he figures out his son is involved he may decide it's in his best interest to just stay out of it," Decebel added.

Dillon nodded his agreement as he pulled out his phone and dialed the Springfield Alpha's number.

When the interrogation had ended and Fane returned to the car, he slammed the door of the SUV, causing the four women waiting to jump.

"Things went that good?" Jen muttered under her breath.

Vasile and Decebel climbed in with less fanfare. Vasile was already on the phone with Sorin as he pulled out of the Denver pack's driveway.

"Sorin, get the plane ready. We're going to Springfield, Missouri." There was a pause as Vasile listened to Sorin on the other end of the phone.

"Yes, we're taking everyone. Get us a hotel. I'm not totally sure about all the details yet so we will need a place to regroup." Vasile ended the call and looked in the rearview mirror at Lilly, who waited patiently.

"Logan has been getting help from a pack mate whose father is the Alpha in Springfield and has some land with a cabin in Ozark. We think this is where Logan is holding Jacque."

"Well, that's good news, right? So what's with the obvious anger?" Sally asked.

"The Alpha is not cooperating. He wouldn't give us the location of the cabin. All he said was that he wouldn't let his son know that we knew their general location," Fane growled out.

"What the hell! Vasile, can't you do anything to this Alpha?

Give him a good shake by the scruff or something?" Jen asked, her frustration obvious.

"Did you just say a good shake by the scruff?" Sally asked her dubiously.

"What? I'm just saying."

"If it comes to that, then yes. But I don't have my whole pack with me and the Springfield Alpha is no weakling," Vasile answered.

"Oh, right. Geeze, this SUCKS!" Jen growled out.

The drive back to the hotel was quiet. The tension was palpable and the waves of frustration rolling off of Fane were enough to cause motion sickness.

They hadn't been back in the hotel room five minutes when Fane collapsed to the floor. He grabbed his head, fighting the stabbing pain. As he squeezed his eyes closed he realized it was Jacquelyn's pain he was feeling. Something was seriously wrong. He reached out to her but she was pushing as hard as she could to keep him out. Fane pushed harder. He got a very brief sense of fear, or terror rather, and then she slammed the walls down even harder.

"Ahhhh!" Fane yelled.

"Fane, what's wrong? Is she okay?" Sally and Jen were both kneeling on either side of Fane, who continued to growl so menacingly that for the first time Sally really was afraid.

Decebel let out his own growl as he gently took Jen's arm and pulled her away from Fane's side.

"Hey, what the-" Jen began to protest, but when she looked up at Decebel's face she shut her mouth. Decebel's eyes were glowing and his canines had lengthened. Something told her it would be better to just sit this one out.

Fane tried again to reach Jacquelyn, *"My love, I'm here."* And what he heard in response tore his heart in two.

"I'm sorry, Fane. I'm so sorry." Jacquelyn's voice in his mind was so broken and helpless sounding. He knew then that he would rip Logan's heart from his chest for being the cause of that.

"Jacquelyn," Fane groaned as he knelt on the floor, the depths of his despair etched in every syllable of her name.

"Fane, please, what's wrong? Is she okay?" Sally asked him gently.

Fane looked up into Sally's fearful eyes. "I don't know." Then he looked at Jen. "I don't know if she's okay."

Jen sat on the park bench and although she looked to be watching some kids play on the playground, her eyes were glazed over, her thoughts far from where she sat. Moisture rolling down her cheek snapped her out of her stupor. She couldn't remember a time when she felt so helpless. Even during the wreck she was at least able to do something to help, but all she could do right now was wait. Wait for Vasile to get the travel arrangements made, wait for Fane to hear from Jacque that she was okay, wait for the freaking world to open up and swallow her because she couldn't imagine a world without Jacque. She wanted to scream at the injustice of it all. Jacque was one of the nicest, most loyal people she knew. Why was this happening to her? Jen closed her eyes and tried to fight the overwhelming fear that threatened to crush her spirit. She felt a big, warm body sit next to her on the bench and for some reason she was not startled or surprised at his arrival.

"What's wrong, Jennifer? I've never seen you so distant." Decebels voice conveyed the worry he was trying to hide.

"I'm tired, Decebel. I'm worried and I don't have any humor left to help ease the tense situation." Jen's face showed the fear that for the first time she allowed him to see. "I know I'm sarcastic and I joke a lot, even in the most serious situations. It's how I deal, how I cope so I don't fall apart. But I don't have the strength to be the one who lifts the spirits of everyone. I don't have it in me to hide the sick ache that threatens to choke me for fear that I will never see Jacque again or that something horrible has happened to her."

Decebel pulled Jen close in a show of gentleness that she was beginning to notice he only displayed with her. "You don't always have to be the strong one."

"That's where you're wrong, Dec. I do, for them. Sally, Lilly, and at times even Fane. I have to be the one who believes so strongly that we will get her back that I *can* be sarcastic. That I have the luxury of bringing humor be it light or dark into this majorly messed up situation. And not that we will just get her back, but that we will get her back whole. There are worse things than death to a woman, Decebel."

Decebel wasn't really sure how to respond to that. He didn't know how to handle a discouraged Jennifer. Sarcastic, bitchy, playful Jennifer, yeah, that he could deal with. But this crushed, fragile spirit he didn't know what to do about it. He pulled her closer and laid his chin on the top of her head. "I would do anything to take the fear from you, to bring your friend back to you unharmed."

Jen pulled back so she could look up at Decebel, taken back by the words that were thick with emotion.

"I believe you," Jen told him as she stared into his eyes.

Decebel leaned forward slightly and for a moment Jen thought he meant to kiss her, but he caught himself. He coughed to cover the awkward moment. "Well, I guess we better get back up to the room and see if they are about ready to head to the airport."

"Yeah, I guess we better." Jen stood and turned to head back to the hotel. Despite Decebel's kind words she felt worse. Not only was her best friend in the hands of a psycho wolf but the guy she was falling for could never be hers. What had she been thinking to even consider a fling with a guy, a man like Decebel? It would break her heart when he found his mate. She wasn't as strong as Lilly. Once Decebel was hers she would never be able to let him go.

Fane watched as everyone boarded the plane .He had reached for Jacquelyn several times since the last time she had contacted him and still she would not let him in. He was beginning to get angry at her rejection. Why would she not let him close to her? Did she not understand how painful it was to be separated from her? Did it not hurt her as well? For the first time since he had met her Fane felt the fear of the possibility that she didn't want him, didn't love him as he loved her. But he knew that couldn't be true. She was his mate, the other half of his soul, she must be feeling the pain at their continued separation. Something had to have happened to cause her to keep him away. As soon as he was alone and could concentrate he would, for the first time, force her to let him into her mind. He knew he shouldn't but enough was enough. He was her mate, how could he help her if she wouldn't let him near?

Sally watched as Jen buckled into her seat on the plane. Her face was devoid of emotion. It was the only time Sally could remember ever seeing her sarcastic, outspoken friend look so lost. She sat down next to her, buckled in, and then took her hand.

"Talk to me, Jen," Sally said.

Jen looked at Sally and to Sally's surprise Jen leaned forward, burying her face into Sally's neck. Sally felt Jen's shoulders shaking and realized she was crying.

"Oh, Jen." Sally wrapped her arms around her broken friend. "Sweetie, tell me, did that wolf hurt you? I'll kill him, just say the word and I'll gut him like a fish."

Jen's shoulders shook harder. Finally she pulled back and looked at Sally. "I'm just so scared for Jacque. What if that piece of crap has hurt her? What if, god Sally, what if..." Jen couldn't finish the thought, it was too horrible to even consider.

"Then we will help Fane rip him apart, and then we will love her so fiercely that she will know we will always be there for her. No matter how long it takes for her to heal, we will be there for her."

Jen nodded solemnly. "In the middle of worrying for Jacque, I think, crap I don't know. I feel something for the big, dumb wolf, but I shouldn't. He will only break my heart."

"Oh, my little Jen. Who would aim for the stars if not for you? Don't give up, not yet, okay?" Sally told her.

Jen just shook her head. She wouldn't continue to hope for something that would never be. She would focus on getting Jacque back, and then she would have to seriously think about whether she could handle being in Romania, where he would be.

Decebel looked over at Jen across the aisle from him. Her face was blotchy from shed tears, her eyes swollen. He felt his chest tighten and an unfamiliar desire to protect her, to rip anything who dared to harm her to pieces. It was killing him not being able to do anything about her pain. How did you fight an invisible enemy? How do you repair an irreparable situation? Decebel growled as he leaned his head back against the head rest and closed his eyes, though he would glean no rest, not while Jen's fear was pulsating over his skin. He wouldn't rest again until he could see the light fill her eyes and the sarcasm roll easily from her tongue once more.

Chapter 31

As Cynthia ran the warm washcloth down Jacque's back, trying to wash off the dried blood, she thought about how when she had finally come to after being knocked out by Logan, she had yelled until Logan had finally come back into the room. She had shamed him for the treatment of his so called mate and he finally had relented and brought her some warm water and a cloth so she could clean Jacque's bloody skin. She had wanted to try and talk Logan into letting her help Jacque take a hot bath, but she hadn't been able to rouse the poor girl at the time. Cynthia imagined she was in shock from the brutal treatment of the wolf. Hell, she herself was in shock. Now that Jacque was awake she feared how her mind would handle all that had happened to her at the hands of Logan.

"Why did he do it?" Jacque finally raised her face and looked Cynthia in the face.

"Oh honey, come here." She pulled the chair her leg was cuffed to closer so she could take Jacque in her arms. Jacque began to cry silently, her face buried in Cynthia's shoulder.

"He made me drink his blood and then he took mine. How will Fane want me now?"

"He will always want you, Jacque. You are his mate, his and his alone," Cynthia told her as she gently rubbed her back.

"I still hurt. I thought his blood was suppose to make me better," Jacque told her.

Cynthia pulled back to look at Jacque. "Really? You don't feel *any* better?"

Jacque shook her head. "No, I still feel like I'm on fire, burning from the inside. He didn't do anything sexually to me but I feel so violated, so dirty." Jacque closed her eyes as tears slowly streamed down her face.

"In some ways what he did was more intimate than sex."

"It was supposed to be Fane, Cynthia. God, it was supposed to be Fane. It wasn't supposed to be like this."

"I know, sweetie. I know. It's my fault, Jacque." Now Cynthia was crying. Cynthia knew what she said was true, it was her fault. She had helped this monster get his hands on Jacque. How could she live with herself ? "I was so angry at Fane for taking my brother, I didn't want him to be happy, to have you. I didn't think Logan would hurt you. I thought because he wanted you as his mate he would treat you reverently as most males do their mate. But you aren't really his, you aren't taking his darkness and it's only feeding his madness. I'm so sorry. I did this and I will deserve any punishment that your Alpha decides."

"I'm not mad at you, Cynthia. I don't have any emotions left to be mad. I just want Fane. I just want my mate." Jacque pulled back and leaned against the chair she was cuffed to.

"Can you still feel him through your bond?" Cynthia asked her.

"Yes, but I don't want him to know what happened. What if he doesn't want me anymore? How will he ever want to touch me after Logan has?"

"Jacque listen to me," Cynthia growled at her firmly. "Fane is your true mate. There is nothing in this world that could keep him from wanting you. He will never stop looking for you. You have to believe that. Let him in, let him love you, that's the only thing that will heal you emotionally and I suspect only his blood will heal you physically."

"What if he doesn't find me in time? What if I die before he can give me his blood?" Jacque thought she would be sick at the idea of never seeing Fane or friends and family again.

"Don't spend this time separate from him. Reach out through your bond. You have to know it's killing him for you not to let him in and I can tell it's killing you."

Cynthia's head jerked towards the door a second before it opened. Jacque couldn't help the whimper that emitted, but steeled herself before she would let her fear over take her. She decided then and there this asshole would not break her. She wouldn't let him take Fane from her.

"You're awake, finally." Logan glared at her, the contempt obvious on his face.

"Yes, well I'm sorry to keep you waiting but it takes a little out of a girl when she's assaulted. You will have to forgive my lack of consideration towards your feelings," she growled out, knowing she shouldn't provoke him but unable to stop himself.

Cynthia placed a hand on her leg, a silent warning.

"Yes, well like I said, you pushed me Jacque. Now you know. If you push, I will push back, and I will always win."

Jacque didn't respond, she simply glared at him, meeting his stare without flinching.

Logan chuckled. "I see you really are an Alpha, good to know. I would hate for you to be so easily broken. Where would be the fun in that?"

"Logan, I told you earlier that if you want her as a mate then you are not going about it the right way," Cynthia tried reasoning with him.

"I will feel better once my mate no longer bears the marks of another. I will have you give Jacque some of that sedative, Cynthia. That way she won't be in too much pain when I have them burned from her body."

Cynthia gasped. "You're not going to touch her, Logan. I will die before you lay another hand on her."

"Oh, don't worry, Cynthia. That can be arranged. But first I thought you would want to see this through, since you helped me and all. Doesn't it feel good to know that the wolf who killed your Alpha will never have his mate? I thought you would be happy," Logan taunted.

"I can't wait to watch Fane rip your limbs off one at a time. I will revel in your screams and then bathe in your blood." The look Jacque gave him was feral and even she was surprised at the bloodthirsty sound of her voice.

"You are a feisty one, I like that. I'll bring your dinner in in a moment and then you should get some rest, love. Tomorrow looks to be a rather trying day for you." Logan chuckled as he turned to leave.

Jacque watched as he shut the door behind him. She doubled over as pain uncoiled in her body.

"Jacque, is the pain getting worse?" Cynthia asked gently.

"Yes, it just hurts. Will you talk to me, distract me please."

Cynthia thought for a moment, trying to figure out what to talk about, then she remembered about Jennifer and her blood.

"I found out what was different with your friend's blood."

Jacque looked up, genuine interest on her face. "Really? What is it? Is she okay?"

"She has werewolf blood."

"Shut up," Jacque responded bluntly.

"Um, okay," Cynthia said, confused.

"Oh, no, I don't mean really shut up. It's more like an 'oh crap' statement," Jacque quickly explained.

"Oh, well then, let me explain. Jennifer has werewolf blood, although just a little bit. There is this thing called the one drop rule. It was actually used to describe the amount of mixed blood a person had back in the civil war days when there was beginning to be interracial relationships and people were beginning to see mixed children between African Americans and Caucasians."

Cynthia spent the next couple hours explaining to Jacque all about the one drop rule, and how it applied to Jen. Jacque couldn't believe what she was hearing and undoubtedly had been able to successfully keep her mind off of her pain. So maybe it was possible that Decebel was her mate?

"Decebel has been acting so protective of Jen. Is it possible he is her mate even though they haven't heard each other's thoughts and she doesn't have his marks?" Jacque asked.

"I guess it's possible that since Jennifer's blood is rather diluted. I guess it could require something more for the mating signs to reveal themselves."

"What do you mean something more?"

"Perhaps a major physical or emotional reaction is required to trigger the mating response," Cynthia explained.

"Huh, that sounds like what I learned in psychology about how people with dormant genes of mental illness sometimes have to have some sort of major life event to bring the gene to the forefront."

"That's a good point, Jacque. It's quite possible it's similar to that."

Both women were quiet after the long conversation, both thinking of the possibilities. Jacque finally laid down, grabbing a pillow off the chair. She turned onto her side facing away from Cynthia, needing some time to think. She felt Cynthia lay a blanket over her and said a silent thank you that the woman seemed to understand that Jacque needed to be left alone for the moment. That alone time didn't last long. She felt a hard push in her mind and could have done nothing to keep him out.

"Jacquelyn, don't shut me out. Please don't ever force me to push into your mind like that again." Jacque could hear the desperation in his voice.

"I'm sorry I blocked you, Fane, but I don't know how to face you right now." Jacque bit her lip to keep from crying. She wouldn't break down before she had told him everything, he had a right to know.

"Tell me, Luna. Tell me whatever you need to, but first hear this: I will always love you, always need and want you. Don't you dare ever doubt that, are we clear?"

Damn that wolf, she thought as tears escaped her eyes. *"Crystal."*

"Good, now tell me."

Jacque decided she just needed to rip it off like a band aid and maybe it wouldn't hurt as bad. *"He forced me to take his blood and then he bit me. I tried to fight him, Fane, I tried, but he was too strong. He clawed my back because he saw your marks."* Before Jacque could stop herself she was pouring everything out. *"He told me that tomorrow he is going to burn your marks from my back. I was afraid you wouldn't want me anymore because he bit me."*

Jacque could feel Fane's rage emanating through their bond and she tried to reassure herself it wasn't directed at her.

"There is nothing that could keep me from wanting you. Nothing you could do or not do would stop me from being with you. You are mine, Jacquelyn. Mine no matter what." Jacque felt the tears run down her cheeks. She felt Fane's lips on her own as he sent her the thought of him kissing her, holding her.

"I miss you, wolf-man," she whispered.

"I'm coming for you. We know where you are."

"What! Where? Where am I? When will you be here?" Jacque couldn't believe what she was hearing. He'd found her. She knew he would, never doubted he would, but to hear it brought a relief she had never known.

"You are in Missouri in the Ozark mountains. We don't know your exact location but we arrived in Springfield a couple of hours ago and are on our way to Ozark now. If I have to search every cabin in the Ozarks I will find you."

"I know you will. I'll be waiting."

"Don't provoke him, Jacquelyn. You survive, do you

understand? That's your job, to survive." Jacque could feel the intensity behind his words and knew what Fane was asking of her. To do whatever it took to stay alive. No matter what Logan wanted, Fane just wanted me alive.

"You just worry about getting here, let me worry about me. I need you, Fane. Be with me now, talk to me, and tell me how my mom is, and Jen and Sally."

Fane told her everything she wanted to know. He told her about how strong her mom was and how Jen was driving Decebel crazy. He told her how Sally had actually stood up to him about going with him to see Dillon's wolves. When he ran out of things to tell her about her friends he began to tell her about the history of the Grey wolves.

"Where did they come from?" she asked him.

"The legend is we were created by the goddess who lives in the moon. She is the great Luna. The wolves in Romania were growing extinct due to hunters killing for their pelts. In order to help save the species she combined the human spirit with the wolf spirit, creating the werewolf. She gave the human the power and strength of the wolf and the wolf the intelligence of the human. Since then the wolves have thrived."

Jacque thought about the legend and wondered if it were true. She figured anything was possible since werewolves even existed. That thought ignited another. *"Fane, are there other things besides werewolves?"*

"Do you really want to know the answer to that, Luna?"

"At this point, wolf-man. the things that go bump in the night are the least of my worries." Jacque couldn't help but think that it was her own species that she needed to fear.

"Then yes, my love, there are other things besides werewolves. But I think right now you need to get some sleep. I will be there soon."

"Stay with me." Jacque yawned then flinched when she felt pain ripple through her body.

"Always, Luna. You are still hurting." It wasn't a question.

"Just hurry, wolf-man."

Chapter 32

Fane felt Jacquelyn slip off into a fitful sleep. He could feel the pain consuming her body and it was driving him mad. More than that was the thought of what Logan had done to his love. Fane was going to rip Logan's fangs from his mouth and then make him swallow them for piercing Jacquelyn's precious flesh. They had just arrived in Ozark, Missouri and Fane was keeping tabs on Jacquelyn's dreams. It was then that he caught glimpses of her memory of Logan, his arm pressed against her mouth, his teeth sinking into her back. Fane let out a howl in the vehicle that had everybody covering their ears.

"Pull over!" Decebel shouted to Vasile.

Vasile looked in his rearview mirror and saw that Fane was on the verge of phasing. He pulled over, and just as the vehicle came to a stop Fane was out the door and phasing in mid-air. Decebel was out right behind him. One minute a man, the next a huge, dark grey wolf with white paws.

Jen's breath caught at the sight of Decebel in his wolf form. It was the first time she had ever seen him. He was magnificent. She grinned at his white paws. She had new material. The wolf had socks. That was too rich!

She and Sally gasped as Fane turned on Decebel and snapped his huge teeth at him. Decebel dodged out of the way just in time. The two wolves circled each other, snapping and lunging but neither making contact. Then there was a third wolf and when he stepped forward and howled the other two hit the ground, heads low and baring their necks. He snarled at them both and then suddenly there were three very naked men standing on the side of the road. Sally squeaked and turned away. Jen had to pry her eyes off of the beautiful muscles that were Decebel.

"Coast's clear," they heard Alina say. "They went into the woods."

"Well, that was invigorating." Jen grinned.

Sally rolled her eyes. "You would think seeing three naked men was invigorating."

"There were three? Cuz, sista, I only saw one." Jen closed her eyes and again saw Decebel's bare back. The wolf markings across his tan skin were breathtaking.

"Fane!" Vasile growled. "What has gotten into you? And Decebel, what the hell were you thinking engaging him while he was like that?"

Fane snarled. "You don't know what he's done to her, what he's going to do if I don't get to her."

"What has he done?" Vasile asked gently.

"I won't disgrace my mate that way. She is mine." Fane turned to Decebel. "My apologies, Beta. I know you were just protecting the females."

"I can't imagine what you must be going through, Fane. No apology necessary," Decebel told him, averting his eyes out of respect.

"Father, I will speak to the Springfield Alpha. I want to know where that cabin is and I want to know now."

"Fane, we will find her," Vasile started but Fane cut him off.

"HE'S GOING TO BURN THE SKIN OFF HER BACK!"

Decebel growled low and Vasile snarled. After Alina had taken the three wolves clothes, Vasile had his phone out and was waiting on Tyler, the Springfield Alpha, to answer. He picked up on the third ring.

"Hello?"

"Tyler, it's Vasile. We need to know where that cabin is now." Vasile continued before the other wolf could interrupt. "He's planning on removing her mating marks. Do you want to be responsible for that?"

There was no response for several seconds. "Fine, here are the coordinates."

"Got it, let's go." He then phoned Sorin with the coordinates and designated a place to meet a couple of miles downwind from the cabin at midnight.

They all climbed back into the car and drove to find a motel in

Ozark to make plans.

Vasile pulled into the parking lot of the nicest hotel they could find. It wasn't the Hilton, but they weren't planning on spending a lot of time there anyways so Vasile wasn't going to be picky. He and Alina went into the lobby to check into a room. Jen could smell the anger coming off of Fane. Wait, smell anger? What the, that isn't possible. Why would she even think that? She felt a large, warm hand on her shoulder and felt warm breath by her ear. "You okay?" Decebel asked her.

Jen turned her head slowly to look at Decebel. It was the first time she had spoken to him since the little scene on the side of the road. "Um, yeah, I'm good. Just mentally preparing for the whole black ops situation."

"Black ops?" Decebel said questioningly.

"She has this weird obsession with military lingo and missions. Just nod your head and move on," Sally told him dryly.

Decebel made an 'ahh' movement with his mouth and then grinned at Jen, who blushed and quickly turned away.

Vasile and Alina climbed back into the car and drove around to the side of the building where the room was. They all unloaded and headed to the designated room.

Vasile, Fane and Decebel spent an hour planning and getting the location of the cabin marked on a map. Once they had the details worked out Vasile addressed everyone.

"The ladies are going to wait in the car in the woods where you drop us off. We're going in our wolf forms and will meet up with Sorin, Skender and Boian. Sorin is calling Dillon and telling him to bring his first four and will meet us two miles from the cabin."

"How will you get Jacque back to us if you are in your wolf forms?" Sally asked.

"I'm hoping that Dr. Steele will be in her human form and she can help get Jacque back. Sorin, Skender, and myself will escort them while Fane finishes off Logan." Vasile looked at Decebel. "It is to be Fane who kills him, it is his right."

"Understood," Decebel responded.

Lilly sat with Alina at the small table. Neither woman spoke but sat in companionable silence as they each thought about the path their children would take tonight.

Finally at eleven thirty Vasile stood. "Let's go." That was all he said and everyone was up and out the door. They drove in silence to the location on the map that brought them closest to the cabin. The tension in the vehicle was palpable and Jen swore if you reached your hand out you would be able to feel it on your skin. After twenty minutes Vasile pulled the car off the road and down into the trees that were the edge of the forest. He pulled the vehicle in as far as he could to hide it from view. Vasile turned to look at his mate. "I will call to you as soon as we have her. You need to stay and protect them."

"As you say, Alpha," Alina responded. "You just make sure you bring my son and his mate back."

"As you say, my Luna." Vasile leaned across the seat and kissed her gently.

Fane waited outside the vehicle while his father spoke with his mother. His skin was itching to phase, his wolf desperate to get out and hunt. He couldn't believe how close he was to her, he could feel her.

"Luna, we are coming. Be ready." Fane could feel her but she didn't respond. Maybe she was still sleeping. He would let her be for a few minutes more, then he would push. He needed her to be alert once they attacked.

Jen got out of the car as Decebel did. "Hey, Dec." He turned around to look at her. "Take care of yourself, okay?"

Decebel's grin was slow, calculated. "It sounds like you care, Jennifer."

"Of course I care. Jacque needs all of you to protect her, so don't go get yourself killed. It could leave her vulnerable." She glared at him.

"That's the only reason you want me to be careful?" His voice was low, and velvet soft.

Jen had to shake her head to clear the fog. "No, there's another reason," she whispered back. She crooked her finger at him, beckoning him forward. He leaned down so she could whisper in his ear. "You remember Matty, don't you? That handsome nurse who helped me out? Well, you still don't know if he changed my name."

Jen couldn't help the wicked grin that spread across her face.

"What do you mean if he changed your name?" Decebel growled and he could tell he wasn't going to like the answer.

Jen's response was to start singing 'Meet Virginia' as she climbed back in the vehicle. She heard Decebel's growl and shut and locked the door just as he lunged for her. She looked at him through the glass and winked.

"Jennifer Adams, what have you gone and done to that poor wolf now?" Sally whispered to her mischievous friend.

"Just gave him some extra incentive to come back alive."

Cynthia strained to hear any little noise she could but there was nothing. No footsteps, no coughing, laughing or breathing, and no heartbeat. Logan had left them alone. Well, he was dumber than he looked, she decided. She reached across and gently but firmly shook Jacque.

"Jacque, wake up, we're getting the heck out of dodge."

Jacque sat up groggily. "What?"

"Logan and his mini-me aren't here. I heard a vehicle leave a little bit ago and thought one of them had stayed behind, but there is no one here. We are getting out of here now."

"How?" Jacque asked.

Suddenly where Cynthia Steele once sat was a medium sized grey and white wolf. The wolf slipped its foot out of the cuff and then Cynthia changed back. Now there was a very naked Cynthia sitting in front of Jacque. "Sorry about the clothes, hazard of phasing."

"No big thing." Jacque tried to be as nonchalant as possible.

Jacque watched as Cynthia began to search the room, she presumed for something to pick the lock on the cuffs. When she couldn't find anything she came back over and examined the chair it was cuffed to.

"Okay, I'm going to try and break the frame," she told her. Jacque looked a little skeptical.

"Hey, werewolf remember?" Cynthia said, slightly offended.

"My bad," Jacque said, holding her hands up in surrender.

Cynthia grabbed the chair where the front legs met with the cross bar of the frame and pulled with everything she had. At first she didn't think it was going to work but then she felt the wood give and then crack! The frame snapped.

"Nice," Jacque said, impressed with Cynthia's strength.

She was able to slide the cuff straight off the broken end of the cross bar.

Jacque stood up and stretched, unable to believe she was free…sort of.

Cynthia grabbed her hand. "Come on, we have to get as far away as possible. Once they are back they will be able to track us so we need to run in circles and then try and find some water to hide our scent."

Jacque nodded her head. "Okay, doc. Let's do this."

Cynthia paused briefly. "Jacque, I truly am sorry."

Jacque held up a hand to stop her. "Save it, let's just get our butts out of here. We will deal with the rest later, okay?"

They held hands as they crept through the cabin as quietly as possible, looking around constantly to make sure the really were alone. As soon as they were sure, they made a bee line for the front door. Once again they crept out silently. Cynthia took in a deep breath, scenting the air.

"They're not here. Let's go." With that she pulled Jacque off the porch and out into the night. They ran hard and fast through the trees. Jacque didn't know how Cynthia could see but was glad that she could, because otherwise Jacque would have become intimately acquainted with one of these lovely trees they were breezing by. Jacque was trying hard to stay on her feet but Cynthia was making it very difficult. Just when they would get in a rhythm Cynthia would make a sharp turn, causing her to stumble a few steps before gaining her footing again. This went on for what seemed like hours but probably was no more than 30 minutes and then they finally found a creek. Cynthia didn't even hesitate as she ran straight for it.

Without pausing she pulled Jacque into the cold water. Jacque's breath caught as the chill seemed to seep into her bones. Cynthia never slowed. Suddenly Jacque doubled over as pain shot through her body.

"Jacque, are you alright?" Cynthia asked as she kept Jacque from taking a nose dive into the creek.

"I don't know. It's hard to breathe, the pain is so intense." Jacque tried desperately to drag air into her straining lungs. She felt Fane stir in her mind.

"Jacquelyn, I can feel you are in pain. Are you alright? We are in the woods on the way to the cabin."

Jacque couldn't hold back the sob of relief that came out. He was here. Fane was here and he would rescue her.

"We aren't at the cabin anymore. Logan and the other wolf left and we broke out," Jacque told him.

"Where are you? How far from the cabin are you?"

"Cynthia, Fane wants to know how far from the cabin we are," Jacque told the doctor.

Cynthia looked off in the direction they had just come from. "Probably about two miles east. Not far enough. Why?"

"They are here in the woods on their way to get us."

"Fane, she said we are about two miles east from the cabin. How far away are you?"

Just then they heard a loud angry howl in the direction of the cabin.

"They're back." Cynthia grabbed Jacque's hand and started to run again. "We have to get farther. Once in their wolf forms they will be able to run fast."

"Fane, Logan is back at the cabin. Where are you?" Jacque knew her voice sounded shaky even if it was in his mind.

"We're about a mile from the cabin. Tell Cynthia we have a car parked two miles west of the cabin."

Jacque was trying again to stay on her feet as they ran through the creek. The water level changed constantly and made it difficult to stay upright.

"Fane said they have a car parked two miles west of the cabin." At her words Cynthia changed direction and crawled out of the creek, dragging Jacque behind her. They paused briefly and Jacque watched as Cynthia stuck her nose in the air and took a deep breath, then cursed low. Jacque heard the rustling and crunch of leaves and knew why Cynthia was cursing. Logan had found them. Without thinking Jacque let go of Cynthia's and took off running. She heard Cynthia shout her name but Jacque didn't stop. She couldn't stop. All she could think was that there was no way she was going to be at Logan's mercy again. She would rather die than go through that again.

Cynthia watched as Jacque ran then turned back to where she could hear Logan running. She made a decision then. She had gotten Jacque into this and she would do anything she could to get her out of it. She phased into her wolf form and waited for Logan to come crashing through the woods. He stopped just at the edge of the creek and his wolf form was huge, much larger than Cynthia's. She snarled at him, showing her teeth. She remembered how he had manhandled Jacque, how he had forced himself on her, and that fueled her rage. She watched as Logan took a couple of steps back and then jumped. He cleared thc creek with no problem and landed several feet from her.

They began to circle one another, looking for an opening. Cynthia knew she unmatched Logan in size but she was fast. If she could keep him distracted so Jacque could get to the car it might be enough. Logan took a step towards her and she growled and snapped her teeth at him. She lunged forward, knowing her boldness would take him by surprise. She was right. She went in low and latched onto one of his legs. Cynthia heard Logan yip and then felt his teeth latch onto her side. She thrashed her body, letting go of his leg and rolled to get out of his bite. She continued to roll until she was up on all fours again. Logan tried to lunge for her before she could right herself but she jumped to the side. He was so close she felt the air from his bite ruffle her fur. He turned quicker than she would have thought a wolf his size would be able to and grabbed her back right leg before she could move. She felt a snap and let out a loud whine. Logan released her leg and backed away. He was taunting her. He knew she could never defeat him. She let out a whimper as she tried to put weight on the broken appendage. Logan lifted his upper lip in a snarl and lunged again. Cynthia tried to jump out of the way but her weight shifted unevenly and Logan was able to grab her left back leg. She twisted and rolled, trying desperately to get out of the death grip he had on her. Again she felt a snap and the pain that raced up her leg to her spine. She realized now he didn't plan to kill her, he just wanted her immobile. She laid on the ground, her body heaving, her two broken legs lying useless. She began to drag herself forward with her front legs. Logan sunk his teeth into her neck and squeezed. He didn't break her neck but as the world around her got fuzzy, she realized he was cutting off her air, and then everything went black.

Jacque ran blindly, her arms thrown out in front of her, desperately trying to keep herself from running face first into a tree. She felt horrible for leaving Cynthia but the thought of Logan getting his hands on her was just too much. She stumbled over a fallen tree branch, falling forward but caught herself on her hands. She pushed herself up again and started forward without bothering to dust her hands off.

"Fane! Logan found us. I freaked out and took off running and left Cynthia behind. I don't know where I am." Jacque reached out for him, hoping that maybe he was close to her.

"We are tracking him. We just passed the cabin about a mile ago. Keep running, Jacquelyn. I will find you."

Jacque nodded her head and then remembered he couldn't see her.

"Please hurry." Jacque heard a loud howl not far behind her. *"He's getting closer."*

Jacque kept running, but fell to the ground when the pain that was becoming more intense wracked her body. She rolled onto her side, biting the inside of her cheek to keep from screaming.

"Luna, what is it? I can feel your pain."

"The pain is getting worse. Whatever is happening to my body, it's getting worse." Jacque squeezed her eyes closed and tried to take slow, deep breaths. Pushing past the pain, she rolled onto her hands and knees and began to crawl. If crawling was all she could do at the moment then so be it but she wouldn't just lay there on the ground and wait for Logan to come rip her apart. Unfortunately, she didn't make it far before she heard a low growl behind her. She turned her head and sure enough a huge black and grey wolf stood there. His head was down low, all his hair on his large body seemed to be standing on end. Jacque turned, not wanting her back to him and fell onto her butt. She began to try to scoot back away from him as he began advancing on her.

"Why are you doing this?" she asked him, hoping maybe to distract him. "Why would you want me when you know I am not your true mate?"

Jacque squeaked when all of a sudden there was no longer a large wolf before her, but a naked man instead.

"Do you have any idea what it's like to be alone? To be empty on the inside and feel like you are being consumed by it? That is why I'm doing this. I need a mate. There are so few females and Fane is still a pup. He has plenty of time before the darkness begins to drive him mad. But me, I'm old. I need a mate."

Jacque kept her eyes firmly planted on his face as she listened to him. She could see the pain on his face but after what he had done to her she couldn't feel sorry for him.

"You have to already realize that I will not make the darkness go away for you. You have to know that only your true mate can do that," she tried to reason.

"It will be better once we mate. That will make us one and then the madness will be contained."

"Logan, it's not going to happen. I am not yours! I will never be yours."

Logan lunged at her, pushing her onto her back. He grabbed her hands and pushed them down into the ground as he leaned forward placing his nose against her neck. Jacque whimpered at his closeness, hating the feel of his skin against hers.

"You don't even smell like him anymore," he growled. "You smell like me. Do you really think he is going to want you once he smells another wolf all over you?"

Jacque looked Logan straight in the eyes. "Fane will always want me no matter what you do to me."

Logan snarled at her boldness but didn't back away. He took her hands and raised them above her head, holding both wrists with one of his hands. He took his free hand and grabbed her chin, holding her face in place as he leaned forward. Jacque realized he was going to try and kiss her and she began thrashing wildly. He held her tighter and she flinched at the pain in her wrists. He gripped her face tighter as his lips came brutally down on hers. She thrashed her body trying to throw Logan off but he was too big. Before he could pull his lips away, Jacque opened her mouth and bit down hard on them.

Logan snarled as her released her mouth. Glaring down at her, Jacque shivered at the feral look in his eyes.

"It's like that, is it?" He asked her as he pulled his hand back. Jacque realized he was going to hit her and tried to move her head out of the way. She squeezed her eyes closed, waiting for the blow. It never came. Instead, the weight that was Logan was suddenly gone as he was thrown from her body. Jacque opened her eyes to see

Fane leaning over her.

"Fane?" she whispered his name as tears began to stream down her face.

"I'm here, love." Fane reached for her but stopped when she cried out in pain.

"It's getting worse," she ground out through clenched teeth.

"We're going to get you out of here just as soon as the others catch up." Fane was cut off when he felt teeth sink into his arm. He growled loudly and turned to face Logan. Fane lunged for Logan and phased in mid air.

"Fane!" Jacque yelled as she watched two large wolves clash in the air. Sounds of snarls, growls, and teeth snapping filled the air. Jacque pulled herself up so she could see the battle that raged before her. She gasped as she saw Logan grab onto Fane's side, but he must not have had a firm grip because Fane slipped away. She was so entranced with watching Fane and Logan that she didn't notice the five other wolves that slowly crept up to her. She startled when she felt a cold nose touch her arm. It was then that she noticed that Decebel was carrying Cynthia in her wolf form.

"Decebel, is she alive?"

"She is. She has two broken legs but I think those are her only injuries," Decebel told her, "Jacque, we are going to take you to the car that is waiting with your mom and friends. Can you walk?"

"I'm not leaving Fane," she said firmly.

The largest of the five wolves growled low at her. She looked at him and knew it had to be Vasile. The power flowing off him was unmistakable.

"I'm not leaving him, Vasile. You can growl and snarl all you waaa..." Jacque couldn't finish as she grabbed her stomach and tried to breathe through the pain.

Decebel looked at Vasile. "Let me help him finish this. It would be over quicker and we could get her out of here."

Vasile shook his big wolf head once and snarled. Jacque decided that must have been a no. They all snapped their heads back to the fight when there was a loud howl. Jacque couldn't believe the amount of blood that matted Fane's fur, it was everywhere. She covered her mouth to keep from screaming out. Surely that wasn't all his blood, she prayed it was not all his blood. She watched as Fane leapt forward and latched onto Logan briefly, then giving his head a quick jerk she saw him tear away fur and flesh as more blood poured out of Logan. As she continued to watch, wanting to turn away but not being able to wrench her eyes away, she realized that every time Fane lunged forward he would literally take another bite out of Logan. There were holes all over Logan's body and blood poured from him. He was weakening from blood loss and she watched him stumble. Fane took advantage of Logan's moment of weakness. He lunged, landing on Logan's back and sunk his teeth into his neck. She watched as Fane began to thrash his head back and forth like a puppy with a new chew toy and then heard a loud snap. Logan's body went limp in Fane's jaws. Jacque realized that Fane had broken the wolf's neck.

Fane dropped the lifeless form and threw his head back and howled. Jacque flinched as the other five wolves and even Decebel in his human form howled in victory with him. As the howls died down Jacque added her own howl, but hers was out of pain as once again she doubled over. Only this time the pain was too much. She held her breath and felt tears seep from her eyes just before she passed out.

Chapter 33

Fane was back in his human form as soon as he heard Jacquelyn's pain-filled scream. He rushed to her side just as she lost consciousness. Taking in the bruises on her face and the teeth marks on her neck, he nearly lost his barely contained control. He reached for her body, pulling her up into his arms, and stood. He turned to look at his father who was still in his wolf form. "No matter Dr. Steele's part in this, right now we need her. We need to know how to fix my Luna."

Vasile gave a small snort and Fane took that to mean that his father would not take any action towards the doctor…yet.

As Fane, Decebel, and the five wolves approached the vehicle his gaze locked with Lilly's. She rushed forward as tears ran down her cheeks, sinking to the ground as Fane lowered Jacquelyn's body. He helped Lilly lay Jacquelyn's head in her lap and then quickly took a pair of sweatpants his mother was handing out for each of the wolves to put on.

"Okay, girls. They are all decent," Alina announced.

Jen and Sally came around from the other side of the vehicle and rushed to Jacquelyn's side. Both girls were crying as they looked their friend over, making sure she was really alive and really here. It took everything in Fane to keep from taking her from Lilly and holding her close to him so he could assure himself and his wolf that she was safe.

Fane turned to his father as Vasile approached. "We need Dr. Steele awake."

"I will force her to phase once we are back at the hotel. Then she can tell us what we need to do to make Jacque well."

Fane watched as one of the wolves that had phased back and was now wearing a pair of sweats approached Lilly. Fane couldn't help the low growl that came from his chest. Dillon Jacobs looked up at the sound of the growl. "She's my daughter, too."

"I understand that. Do not touch her while you check on her. I know that you want to make sure she is okay, but no male is to touch her." Fane's voice was lethal as he issued the order.

Dillon nodded in acknowledgment of Fane's request as he knelt down next to Lilly.

Vasile gave everyone a few more minutes before he announced they needed to be getting back to the hotel.

"Dillon," Vasile said, turning to face the other Alpha. "You may come back to the hotel but I would ask that your other wolves stay away. Fane will not be comfortable with other wolves around Jacque right now. As it is, he is on the verge of losing it."

Dillon agreed to this and told him that he would meet them at the hotel after he dropped his wolves off.

Fane went over to Lilly and knelt down. "Can I take her, Lilly?"

Lilly watched as Fane shook with the need to be close to his mate. Lilly gently lifted Jacque's head so Fane could slip his arm underneath it, and his other arm came under her knees as he stood up with her. He carried her to the SUV, not waiting for anyone else, and climbed in with her in his lap. He looked down at her face, brushing hair away from her once-pale cheek now marred with a bruise, and reached for her mind.

" Meu inimă, can you hear me?" Fane continued to run his fingers across her cheek as he waited for her response.

"It hurts, Fane." Jacquelyn's voice was soft in his mind.

"We are going to make you better. Can you open your eyes for me, love?"

He watched as slowly her eyes began to flutter and then open. He sheltered her with his large body, not wanting anyone else to see she was awake, needing a few moments of her all to himself. He leaned forward and kissed her lips gently and whispered, "Don't move right now, just let me look at you."

"Someone would have to pry me from your arms, Fane," she whispered back with a small smile, which quickly turned to a grimace as her body throbbed.

Fane's heart clenched as he watched pain fill her eyes, hating that he could do nothing for her.

"Just rest, my love."

Jacquelyn closed her eyes and Fane pulled her close to his body, sharing his heat with her.

Just as they had arrived at the woods in silence, their trip back to the hotel was just as quiet.

Alina laid a blanket over Cynthia Steele's wolf form lying on one of the hotel beds. Vasile, Fane, and Lilly stood over her as they watched her begin to phase back to her human skin. Jen and Sally sat on the other bed next to Jacque's supine form and Decebel leaned against the back wall, his arms folded over his chest, looking even more ominous if that were possible.

Cynthia blinked several times as her eyes opened. She didn't know where she was, she just knew she was no longer in the woods, and she was alive.

"Cynthia Steele, we need your help," she heard a voice say to her.

She began to sit up. Her arm and leg that had been broken healed during her phase but they remained stiff and still ached. She felt the warm fabric against her skin. Realizing it was a blanket that covered her very bare self, she clutched it to her as she sat up fully to look at the room full of faces staring holes into her. She began to recognize the faces and then everything that had happened came rushing in.

"Where is Jacque? Is she okay? Is Logan still alive?" Questions flowed from her mouth like water from a faucet as her eyes darted from person to person.

It was Fane who answered her. "Jacque is alive but in severe pain. Please tell me how to heal her."

"She needs blood," Cynthia told him.

"She has already had blood." Fane's voice was deadly. "Logan forced his blood on her, she is not better."

"Not just anyone's blood, Fane. She needs your blood, the blood of her mate."

Fane stepped towards the bed as hope began to inch its way into his heart.

"You're sure?" he asked.

"Scientifically, no, I'm not. But Fane, we are werewolves, science cannot explain us. In my gut I know it is your blood she needs. I don't think one bite will do it since she has gone so long and her body has slowly been attacking itself. She will probably have to bite you several times over the period of a few days."

Fane turned to his mother. "Get her some clothes, please."

Alina brought Cynthia some sweatpants and a shirt and all the males stepped out of the room. Lilly and Alina helped Cynthia dress. Although her broken bones had mended when she phased, her body was still very stiff and sore. Nobody spoke as Cynthia dressed. Alina opened the doors and let the wolves back in. Fane walked over to Jacquelyn's side and stared down at her in silence. Everybody in the room waited, watching to see what he would do. Fane made a decision.

"Everyone, please leave," he requested without ever taking his eyes off of his mate. "She wouldn't want anyone to watch this."

Without a word, the room emptied and as soon as Fane heard the click of the door he sat down next to Jacquelyn on the bed.

"Luna, can you wake for me?"

Jacquelyn turned her head in the direction of Fane's voice. Her eyes opened. "Am I really here? Are you really with me?"

"Yes and yes," he answered as he lay on his side next to her.

She reached her hand to touch his face but pulled back in pain. Fane gently caressed her face as he turned her face to look at him.

"Dr. Steele says you need my blood, that you will have to bite me several times in order to fully heal." Fane paused before he continued. "Do you think you can handle biting me or would it be too much since you were forced before?" His voice got softer and softer as he spoke, his eye lids shadowed his eyes and his lips were held in a tight line.

"Fane, I didn't bite Logan. He bit himself and poured his blood into my mouth. Biting you will be weird but not because of Logan." Her mouth turned upwards as she tried to reassure him but she must not have succeeded because he still looked stricken.

"Fane, tell me what to do. Unless," she said, looking away from him as her voice quivered, "unless you don't want me to bite you."

Fane growled. "Why would I not want my mate to bite me, to take my blood?"

Jacque shivered at the anger she heard in his voice. "Because I've had his blood, because he tainted me," she sobbed out.

Fane began to wrap his arms around her but as his hands

touched her back she cried out in pain.

Fanes eyebrows rose as he jerked his arms away. "What is it? Where are you hurt, love?"

Jacquelyn's eyes fell as her lips trembled. "He clawed my back when he saw my markings," she whispered.

Fane gently tugged her forward so that she was lying on her stomach. He began to raise the hem of her shirt. "I will be gentle," he told her, his voice tight and strained. As he continued to pull her shirt up, revealing more and more of her skin, he finally saw the angry red slashes that marred her beautiful body. They sliced from her neck to below her bra. Fane couldn't stop the low growl that rumbled in his chest at the sight of his beautiful mate's precious skin so angrily torn.

"His death was too merciful for the pain he caused you." His voice trembled, exposing the depth of his hurt for her. Fane leaned forward and gently kissed her injured back and neck. Pulling back and lowering her, shirt he helped her lay back on her side.

"I want you to take my blood. I am your mate. You will take my blood so you can get better and then you will take it so we can complete the Blood Rites."

Fane tilted his head back, bearing his neck to Jacque. "Your instincts should help you out, love. Just close your eyes and bite."

Jacque looked at Fane's neck, his beautiful smooth skin and the markings that ran across it. She couldn't believe she was going to do this, but she was in so much pain that she no longer cared. She did as Fane told her and closed her eyes. She scooted closer to him, leaning forward and gently touching her lips to Fane's neck. She kissed him once before parting her lips and pressing her mouth down. As her teeth began to apply pressure to his skin, to her surprise, she felt her incisors lengthen and then she was able to pierce his skin with almost no resistance.

She squeezed her eyes tight as the taste of Fane's blood hit her tongue. Instead of thr metallic taste she had been expecting there was almost a spicy quality to Fane's blood. She felt him pull her tighter against him and she tightened her mouth as she continued to swallow his blood. It should have grossed and freaked her out, but instead it felt right.

Fane closed his eyes as he felt Jacquelyn's mouth on his neck. His body stiffened briefly as he felt her teeth sink into his flesh. He couldn't describe the feelings stirring inside at the pull of her mouth if he wanted to do. It was something so private and special between mates. He let her continue to take in his blood for several minutes. When he thought she had gotten enough for this time he reached into her mind. The thoughts he found there gave him pause before he finally spoke to her.

"Love, it is enough for now. You may stop."

Jacque slowly pulled her mouth away from Fane's neck. She blinked several times as Fane's face slowly came into focus. His breath caught as he saw Jacquelyn's teeth. He lifted her upper lip to look at the incisors that had lengthened. "Interesting," he muttered. As he pulled his hand away he watched them retract.

"That was," Jacque paused as she swallowed and caught her breath, "intense."

Fane grinned at her, rubbing his hands up and down her back. "That's putting it mildly, Luna."

She looked into his eyes, enjoying being so close to him, once again being able to touch him, smell him, and taste him. "Will it always be like that?"

Fane cocked his head to the side at her. "I don't know, but you are welcome to find out anytime you want." He grinned and was encouraged to see a little smile on her lips.

"How are you feeling? Any better yet?"

"The pain has actually dulled quite a bit. It's still there but it's not keeping me from breathing."

"Do you think you can move?" he asked her gently.

"As long as you aren't asking me to run through the woods from a crazed wolf," she teased. Fane didn't find it funny as he growled at her.

"I'm ready to take you home, to Romania. I want to be bonded to you, Jacquelyn. I want to complete the Blood Rites. If you are up to it, we were going to fly out tonight."

"What about my mom? Jen and Sally?"

"They are coming with us. My mother and your mother somehow convinced their parents. Do you think you can travel, Luna?" Fane was really hoping she would say yes. He wanted out of this country. It seemed like only bad things happened to Jacquelyn here. He wanted her home with him, where she belonged.

"I'm ready to be bonded to you, too. Let's do this." Jacque winked at him and he felt that wink all the way to his soul.

Fane stood up and began to go towards the door."Wait, where are you going?" Jacque asked him. He turned to look at her face and saw panic in her eyes. He realized then that his brave, sarcastic, fierce Luna had not walked away from this unscathed.

"I'm just going to let everyone back in to tell them we are going." He sat back down on the bed next to her and took her hand. "What is it, Jacquelyn?"

She hesitated but then looked him in the eyes with her chin held up. "I hate to be weak and to feel helpless, and I refuse to always be this needy, but right now the idea of you where I can't see you terrifies me. If that makes me pathetic then so be it." Fane could tell it took so much of her to admit her fear to him.

"None of what you just told me could ever make you pathetic and if you think that then you are going to think I'm completely psycho, because I'm never letting you out of my sight again, nor will another male ever be close enough to touch you."

Jacque couldn't stop the small laugh that escaped her lips.

"Why do you find this funny?" Fane asked, truly confused by her response.

"You can't very well keep every male away from me forever."

"Yes I can. I am the next Alpha in line. I'm the prince of the Romanian Grey wolves. If I say they are to stay fifty feet away from you at all times then that is what they will do."

Mischief glimmered in Jacquelyn's eyes. "Fifty feet? Are you sure that's enough? Maybe you should make it, I don't know, several hundred feet. That may be more reasonable."

"Are you making fun of me, Luna?" Fane asked with a low growl.

"Why yes, Fane, I am. However could you tell?"

Fane glowered at her as she smiled innocently, then surprised her by kissing her on the nose. "I'm glad to see that you haven't lost your sense of humor."

"Wolf-man, if you keep making outrageous statements like that then my sense of humor will only improve because I will have you to make fun of."

Fane stood and walked again towards the motel room door and

as he pulled it open he said, loud enough for everyone to hear, "So glad I could be of service to you, Jacquelyn."

Jacque turned bright red as everyone filed in, their eyes darting between the two.

"Is that what they're calling it these days?" Jen asked. She looked at Sally. "That's what I've been doing wrong. I haven't been saying I wanted to be serviced."

Every male in the room coughed to cover up laughs as Sally swatted Jen's arm.

"I'm just saying, you learn something new every day," she said, winking at Jacque.

Fane shook his head, a smile on his face simply because his Luna was smiling.

Vasile was the first to recompose himself as he looked at Jacque. "How are you feeling?"

"A little better. I was telling Fane the pain is bearable."

"So you think you can travel? It's a long flight to Romania," Vasile told her.

"Yeah, I'm good. I'm ready to get off this continent. I'm convinced it has something against me."

Fane looked at Cynthia, who stood off to the side looking like she wanted to crawl in a hole. "Do you think it is okay for her to travel?"

Cynthia looked at Jacque and then at Fane. "If she says she feels up to it then, yes. If she begins to hurt badly again you will just need to give her more of your blood."

Jacque blushed as Fane looked at her with a wicked grin.

Jen looked between the two and then at Sally. "Do you see that fine wolf grinning wickedly at our best friend?"

Sally looked apprehensively at Jen. "Yes," she answered cautiously.

"I thought I told you I wanted one. Where is he?" Jen asked dryly.

"And I thought I asked if you wanted fries or tots with that and you said you preferred whipped cream. Much as it pains me to tell you this," Sally took Jen by the shoulders and looked into her eyes in all seriousness, "and you might want to brace yourself, apparently wolves don't do whipped cream. They all said it makes their hair sticky."

Jen grinned at Sally as the entire room erupted into laughter, holding out her fist for her to bump. "Niiiiiice."

Vasile turned to Fane still grinning, obviously enjoying the lightheartedness after so many days of worry and fear. "Get them ready to go, Sorin has the plane waiting."

Fane nodded, still smiling. "As you say, Alpha."

Chapter 34

Jen and Sally boarded the private plane Vasile had charted. Jen whistled while Sally's jaw dropped open at the sight of such luxury.

"Sally, I take it back. I don't just want a wolf and whipped cream. I want a *rich* wolf with whipped cream.

"Ok, let me just write that down for you since you seem to think I'm your personal assistant," Sally responded, her tone clipped.

"You ever noticed how assistant starts with ass? Do you think that's a coincidence?" Jen shrugged her shoulders as she raised her eyebrows at Sally.

"Oh, how I've missed my two snarky best friends," Jacque quipped as she boarded the plane, closely followed by Fane.

Jacque had begun to follow Jen and Sally when she felt Fane tug her hand. She turned back to look at him.

"Let me check the plane before you and your friends go exploring." He gave her hand a quick squeeze and then walked towards the back of the plane. Jacque noticed that there was a small hall that was blocked off from the front of the plane.

"This thing is huge. Where do you think that goes?" Sally asked pointing in the direction Fane had disappeared down.

"I don't know, but I intend to find out," Jacque said to her friends with a wink.

The three girls sat down on a plush seat that ran the length of one side of the plane. On the opposite side of the plane were bucket style seats, two to a row. Each set of two faced opposite another and there was a small table in between each set. Jacque counted three sets. To the right of her on the wall that separated the back of the plane from them was a large flat screen television and below that was a bar with various drinks in the glass case.

Fane came and stood next to Jacque, apparently finished with his inspection. Jacque, Jen, and Sally watched as the others began to board the plane. Alina and Lilly took one set of the bucket seats while Sorin and Vasile sat across from them. Jacque had to pinch Sally when she started laughing because Boian had attempted to sit on the bench seat next to Jen, and Decebel snarled something in Romanian at the poor wolf, causing him to pale and jump up so fast it looked like he had been stabbed in the butt with a hot poker. Jen acted as if she didn't notice.

Cynthia sat next to Skender across from the now trembling Boian and the frowning Decebel. Fane reached down and grabbed Jacque's hand, tugging at her as he indicated the bucket seats for them to sit in. Jacque stood up, motioned to Jen and Sally to join them in the seats across from each other.

With everyone safely buckled in, the plane began its journey down the runway, picking up speed until finally Jacque felt her stomach drop as the plane's wheels left the ground. As the plane rose higher into the sky Jacque felt like she was finally getting away from the nightmare that she had been living this past month. That is until the pain ripped through her again.

She leaned forward in her seat, arms wrapped around her middle as she laid her head on the table in front of her. She heard startled voices but could not make them out. Not with the sound of blood rushing in her ears as she tried not to scream out. She thought that since she had taken Fane's blood that she was better, but Cynthia was right when she said it would take more than one time. She felt someone undo her seat belt and then strong arms were around her lifting her. She curled her body into the strength that she knew had to be Fane.

Jacque didn't open her eyes until she felt him laying her down on a soft surface. She didn't bother looking around, the only thing she wanted to see were Fane's eyes. She watched him as he stretched out beside her never taking his eyes from hers.

"You need more blood, Luna," he told her gently.

Jacque watched as he unbuttoned the first three buttons on his black shirt and pushed the collar back to expose his throat. As the pain continued to course through her body she barely registered that her canines had lengthened the moment Fane bared his throat to her.

Fane gently wrapped his hand around the nape of her neck and guided her mouth to his skin. This time Jacque didn't hesitate. As soon as her teeth met his flesh she pierced it without a thought. Once again Fane's spicy essence poured into her as she closed her eyes and welcomed his healing blood.

Fane pulled Jacquelyn close, sheltering her with his body as she took what he offered.

He whispered in her ear using his native language, telling her how much she meant to him and how he could never imagine a life without her. And when he told her he loved her he felt her body tremble in his arms. She pulled back this time on her own and Fane saw the tear tracks down her cheeks.

"Why do you cry, love?" he asked her gently.

"I knew you would come for me, but I didn't know if I would be the same person when you found me."

Fane watched as she moved forward and he felt her tongue run across where she had just bitten him. As she pulled back he saw that her cheeks were tinged a soft red and as he ran his fingertips across her face he felt the heat on her skin.

"Sorry, there was, um, some blood." She let her words trail off.

Fane chuckled as he wiped away the evidence of her tears. "You don't have to be embarrassed, Luna. You can run your tongue across my neck anytime. I assure you I will never object." He laughed as she swatted at him, but was glad he had gotten a smile out of her.

"How are you feeling now? Has the pain lessened?" he asked in a much more serious tone.

Jacque took a deep breath and let it out slow. She closed her eyes, concentrating on her body. She could still feel a dull ache but it was even better than after the first time he had given her his blood.

"I feel much better," she told him honestly. Her brow furrowed when she asked, "Fane, will this affect the Blood Rites since I've taken your blood?"

"No, Luna. Because I have not taken your blood, the Rites are not complete yet."

Jacque nodded her understanding. She rolled onto her back and for the first time looked around at her surroundings. She realized they were in a small but luxurious room. There was soft overhead lighting along the edge of the room. They were lying on a queen sized bed that almost completely filled the space.

"Is this the back of the plane?" she asked him.

Fane nodded. "This is the only cabin on the plane. I came back here when we first boarded to make sure it was ready should I need to give you blood again."

Jacque's face once again took on the rosy red coloring. "I suppose they," she indicated with a nod in the direction of the front of the plane, "all know why we came back here."

"Well, I'm sure they are assuming it's because you needed my blood, but we could give them a reason to believe it was for something else," Fane teased as he started tickling her and she couldn't hold back the soft laughter that came pouring out of her.

Jen and Sally sat tensely in their seats as the wondered if Jacque was okay. She had been so pale when Fane had carried her off. Alina kept trying to reassure them that Fane would take care of her. Still, they couldn't help worrying. About the time the plane hit cruising altitude they all heard a gentle giggling from the direction Fane had carried Jacque. Jen rolled her eyes as she unclipped her seatbelt.

"Oh, for crying out loud," she said as she stood up. "If Jacque gets to get her freak on at 80,000 feet, I'm at least going to get my game on." She turned to look at the other wolves. "Skender, Sorin, Boian," but was interrupted before she could finish.

Decebel stood up, nearly ripping the seatbelt before he remembered to unbuckle it. "Jennifer," his voice was deathly soft, "what the bloody hell do you mean to get your game on with three of my pack mates?"

Jen had to slap Sally on the back as she started coughing at Decebel's words.

"Well, when you put it like that it does sound pretty bad. But those were your words, Sparky, not mine." She turned to Alina, ignoring the daggers that Decebel was glaring at her. "Do you have a deck of cards on this ride?"

Alina's eyes crinkled as she smiled. "I bet we could find some." She unbuckled her seat belt and started going through various compartments that didn't look like compartments until she started hitting buttons that made them open. Finally, after a few moments Alina held up a deck of cards triumphantly. "We're in business," she said, smiling at Jen.

Jen took the deck as she looked at Sally. "You in?"

"Always."

"Okay, boys. Let's see what you got," Jen taunted as she sat down on the bench seat across from the others.

The three wolves looked tentatively at Decebel.

"Oh, for crying out loud, Dec. Tell them you won't beat them if they play cards with the two humans." Jen glared at him.

Decebel had not taken his eyes off of Jen since she had declared she wanted to get her game on. Finally he relented and turned to his pack mates, who all cringed under his scrutiny.

"No touching," he said,as he sat back rigidly, angled so he could watch every move of the game.

The three wolves joined Jen and Sally. Uncertain of where to sit they all sat right on the floor in front of the bench seat Jen and Sally occupied.

"So are we playing hold 'em?" Skender asked Jen.

Sally snorted as Jen continued to deal the cards. "Hold 'em's for sissies," Jen teased with a wink. "We're playing something a little less civilized."

"What would that be…exactly?" Sorin asked his eyebrows raised and his lips slightly down cast.

"Strip poker, of course," Jen said innocently while all three wolves coughed into their hands. "But remember," she added with a wicked look directed at the brooding wolf sitting behind the other wolves, "no touching."

The low sound that rumbled from Decebel's chest had the other wolves cringing. "Jennifer," Decebel growled in warning.

"Fine. Strip poker is out, go fish is in." Jen glared at Decebel. "Who invited you to this party, anyways? Can't your invitation be revoked?"

"That only works with vampires, Jennifer." His eyes narrowed.

"Well, it would be a little more convenient if some things were universal in the supernatural world," she snapped.

"Some things are universal. For instance, there isn't a being in existence that couldn't possibly want to take a bite out of your mouthy hide." Decebel winked at her as she sat in mid-shuffle, her mouth dropped open. Sally reached over and pushed Jen's chin up, effectively snapping her mouth closed.

"Jen, how 'bout I just take over the shuffling, k?" Sally cautiously took the deck of cards from her while Jen continued to glare at Decebel.

Fane lay next to a sleeping Jacquelyn as the quiet hum of the plane engine hummed like a lullaby and noticed how much she seemed to have improved after taking his blood twice. The bruise on her cheek had faded to the soft green color they get just before they disappear. He hadn't looked at her back again to see if the claw marks had begun to heal. Fane didn't know if she would have scars or not since she was only half Canis Lupis.

She looked beautiful lying next to him. He gently picked up a lock of her hair and brought it to his face. The soft strands against his skin were like silk and the scent he breathed in from them was like little piece of heaven to him. He couldn't begin to express his thankfulness and joy at having her back with him.

The plane gave a jerk as it ran into turbulence, the disturbance causing Jacquelyn to stir. Fane watched as her eyes fluttered open and then collided with his own. His breath was drawn from his lungs at the softness and love that he saw reflected in Jacquelyn's beautiful emerald eyes. He saw her eyebrows draw together as a questioned formed on her pink lips.

"Why did your parents only have one child?" she asked him.

Fane took a deep breath as he thought about her question. "They tried to have more but my mother kept losing the pregnancies."

"Oh, Fane, I'm sorry. That must have been hard for her." Jacquelyn took his hand and brought it to her lips as she gently kissed his palm.

"You should know, just in case in the future you want to try, it is difficult for our kind to conceive. We don't know why, but it's not common for mates to have more than one or two children."

"Maybe Cynthia could help," she told him as her eyes brightened.

Fane smiled at her forever optimism, but then his eyes narrowed. "Cynthia has a lot to answer for."

"Oh, Fane." Fane watched as Jacquelyn's face softened. "I know what she did was wrong but I understand that she was hurt and angry. She got me out of there and she could have died fighting Logan so that I could get away. Please don't hurt her."

He tilted her chin up so he could look into her eyes. "You really forgive her, even after all you endured?"

Jacquelyn nodded as she searched his face."I forgive her," she said simply.

Fane closed his eyes briefly and pressed his lips gently to hers. "I will discuss it with my father."

He watched her lips turn up and her eyes lighten. "Thank you, wolf-man."

He inclined his head to her, never taking his eyes from hers.

"Jacquelyn, how did things go with your father? I didn't listen in on your conversation with him when you parted ways." Fane's eyes softened and his mouth turned up in a reassuring smile.

"It was okay. He really felt like he needed to get home and talk to his mate about everything. Apparently she doesn't know a thing about me. I'm glad I got to meet him. I'm glad that I know he cares about me but he isn't who I need right now. The time for me to have a father has passed, Fane, and Dillon understands that. He is happy for us and that means a lot to me, but it's my mate that I need now."

Fane leaned forward and kissed her forehead gently as her words seeped into his heart.

"Can I ask you a question?" she asked when he pulled back.

"I could deny you nothing, Luna. Perhaps you will allow me to look at the marks on your back to see if they are healing as quickly as the bruise on your face while you satisfy your curiosity," he bartered.

She rolled onto her stomach and let him pull her shirt up so he could examine her skin.

"Do you ever wonder if the Canis Lupis want a king or Alpha? Do you think that they have ever wanted to be, like, a democracy?"

Fane chuckled as he ran his fingers lightly across the claw marks that were now red slashes, the skin already closed.

"Where did this question come from?" he asked as he pulled her shirt back down.

She rolled back onto her side, her eyes down cast sheepishly. "I'm just really scared that your pack isn't going to want me as their female Alpha. What if they would rather be a democracy than have a half-breed as a leader?"

"There are flaws in your logic, my love." Fane relaxed on his back, his arms folded behind his head. "First, Canis Lupis, like our cousins the natural wolves, thrive under the leadership of an Alpha. Because of our violent and dominating nature we need the leadership and direction of one that is stronger and more in control than each of us. Without an Alpha there would be chaos and anarchy. We aren't human, Jacquelyn, not even you. We would not survive if we tried to live as humans do. The pack will respect you and follow your leadership. You are strong and that is what they look for in a leader. This also explains why a democracy wouldn't work, why Canis Lupis could not elect a leader. Wolves only follow the strong; the leader has to prove he can lead. His strength cannot be based on others' opinions. He has to be able to demonstrate that he is the most dominant and most capable to care for the pack. The female Alpha, by nature's design, comes into this position naturally because she is mated to the Alpha. You were chosen by fate to be my Luna and because of that it proves you are strong enough to lead, strong enough to take control when others would try to bring disarray into the pack."

Jacque was quiet for a few minutes after Fane had finished talking. She thought about what she had gone through since meeting Fane and wondered if it was fate's way of showing her that she was indeed strong enough to lead, to take control. After all, she had survived two psychotic Alphas and although she hadn't walked away unscathed, she remained whole. She was still Fane's mate, she was still strong. She looked down at Fane who was patiently waiting for her response. His eyes softened as they met hers and she couldn't help but let her eyes wander on his beautiful face. They traced over the markings that flowed across his neck and disappeared under his shirt and then met his eyes once again.

"I can do this. I'm not saying that I'm not scared, but I got this. As long as you are by my side, wolf-man, I'm game."

Jacque curled up next to Fane, content to be in his arms and continued to think about her future, about their future. She wasn't going to worry, she was going to trust Fane and herself and she would give it her all and be the best mate and Alpha female when her time came.

"You will be amazing, Luna, never doubt that." She heard Fane's voice and the love he poured into his words in her mind.

"I wouldn't dare," she replied confidently. His response was a gentle squeeze and low chuckle under his breath.

Chapter 35

Jacque stood in the room that she was sharing with Jen and Sally in the mansion where Fane and his family lived. It had been a week since they landed in Romania and the whirlwind of preparing for the bonding ceremony had begun. Tonight, in a matter of less than an hour, those preparations would finally bear the fruit of their purpose. Tonight Jacque would tie herself to Fane for all eternity. Needless to say she was a little anxious, and it would be a lie if she didn't admit that she was a bit jumpy feeling that at any moment some crazy wolf would jump out of the woodwork to steal her away in some freakish attempt to make her his mate. Okay, if she took a minute to really think about those fears she just might break down into hysterical laughter knowing that three months ago she didn't even know werewolves existed. She looked in the mirror at the simple, green gown adorned with embroidered flowers stitched in a darker green thread, with gold thread mingled in working its way up from the hem of the dress up and growing sparser the higher up the dress it went. It was cut low in the front but had a high back that would cover her markings. Alina chose this dress as the replacement for the original one ruined in the accident. The green accented her eyes and complimented her red hair and although it wasn't the first dress, it was still just as stunning in its own way.

Today was not only the Blood Rites ceremony, it was also her eighteenth birthday. Who would have thought that on her eighteenth birthday she would be in Romania getting ready to bond with a werewolf? Ya, her either.

"How you doing of there, wolf princess?" Jacque heard Jen ask from the bed she was lounging on while Sally finished painting her toenails.

Jacque turned to face her two best friends, thankful beyond words that they were here to support her and if nothing else, give her sarcastic remarks to help keep her nerves under control.

"I'm nervous, but honestly I'm so beyond ready to be bonded to

Fane."

"Well, believe us when we say we wish you would hurry up already because the whole 'crazy Alphas knocking down your door to get in your pants' is getting old," Jen told her dryly.

"Classy, Jen, real classy." Sally rolled her eyes.

"Well, better Jac than me, that's all I've got to say."

"Wait a minute," Sally began. "If I do recall, inebriated Jen was all about some wolf to be her man. What happened?"

Jen rolled her eyes, her mouth going tight. "We all know that's never going to happen. Besides, I'm beginning to think I wouldn't look good in fur anyways." Jen snorted at her own comment. "Get it? Fur? Wouldn't look good in fur? No, no takers, huh? Ok then, tough crowd."

Jacque walked over to Jen and knelt down in front of her, her eyebrows raised. "Jen, um, about that. I need to tell-" Just then the door to their room opened and Decebel stepped in.

Jen jumped up off the bed, causing Sally to fling nail polish all over. "Decebel, how good of you to join us in our private room, where we could be naked at any given moment. I was just saying to my two friends here how badly I wished that a grumpy, cocky, condescending, conceited werewolf would barge in uninvited. So thanks for that. Really, thanks."

Decebel just stared at Jen amd his eyes took her in from head to toe. Jen felt heat rise in her face under his scrutiny. "What, have you never seen a girl in a dress?" she snapped.

Decebel growled low. "Not a dress like that. Is it missing a jacket or some material?"

Jen's jaw dropped open, her eyes going wide. Sally coughed into her hand and Jacque just flat slapped her hand over her mouth.

Jen looked Decebel straight in the eyes as she pulled her already low cut dress just a tad lower, daring him with her lethal glare to make another comment.

Decebel walked over to her, standing directly in front of her. Jen had to lean her head back to look up at his towering form. "This conversation isn't over, Jennifer, and you aren't leaving this room until you put on a sweater or robe, or a parka for all I care. But you are not going out there like that." He then turned to Jacque. "It's time. He is waiting for you. Once Jennifer adds some material to her body I am to lead you and your friends to the gathering hall." Without another word he turned and walked back into the hall, waiting for them to follow.

Sally was already pulling out a soft cream short waist sweater that would go with Jen's navy blue dress. "Just put this on and lets go. It's Jacque's day, okay?" Sally whispered to her fuming friend.

Jen snatched the sweater from Sally and jerked it on, never taking her eyes from Decebel's stiff form. Finally she wrenched her eyes away and looked at Jacque. Her face immediately softened. "Okay Jac, let's do this. I've got your speech thingy so we're good. And you look amazing!"

Jacque beamed at the compliment. She nodded her head, taking a deep breath, and turned to follow Decebel out to where Fane waited for her.

As they approached the gathering room Jen and Sally both gave Jacque a hug. Neither spoke as they had already said all that needed to be said. Jen handed Jacque the sheet of paper that had her vows and gave her a quick wink. Decebel escorted Jen and Sally into their places in the hall, leaving Jacque standing there alone.

As Jacque stepped up to the entryway and looked into the hall, she saw that it was dark. As she continued to watch, one by one small lights lit up on the floor. She realized it was candles being lit and they created a circle. All around the circle were people. She could see the first couple of rows but then the rest of the faces faded into the darkness that the light of the candles didn't reach. She also saw that in the center of the circle was a chair, a basin of water, and towels. But the most important thing standing amidst the soft candle light was Fane.

He was wearing relaxed jeans and a white button down shirt untucked, the long sleeves rolled up, showing off his strong forearms. And he was barefoot. She could see his tattoos like a vine crawling up from beneath the collar of the shirt, hugging his neck and face in a loving caress. Jacque took a deep breath and then walked into the hall. With every step she took a candle was lit on either side of her on the floor, creating a lighted path. It was quiet, unlike a wedding there was no music for her to enter in to. But that didn't matter because all she could hear was her heartbeat getting harder and harder until she was standing in front of Fane. She looked at his handsome face and a big grin broke across it. Jacque giggled, remembering how he had told her he would be the one with the big goofy grin. Only he didn't look goofy, he was breathtaking.

"Hi," she whispered breathlessly.

"Hello, Luna." His voice was a caress across her face. Fane took her hand and then turned to face Vasile who had been standing there the whole time, but Jacque only had eyes for Fane.

"Fane, Jacquelyn," Vasile began, his voice strong and deep, "you are here today to complete the mate bond. Though fate has brought you together and destined you for one another, you have both chosen of your own free will to be here to profess your love and commitment to your mate."

"We have," Fane answered for them. Jacquelyn looked up at him and he squeezed her hand in reassurance. *"As the Alpha I will answer for us as a mated pair. When my father addresses you directly, then you will speak."*

Jacquelyn nodded her head once in acknowledgment to his thought. Fane returned his attention to his father just as Vasile said, "Fane, it is time for you to recite the formal vows to your mate. Jacquelyn, you will sit in the chair while Fane recites the vows and while doing so he will wash your feet. This symbolizes his willingness as the leader and Alpha to serve you, his mate. To care for your most basic needs no matter how big or small, and to give you the honor you are due as his Luna. Once she has answered you, Fane, you may stand and recite the vows you have written."

Holding her hand, Fane led her over to the chair for her to sit down. Jacque pulled her dress up, baring her calves and feet. Jacque watched as he brought the basin of water and set it on the floor next to her. Next he removed the slippers she had been wearing and took one of the towels and placed it under her feet. She watched in awe as he took a small cloth and dipped it in the water, picked up her foot and began to wash it with the cloth. As he washed her feet he spoke, "On this day I kneel before you, as a servant to my mate, to ask if you will make me whole. Will you give yourself to me? Finally calming the beast inside, bringing order to chaos, shining light where there has been only darkness? Will you bind your life to mine, your fate to mine, and your soul to mine and in doing so complete the mate bond?" As Fane waited for Jacquelyn's response he rinsed her feet and began to pat them dry with the final towel. When she finally did respond it knocked the breath out of him.

Jacquelyn got down on her knees so that they were face to face. She placed her hands in his, holding his gaze with hers and recited the response that Alina had taught her. "On this day I kneel with you, my mate. I will make you whole as you will make me whole. I will give myself to you, calming the beast, bringing order to chaos, and shining light where there has been darkness. I will bind my life to yours, my fate to yours, and my soul to yours and complete our mate bond. I will take you for my own, my mate, and my Alpha." Fane couldn't breathe and for a moment his mind went blank as he stared into the face of his own personal miracle. He realized he had been quiet too long when Jacque squeezed his hands to get his attention. She waited patiently for him to read the vows he had written to her. Neither one of them stood but instead remained on their knees, staring into each other's eyes. He cleared his throat and then he spoke.

"Jacquelyn, Luna, Mate. You have many names. Each of them holds a special meaning, but the only thing I want to call you is mine." Fane paused briefly, watching the emotions play across Jacquelyn's face. He wanted to look into her mind and see what she was thinking, instead he continued to look into her deep green eyes. "I wasn't sure how to tell you all that I feel for you and the depth of those feelings, but someone very wise helped me and so I pass on her words and add some of my own. I don't know if there is any way to explain or truly understand the bond between mates. It's not human; it's beyond the realm of reason and that makes it hard to believe it is even possible. I know I haven't known you long. I know we are both young. But we will grow closer faster than either of us can imagine. You will become my best friend, my lover, and I will become yours. Even now I know you feel it, that no one in this world will ever love me as you will and no one will love you as I will. We were born to love each other and that love will grow stronger as time goes on. I worry that I won't make you happy," Fane's voice was so soft, laced with tight emotions, "but that wise voice helped me see that I will. I will also make you mad, sad, annoyed, and probably a little claustrophobic at times." Jacquelyn grinned at him, full of adoration and he pressed on encouraged by her response. "But I will do everything in my power to make you happy. My wolf will step in when my human side steps out of line. The wolf only sees black and white. All he understands is that you are our mate. He will love you, protect you, provide for you, play with you, and make you content while my human side fills in the gaps of emotions the wolf does not understand. You will make me a better Alpha, a better man. I will give you what no other man ever could, the other half of your soul." When Fane finished he saw that Jacquelyn had tears running down her cheeks, her eyes full of love. He reached up with the hand that was holding hers and gently wiped the tears away.

"Jacquelyn, it is time for you to recite the vows you have written to your mate," Vasile told her gently, mindful of her emotions.

She had to let go of Fane's hands as she unfolded the piece of paper she held in her hand. When she looked up and saw Fane watching her she grinned. Fane winked at her which made her heartbeat pick up. *"Easy, love. It's just me, just us. Talk to me,"* Fane whispered in her mind, helping to calm her so that she could unfold the paper and read it to him.

"Fane, there is so much I don't know about you, so many secrets I have yet to discover, but there are a few things that I do know. I know that your face is the first thing I want to see in the morning and the last thing I see before I close my eyes at night. I know that your smile is the one I want to see when life fills you with joy. I know that I want to be the one to hold you when you are hurt or discouraged, and when life knocks you down I want to be the one to help you get back up. I know that if we are so blessed, I want you to be the father of my children, and I hope they have your beautiful blue eyes. I know without a doubt, out of the millions of people on this earth, you were created for me and me for you. All these things *I* know. What *you* need to know is that I am yours and yours alone. You hold my heart. You have the power to fill it with love and you have the power to destroy it. You need to know that not a day will go by that I don't thank God that you are mine. You need to know that I will get mad at you, I will give you hell when you need it, but I will also love you unconditionally and without reservation. I will give you everything I am and I expect nothing less from you." Fane looked at his mate, speechless at her precious words. He didn't even realize his father was asking him a question until Jacquelyn turned to look at Vasile.

"Fane, what offering do you bring your mate to show her you will provide for her and care for her needs both physical and emotional?" Vasile asked him.

Fane stood up and brought Jacquelyn with him. He reached into his other pocket and pulled out a little black box and heard Jacquelyn's breath catch.

Fane opened the black box and knelt back down on one knee. He took Jacquelyn's left hand into his and felt her shaking. He brought her hand to his lips and kissed it and held it to his lips until the shaking stopped. "I have brought a ring. There is no other like it in all the world just as there is no other like my Luna. Engraved all the way around the band in Romanian are the words: finalizarea (complete), for without you my soul is incomplete; absolut (absolute), that is how my love is for you; chiar (unmovable), there is nothing on this earth that will separate me from you; and intreg (whole), you have filled the void in me making the man and the wolf whole. In the center is a very rare red diamond. I chose red for two reasons. One, you are my *micul incendiu (*little fire). And two, it is a reminder of this day when we both shed blood to bind our souls to each other." Fane looked at Jacquelyn, pleading with his eyes for her to understand how much he needed her. "Jacquelyn, I love you. You are my mate and from this day forth every wolf will know that you are mine. But because I am selfish and a barbarian just as my mother called me, I don't want just the wolves to know you are mine. I want every man to know you are taken. I realize you are not ready to marry me right now. That is okay, I will wait. But I am asking you to tell me that you will be my wife in the human sense of the word one day. Wear this ring as a symbol that your heart is spoken for. Jacquelyn, will you marry me?"

Jacquelyn's eyes were closed and when she opened them he saw them glisten with unshed tears. Fane stood up and pulled her close to him. He pressed his lips to her ear and whispered, "Please tell me those are tears of joy."

Jacquelyn nodded her head but that wasn't good enough for Fane. He needed to hear it from her lips. *"I'm going to make you say it out loud, my love. I need to hear it from you."* Fane sent her his thought and then waited for her response.

She pulled back away from him so she could look into his eyes,

"I will marry you, Fane."

Fane could see a little sparkle of mischief in her eyes; she had something up her sleeve. "When Luna? When will you marry me?" he whispered.

"I would marry you now, here, in this place," she told him, her eyes filled with determination.

There was a gasp that rippled through out the room, reaching far into the darkness where the faceless stood. Fane's breath caught, he couldn't believe what he was hearing. He turned to look at his father. "Alpha, marry us," he said firmly. Jacque laughed at the urgency in his tone. He turned back to look at her. "I don't want you to have the chance to change your mind." His voice was playful but Jacque could see in his eyes that he was serious, he wasn't ever letting her go.

Vasile's voice brought them both from their private world back to where and what they were doing. "Before the marriage vows are spoken, that is only one offering, Fane. Where is your second?"

"I have another offering but I wish to give it to my mate in private when we complete the blood rites."

Vasile turned to Jacquelyn."You accept this request?"

"Yes," Jacquelyn answered, her eyebrows raised as she looked at Fane.

"Alright, I suppose now we will do the marriage vows," Vasile said as he grinned at Jacque.

"Hey, it seemed a good a time as any," she told him as her cheeks flamed with heat. "Oh, and you can do the quick version. I'm pretty sure what we've already said covers all the rest." The crowd laughed at her words and then quieted when Vasile looked out into the darkness. Bringing his attention back to Fane and Jacque, he spoke the marriage vows and everyone listened once again as Fane and Jacque bound themselves in the human way as well.

"I now pronounce you husband and wife." Vasile finished the wedding vows and then added, "Fane, it is time for you and your mate to perform the blood rites. Once done your bond will be complete."

Fane turned to her and took her face in his hands and kissed her soundly on the mouth. The kiss seemed to last forever and Jacquelyn was sure that even Jen would be blushing. When he finally pulled away he placed one more soft kiss on her lips and said, “Mate, come. I have waited long enough.” Jacquelyn’s eyes popped open as she looked into the face of her mate, the face of her wolf.

Chapter 36

Jacque couldn't say that she wasn't nervous as Fane led her to his suite in the mansion. When Fane had ended that kiss and spoke to her, she realized that Fane had been out of commission and the wolf was in control. As they reached the door, Fane turned and looked at her. "Don't be afraid, I am here. I am in control but the wolf has pushed forward because the blood rites is a bonding between the wolf and his mate, you. We will not hurt you, Jacquelyn."

Jacque smiled up at him and leaned forward to gently kiss his lips. She whispered, "Mate, I trust you."

A low growl rumbled from Fane as he gently pulled her into the suite. Jacque could smell flowers and when she looked down at the floor she knew why. There was a path of rose petals that lead into the suite. She had been in his room several times over the past two weeks. It was basically like a hotel suite, only very fancy.

It had a sitting room with a fireplace, which Jacque noticed had a blanket spread out in front of it with a basket full of food. The suite also had a small kitchen and dining area. As they followed the path of flower petals on the floor she found herself in awe of all the candles lit everywhere giving off a soft glow. Arriving at the room Jacque knew to be where Fane slept, she felt her stomach drop to her feet and her breathing increased.

Fane pushed the door open and the sight momentarily took Jacque's mind off her fears and took her breath away. There were candles of all different shapes and sizes around the room. There had to be 50 or more. The bed had been covered in a bedspread Jacque had never seen; it was a quilt with two wolves in the center. One larger than the other. The smaller wolf was tucked into the front of the chest of the larger wolf as he sheltered her. It was a beautiful quilt and it spoke volumes. As she looked around the room Fane stepped away from her. She watched him take a basin of water that was on a warming plate and place it on the bedside table. Next to it he placed several towels. He must have felt her confusion because he turned and grinned at her. “It’s to clean the bite marks, love, that’s all.” Jacque felt heat rush up her neck and face as he had picked up on her thoughts.

She sat down on the bed and looked up at Fane, surprised by her own confidence as she stared into his beautiful eyes. "So how does this work?”

"You will need to remove the dress, love." Fane told her, eyes twinkling wickedly. Then he added, "If you want you can go into the bathroom and there is a robe for you."

She grinned at him. "You're bad, you know that? Trying to scare an innocent girl, you ought to be ashamed."

Fane grabbed her hand and kissed it before she could walk away. "I should be, but I'm not." Jacque felt Fane's eyes on her as she retreated into the bathroom to change.

A few minutes later she stepped out in a plush white robe that came to her knees. With her head bowed, eyes hooded by her eyelids, she couldn't help but feel vulnerable knowing there was nothing under the robe. But she reminded herself again, as she had a hundred times while in the bathroom, Fane was her husband and her mate. She heard the intake of Fane's breath and she finally looked up. His jaw had dropped, his eyes wide as he took her in from head to toe and back again. Jacque had never felt more beautiful.

"You have never been more beautiful, love." She heard Fane's words and even in her mind they sounded breathless.

He took a deep breath and ran both his hands through his hair. Jacque could feel how restless he was and how desperate he was to complete the blood rites, but he was trying to be gentle with her.

She walked over to him and took his arms, pulling them around her waist to encircle her. She didn't know what to do so she just let instinct take over. She looked up into his eyes with all the trust in the world. She tilted her head and exposed her neck to him. She saw his eyes glow brighter and heard a low growl. “You are sure you are ready?” Fane asked her, his voice rough with emotion.

“Fane, I trust you.”

She felt him pull her closer, and then his hand came up and pulled the robe gently until her neck and shoulder were exposed. His fingers traced the mating marks on her back, no longer marred from the claw marks, completely healed and whole. Small chill bumps erupted all over Jacque's skin and she shuddered under his touch. He cradled the nape of her neck and Jacque felt him place his nose against her skin and heard him breathe in deep. She heard a rumble from his chest. She tensed briefly and then relaxed as she felt his lips on her skin. He gave her gentle kisses from her chin to her shoulder then back up to her neck just below her ear. Jacque felt his lips part and a stroke of his tongue, then she heard a deep growl just as a sharp pain pierced her neck, then it was gone. She could still feel Fane's mouth on her, but where she first felt pain she now felt pleasure. It was making her stomach do weird things. She felt herself pushing against Fane's body and heard soft moaning. A moment later she realized the moaning was coming from her. She should've been embarrassed but she couldn't bring herself to feel that when this was her mate, the other half of her soul who held her.

Then Fane was pulling away. She wrapped her arms around his neck. desperate to pull him back, but Fane was stronger and continued to pull back until he could see her face. Jacque saw the tears that ran down his cheeks and felt the intensity of his stare into her heart. The look changed abruptly to concern as he looked at her neck. He reached for one of the towels he had laid out and dipped it in the warm water, squeezed out the excess, and brought it to her neck to clean away the blood. She couldn't help the wince that crossed her face as the water touched the wound. Fane gently turned her face to his. "Did I hurt you?"

"No. I mean, it hurt for a moment but then..." Jacque didn't know if she could even put into words how it had felt once the pain had subsided.

"Then what, my love?" he asked.

Did he not know? Could he not hear her moans and feel the emotions rolling off of her? Fane stepped closer, his body brushing up against hers. "I felt your desire," he whispered. "I heard you, my love. I just want to hear you say it. You so often avoid this topic altogether I was beginning to think maybe you weren't attracted to me."

Jacque let out a breathless laugh. "Liar," she teased him.

"After the initial pain, it felt good. No, it felt freaking awesome." Fane chuckled at his mate, but Jacque continued on undaunted. "I have always desired you, Fane. I've just never been comfortable talking about it. But rest assured after feeling your mouth do that on my skin," Jacque shuddered at the memory, "I without a doubt desire you, wolf-man."

Fane decided not to torture her any more with questions about her physical affections for him. Instead he reminded her that the blood rite still wasn't complete. "Are you ready, Luna?"

Jacque took his hand and led him over to the bed. She pushed him down to sit on the edge. With him sitting and her standing, her face was level with his neck. Jacque watched as Fane undid the buttons on his white dress shirt until they were all open and then shrugged the shirt off. She looked at him and although she had already done this twice, this time it felt different, more intimate. Fane turned and exposed his neck as she had done for him. Something deep inside Jacque stirred at the sight of the bared neck. She felt a desire to mark it, claim it, to claim him. She leaned towards Fane and placed her arm around his strong shoulders. She kissed his cheek and down his jaw to his neck just as he had done. She kissed him down to where his neck met his shoulder. At that point instinct took over, the wolf blood in Jacque came forward to claim their mate. Once again, as she had felt the first two times she took Fane's blood, Jacque felt her teeth lengthen just a little and when she ran her tongue across them she realized they felt much sharper. Before she could stop to think about it she opened her mouth and sunk her teeth deep into Fane's flesh. She heard a groan coming from Fane's chest and then the low growl she had become accustomed to. Fane wrapped his arms around her waist and pulled her close. Jacque closed her eyes as she tasted Fane's blood. She felt something, like her very soul was being knitted into Fane's. The bond, she thought, the bond was complete.

After a couple of minutes she felt Fane pulling her away, reluctantly she relented. Neither of them spoke for several seconds. Jacque kept her eyes closed as her breathing slowed. When she opened her eyes to look at Fane she saw the blood running down his neck. Just as he had done, she wet one of the towels and gently wiped the blood away. Fane sat there quietly, watching every move she made. Finally Jacque couldn't handle the silence anymore. "What are you thinking?" she asked him.

"You don't have to ask, Luna, you could just look."

"I know, but I want you to tell me. I want you to share your thoughts with me without me invading your privacy," Jacque explained.

"I am your mate, Jacquelyn. We are bonded. You have every right to invade my mind, but if you want me to talk then that's what you shall get." He grinned at her and grabbed her hand to pull her on to the bed next to him. Fane scooted until his back was against the headboard of the bed.

When he reached to pull Jacque up against him she started to resist. "I want to be able to look at you while we talk."

"In a moment, Luna. First let me hold you. I can feel our bond growing stronger now that we have shared our blood. My blood is in you now and you will always carry my scent. Let me and my wolf hold you and enjoy our scent being all over you."

Jacque rolled her eyes but acquiesced to his wishes. "Your mom was right when she said you were possessive, overbearing barbarians."

"I never claimed otherwise, my love," Fane teased her.

He pulled her close and she rested her head on his chest, her legs tucked up against his side. Jacque felt a rumble in his chest and a smile quirked her lips as she thought about her telling him he purred.

"I do not purr, mate, I rumble."

Jacque glanced up at Fan., "Your wolf is doing that more and more you know?"

"The bond is strong now. You will feel him and hear him more easily now. He is very smitten with you, you know?" Fane told her. Jacque laid her head back on his chest and enjoyed Fane's hand rubbing up and down her arm.

"You were supposed to tell me what you are thinking, remember?" Jacque asked.

"I'm thinking about how in awe I am of you, of your ability to take all that has happened since we met and still smile, tease, take me as your husband and mate. You could have turned away from me, running for your life." Fane paused for a moment and Jacque just waited patiently to see if he would say more. "I'm thinking that I am the luckiest wolf in the world to have found such an amazing mate."

"Funny that," Jacque said. "I was thinking the same thing about you." She felt Fane kiss the top of her head and she snuggled closer.

Jacque held out her left hand and studied the writing on the band. She remembered the words that Fane had said were engraved on it and she felt warmth fill her. "It's the most precious thing I have ever received, Fane." Jacque's voice was filled with awe at the beautiful gift he had given her. She remembered then that he had told his father that the second offering was something he wanted to give her in private. "So where is my second offering, oh wolf of mine?" Jacque asked him in the haughtiest voice she could muster as she sat up and turned to look at him.

"Oh yeah, about that," he began.

Jacque interrupted him quickly. "Don't you even try to act like you don't have something, fur ball." She slapped his leg playfully.

"Have I ever told you that you are a violent little thing?" Fane asked her as he reached to open the bedside table drawer. He handed her a box wrapped in purple paper with a simple ribbon tied around it. Jacque untied the ribbon and unwrapped the package to find a shoe box. "Um, shoes. Great, thank you," Jacque said, trying hard to keep the confusion out of her voice, knowing she was failing miserably. Fane's face was blank. Jacque could read no emotion on it nor could she pick anything up from their bond.

"The shoes represent my ability to provide foot coverings for you and maybe one day our children." Fane cleared his throat and continued, fumbling along as he went. "You see, it is important that you know that you won't be without something on your feet, so-"

Jacque held up her hand to stop Fane from going any further. "There are no shoes in this box, are there?"

Fane shook his head once. "Not one."

As Jacque began to open the box Fane heard her mutter under her breath, "Furry little liar." He started to say something in response but stopped when he saw Jacque's face light up as brilliant as the sun breaking through the early morning dew. "Fane! I can't believe you remembered!" Jacque pulled out the first edition copy of *Where the Sidewalk Ends* by Shel Silverstien. She held it so reverently and ran her hand across the cover.

"Open it," she heard Fane tell her. When she pulled open the cover she could feel the binding bending for the first time, the newness of the book apparent. If it was possible her face got even brighter as she saw the hand written autograph on the cover page.

"This is so freaking awesome," Jacque told him as she closed the book and flung herself into his arms. Fane was surprised by the motion but caught her easily and held her tight. “Thank you, thank you, thank you,” he heard her whisper.

“If I had known you would react this way to a book I would have proposed with it instead of a ring,” he teased.

“The book is amazing, no doubt. But that you remembered something so random, yet so important to me means so much to me. You got skills, wolf-man. Serious, mad skills.”

Fane kissed her gently on the lips and then let her pull away from him. She sat flipping through the book and he was content to just watch her. Jacque finally looked up from the book when she felt Fane begin to rub her back. She couldn’t help the big grin that spread across her face. He was hers; she could feel the mate bond growing stronger now that the blood rites had been completed.

“Will it continue to grow stronger?” Jacque asked him.

Fane's brow furrowed as he thought and was quiet for a moment. “From what my father has told me it will be stronger because of the blood rites, but once we consummate our mating it will be its strongest.”

Jacque's eyes widened at his words, and Fane realized how that had sounded. “Jacquelyn, I’m not trying to rush you. I know you said we would make love once we were married but if you aren't ready I will wait for as long as you need. I will never pressure you. Do you believe me?” Fane asked her and desperation coated his voice.

Jacque looked up at him. “I believe you and I love you all the more for your patience. But it's not necessary. I'm ready, Fane. I'm ready to be yours in every possible way.”

Fane sat frozen at her words, then a slow grin stretched across his face. Jacque felt that grin from the bottom of her feet to the tips of her red hair. He stood up and Jacque watched as he began blowing candles out until there were only four left burning, one in each corner of the room. Fane stepped close to Jacque. She tilted her head back to look up at him as the candle light danced shadows across his face. Jacque's breath caught as she saw Fane's eyes glowing wolf blue.

He took her face in his hands and kissed her gently, then whispered to her, "I can't believe you're here, and you're mine." His body shook with emotion as he stared into her eyes. "I love you, Jacquelyn Lupei. I will love you until my last breath."

She took a shuddering breath as she felt him untie the robe and slowly push it off her shoulders until it fell in a gentle heap on the floor at her feet.

Fane never took his eyes off hers as he pulled her into his arms. As his lips met hers Jacque trembled at the skin to skin contact. She felt his hands on her back, his fingertips lightly moving over her skin. Fane pulled back and they were both breathing hard as he continued to torture her with his gentle caresses.

Fane chuckled at her thoughts. "It's not meant to be torture, love," he told her gently. He pulled her closer to the bed and then tilted her chin up with his fingers to look him in the eyes.

"I would make love to you now, Luna." Fane's eyes continued to glow as he stared intently at her. And as Jacque felt his love pouring through their bond, wrapping around her and filling her up, she knew she was ready, ready to be Fane's mate. Finally.

"Then why are we still talking?" Jacque whispered. He pulled her onto the bed with him and into his arms, arms that would always hold her, always protect her, and always wrap her in love.

Epilogue

Jen and Sally sat at one of the tables in the gathering room, the celebration slowly coming to an end. After Fane and Jacque had left, Alina and Vasile had thrown one hell of a party in honor of their son's mating. Jen had danced until there were blisters on her feet. She had eventually taken off the ridiculous sweater that Decebel had demanded she wear but she had felt the weight of his stare on her all night. Even now as she listened to Sally ramble about all the pack members she had met she could feel his eyes on her.

Jen looked around the room for what felt like the hundredth time trying to find the gold eyes that she knew kept her in their view. But just like the other ninety nine times she could not see him.

"Are you listening to me, Jen?" she heard Sally ask her. Jen turned back to her friend and saw her eyes narrow. "Who ya looking for, chicka?"

"No one," Jen lied.

"Uh-huh, sure. And I'm your freaking fairy-god mother."

"Well, I wish you would get on a couple of my requests then instead of sitting around here yapping," Jen teased, hoping Sally would just drop it.

"He's awfully protective of you, and possessive," Sally continued, ignoring Jen's attempt to change the subject.

"Sally, it's not going to happen, okay? In case you've forgotten he happens to be a werewolf and I am human. So," Jen didn't get to finish as she was interrupted by a voice from behind her.

"That's not completely true." Dr. Cynthia Steele pulled out one of the chairs at their table and sat down.

"What's not completely true?" Jen asked cautiously.

"You aren't human…"

Books by Quinn Loftis
Prince of Wolves
Blood Rites
Just One Drop
Out Of The Dark

Now please enjoy Chapter 1 from
Blood of Anteros
The Vampire Agápe Series #1
By: Georgia Cates
Published by Georgia Cates

Chapter 1

July 11, 1989

Los Cabos, Mexico

Humans chased eclipses so they could say they were witnesses to them, but we chased the darkness of the moon covered sun because it coincided with spectacular supernatural events for our kind. The greater the eclipse, the greater the outcome, and this was predicted to be the grandest total solar eclipse since 1955.

We arrived at our resort, under the cover of darkness, the night before the eclipse. Marsala, my maker and eternal captor, studied the prediction of the paramount eclipse, along with the history of others, to predict the best location for us to experience it's projected greatness. Because the narrow path of the eclipse was limited to tropical locations, we were required to leave the safety of a cooler, darker climate and she carefully chose Los Cabos, Mexico as our location. She never revealed the nature of her rationale, but her secrecy came as no surprise; it was her way. Unlike other guests at this tropical destination, pleasure wasn't what drew us to this all-inclusive beach resort; Marsala had ulterior motive in mind.

It was no surprise to learn Marsala made arrangements for she and I to share a suite. She assigned the other half of our foursome, Wythe and Madon, to a suite down the beach from us and ordered them to remain there while she and I experienced the eclipse together, as a couple. She was shameless in her show of partiality for me, but her efforts to win my heart were pointless; she refused to see my deep loathing for her.

Wythe and Madon were captives like me, with one exception; they loved Marsala unconditionally. She always chose me first, leaving them to battle for second place, while the loser settled for third. Both were completely unaware it was a competition I had no desire to win.

She sought their love and intimacy, only after failing to capture my heart. She toyed with them, playing one against the other as she coaxed them to fight for her affections, promising her love as a prize for the winner. She used their competition as entertainment and it was one of many cruel ways she made herself feel wanted and worthy.

Wythe and Madon shared a common loyalty and devotion to Marsala, along with jealousy and hatred for me. They were furious because she had chosen to experience the supernatural event with me, while they were ordered to not interrupt, and her wrath was the only reason they didn't kill me. I wished they would, but they weren't kind enough to put me out of my misery, leaving me forced to do it myself.

I spent the evening avoiding Marsala, along with her romantic advances. She finally conceded and left the suite, giving me a few hours of peace before she returned, shortly before dawn. From refuge in the bedroom, I smelled a human and recognized it as another one of her games. The warm, fresh blood was intended to taunt and punish me for resisting her romantic advances.

I spent the day in the dark bedroom, away from the sinister devil that refused to release me from her hold, and waited for the moon to cover the sun. Eclipse watchers gathered on the beach and their excitement could be heard inside the safety of our suite as the darkness approached. I left the bedroom and entered the living room to find a young, Mexican woman sitting quietly on the couch. Marsala stood across the room and said, "Curry, I have something special for you."

I looked at the woman sitting on the couch and saw no fear on her face, a sign she didn't realize Marsala was a vampire with plans in store for her.

"I don't want your gift," I replied, dryly.

"You can be so inconsiderate at times. I went to a lot of trouble for this one and I know you thirst for her blood; I see the desire all over your face," she taunted.

"You know how I feel and I grow tired of repeatedly explaining the fact that we no longer need to kill humans to survive."

She ignored my words and attempted to taunt me further by saying, "Can't you smell the richness of her blood?"

"Why is it impossible for you to take no for an answer? It's exhausting. You are exhausting."

"Curry, we've waited for this total solar eclipse since 1955. Something spectacular is about to happen and that means this is a time to celebrate." She walked over to the young woman sitting on the couch and lifted her wrist in my direction, offering the first drink to me. "Please join me in drinking from her. I chose her, just for us, because I know she will be delicious."

Bewilderment flooded the young woman's eyes as she looked to me for some kind of reaction since she didn't understand English. She was confused by Marsala's gesture, but I gave her a false smile of reassurance and was glad she didn't comprehend what was about to happen to her.

I was powerless to stop Marsala, but I refused to watch her prey upon this innocent woman, so I stood to leave the inevitable scene and heard Marsala whisper her patented line. "Know the truth, but whisper lies." It was what she always said, the moment before she devoured her prey.

I entered the suite's bathroom and shut the door before the young woman's screams invaded my sensitive ears. I looked at the stranger in the mirror staring back at me and wondered who he was. His image stood just under six feet tall and his hair was dark, nearly black, like his heart. I leaned closer to the reflection, attempting to see a glimpse of myself within the monster standing in front of me and searched his eyes, the so-called windows to the soul. I looked beyond the flecks of light blue and gold of his irises, but found no trace of the soul I was told no longer existed and wondered, "Who is this demon mocking my every move?"

Shortly after the woman's screams stopped, I felt the arrival of the darkness and silence swallowed the noise of the crowd's loud anticipation. Marsala anxiously called for me from the other room. "Come, Curry, it is time."

With one last glance, I bid farewell to the stranger in the mirror and walked through the living room to see the lifeless body of the young woman with a large, bulging abdomen stretched awkwardly on the couch. Unaware it was a possibility, my revulsion for Marsala grew greater. "How could you? She was pregnant," I disgustedly said.

"Don't be so quick to judge. She thought she was here to negotiate a price for her unborn bastard." She offered me a glass filled with the blood of my gift. "Here! Drink it before it cools."

"Monster! Are there no bounds to the depravity of which you have so freely given your soul?" I asked, as I walked past her. I jerked the terrace curtains open, revealing the darkness of the eclipse and she stepped in front of me to place her palms on my chest.

"Curry, things are going to be different after this; I'm going to give you something you have always wanted and it's going to change everything. We will be happy, you'll see."

"My hatred for you runs so deep it drowns in my very marrow and the only happiness I'll ever know is when I am released from your hold." I bit my tongue to withhold from saying more, not wanting to clue Marsala to my plan.

She flashed her familiar, evil smile and said, "We shall see." She cautiously stepped out into the darkness where she was shielded from the dangers of the sun. I followed her onto the terrace and took my place, propped against the wall with my arms crossed and waited for my beautiful end.

She lifted her fair Creole face toward the moon covered sun with her eyes closed, concealing the pale peridots behind her lids. Two thick braids met just below the crown of her head and light brown curls hung close to her waist. She stood with her feet together and arms stretched wide, like the crucified, with her body motionless in anticipation of something I didn't dare imagine.

I waited against the wall while the eclipse passed quickly and she unsuccessfully shielded her disappointment, as she wore her crushed hope like a flashing neon sign. We exchanged no words as the end of the eclipse drew closer, and with a last desperate attempt, she ended her silence saying, “I conjure you, Hecate, because you are the goddess of magic, witchcraft, the moon, the night, ghosts, and necromancy. I ask you to wrap your arms of favor around me. I compel you, Hecate, to bequeath me a viable womb. I call upon Rhea, the titaness of female fertility, because you are mother to powerful gods and I implore you to grant me fertility and fruitfulness of my womb.”

As she revealed her dark desire, I realized drinking the pregnant woman’s blood was no coincidence and I recognized her pathetic attempt to make me love her. “You can stop now, Marsala, because a child could never change the depth of my disdain for you. Are you really so far gone that you can’t see how bringing a child into this would be the worst form of evil?”

She raised her voice and began to scream her challenge, “I petition you, Hera. You are the queen of marriage, women, childbirth, heirs, kings and empires and I command you to bestow my body with a supernatural pregnancy. These things I command of you! I demand it!”

The sunlight slowly began to spill from behind the moon and death couldn’t claim me quickly enough. She didn’t want the eclipse to end and I took joy in her disappointment. With only seconds to spare, I gladly said the words she didn’t want to hear, “It’s over, we must go inside.”

Strangely, I was at peace with my plan for an elective demise. I was uncertain what awaited me on the other side, or if there could be anything other than Hell for someone like me. In the unlikely event my lost soul had a place to rest peacefully, I took my last opportunity to repent and although I held my tongue, my heart couldn’t remain silent. “All this time, I can’t make right. I am hollow by what remains inside and I ask to be saved from the nothingness I have become. I ask that my misplaced heart no longer wanders, lost and wounded, and finds it’s way into the arms that love me. I beg the forgiveness of the ones I’ve wronged and of the One listening.”

My last moments were interrupted by Marsala’s words, “The goddesses and titanesses have heard my demands and I feel something happening.” She placed her hands to her abdomen and looked up at me with wide eyes saying, "I know you'll love me when I give you the child you have always wanted."

She was happy with herself, believing she had won the battle between us, her obsession victorious over my hate, and she would never understand that this had nothing to do with a child. I could never have feelings, other than hatred, for her because she had taken too much away from me by stealing my life, my happiness, my future, even the light of day.

"Look, it's a sign," she said, as she pointed to my crossed arms.

I lowered my head to see the source of her delight and saw a pair of butterflies sitting upon my crossed arms, their bright wings growing redder as the sun began to peak around the moon. They softly, and whimsically, fanned their wings back and forth and I sensed she was right; something was happening. I felt a force of adrenalin coursing through me, along with a euphoria I'd never known, and was engulfed with inner strength as years of heaviness lifted from me. My invisible shackles were unlocked, tossed aside and the bondage holding me to her was dissolved.

"No! No! No!" she screamed, as she fell to her knees. "What have you done?" she hissed at me. I backed away as she crawled toward me with her hand outreached. The exposure of the sun grew as the seconds ticked by and the time for my death arrived. I lowered my head to meet her eyes, one last time before the sun aided me in my eternal escape of her. I saw the burning pain on her face, along with something else in her narrowed eyes and I recognized her look of jealous fury; it could be mistaken for nothing else.

She hissed, "I don't know how you did it, but you'll never have her. I will serve her heart to you on a platter and make you enjoy eating it."

She had completely lost her mind and I laughed before saying, "You are mad! You don't even know what you're saying."

"No! It's you that doesn't understand, you stupid fool! She has arrived, but listen well and never forget my words! You'll never have her!" she screamed.

I didn't understand the mystery of her words, but I suspected she, too, felt the dissolution of our bond and realized my intentions. Fortunately, she didn't have time to act and was forced inside by the sun's rays before she could drag me inside with her.

Seconds later, the sun was completely unobstructed by the moon and I was entirely exposed to the beaming rays. I felt the warmth on my face and waited for the burn that would end my existence. She frantically called for me from inside the suite, but I refused to answer, allowing her to believe I was incinerated; I would be soon enough. Luckily, her misplaced, distorted love for me would never be reason enough for her to risk her safety in place of mine.

I waited in vain for the anticipated burn as I only felt the mercy of the sun, and didn't understand why. I was afraid to move, yet afraid to remain still and I had no idea how much longer the sun would show me grace. I took a few steps, testing my boundaries like a child, and gave thanks for the arms of protection surrounding me, then made the decision to run. This was a gift and a blessing I didn't yet understand, but one thing I knew for certain; now wasn't the time to understand, it was the time to escape.

Georgia Cates Links:
Georgia Cates Blog
Georgia Cates on Facebook
georgiacates on Twitter
Blood of Anteros on Goodreads
Book_Trailer

Links to Purchase Blood of Anteros:
Amazon
Barnes&Noble
Smashwords
iBooks

Made in the USA
Middletown, DE
08 October 2016